DAYTON AND DAUGHTER

DAYTON AND DAUGHTER

Tessa Barclay

HEADLINE

First published in 1999
by HEADLINE BOOK PUBLISHING

10 9 8 7 6 5 4 3 2 1

British Library Cataloguing in Publication Data

Barclay, Tessa
Dayton & daughter
I. Title
823.9'14 [F]

ISBN 0 7472 2259 2

Typeset by
Letterpart Limited, Reigate, Surrey

Printed and bound in Great Britain by
Mackays of Chatham plc, Chatham, Kent

HEADLINE BOOK PUBLISHING
A division of the Hodder Headline Group
338 Euston Road
London NW1 3BH

www.headline.co.uk
www.hodderheadline.com

Dayton and Daughter

The eldest Dayton son has always been an architect!'

'But I'm not the eldest son, am I? I'm the next best, the one who was usually allowed to have a career of his own while his brother took on the family fame. Well, the career I choose is medicine, and if you think I'm going to change now just to please you, you've another think coming.'

The row had rocked the family for weeks. Robert had proved stubborn as a rock, had taken his A levels sufficiently well to get into medical school, and moved out. A legacy from a great-aunt financed his studies when Daniel refused his help. Daniel had disapproved loudly and for a long time; but when after qualifying Robert announced his intention of going overseas with a charity organisation, his father yielded to his mother's tearful pleas and 'forgave' him.

That's to say, he muttered a few words of congratulation, and went to wave him off at Heathrow.

Now there arose another family conflict. Though it seemed a complete waste, since she would marry soon and start a family as any sensible girl should, his daughter Bethany said she wanted to go to university. Not only that – she said she wanted to study architecture.

'Study architecture? I'm not wasting money on fees for that!'

'It wouldn't be a waste, Dad,' Bethany pleaded. At nineteen she still found it hard to put herself in opposition to that godlike personage who had ruled her childhood. 'When I get my degree I can come into the firm and – and—'

'And take Dennis's place?' The bluff, open features darkened with ire. 'Nobody can ever take Dennis's place so don't waste your time!'

'I didn't mean that, Dad. I know no one could replace Dennis – what I meant was – it would continue the tradition – there would be another generation of Daytons carrying on the tradition.'

'Don't be presumptuous! The firm has always been handed on to a son. And say what he likes, Robert will get fed up with this doctoring business. A few years in Africa plagued with mosquitoes and drinking swampy water will bring him to his senses. Of course it would be better if he had architectural training but I can stay on a bit longer than I intended to, to teach him the ropes, and I can easily hire someone good to act as second in command when I retire—'

'But there's no need for that, Dad! I can do all that – I can learn from you and be a help as long as you need me and of course I would hope that by and by you'd accept me as—'

'As what? As an architect? No woman's ever been any good as an architect, all they're good for is itty-bitty things like houses and retirement homes.'

'I'm not going to be like that, Dad. You'll be proud of me, I promise you will!'

Looking back now, from twelve years of experience, Bethany Dayton knew she should have had more sense. No matter that she took an

3

honours degree, or that she won the University's Lutyens Prize for Architecture, Daniel Dayton refused to be impressed. He didn't offer her a job with his firm. He had never had a woman working for *Dayton & Son* in any capacity higher than secretary and he wasn't about to do so, Lutyens Prize or no Lutyens Prize.

Bethany was shocked, she was hurt, but she wasn't going to let him know it. She'd had one or two offers when the architectural magazines featured her university prize, so she accepted the one she liked best, with Harald Gernsen of Copenhagen.

She lived in Copenhagen so long she began to think of herself as a Dane. Six years of hard work, of learning through hands-on experience, of extending herself by matching her work against that of others in the active European style . . .

Not exactly an exile, for she came back to York from time to time, chiefly to see her mother. She would stay in the family home, eat at the family table, make polite and even sometimes genial conversation with her father. Yet he never seemed to warm to her, and after a time she ceased to expect it. A genteel armistice – that was the best she could hope for.

It wasn't until her thirtieth birthday that she returned home in the generally accepted sense. Several events led to the move. A long-standing relationship with a Danish colleague came to an end when Ewe decided to accept a teaching post in Canada. Bethany didn't much want to go to Canada and all Ewe's pleas were in vain – which seemed to suggest her feelings for him weren't strong enough. Good sense indicated that it was time to call it a day.

Her mother had been carrying on a campaign on her behalf, and unexpectedly wrung a concession from Daniel while she was laid up with a broken ankle. 'Other women can have their daughters around them at a time like this,' she mourned, 'but I have to rely on the cleaning woman and the goodwill of neighbours . . .'

It was too much for Daniel, who for some time had been feeling he looked like an ogre to his friends and acquaintances. What, not on friendly terms with his own daughter? And her so fine and clever, with a degree and all that!

So he telephoned Copenhagen, told Bethany her mother needed her and that she should come home like a good daughter – and Bethany obeyed. A few weeks later, when Mary was walking around as good as new, Daniel offered his daughter a job in the family firm. 'Just on trial, you know,' he insisted, 'for I've never had a woman working for me and there's no way of knowing if I'll like it.'

It wasn't exactly an offer she couldn't refuse. She was on leave of absence from Harald Gernsen, who was reluctant to let her go. But Mary Dayton pleaded with her daughter. 'Don't you want to come into the firm, Bethie?'

4

'You know I do. It's what I've always wanted – to do something that would increase *Dayton's* good name.'

'Well, dear, don't you think you're more likely to do that if you're here on the spot rather than miles off in Denmark?'

'We-ell . . . I suppose there's something in that. But if he starts treating me like a secretary, I'm off.'

Luckily there had been urgent projects at *Dayton's* needing exactly the talents Daniel expected his daughter to supply. There was a co-operative housing association that wanted to hire a sympathetic architect, there was also a mining community hoping to turn a row of ex-miners' cottages into a leisure centre. Bethany took them on without complaint – in fact with an eagerness which brought not only success but good public relations. The local papers took an interest, published photographs; Yorkshire Television interviewed the satisfied clients, and other work came to the firm as a result.

From these beginnings Bethany had worked her way up to bigger things though always in consultation with the firm's Planning Department. One day, she hoped, her father would give her a free hand. She told herself every day that compared with most architects, she wasn't doing badly. Not everybody could be a Frank Lloyd Wright or a Mies van der Rohe. All the same, like most architects, she longed for the chance to prove herself on some big project.

Never likely to happen. But tonight's announcement was at least a step in the right direction.

Her father was tapping a Parker pen against a wine glass to get the attention of the gathering. The faint chime of the note caused heads to turn. People moved towards the far end of the room where the publicity people had set up a display – architectural drawings of buildings under construction, a list of past achievements. These were mostly modern housing estates and, if the truth were told, not much to Bethany's taste. Tall housing blocks of concrete tricked out with a few lines of coloured tiles for decoration, a revamped railway station she'd always thought unfriendly despite its efficiency . . .

'Ladies and gentlemen,' began Daniel. 'Friends, Yorkshire folk and countrymen, lend me your ears!'

It became clear to Bethany that her father had had a Scotch or two, or even three. She glanced about for her mother, but Mary Dayton gave a muted smile and a faint shrug, as if to say, 'Nothing to be done about it.' True enough. Short of going up to the display area and dragging him away, nothing was going to stop Daniel Dayton making a speech. He had an announcement to give and by George he was going to give it.

He was a commanding figure in his dinner jacket and black tie. Tall, burly, his thinning grey hair well barbered, he was growing a little thick about the jowls but was still a handsome man, and he knew his own worth as a master of ceremonies.

'Y'all know why you're here this evening,' he told them. 'It's there on the invitation – "to announce the inception of the partnership *Dayton & Daughter*". That's my daughter over there, the tall handsome lass looking modest. C'm over here, Beth, and let's give you a cheer.'

Bethany would have resisted this invitation but other hands urged her forward. The guests were the great and good from the business world of Yorkshire and their wives – most of whom Bethany had known all her life. She'd gone to school with their sons and daughters, some of whom were also here, ready to add their voices to the buzz of approval that greeted her as she joined Daniel.

The representative from the publicity firm handling the event for *Dayton & Daughter* was less pleased. Iris Weston frowned to herself. She'd arranged with Daniel that he'd say a few dignified words. Misquotations from Shakespeare and invitations to raise a cheer didn't come under that heading. She began to work her way towards the front of the gathering, just in case she needed to take control.

No one would have known she was in the least perturbed. There was a smile of approval on her glossy lips; her black eyes seemed to gleam with enjoyment. On second thoughts, she told herself, it didn't matter if Daniel made a fool of himself. None of the national press were here, the event would only interest the professional journals and perhaps some of the building trade periodicals. A waste of her time to come up from London, really.

The two women who joined Daniel Dayton couldn't have been more different. Bethany's fair tall Saxon image was in total contrast to Iris Weston, whose smooth dark hair fell on either side of her oval face in Mona Lisa wings. One or two of the men began asking each other who she was: that was the kind of effect she always had on men. But on this occasion it suited Iris to stay in the background.

'Y'all know,' Daniel resumed, putting his arm round Bethany's shoulders, 'that the firm's always been called *Dayton & Son*, but Robert's a doctor now, and he's over in Albania at the moment, helping to pick up the pieces there. Luckily, Bethany here had more sense so I ask you to raise your glasses now in a toast . . . Here's to *Dayton & Daughter*, and God bless all who sail in her!'

There was laughter and cries of 'Hear, hear!' Iris Weston hastily waved at the waiters to furnish drinks to anyone who didn't have one. Bethany smiled for the photographer. She caught her mother's eye; Mary raised her glass. But both women had noticed that Daniel had made no reference to the son who had died, the one who should really have been here tonight to celebrate the beginning of a new father-and-son partnership.

Bethany knew that she wasn't the partner her father wanted. She wasn't second best, as Robert would have been, or even third best. He had accepted her reluctantly, partly because there was no one else in the

6

family to carry on the firm and he needed to train her in the way he thought she should go. At fifty-nine, retirement was looming for Daniel. So he had agreed at last with his wife that Bethany should be a partner – but that didn't mean he was pleased about it.

'Speech, speech!' demanded the audience. Bethany shook her head, tried to move away. Her father held on to her 'Goo on, luv, don't be shy!' The publicity girl murmured in her ear, 'Say a few words, just to humour him.'

Mary Dayton was nodding at her too. Mother and daughter knew it was best to fall in with Daniel Dayton's wishes at moments like this.

'Thank you very much,' said Bethany, raising her glass. 'Here's to *Dayton & Daughter*, especially the Dayton part!'

Perhaps it wasn't the most graceful tribute Daniel had ever received but it pleased him. Beaming, he accepted the toast and the moment was over. Bethany was given a big fatherly hug for the sake of the cameraman, then was allowed to step back among the guests.

She almost collided with a man standing a yard or two away. 'Oh, sorry!' they both said, catching at drinks to prevent them splashing over.

'Congratulations,' he said, raising his glass.

'Thank you.' He was a stranger to her, tall, thin, with a set of rather severe features which had lit up as he smiled his good wishes. 'I'm afraid . . . er . . . I don't know you,' she murmured.

'No, I'm fairly new in town and I'm only here escorting Mrs Crowther – she's a client.' He offered his hand. 'Peter Lambot – I've joined *Pesh, Samuels & Company*.'

He had named a well-established law firm in Barhampton, an industrial town about twenty miles outside York. Mrs Crowther was a wealthy old lady who always expected to be invited to anything that went on in York and generally pressganged some suitable man into squiring her. Bethany smiled her sympathy. Looking after Mrs Crowther couldn't be much fun, but she guessed Lambot wouldn't let himself be tricked into that role again. He looked the kind of man who caught on quickly.

Ossie Fielden came bustling up to give her a kiss of congratulations. Others followed, and Bethany lost contact with her new acquaintance in the press.

'That was nice, what you said, Bethie,' Daniel remarked. 'You're a good girl, y'know.'

'Of course she's a good girl,' Mary said fondly. 'Better than you deserve, my lad!'

'Now don't you start on a lecture, our Mary,' said her husband. He was just a little too jovial and his Yorkshire-isms were becoming more marked. Mary looked around for a waiter to make a quiet request for some black coffee.

Most of the guests were inspecting the buffet table where the savoury items had been replaced with desserts. Bethany, her parents and Ossie

7

Fielden formed a little group on their own. 'Was that Peter Lambot I saw you talking to a minute gone by?' Ossie asked. 'He's recently joined *Pesh, Samuels.*'

'So he told me.'

'Happen they'll get some of the legal work over that big building project of ours,' Ossie said with some pride. As a former Mayor of Barhampton he took a continual interest in all that concerned the town; he was fond of saying 'My spies are everywhere' when he came up with little nuggets of information about what was going on. Now he added, giving Daniel a nudge, 'I hear you're putting in a design for the town centre site?'

'Wouldn't miss a chance like that, now would I! My Planning Department's got something almost ready to submit.'

'Aye, so I hear . . .'

Despite the fact that he'd taken a few drinks, Daniel didn't miss the lack of enthusiasm in his old friend's tone. 'What d'you mean, "so I hear"?'

'Your usual sort of thing, I suppose.'

'What if it is?'

'Concrete tower blocks, is it?'

'There's no need to say it in that tone of voice! Concrete's the building material of the century and don't you forget it!'

'Not likely to, are we?' grumbled Ossie. 'It's all around us, wherever we look. Have you had much to do with the new lot that's got in at Barhampton at the last election?'

'I've met some of 'em here and there. Why d'you ask?'

'I ask because those councillors were voted in by folk that live in concrete tower blocks, and they've had enough of it! As far as I can tell, the message is: "Let's have something that's more like a home and less like a prison." '

'Now hang on, Ossie – nothing I've ever built is like a prison and—'

'You've never had to live in 'em, Daniel,' Ossie said, putting a hand on his friend's shoulder to lessen the criticism. 'When I were Mayor, I heard a lot of complaints, and sad it is to say I paid very little heed because "experts",' here he sighed and nodded, 'aye, "experts" told me that was the only way to provide housing at an affordable price.'

'Well, so it is,' cried Daniel, prepared for an argument he'd often had before. 'If you make a comparison, the cost per square foot—'

'Nay, lad,' Ossie broke in. 'The cost per square foot doesn't take in human misery.'

'Oh, come on, you're talking like a Greek tragedy! And besides, the bidding for the town centre isn't only about housing. There's shops and offices and new pedestrian areas and—'

'I don't need to be told what's intended for Barhampton town centre, lad. It's my home ground, and I know for a fact that the folk of

Barhampton are expecting something a sight better than more concrete. So think on, Dan lad.'

Daniel Dayton stared at his old friend. 'Are you saying,' he ventured, 'that my design doesn't stand a chance?'

'I'm not saying that, Daniel. I only hear snippets from the council's Planning Department. But what I do hear makes me think they want something more . . .' he hesitated, unwilling to hurt his old friend's feelings, but at last had to say it. 'They're looking for something more *human* than what they've used in the past. If I were you, I'd have a good look at the blueprints before you send 'em in.'

Daniel groaned. He was rapidly recovering from the effects of his several whiskies. 'You're saying I haven't got a chance.'

'Not unless you come up with something a bit different from what I've seen in the past.'

'But there's no time, Ossie! The designs have to be submitted by the end of next month!'

'Well, couldn't you make a few alterations in—'

'A few alterations? What d'you think architecture is? Playing with building bricks? There's no way I could alter those plans, even if I want to.'

Bethany, who had listened to all this, had smothered a laugh when Ossie Fielden suggested some quick alterations to her father's designs. She was only too well aware of them – imposing, grand, announcing to the world that these buildings were taking over the terrain without opposition. To alter them in the way Ossie implied was impossible. They defied any attempt at tinkering.

Ossie said: 'It's a big project, Daniel. It'd be a pity if *Dayton & Son'* – he broke off – 'sorry, *& Daughter* didn't have something in as a bid. Haven't you got a piece of work – a sketch that was discarded, or a try-out for some other site?'

'I've got a design, Dad,' Bethany said.

'You what?'

'A design. For the town centre site.'

'What are you talking about?' her father demanded in irritation. 'How can you have a plan for a site that big?'

'I was doing it in my spare time, Dad.'

'But what on earth for?'

'Well, I . . . I like to do things on my own . . . keep my hand in . . . not that I ever thought you'd want to see it, but . . .' She pulled herself together so as to make a better sales pitch. 'Do you remember that prize I won in Copenhagen?'

'What prize?'

'The chief architectural magazine set out a list of conditions for a town centre reconstruction and competitors had to design according to those conditions. I won the prize, the equivalent of a thousand pounds or so. Don't you remember? It was about four years ago.'

'Um . . . er . . . it does seem to strike a chord,' Daniel acknowledged, 'but what of it? A scheme for some imaginary Danish town is hardly going to fit Barhampton!'

'No, of course not,' she agreed. 'But it's not that design exactly. I told you – I'd been working on it in my own time and with Barhampton in mind, just to see how it might look. And I must say . . . it doesn't look bad.'

Ossie was eyeing her with wonder. 'No concrete?' he asked.

'Well, there *is* some. You can't build thousands of square feet of a modern town without using it. But on the whole I've tried for the vernacular—'

'What's that mean?' Ossie asked.

'It's when you use traditional materials or their equivalent to get the kind of appearance that fits the surroundings. Old Barhampton was built of brick, mainly—'

'You're never suggesting that you could bring in a new town centre at any sort of realistic price using *brick*?' snarled Daniel. 'Don't be silly.'

'Hang on, hang on,' Ossie said. 'Hear the lass out. This competition you won – did it impose cost restrictions?'

'Of course it did. And I had that in mind when I reworked the plans.' She glanced appealingly at her father. 'It isn't being silly to say that you *can* use a variety of building materials. It's true that it puts the cost up and that this design wouldn't be the cheapest that could be submitted. But it seems to me that always going for the lowest-cost design has led us into mistaken town planning in the past. I just thought I'd work with my old design and see if it could be brought in at an estimate within the suggested limits.'

'And could it?' asked Ossie.

'Well . . . I only ran it through my home computer . . .'

'Seems to me you've made quite a career of it,' her father said in annoyance. 'By all means, use the office computer for your little hobbies!'

'Now, now, Daniel,' Ossie soothed. 'Don't get your feathers in a fandango. I've just been telling you that I don't think your usual kind of plan is going to get you anywhere with the new councillors in Barhampton, and here's your lass with a different plan that might stand a better chance. At least take a look at it.'

'But my Planning Department has spent months on the drawings I'm going to submit.'

'Haven't I just been telling thee, lad, that your usual sort of thing won't fit the bill? I actually heard one councillor say, "No more forbidding concrete." So think on! You've got – what – five weeks to alter your own designs or find alternatives. Here's Bethany with something ready to look at. Where's the harm in casting an eye over it?'

10

Daniel glared at his old friend. He longed to tell him to mind his own business. But in the past Ossie had put a lot of projects Daniel's way; to tell him now that his suggestions were unwanted would be ungrateful – and what was worse, might be bad for business.

For generations the Daytons had been at the forefront of architectural planning in the North. He didn't want to miss out on the chance of the Barhampton project. He wanted their name there, among the entries for the new town centre. If he put in his own designs, it sounded as if the new brooms on the town council would sweep them and him away.

As Ossie said, where was the harm in casting an eye? Of course the thing wouldn't be suitable – the girl had no real experience – but then there might be something there that he could use, adapt, improve . . .

'Where are these drawings, then?' he asked.

'At home, in my room.'

'Well, then, might as well take a look,' he agreed grudgingly. 'Mind, if it's fancy Continental nonsense, I'll throw it out the window.'

'I wouldn't be too quick to do that, lad,' warned Ossie. 'Mebbe a touch of the Continental is what Barhampton's after these days.'

Mary Dayton had remained silent throughout the entire discussion. She'd been holding her breath, praying that her husband would at last agree to take Bethany seriously. She knew it was no good to urge too strongly. Daniel would have told her to be quiet. But from another man, and an old and valued friend like Ossie, he would accept suggestions.

Nothing might come of it. Mary had no idea whether Bethany's design was a good one – she couldn't read architectural drawings. But she'd seen the glow of enthusiasm in her daughter's blue eyes as she sat at her drawing table in her room at home. Her motherly intuition told her it meant a lot to Bethany. She wanted the girl to succeed, almost more than anything in the world.

For her husband actually to agree to take a look was a tremendous victory. She turned away so that her smile of delight wouldn't be too obvious to Daniel. Her gaze lighted on the dark young man who was bringing a glass of wine to old Mrs Crowther. He paused, smiling back. 'Anything I can do for you?' he enquired.

'No . . . no, thank you . . . You're . . . you're Peter Lambot, aren't you?'

'At your service. And you're Ms Dayton's mother – I can see the resemblance. Congratulations on the new partnership, you must be very proud of her.'

'Oh, I am,' she said with perhaps more fervour than was called for. She saw Peter's look of surprise and added hastily. 'This is a big night for us.'

'I can tell it is. Ms Dayton looks all aglow. Have this glass of wine to celebrate!'

'But it's for Mrs Crowther, isn't it?'

'I'll fetch her another.'

'It's very kind of you, Peter.' Truth to tell, she was glad of the wine. Her throat was dry with apprehension after Ossie's intervention. She hadn't been sure Daniel would accept it in good part and to have had a noisy row tonight of all nights would have been unthinkable.

Peter made a return trip to the bar for Mrs Crowther's wine. What a nice lad, Mary thought to herself, and turned back just in time to greet old friends who had come up to join the group.

The evening seemed to Mary to go on for ever. Daniel, who had put on a good front when announcing the partnership, maintained the impression of being pleased with life. But his wife knew him too well to be taken in. He had been shaken by Ossie's words and was probably in two minds about looking at Bethany's work. Any chance remark might start an upset. But in the end they saw all their friends off, then drove home to their house out beyond the University.

It was late, they were all tired. They went to bed. Mary was aware that her husband lay beside her wide awake for hours. He was trying to come to terms with the idea of taking Bethany seriously as a partner.

In her own room, Bethany too was awake. Was it really true? Was her father going to look at her work with any real intention of using it? She was tempted to get up and open the big folder that held the drawings, to see if there was any last-minute improvement she could put in. But no, that would be childish. She was a fully grown woman, she must stand or fall by the work she had done so quietly over the last few months.

In the morning while Mary Dayton was making breakfast, Daniel in his shirtsleeves tapped on the door of his daughter's room. 'So what about these plans, then,' he said.

'They're here, Dad.' She'd been up for hours, bringing up 3D images on her computer, fidgeting about with the order of the sketches, going over her estimate of costs, unsure now of facts she'd verified a hundred times already. She was still in her dressing-gown, her long fair hair falling over her shoulders unbrushed, barefoot, completely without the armour of business attire and make-up.

Daniel stood at the drawing table, where the sketches were laid out. He saw office blocks spaced among lawns, a cinema and parking lot with restaurants whose windows looked out on the River Barr. He saw department stores with oval windows and open-air balconies for fine days. He saw housing several storeys high, protected from the winds that rushed down from the moors by mature trees and from the midday sun on the south side by metal canopies over the windows.

If Bethany had set out to design something utterly different from anything he could have conceived, she had succeeded. It was so strange and new that it almost shocked him.

He understood at once that any intention of adapting or altering the architectural conception was futile. This was a thing complete in itself, unified by its scale and its care for the surroundings. Bethany had used the river, the moors, the shallow valley in which the old town stood, the open aspect towards the west, the slope of the land, to best effect. There was a natural flow between the housing estates and the shopping malls, between the office blocks and the public transport depots.

But there was more than that. There was a warmth, a kindness in the design, an acknowledgement that human beings would live and work in these buildings. It was something Daniel had never even thought of including in any of his work, and it took him completely aback.

He stood staring down at the sketches. He had three choices. He could send in his own plans, worked up for him by his Planning Department and probably meet with rejection. He could submit his daughter's work. Or he could refrain completely.

His own work, he knew, was unlikely to find favour. Ossie had made that clear enough. Not to take part went against his nature; *Dayton's* had always tendered designs for anything worth designing in the North. And he had always upheld tradition.

Bethany's designs . . . Well, Bethany's designs were beyond him. He had no idea whether they were good or bad because they'd surprised him so much. His own instinct was that wary town councillors would find this project unserious, almost light-hearted, not at all what they ought to spend money on.

But it was complete, detailed, ready to be seen. No amount of nipping-and-tucking could make it better. They could perhaps work on the estimate of costs, where his long experience of materials might be of use. But in the main Bethany's work needed nothing done to it.

He took a deep breath. 'All right,' he said, 'we'll submit it.'

And Bethany's whole world was bathed in light.

Chapter Two

The months that followed weren't an easy time for anyone connected with *Dayton & Daughter*. Daniel set himself to cost Bethany's specifications for her design, and what he saw on the computer screen didn't please him. The price of building according to his daughter's views was at least a third higher than for his own, and experience had taught him that during any construction scheme, costs are likely to increase. Experience had also taught him that town councils tended to go for the most economical project. Ossie Fielden had said this wouldn't be the case with the new batch of councillors at Barhampton – but could he rely on that?

Harried by doubt, secretly humiliated at having been told his work would fail to please, Daniel had to strive hard not to lose his temper a dozen times a day. Added to that was the suspense. Bethany's plans had been submitted by the final entry date. Rumour said that seven other firms had submitted plans and some were very big names in the architectural world. The competition seemed fierce.

Daniel bewailed his decision to back his daughter's work – it was too outlandish a design, it cost too much, her reputation wasn't influential . . . He almost wished he could withdraw it, but that of course was impossible.

'Stop worrying about it, Mr Dayton,' said Alan Singleton. 'I've been over that area half a dozen times with Bethany's plans, and I can tell you they fit the ground contours beautifully.'

Alan was chief of the Surveying Department of *Dayton & Daughter*, which made his views important. All the same, fitting the landscape wasn't the most important point about a construction plan.

'The costing's too high,' Daniel mourned. 'The minute the Town Planning Committee see those noughts after the pound sign, they're going to chuck it in the waste-paper basket.'

'No, no,' urged Alan. 'It's an attractive set of sketches from the very first glance. That front elevation of the cinema and restaurant complex is really intriguing. They'll sit and study it and think how nice it is, and when they come to look at the figures they'll say, "Well, it's worth spending a bit more to get something as good as that." '

'A bit more! Alan, we're talking *millions* here! And they'll guess that

14

the estimate isn't likely to stay the same. They know how prices escalate and this thing is going to take more than two years to complete – *two years*. In that time, who knows what timber's going to cost? And all that brickwork . . . Bricks! I should never have let it go through!'

'Bricks are good,' Alan insisted. 'Bricks are fashionable. And the new set of councillors seem to be a trendy lot. It may be just the kind of thing they'll go for.'

Daniel had to pay attention to Alan's opinions. He'd been with the firm for over five years, bringing efficiency and more modern methods to the Surveying Department. He it was who had had the computers installed, so that now instead of relying on blueprints and contour maps, a 3D image of the ground could be called up. He it was who had worked up a database of all the firm's maps and plans, all their previous buildings and their ongoing projects. His qualifications were impressive: he was as much a scientist as a surveyor, with a vast knowledge of geology to help in understanding ground and rock formations.

In addition, he was rather good-looking, which helped when he was explaining problems to worried clients. Tall, thin, with a narrow intellectual face and calm brown eyes, he somehow managed to reassure house-owners who'd been told there was an underground stream running below their wine cellars.

Alan was most definitely on Bethany's side in the battle over the design for Barhampton's town centre. When he joined *Dayton's* he had known it was an old-fashioned firm, but that hadn't been an issue. He'd always intended to influence it towards modernisation, and as far as office procedures were concerned he'd succeeded.

But he'd begun to be aware after his first year with the firm that it was wedded to the architectural outlook of the 1950s and 1960s. These were the traditions Daniel had studied at university, these were the traditions that had served him well in gaining lucrative contracts with various councils and governing bodies.

When Bethany arrived back from Denmark to join the firm, it was like a breath of fresh air. Alan made it his business to do the surveying for the various small projects she was allowed to handle, and approved of everything she proposed. Now she had put her mind to a big project, a huge project, involving millions of pounds and Alan still supported her. True, the Town Planning Department of Barhampton might not like the airy, friendly designs. They might dismiss them at once. Or, if they liked them, they might be frightened off by the cost. Well, too bad. That didn't change the fact that Bethany's work was outstanding, far superior to her father's both in originality and in its concern for the environment.

There was also the fact that Alan found her attractive. Her tall, Saxon good looks were very appealing. She would drive up to a construction site in her little jeep-like vehicle, leap out, and stride around with a sparkling energy that invigorated everyone who saw it.

Building a sheltered housing block or a market garden centre on a small site can be a wearisome business: in bad weather the ground becomes a morass but there's no space to work elsewhere, there can be delays in delivery of vital components but a lack of other work to keep the men busy. It's then that they grow careless, drift away to smoke a secret cigarette, waste time by skiving off to the nearest caff to read the sporting page. Somehow Bethany was able to brighten up the situation. Somehow she smoothed away problems, chatted up the contractor, got things going again.

Alan Singleton had grown fond of Bethany. Now and again he even entertained thoughts of falling in love with her. He was a divorcé, fancy-free but chary about getting entangled again. Still, with Bethany it might be possible to have a rewarding relationship without the irksome feeling of being shackled. But it would complicate his life; she was, after all, the boss's daughter. Best not to get involved . . .

For her part, Bethany was deeply grateful to Alan. She knew how much she owed to his support. During her two years with the firm, when she'd known very well she was on probation as far as her father was concerned, Alan had been a good friend. One of the things she liked about him was that he'd never resented her. It would have been quite understandable if he had, for after all she'd arrived back from Copenhagen and then a few weeks later she was part of the firm, assistant to her father, someone who had to be considered important in office politics.

But the fact was, they were on the same side. Alan had always wanted to update the firm's image, and Bethany wanted to produce buildings that would still look good well into the twenty-first century. Without ever putting it into words, they were allies.

So during the long wait for the decision on Barhampton, she relied on Alan's support. And when at a reception in the old Town Hall in Barhampton it was announced that *Dayton & Daughter* had won the design contract, she threw her arms around Alan and hugged him.

The reception laid on by Barhampton Council was a high-class affair. Daniel Dayton, when he got the elaborate invitation, decided that it would be a good idea to get some publicity out of it even if his firm didn't win the design contract. So he called the public relations firm in London to ask them to send someone, and because she'd handled the party for the partnership, Iris Weston was sent again.

She wasn't best pleased about it. Barhampton to a girl like Iris was practically tiger country. A preliminary chat with Daniel had led her to believe he expected very little from this affair. A total waste of her time. So she'd got herself a drink and begun to 'mingle', because it was always useful to pick up contacts even in a one-horse town like Barhampton.

As she drifted among the guests, she came across a tall, thin, elegant man who looked as if he might be a stockbroker or a financier. 'I'm Iris Weston,' she said, holding out her hand. She was disappointed when he

told her he was the head of the Surveying Department for *Dayton &
Daughter*. She was about to give him ten seconds' attention when
something about him stirred a response in her. Something . . . He wasn't
really her type; normally she went for younger, more streetwise men.
Yet it couldn't do any harm to stay with him and be friendly.

She was very much surprised how much she resented it when
Bethany Dayton threw her arms round Alan to give him a big hug after
her firm was declared the winner. Perhaps from that moment, Iris began
to dislike Bethany.

However, it was her duty to ensure good publicity. She hovered close
by as the photographers got their shots. Even the big, spontaneous hug
between Bethany and Alan Singleton would be useful – they were both
good-looking and it was the kind of thing the broadsheets might take.
Certainly the trade and professional journals would use it, for after all
this was an important project for this fading northern town, involving
very large sums of money and using a totally new name in architecture.

So it wasn't going to be a 'nothing' enterprise. Her firm, *Seymour PR*,
had given the account to her, and though it meant scurrying up the
motorway from time to time, she could live with that. Particularly if she
could cultivate Alan Singleton on her visits.

She worked hard for the rest of the evening and Bethany, watching
her, marvelled at her skill. Iris seemed to have the gift of handling
people; she had Daniel eating out of her hand, and all the cynical
reporters allowed themselves to be pulled into conversations with
Dayton & Daughter. Daniel enjoyed the limelight but Bethany found
it less pleasing. The pressmen were more interested in the fact that a
woman had won the design contract than in the design itself.

They wanted to talk about her private life. 'You've never married? Is that
because you're dedicated to your career? Is there a man in your life
currently? What are your hobbies? Do you buy your clothes locally or in
London?'

Smiling to hide her embarrassment, Bethany did her best to give them
what they wanted. Iris decided that she must cook up a résumé of
Bethany's career the minute she could get at her Compaq computer so
as not to be at a loss on future occasions. *Seymour PR* had plenty of
human interest stuff on file about Daniel and even a little about his wife
Mary, but almost nothing about Bethany. And it would be Bethany who
would figure in any news story coming out in the morning.

Perhaps it would be better if Iris stayed overnight in Barhampton; she
could do a get-together résumé of the staff of *Dayton & Daughter*. She
could fax it out as background info to all the building trade journals and –
though this was a side issue – it would give her the chance to see more of
Alan.

She might even invite him out to lunch. She'd put it on her expense
account, of course.

Alan was flattered by the invitation, especially when she mentioned the very posh pub – a place outside York which had earned itself a reputation for excellent food. But he was puzzled too.

'Don't quite understand why we're doing this,' he commented the next day as they waited for the hors d'oeuvres. 'I'd have thought Bethany would be the one you wanted to chat with.'

'Yes, you're right, but I'm seeing her this evening,' Iris said, making a mental note to call Bethany and make the arrangement. 'I wanted to get the outlook of a member of the firm.'

'There are others who've been there longer than me.'

'But I gathered from things I heard that you're regarded as the moderniser.'

'Well . . . all I did was bring in a few specialised computers. Daniel was ready for it, because he'd seen the way things were going, so there was no problem. And anyhow, when Bethany came back, she'd have got him into modernisation. Bethany's a great girl,' he added, partly because that was his opinion and partly because he felt this PR girl was looking for information to flesh out her press release. 'She maybe didn't think so at the time, but going to Denmark was a good move. Architecture's taken seriously in Scandinavia – she learned a lot there.'

'Yes, yes,' agreed Iris, who didn't really want to talk about Bethany. 'So how long have you been with the firm?'

He gave her the information which she already had on file from a handout by the Personnel Department. She listened to the story of his career while they worked their way through melon slices with raspberry coulis, and then smoked duck and salad. By the time they got to the brown-bread ice cream she'd reached the point she'd been aiming at since they sat down.

'And you yourself,' she prompted. 'I suppose you and your wife have a splendid house you designed to suit the family?'

He laughed. 'My wife has a house, not particularly splendid and in Sussex, which is where we used to live before the divorce.'

'Ah . . . Your children live with her?'

'No children. We were both too busy career-building. Just as well,' he said, with a sigh that told her he had no very serious regrets.

That was a relief. She tried not to get involved with married men. And even divorced men could be something of a bore if they were always worrying about access to their children. Iris herself had never been married – she'd never liked the idea of being tied down and even a live-in partner could cause problems. Because when the thing ended – as it always did – it could be messy, the breaking-up.

But here was a man who for some strange reason attracted her, whom she could see from time to time when she felt like it, and all with no strings attached.

They walked out to the car park after the meal arm in arm, and when she dropped him back at the office she gave him a little brushing kiss on the cheek in farewell. He was surprised, but pleased – who wouldn't be pleased at a kiss from a beautiful, clever and obviously successful young woman? He was smiling to himself as he went into *Dayton & Daughter's* handsome building in the Aldwark.

'Looking pleased with yourself, aren't you?' Daniel Dayton remarked as they passed in the hall.

'Why not? It's a lovely bright day, I've just had a slap-up lunch, God's in His heaven, all's right with the world,' Alan said.

'What's got into you? You don't usually wax poetic about food.'

'That's because I never ate at the Old White Rose before.'

'You've had lunch at the Old White Rose? What is it, your birthday?'

'As a matter of fact, Miss Weston invited me.'

'Miss Weston? So that's the way the wind's blowing?'

Daniel was aware of a little stab of resentment. If Iris Weston was going to invite anybody to lunch, it ought to be himself, the head of the company.

'No, nothing like that,' Alan protested, laughing. 'She just wanted some background on the firm.'

'Huh. And I suppose that's going to come out of her PR budget, which *I'm* paying for.'

'There you are then. You paid for my lunch. But it was all in the good of the cause, you know, so she can write nice things about us for the papers.'

'Write nice things,' grunted Daniel. 'All this fol-de-rol . . . We've won contracts for public buildings before now without having to put on an act for the papers.' He shrugged his heavy shoulders before striding on his way to a meeting. He was headed for a confidential chat with some of the building contractors who were tendering for construction work on the Barhampton job, a meeting in a far less public place than the Old White Rose.

All through his conversation with Billy and Emmett and Vernon a certain disgruntlement remained in the background. Why should the girl from *Seymour PR* want to talk to Singleton? Daniel was the backbone of the firm, Daniel was the one who could give her the history going back to 1742 . . . but then he supposed she'd wanted to talk about those confounded computers with their new-fangled programmes that could show everything in 3D . . .

When he got back to the office his secretary told him that Bethany had been trying to get in touch. Still unsettled, unwilling to sit down to the work that would get Bethany's winning design off the drawing-board and into the real world, he tramped along to her office.

'You wanted to speak to me?'

'Oh, there you are, Dad. I wanted to ask if it's all right to have that PR girl to dinner tonight.'

'Miss Weston?' Daniel said, as if there were several PR girls in question.

'Yes, she rang to ask me out for a drink after work tonight.'

'She did, did she?' So after all she hadn't chosen Singleton before the head of the firm. She'd chosen Bethany – and that was only reasonable, because after all Bethany was the winning architect and, he had to admit, something a bit special in that she was a woman.

Luckily he didn't enquire at what time Iris Weston had rung and Bethany didn't think to tell him that it had happened about an hour ago. As far as Daniel was concerned Miss Weston had had no special preference for Singleton, and that was what had been rankling with him.

'So I thought I'd rather not have a one-to-one with her, Dad, because I had a feeling she'd want to go on about what it's like to be a woman in a man's world and so on, so I asked her to come to dinner – I said eight o'clock – is that all right with you?'

'What's your mother say – about catering and all that?'

'Oh, you know Mother can always whip something up if she's asked to. She said it was all right. Is it okay with you?'

'Yes, why not?' grunted Daniel, and felt a little thrill of pleasure at the thought of having the company of Iris Weston for a whole evening.

Mary Dayton was adept at coping with unexpected guests. She was quite accustomed to her husband bringing home business acquaintances at very short notice, sometimes at no notice at all. Years ago, Mary had been a teacher with ambitions to become head of a grammar school. That was before Daniel Dayton swept her off her feet and into matrimony. Thereafter three children had kept her at home, and when they were old enough to be, as they say, off her hands, Daniel had been very discouraging about any resumption of her teaching career.

Moreover, she'd have had to go for some retraining. Education had changed while she was away starting her family. And she was invited to go on the committee of first one charity and then another, and of course the British suddenly began taking an interest in food so as a hostess she had to take a Cordon Bleu course, and then she was asked to do the flowers at the local church so she took flower-arranging classes, and one way and another the idea of being anything except wife and house-keeper had faded away.

But the skills she'd learned had been learned well. The meal she set on the table that evening was better than the lunch Iris had paid for at the Old White Rose. The wine was superb; Daniel prided himself on his cellar and Mary knew how it should be served. Iris was a little taken aback. Mary Dayton with her still-blonde hair beautifully cut, her big-boned figure still looking good in a soft wool dress that had clearly been made for her ... She'd been viewing the Daytons as a bunch of provincials but now she saw her mistake. She particularly noted that Daniel was miffed about the lunch with Alan Singleton.

A little jealous, was he? So much the better. It was always a good thing to have a male client a little attracted to her. It made them easier to handle. And this, she now saw, was a trickier situation than she'd thought.

Daniel couldn't quite disguise the fact that he was both pleased and displeased about the Barhampton contract. He had wanted his firm to win it, but she could tell he would have preferred his own design to succeed.

'I can tell you, costing it out, we'll be lucky to come in at the price Barhampton has agreed. I don't suppose you know, Miss Weston—'

'Iris. Call me Iris.'

'Yes, well . . . You have to understand, Iris, that weather plays a very important part in construction work. Hard frost makes it difficult to set concrete, rain makes the ground messy for heavy equipment—'

'But surely you with all your expert knowledge, Mr Dayton . . .'

'Ah, sitha! If I'm to call you Iris, you're to call me Daniel, that's only fair.'

'Well, if you're sure that's all right? Some clients don't like to be on first-name terms but, of course, we'll be working together perhaps for as long as a couple of years.'

'Sure thing! You'll be like a member of the family by that time!'

Mary, watching her husband's eyes gleam with pleasure at the thought, sighed to herself. Daniel was about to fall for the beautiful young woman with the Mona Lisa look.

Probably nothing much would come of it. He never became deeply involved. It was just that he liked to have a pretty woman in his life, someone who would admire him and laugh at his jokes. With one or two in the past, things had gone a little further; there had been occasional weekends when he went away 'on business' and came back with his shirts faintly redolent of someone else's perfume. But whoever the girl might be, she never seemed to cause any trouble. Perhaps Daniel laid out the ground rules before he let things go beyond a little innocent flirtation.

Mary had learned to view it all with tolerance. Daniel was after all an impressive man in his big-bodied, domineering way. It was quite understandable if a young woman or two fell for him.

Yet with this Iris Weston it might be different. Mary sensed that *this* girl wasn't likely to be overwhelmed by a middle-aged man from a Northern city. So of course all her admiration, all her appearance of thinking him a supreme expert, was an act. Well, fair enough. Iris's role was to steer *Dayton & Daughter* through the uncharted waters of being winners in a competition that would attract nationwide attention. If flattery was one of her methods, so be it.

Bethany Dayton hadn't yet picked up the vibrations that her mother sensed. She was too busy fending off personal questions about her girlhood and why she'd never married.

'I'm rather hoping you can get the press to play that down, Iris,' she remarked. 'It's true that women haven't taken a big enough part in the world of architecture in the past, but that's all changing now. I'm by no means the only woman who's had success.'

'But most of the others seem to be in America or on the Continent,' said Iris, who'd looked it up. 'I can see you're not keen on the personal angle, but it's a fact that this is a big event.'

'It's a big event for the *firm*,' Bethany insisted. 'And it's the firm you're supposed to publicise.'

Daniel was nodding agreement; Bethany was looking irritated; Iris was smiling a little too sweetly. Mary saw that it was time to produce a diversion. 'Well, now, if no one wants any more ginger meringue I think we'll go into the drawing room for coffee. Iris, have you any preference? Italian, French – or do you take decaffeinated?'

She led the way out of the dining room, and was aware that her husband loosely linked his arm with Iris to lead her in the right direction – quite unnecessary, since the drawing room was straight across the passage from the dining room. 'Stir the fire up a little, will you, dear?' she asked, to detach him from his lady. 'It's not really cold tonight but it's nice to have a little bit of a flame.'

She heard her daughter cough to cover a little chuckle at the use of the word 'flame'. She knew Bethany had seen the linking of arms and understood what it meant. But Daniel was too busy clattering the fire irons to catch on. His attention was next taken up with offering brandy or Armagnac. Iris in her short silk dress was shown to the sofa where, sinking in, she displayed a length of very elegant leg.

Oh Lord, thought Bethany, why couldn't we have had a man as our PRO? But she comforted herself with the thought that Iris wouldn't be permanently based in York. She had other accounts to look after. Head office for *Seymour PR* was in London, so she would only come North infrequently.

Not so. Even as Bethany was saying this to herself, Iris was asking how the construction of the new Barhampton Town Centre would be planned.

'Ah, we've had experience in that kind of thing,' said Daniel, turning from the drinks tray to bring her a brandy. 'Not on as big a scale as this, of course . . .' He paused, struck for the first time by the money involved. He had put up tower blocks and hospitals for town or county councils, but this time it wasn't just a million or two – it was hundreds of millions. In a way, that made it worse. That a chit of a girl should win this contract . . . That he, after all his years of experience and service to the community, should have been warned off as being too old-fashioned . . .

Still, he was at the head of the firm. He would see that he kept as much control as possible.

It all passed through his mind in a flash. He went back to fetch his own drink.

'There'll be a steering committee,' he went on, settling on the sofa beside Iris. 'It'll include the architect – in this case, our Beth here – and another member of our firm, probably Alan Singleton.'

'Why not you?' Iris asked, turning to give him a smile from admiring black eyes. 'After all, you're the mainstay of the firm.'

'And that's exactly why.' He was pleased that she should pick up that point. It let him express aloud something of what he'd just been thinking. 'You see, though Barhampton's big business for us, it's not by any means the only thing on our books. Of course I'll always be available for immediate consultation if any problems arise.'

'My word, I should think so! With all your experience!'

'Ah, but . . .' now he could say as a joke what he felt was the real truth, 'I'm a bit of an old fogey these days, tha knows. My kind of design is going out of fashion.'

'What nonsense! Don't forget I've looked through all your brochures and photo-files. I know people still like solid, well-constructed buildings no matter how trendy glass and steel may seem for a while.'

Daniel looked pleased and took a sip of his drink. His wife rose to fetch the after-dinner mints. With her back to her guest, she allowed herself a stifled sigh. She quite understood that a PR executive had to do a good deal of buttering-up, but need it be so blatant? And did the recipient have to lap it up so readily?

Mary took care not to let her eye meet her daughter's. She knew Bethany was thinking the same but it didn't do to fall into that trap, mother and daughter against philandering father. Daniel was at heart a good man, happy in his marriage, and this beautiful young thing was too sophisticated to let matters get out of hand. No need to get in a flutter about it.

Rather to her surprise, Iris started on a different topic as she shook her head at the proffered chocolates. 'You say Alan Singleton will be on the steering committee? That means you put a lot of trust in him, I suppose.' This question was addressed to Bethany, who fielded it expertly, glad to get away from the insincerity of the last few minutes.

'Of course we put a lot of trust in Alan. He's been with us – how long, Dad?'

'Upwards of five years, I think. Good lad, is Alan, though I must admit he and I have locked horns more than once over his "modernisations".'

'He told me he'd brought in some new equipment.'

'Yes, I saw his point about that. And when Bethany got back from Copenhagen she said it had been in use at Gernsen's for quite a time. Oh, he's all right, is young Alan – as you'd expect from the head of my Surveying Department.'

'And that's another reason why he in particular should be on the steering committee,' Bethany put in. 'Surveying is very important before and during construction. All kinds of problems could crop up, you know. Barhampton's an old town, and some of the plans for the old buildings have been lost, or were inaccurate in the first place, because we've learned a lot about sub-structure and soil-complement in the last few years. So Alan will be on hand if there are any glitches.'

'And then of course there'll be people from Barhampton Town Council – planning officials, legal bods, an accountant to keep an eye on expenditure . . . Who else, Beth?'

'Representatives of the construction firms.'

'Oh, aye, mustn't forget them. It may be they're the most important of the lot!'

'You only say that because they're your cronies,' laughed his wife.

'You know very well, Mary, that if one of the firms had a strike on its hands or got in a mess over materials, the outcome could be disastrous for the time-schedules. The heads of the construction firms have got to be able to consult over any emergency.'

'That's what he says,' Mary said to Iris. 'But the fact of the matter is that they play golf together and belong to the same social clubs so of course he likes to have them on the steering committee.'

'No, now, luv, be fair, what good is it going to do me this time? It's true I'm usually on the steering committee of any project but this time it's Beth's design, so she's the consulting architect, and what good does it do me to have Billy Wellbrow and Emmett Foyle there?'

'They'll report back to you at the nineteenth hole, of course,' teased Mary. 'And if anything is going on that you don't approve of, they'll put a stop to it for you.'

Iris Weston was far from disapproving of a little sleight of hand on committees. But what she was interested in was something else. 'And Alan Singleton – he'll support you, Bethany, in any arguments?'

Bethany was surprised. 'I suppose he will, if he agrees with me over whatever it is. And we do generally see eye to eye. Alan and I have had many a long discussion about how buildings should look. He took a big interest in getting my designs ready for consideration.'

Iris was thinking it sounded as if they were close. She felt yet another twinge of vexation with Bethany. Why did this girl have to be there first with the man she fancied? Bethany might lack polish, might have too much of an outdoors look about her, but she was good-looking, intelligent, and involved in the same kind of work as Alan. Shared interests, Iris knew, could make a very firm tie.

Clearly it wouldn't be a walk-over, getting Alan for herself. It couldn't be done on a piecemeal basis, with occasional visits to York when she could fit them in. Besides, the whole thing was turning out to be bigger than she'd ever expected. Quick to pick up hints, she'd caught the momentary hesitation when Daniel spoke of the Barhampton project as being on a bigger scale than he was used to. She tried to call to mind exactly what kind of money was to be spent. She'd glanced at the figures but hadn't paid close attention because frankly she'd never expected *Dayton & Daughter* to win the contract.

But clearly it was very big business indeed. Which meant she could justify to her employer the idea of spending more time in the North than expected. Which also meant that she would get a chance to build up a relationship with Alan. All she needed was the opportunity. With luck, Bethany would be busy playing with her building blocks, especially at the outset of such a long-term scheme.

Now was the time to put in some effort, if she really wanted to capture Alan Singleton. And she did, although why he appealed to her so much was still a mystery.

'You know,' she said to Daniel with a smile that seemed to say it was for him she was going to do it, 'I think I ought to stay in York to meet the steering committee.'

Chapter Three

Before she went to bed that night, Iris Weston faxed through a lot of material from her hotel bedroom to *Seymour PR* in London – human interest stuff, the kind that might catch the attention of gossip columnists. Too late of course for anything to be done with it tonight, but the next day was Friday, and if her assistant got busy he might get something into the Sundays.

Bethany picked Iris up at her hotel next morning to drive her to Barhampton for the steering committee. Her first sight of the old town filled Iris with dismay. Derelict woollen mills, whose owners had long since 'rationalised' their businesses, amalgamating in new premises that could handle new machinery and new products. Once-prosperous suburbs, Victorian houses interspersed with a few late-Georgian ones, mostly split up into flats, their front gardens left to the tender mercies of anyone who wanted to take on the chore.

Even in the spring sunlight, it had a melancholy air. Sensing Iris's disapproval, Bethany felt compelled to defend the town.

'They've had hard times here for ages,' she said. 'During World War Two they couldn't get the wool from Australia because of U-boats and so forth, so the mills were turned to making the material for army uniforms. Then when the war ended, man-made fabrics were coming in and the machines had to be adapted again to cope with that. But it wasn't satisfactory so in the end it was better to start again, with new machines, and it was cheaper to go to a new site than try to adapt the old premises. So of course everybody that could go moved with the work. The population has gone down a lot.'

'And the town centre? Is it as bad as this?'

'They were just nosing into it, and Iris could see that though not as melancholy as the outskirts, it was a mess: shopping streets with old façades that had gone through various versions of modernisation, car showrooms with a frontage to suit the cars rather than the neighbourhood, launderettes, small workplaces for silversmiths and picture-framers, doctors' surgeries and charity shops.

The old Town Hall still dominated the surroundings, a handsome building put up when money was plentiful but now costing a mint in upkeep. The magistrates' court and the main police station had been rebuilt in utility 1950s style, pre-fabricated concrete block. The two churches, St Mary's and Trinity, were Victorian Gothic, not unhandsome but sombre with a century of mill-town grime. The town's department store, formerly Natbroome's but now a branch of a national chain, had twentieth-century windows at street level and nineteenth-century brick above. Two or three long blank façades bespoke the presence of old warehouses backing on to the River Barr, where once wool bales used to be unloaded for the mills. Alongside these, two tall chimneys loomed, their factories long inactive and used now for storage only.

The usual food stores and clothing suppliers were scattered round the perimeter of the main square, whose centre was a garden of lawns and shrubs criss-crossed with asphalt paths and benches.

Because it was mid-morning on a Friday, shoppers gave the scene some liveliness. The sky was bright, strong sunlight bursting out from behind pompous white clouds to bathe the scene and give colour to the tubs of Siberian wallflowers on the traffic islands. But the light also pointed up the drabness of sooty brick, the grimy windows of the disused factories, the harshness of scarred walls and untended pavements.

Iris surveyed it with ironic interest. Nothing would *ever* have induced her to live in a place like this. If she'd been born here, the first thing she'd have done when she left school would have been to thumb a lift out.

'How much of this is going?' she enquired.

'Practically all of it, except the churches and the Town Hall. The Chamber of Commerce has done a good job getting firms interested in coming here—'

'To do what? Not to go back to making cloth, surely?'

'No, no – it'll be service industries, insurance HQs, that sort of thing. The new council – you'll meet some of them this morning – they were voted in on a promise to make a fresh start. For quite a long time councils have been going down the wrong road, trying to tempt companies to come in and take over the mills you saw . . .'

'Fat chance!'

'Exactly. Now they've seen the light, those days are gone. It's sad, of course, because they made a first-class product here by all accounts but the industry's left, the buildings are hopeless by modern standards, except for one or two of the old warehouses. I'm planning to adapt them for what's called "loft-living" these days.'

'Oh yes, I wouldn't mind something like that – not here, of course,' Iris said with a shudder.

'You might like it here once I've tidied it up,' said Bethany.

Iris was spared the need to say that she was sure Bethany would make a vast improvement. They were now drawing into a dismal parking lot which served the Town Hall. A moment later she was following Bethany

27

into the big old foyer, impressive if not inviting in its mottled grey marble. An elderly concierge directed them to the lift, which took them in stately ascent to the first floor where a secretary awaited.

'This way . . .'

The boardroom was a vast chamber more suited to the meetings of the previous century than the present day, although this morning's muster would use up most of the chairs at the table. One end had been set up as a coffee stand; a silver urn, cups and saucers, and plates of croissants were set out on gleaming old napery with the town's coat of arms woven into it. Remnants of past glories, Bethany thought sadly as the Mayor of Barhampton urged refreshments upon them.

The Mayor was a youngish man, with a seriousness about local politics which he disguised under a sprightly manner. He made introductions between the newcomers and the men assembled to get the project moving. Except for Bethany and Iris, there were no women; even the minute-taker turned out to be a man. Portraits of former councillors frowned down upon them from the walls – dark suits, stiff collars, pince-nez and beards.

Bethany wasn't cowed. She knew most of the men in the room, old friends of her father's, themselves fathers of her school-friends, their wives the givers of birthday parties, organisers of picnics, and indeed co-workers with her mother in local charities. She shook hands with them, allowed herself to be hugged by some.

For Iris it was different. She was used to coping with strangers, but in general she made an immediate and favourable impression on men. Those she was now meeting seemed a different breed from the London executives she habitually charmed. They were polite in a gruff, casual way; they seemed to study her with something that might have been criticism. She found it hard to catch the speech rhythms of some, and certainly didn't understand their poker-faced jokes.

The fact was, they thought her a very pretty, smartly dressed lass, but they were fairly sure she was here as moral support for young Bethany. It was Bethany they were interested in. It was Bethany who was going to have to prove herself today and in the days to come so, in their view, the importance of the 'publicity girl' was negligible.

The one friendly face for Iris was Alan Singleton. He gave her a warm welcome. Unfortunately he also gave Bethany an embrace and a hearty kiss on the cheek. 'I bet you're thrilled to bits this morning,' he remarked. 'A big day!'

'I hope they're all in a good mood.'

'You'll sort them out if they aren't,' he said confidently.

Which made it seem all the more like some kind of plot on Bethany's part to make Iris feel *de trop*.

The Mayor called the meeting to order. They took their places around the long mahogany table. 'I'm only here as a welcoming committee,' he told them. 'The Council of Barhampton thanks you all for agreeing to take part in the Steering Committee for the new Town Centre. Most of you know each other, I'm sure, but I'd just like to introduce Miss Iris Weston, who is taking care of publicity for *Dayton & Daughter*. Miss Dayton rang to ask if Miss Weston could sit in on this morning's proceedings but I'm sure she understands that although anything you say is fair copy, she may be asked to vacate her place if finance is discussed. All right, Iris?'

'Of course.'

'Righto then. I'll hand over the Chair to the Deputy Head of Town Planning for Barhampton, Councillor Cyril Ollerton. The council have appointed him Chairman of Steerco, and also Project Manager for the new Town Centre. In his capable hands I'm sure this morning will make a good start on our tremendous undertaking, and myself and other members of the council hope to meet you at a buffet lunch when you conclude. Bye for now.' And with this cheery exit line the Mayor took his departure.

The Steering Committee consisted of a group from the Town Council: Cyril Ollerton, now announced as Chairman; Josh Pembury, Head of the Landscaping Department; various members of the Legal and Accounts Departments; then there were the heads of the firms involved in the construction – including the cronies foretold by Mary Dayton – and one or two representatives from social services and churches and chapels. *Dayton & Daughter* were represented by Bethany as the consulting architect, and Alan, who had been appointed Construction Manager.

His would be a very onerous role. Private developers hire specialists to manage the construction of a big building; the job is to order structural steel, masonry such as bricks and prefabricated sections, components for piping, lighting, ventilation, roofing, windows, glass, and anything else that has to be on site from the beginning to the end. But because the developer in this case was Barhampton Town Council, it was the Town Planning Department who chose both the Project Manager and the Construction Manager. In an effort to keep within budget, the Head of Town Planning had appointed one of its own officers to handle the progress of the work, and a member of *Dayton & Daughter* to supervise the provision of materials not already budgeted for with the contractors.

If all members attended every meeting, it might prove unwieldy. But Bethany knew from experience that people began to drop off in attendance quite soon unless the topic for discussion really mattered to them. Technical discussion of drains and lighting cables soon bored them. Bethany herself was apt to skip a meeting about finance.

This being the first meeting, the talk was general. Plans and sketches of buildings were handed round, reports on water levels and soil layers, methods of progress-supervision, schedules of work – a pile of paper soon lay in front of every place. Iris could take little part, and got nothing that could be used as a handout for a general readership, although technical journals would no doubt be interested. But she hadn't expected to get much; if the truth be told, she was here simply to watch what went on between Alan and Bethany.

Cyril Ollerton declared the meeting closed at ten minutes to one. They had all expected this; the first meeting was always brief, an exchange of documentation, really. The getting-down-to-business meeting was scheduled for the following Monday and might last all day. But having got the show on the road, they broke up in good humour, heading for the Mayor's Anteroom where drinks and lunch awaited them.

Now was her chance to get close to Alan, thought Iris. In the course of helping herself to cold game pie and salad she managed to be at his elbow, so naturally he led her to a little table and a set of chairs where she could eat in comfort. This was much better than the boardroom where, seated at an awkward angle, she'd been unable to exchange so much as a glance with him.

But when the game pie and white wine had been disposed of, who should appear but Bethany, come on purpose to break it up – or so it seemed to Iris. In fact Bethany thought she was carrying out Iris's wish, expressed the previous evening, of meeting the members of the steering committee. She took her from one to another of the members. Iris summoned up all her social skills to smile sweetly and seem interested but inwardly she was fuming; how dared this provincial nobody interfere in her affairs!

The men were kinder to Iris than at their first introduction. In the first place she'd held her tongue through the first meeting of Steerco, and secondly they'd got a little used to her being among them. Lastly and most importantly, a couple of glasses of wine had mellowed them. So they paid her a few clumsy compliments which she received as if she were delighted, all the time thinking, Dimwits!

They for their part thought she was pretty but useless. This opinion was altered radically over the weekend when they read the Saturday issue of *The Financial Times* and the heavy Sundays. The material Iris had faxed back on Thursday night had been well received. There was coverage in the business sections and even one mention in editorial columns. And moreover, one of the tabloids had picked it up for the 'woman in a man's world' aspect, dwelling on Bethany's success both at home and in Denmark.

So when Steerco reassembled on Monday, they were not only delighted to welcome Iris back but sought her out at the lunch-hour to do a bit of business on their own behalf. Most of the contractors had press officers on their staff but only to deal with local pressmen and such officials as had to be soothed or argued with. Now, they saw, they were to be associated with a project that would bring them national, perhaps worldwide attention. And here was a young woman who knew how to handle it.

She received several invitations to lunch at the best hotel in Barhampton – but that wasn't saying much because the Victoria, once splendid, was now in the 'eat as much as you like for a fiver' class. She solved the problem neatly by saying that she had to drive back to London in time for a four o'clock appointment but if anyone cared to ring her – and here she handed out business cards – she'd be in her office from five until eight that evening.

It wasn't at all what she'd wanted to do. She'd thought she would get Alan to herself over the lunch break. She'd hoped for a last chance to chat him up before she had to dash back to London for a catching-up session at work. It was really too bad. What made it worse was seeing Alan and Bethany head for the Victoria together.

Bethany was quite unaware of the animosity she was arousing in Iris. Nor did she have any forewarning of the trouble it was going to cause.

The next few weeks were very busy for her. Barhampton Town Council already owned much of the land which was to be redeveloped and were winding up negotiations for the remaining parcels. Alan had surveyed all of it already so that the architectural plans could be finalised. If you dig a hole anywhere in the British Isles, you're likely to come upon Iron Age, Bronze Age, Roman, Saxon or Viking remains. Luckily the Victorians had already dug, and had removed such finds to the local museum, but in their place they had left a veritable bowl of black spaghetti – sewage pipes, water pipes, gas pipes, and later electricity supply cables and telephone lines.

Once again, for economy's sake, the council had decided not to replace this jumble with new services. Instead they had made an agreement with the construction firms that they would respect existing pipes and cables. Alan had had a terrible time in the Planning Department's archives trying to find out where these lines lay, but on the whole he was satisfied he had identified everything.

Such lease-holders or private property owners as remained on the site were moving out; shops put up notices saying they could be found at premises outside the redevelopment zone, businesses sent out flyers and pamphlets explaining how they would cope until they could reopen in the new Town Centre.

Bethany didn't have much to do with the business side of the firm. She didn't attend as many of the meetings of Steerco as she should have, although she tried always to read the minutes. These were as dull as committee minutes usually are, but by and by it dawned on her that considerable leeway was being given to the demolition contractors. Naturally *William Wellbrow & Company* had to be first in the field because until the old buildings were demolished, nothing could be done to prepare the ground for new construction.

Yet did they have to have their cheques sent so much ahead of everyone else? The excavators which came in almost immediately behind the bulldozers belonged to another firm, whose money seemed not to be paid over until two or three weeks had gone by.

'Why do *Wellbrow's* get priority, Dad?' she enquired on coming back to the office after a day on site. 'James McGuire asked me about it over a cup of coffee in the site office.'

'Probably made a special arrangement with Barhampton's accountants,' grunted Daniel.

'But why should the accountants make special arrangements for *Wellbrow's*? McGuire has as much right, surely?'

'If you paid any attention to finance you'd remember that budgeting schedules are set up at the beginning of the work. If McGuire had thought to ask for payment-by-result he could have had it.' Daniel rustled some papers to let her know he was busy.

'But he couldn't ask for it until he knew he'd got the contract, now could he?' Bethany persisted.

'Of course not.'

'But as far as I can make out, Wellbrow was in there the minute contracts were signed, before he could even have had time to tell his accounts department to ask for priority.'

'Well, he's a better businessman than McGuire, obviously,' said Daniel, his brow darkening.

'It seems almost as if he had advance warning, Dad.'

'Well, there's always a lot of gossip in the business about things like this.'

'McGuire says Wellbrow had inside information.' Now it was out, what she had come to say on behalf of James McGuire, who had shared milky, sugary coffee from his vacuum flask as a pretext for having a word with her.

'Well, he would say that, wouldn't he?' her father said, lightening his voice for the well-known tag. 'He wasn't quick enough off the mark and so now he's finding excuses for himself.'

'I don't think that's true. He says his accountant rang the morning after contract-signing—'

'Look here, girl, you're an architect; keep your mind on that. You've no head for business and never had.'

'My head's clear enough to see that there's been some sort of fiddle here. You and Billy Wellbrow have been friends for years, you understand the kind of thing he gets up to.'

'Yes, and when you've been in this world as long as I have, you'll realise that friendships are important in business.'

'Not if it involves you in doing something underhand – and you must have had a hand in it, your friend Ossie Fielden probably gave you advance warning about who'd won the contracts.'

'Underhand? What's underhand about helping an old friend to get his money on time? You know the delays that can crop up during a long construction job. It makes sense to iron them out in advance.'

'No matter that it's unfair on people who don't happen to be part of the Old Boys' Network, who don't know Ossie Fielden and his Barhampton buddies?'

Daniel had reddened at the scorn in her voice, but he kept control of his temper. 'Bethany, half of the business in the world gets done through personal contacts. Connections are important – everybody knows that. McGuire's fairly new on the scene and it's only because Barhampton's new council have this policy of spreading the opportunities that he's in there at all. He ought to be grateful, not filling your ears with spiteful gossip!'

'There wasn't anything spiteful about it, Dad, he simply asked me if I knew how he could get on the first-line payment list because he'd heard that other people were on it. I said there was no such thing and he said "Oh yes, there is" and told me that *Wellbrow's* banked their cheques at least two weeks before he got his. And two weeks means a lot to a man like McGuire. He can't pay his wages if there's a hold-up.'

'Soppy little firm, what's he got, four excavators, a back-hoe, and eleven trucks? He ought to think himself lucky he's in there at all. *I* wanted all of the excavation work on that sector to go to Emmett Foyle.'

'I bet you did,' Bethany said grimly. 'Another of your cronies. Is that what it comes down to? You and your pals get together and sort out who's to get what before ever Barhampton considers the tenders?'

'We have conversations about it, if that's what you mean. What do you expect? We come across each other almost every day in the course of normal life. It would be odd if we didn't talk about it.'

'And make arrangements? That's part of it too, isn't it?'

'We try to smooth the road ahead – what's the harm in that?'

'Grease the road ahead, you mean. A few palms get greased as well, I imagine.'

'You mind your tongue, young lady! If you're suggesting bribery—'

'No, but it's all part of the Old Pals' Act, isn't it? You and your buddies sort things out so that you get the juicy bits—'

'There's nothing wrong in what we do! We only guide—'

'I'm not saying any money changes hands, Dad – it's more subtle than that. But it's underhand just the same.'

'Don't stand there like a mealy-mouthed missionary telling me how to run my business! This firm has flourished—' His gesture took in the handsome room, its fitments of walnut and cherry-wood, the chart cabinets which housed the plans of former successes, the photographs of Daniel with hospital governors, school heads, titled landowners, mayors, councillors – 'It's flourished because we had friends all through the northern counties. Life's going to be hard enough for you when you come into the chairmanship, simply because men find it awkward dealing with a woman. If you're going to take up a holier-than-thou attitude to a bit of good networking, you'll soon find doors closing in your face!'

Who does she think she is, he snarled inwardly. Standing there with her head thrown back, challenging like a Viking warrior maiden . . . ! He was furious with her, and yet in some way with himself too, for her anger struck a chord in him, conjured up a picture he wanted to forget. The young Daniel Dayton had once stood before *his* father in just this way, objecting to dishonesty and demanding explanations.

Yet things really had been bad in those days. Actual cash was handed about in manila envelopes, thick wads of ten-pound notes for services rendered. To complain about what was happening now was naïve and childish. Of course friends helped each other through the labyrinthine paths of local government finance. If newcomers felt left out, let them wait until they'd built up contacts too; everybody did it, it was the way the wheels were kept turning.

'How many others are on your list of favoured firms?' Bethany insisted, disregarding his appeal to family tradition.

'None of your business! You pay attention to the architecture and I'll pay attention to the finance. *Dayton's* have other projects on the books. *Somebody's* got to make sure the funds come in to back up the work. We can't all be worrying about traditional detail on the brickwork and eco-friendly lighting for the footpaths.'

She gave a little shiver, her shoulders moving inside the wind-cheater she was still wearing. 'You really hate my design, don't you?' she muttered. 'You never really wanted to enter it.'

'That's neither here nor there. We're stuck with it now, and we've got to cost it out so that we don't overspend the council's specification. If you don't mind, that's what I'm doing now and I'd like to get on with it.'

Without another word she turned and went out. He stared at the closed door, his hand rubbing at his chin in a gesture of doubt. What had he said? He'd let his tongue run away with him a bit, hadn't he?

Well, so what. It was time she learned that the business world was no bed of roses, that even idealistic architects had to be careful about money. But if she told her mother about their argument, Mary would give him her 'troubled' look. Mary often implied he was unfair to Bethany. Stuff and nonsense. It was perfectly true that, in his opinion, women weren't good architects. He had always believed that and he said what he believed. Winning the contract for the Barhampton Town Centre had astonished him but he still maintained (though of course it would be bad business to say so) that it was a silly design.

Let's just wait and see, he thought. When the first buildings are completed, let's see if everyone still thinks them so marvellous. Too playful, too feminine by half. What's wanted in a town centre is solidity, dignity, not oriel windows and contrast pointing.

Bethany moved out of the family home the following week. She felt the antagonism between herself and her father would only increase if she stayed. She had a perfectly good excuse; rising at five each morning so as to be on site by seven in Barhampton was a strain. By taking a flat in Barhampton she could have an hour longer in bed and if need be stay at work until late evening.

Her mother protested but only for a while. She saw the sense in what her daughter said and, moreover, she could feel the tension between Daniel and Bethany. She thought it was simply Daniel's envy over Bethany's success: neither of them mentioned the quarrel about dishonesty.

'And of course I'll be here a lot anyway,' Bethany promised. 'I'll have to come into the office on business and there's stuff I'd like to leave up in my room, if you don't mind.'

'Of course not! And I want you here for Sunday lunch. I know what it's like for you singles living on your own; you eat out of packets and go to fast-food places. You'll have one good meal a week or I'll know the reason why!'

'Yes, Mother,' Bethany said in a tone of a little girl accepting judgement.

Mary laughed. 'All right, but mind what I say – look after yourself properly.'

Bethany had no trouble finding a flat among the houses she'd pointed out to Iris Weston as they drove into Barhampton. She chose a four-storey building of some character, with bushes of forsythia brightening the small front garden. The top floor had been the maids' attics and was now used for storage. The third floor where Bethany had her flat had high ceilings and tall windows, giving plenty of space and light for her drafting table and a handy nook for her computer. She furnished the three main rooms from the local furniture stores in one afternoon, working from a list drawn up from her expert knowledge of house interiors. It didn't matter that the result lacked character; she would only be here for as long as it took to see the centre of Barhampton completed. Once that was done, she'd think about where she wanted to live. She certainly wouldn't go back to the parental home. It was absurd, a woman in her thirties still living with Mother.

When Iris Weston heard that Bethany had moved out of York, she was pleased. To her it meant that she had withdrawn from the field of battle over Alan Singleton, had conceded defeat. The fact that Bethany didn't even know they'd been in competition never occurred to her. She'd been convinced from the outset that Bethany was her rival and that she now understood she couldn't win.

Iris had come North intermittently since the establishment of Steerco but no longer attended its meetings. There were plenty of excuses.

Several of the contractors had engaged *Seymour PR* – a nice piece of business, greatly appreciated by Iris's boss and resulting in a nice little bonus at Easter. She would drive to York with advertising sketches in her briefcase, rough drafts of publicity hand-outs, statistics on results so far. On almost all of these visits she saw Alan.

Better yet, she invited him to London. She invented reasons at first: someone had given her two tickets for the latest Stephen Sondheim; she needed an escort for a business banquet; would he like to take part in a charity bridge tournament.

But quite soon there was no need to invent reasons. He stayed with her at her flat overnight – it seemed only sensible, why should he keep paying for a hotel room? When they became lovers, she was delighted by the fact that he took the initiative – although she'd intended to share a bed with him no matter what.

It became an accepted fact among Alan's friends and acquaintances in York that he and Iris were an item. If one or two were surprised that he'd chosen a girl with such different tastes from his own, well, love's like that, isn't it? No one could expect Iris to go on geological hikes over the moors, nor take an interest in his collection of antique surveying instruments. But on the other hand, no one had expected Alan to alter so much. He began to appear in suits instead of the corduroys and sweaters of old. What was more, the suits were Armani-style. When he changed his handy little Japanese runabout for a new car, he bought a fine second-hand Merc. The old Alan gradually disappeared and in his place came the man that Iris wanted him to be.

And in changing him, she made him all the more her possession, to be cared for and defended in a way that was new to her. She was very much in love, rather to her own surprise.

Now that he was so clearly involved with her, she didn't mind the continuing friendship with Bethany. And Bethany needed friends, needed someone to confide in.

After a lot of doubt and delay, she asked Alan to meet her for a drink on a day when he had come to Barhampton, and cautiously enquired what he felt about preferential treatment among the contractors.

'How d'you mean?'

'Well, I found out that some of them are at the front of the queue when the cheques are sent out, and some are at the back.'

'But that's got to be so, Bethany. You don't expect Barhampton Council to keep all the cheques in a drawer and send them out in one fell swoop?'

'I don't see why not. It would be fairer—'

'Maybe, but I think it would be a strain on the book-keepers. And surely it's better for some of the contractors to get the advantage of cheques in the bank earning money as soon as possible rather than sitting in the council's account?'

'I suppose so . . .'

'What's brought this on, anyway?'

'Jim McGuire mentioned it to me. He seems to be right at the end of the queue.'

Alan nodded. 'He's a newcomer on the scene, of course. He's got to make his way as best he can until he can get a friend at court.'

'Is that how it's done? You have to do a bit of wheeling and dealing?'

'Bethany, there's got to be give and take on a big scheme like this. If you do everything strictly by the rules, allowing no favours to old and reliable firms, it would take about a century to get the centre of Barhampton rebuilt.'

'I thought of coming to the next Steerco and bringing the matter up—'

'Don't do that,' he said hastily. 'That would really bring the roof down on us.'

'But all it needs is an agreement to accept the same payment day for everybody.'

'And you'd have to make an application to Barhampton's Accounts Department, and you'd have to explain why, and they'd be offended at the idea that they'd been playing favourites and had to change, and their computer would have to be reprogrammed—'

'All right, all right, you've made your point!' She put her hands over her ears, half-laughing. 'I can see it was a silly idea.' She hesitated. 'My father says I'm silly and naïve to bother . . .'

'He might have expressed it more kindly,' said Alan. 'But you've got to accept that in a big project like this, money can't rush out like water from a dam – it comes out in little dribbles when the accountants feel that have to let it go. Don't forget, they have a vested interest in holding on to it because while it's in their account it's earning four per cent – and that's a substantial sum, the interest on big payments like those.'

'Yes.' She sighed, admitting defeat.

'Besides,' he teased, 'you've done a bit of jockeying for priority yourself.'

'Me? What on earth do you mean?'

He hastened to take away any hint of offence. 'Oh, not about money! But didn't I hear you and Josh Pembury plotting in a corner after the last Steerco, about bushes or trees or something?'

She coloured up and laughed. 'Oh, that. He's managed to get the council to agree . . . you see, we need mature trees for the Riverside Walk. We can use saplings elsewhere and the Landscaping Department can get those from the council's plant nurseries. But to attract big companies to the offices along the riverside we've got to give them the landscape we promised in the sketches and that calls for mature trees – so he's going to go over budget on those and he's actually got the council to agree.'

Alan waved an admonishing finger. 'So now, my lass, aren't you ashamed of yourself? It's all right to use an insider to help you get environmental goodies, but it's all wrong for a hardworking contractor to make sure he gets his payments promptly. What have you to say for yourself?'

'I can only plead guilty, Your Honour.' She was half-laughing but not totally convinced.

'He's all right, is Josh. I'd never met him until we set up Steerco. He's one who doesn't take up time with unnecessary chit-chat.'

'That's because he knows most of the other members think all this emphasis on a green environment is a bit daft. But I think it's vital, Alan. We don't want just to build a lot of housing blocks and offices, we want to enhance the quality of life in Barhampton.'

'Well, so long as you know it's not a first priority with most builders, love. If you and Josh can bring it off, that's all to the good. But my advice is, stay within the budget or you might run into trouble.'

Alan spoke blithely about running into trouble. He might well have taken the words unto himself, for trouble was brewing for him in his role of surveyor to the rebuilding of Barhampton Town Centre.

He'd taken it for granted, as had everyone else, that the Town Planning Department had obtained all the land for the construction work. He had surveyed the terrain and made his report about geological strata and underground water and the whereabouts of pipes and cables.

What he hadn't done was check carefully that every square foot of land on the maps was certified as legally available.

The blow fell on a Tuesday morning. Billy Wellbrow's bulldozers arrived at Royal Terrace to begin work on knocking down the old Georgian houses – some turned into offices with shops on the ground floor, one or two until recently occupied as dwellings.

The foreman on the demolition team got out his mobile phone to ring the home office. 'Is that Mr Wellbrow? No, I don't want to speak to his secretary. Tell Mr Wellbrow I have to speak to him, it's important!'

Angry at being interrupted over the morning's correspondence, Billy Wellbrow picked up his phone. 'What's up then, Ernie?' he demanded.

'Mr Wellbrow . . . Mr Wellbrow . . . I've called off the rigs.'

'Called 'em off? Are you daft? Get going on that block or we'll be falling behind schedule.'

'Mr Wellbrow, I can't! The schedule calls for me to start at the west end of the row.'

'Well, get on with it, then.'

'I can't, guv'nor – I really can't! The first house has got somebody still living in it!'

Chapter Four

Billy Wellbrow stared at his receiver as if it had spoken in tongues. 'Don't talk rubbish! That row's been empty for months.'

'No, it hasn't! I tell you there's someone still living in number fifteen.'

'That's impossible, Ernie. Town Planning owns all that row and they made sure lease-holders went by the end of March.'

'Guv, I'm standing here on the pavement outside the house. There's fresh lace curtains hanging in both bay windows and one set of 'em's a bit parted and I can see a big fat old cat sitting in front of a one-bar electric fire, washing its paws!'

'Ernie, it can't be!' shouted Wellbrow.

'Don't blast my ear off!' shouted Ernie in return. 'I tell you I'm looking at it and it's no stray cat that's wandered into a derelict house for shelter. Full of milk and fish, that cat is. *And* there's an aspidistra in a brass pot in the other window and I tell you this for nothing – that pot was polished not more 'n a couple of days ago.'

'Polished?' breathed Wellbrow. He'd had trouble before with squatters who somehow gained entrance to empty houses, but squatters weren't the sort who had aspidistras in brass pots. And they certainly didn't polish anything.

'Go and try the door,' he instructed. 'I'll hang on.' He sat in tense silence for three or four minutes until he heard Ernie pick up his mobile again.

'Mr Wellbrow?'

'I'm here, come on, get on with it!'

'An old lady came to the door and shouted at me to get my machine away from in front of her house!'

'An old lady? What old lady?'

'How do I know, guv?' protested the foreman, annoyed. 'She's there in the house, and I reckon it's her cat and her aspidistra, and I'm not doing no wrecking on this site until you get here and get her out!'

Wellbrow was already on his way out of his office without even bothering to hang up his phone. To his astonished secretary he yelled, 'Get Bigsby – tell him to meet me at Royal Terrace – tell him it's urgent!' And with that, like a tubby whirlwind he was gone.

Royal Terrace had once been an attractive place, inhabited by the well-to-do of Barhampton when it was a pleasant country town under the happy reign of the Hanoverians. There had been trade, goods coming up the River Barr for distribution by cart throughout the region, and farming produce coming to the river to be carried by barge to the Ouse and beyond. There had been a theatre, an Assembly Hall; there had been balls and summer fairs.

People with money had built the Georgian houses still to be seen throughout the town and its southern suburbs. Royal Terrace had been one of the last to emerge, a tidy little row of fifteen houses put up for the lesser gentry, owners of shops and small businesses, with money enough to buy furniture from Hepplewhite but not to need a carriage-house and stabling.

Across the road from the houses was a tiny public garden, intended to make up for the lack of space around the houses themselves and available only to the residents. Beyond that lay the backs of some of the shops in the main shopping centre, the coming and going of vans and lorries screened by the ageing laurels and viburnums which were all that remained of once elegant plantings.

When Billy Wellbrow's car screeched to a halt against the garden railings, he found the team of demolition vehicles standing like dinosaurs in the roadway. His foreman came to greet him.

'She's there, boss, standing behind the aspidistra pot, watching us.'

'Can't see her,' grunted Wellbrow, glaring at the house.

'She's there. She fidgets a bit from time to time, you can just glimpse it.'

'What's she like?'

'Dunno. She didn't open the door when I knocked, she spoke to me through it.'

'So how d'you know she's old?'

'She sounded old. And the aspidistra, tha knows.'

'This is damn ridiculous!' grunted Wellbrow. 'According to the schedule, this whole row was emptied at the end of March.'

'So you said, guv. But she's there, isn't she?'

Still half-convinced that his foreman was under the influence of pot or beer or some other hallucinant, Wellbrow stamped up the three steps to the door of No. 15 and seized the handle. It turned, but when he tried to open the door, it resisted.

Bolted on the inside.

'Open the door!' he demanded.

'Go away!'

'Open this door at once! This house is condemned and is about to be demolished!'

'Just try! I'll have the law on you if you damage so much as a single brick!'

'The law? Let me tell you, madam, the law requires you to vacate these premises at once.'

40

'Don't stand on my doorstep spouting high-flown rubbish at me! And get those hideous machines out of here, they're spoiling the view.'

Although her words weren't audible to Ernie or his drivers, they could guess by Wellbrow's reaction that he wasn't having any success. 'Well, our Billy's not doing too well, is he?' they remarked to each other and didn't bother to hide their amusement.

'Our Billy' shook the handle in vexation. 'Open this door at once, madam!' When there was no response he banged on the door panels. 'Open up at once! My machines need to start work!'

No reply. Nothing. It seemed as if the speaker from within had retired to the interior of the house.

Wellbrow was saved from further humiliation by the arrival of Raymond Bigsby, the solicitor for Barhampton Town Council with whom Wellbrow had to keep in touch over legal matters. He came hotfoot from a case he'd been handling at the Town Hall.

'What's all this about, Wellbrow?'

'What's it about? I'll tell you what it's about! Confounded inefficiency, that's what it's about! Didn't your department tell Town Planning that all the leases had fallen in and the premises were to be emptied? And didn't Town Planning tell me everybody's gone?'

'Yes, of course. End-March, that was the official date, but a lot went earlier.'

'Well, your tenant at number fifteen didn't go. She's there now, with the door shut fast, and my team can't get on with their work!'

Bigsby stared at him. 'You're joking.'

'Do I look as if I'm joking? Two demolition tractors and a fleet of trucks waiting to knock the place down and clear it, and they're just *standing* there, doing nowt.'

'There's some mistake,' said Bigsby. 'Someone's playing a trick.'

'Oh, really? You try then. Go on, go and tell her she's playing a trick on us.'

Bigsby, a man inclined at all times to think he was right, approached the door of No. 15 Royal Terrace. He raised the well-polished knocker and let it fall, twice. Standing waiting for an answer, he looked at the knocker. It shone back at him, a worn but well-polished lion's face in brass. For the first time, he began to suspect there was some truth in the tale Wellbrow had just told.

A voice, thin and old but firm, spoke. 'Yes?'

'Er . . . madam . . . I'm Raymond Bigsby of the Legal Department of Barhampton Council. Madam, I'm afraid you're in contravention of the Town Planning regulation of the 11th April last year, in that the council's property called Royal Terrace was to be vacated by the end of March this year.' He paused. 'Madam?'

'I'm not in contravention of anything, Mr Whoever-you-are. Always told those others I'd no intention of going.'

41

'What others?'

'Those that packed up and left.'

'They were obeying the law, madam. The council's ruling under the Town Planning Act—'

'There's no law that says I have to leave my own house.'

'But there is, madam.' Bigsby, unaccustomed to talking through two inches of oak, drew a breath and said with great formality: 'May I know to whom I'm speaking?'

There came a little cackle of laughter from beyond the sturdy oak panels. 'So much for the Legal Department and the Town Planning Act! You don't even know who I am! Why don't you go and find out before you bother me again, young man?'

And though he knocked and pleaded, she made no further response. He retreated to the side of the caterpillar tractor, where the demolition ball swayed lazily but uselessly at the end of its metal arm, and got on his mobile phone.

Within half an hour word spread from the Legal Department to the Town Planning Department, to the Finance Department, to every other department in the council offices. Josh Pembury rang Bethany Dayton with the news. She threw herself into her Suzuki. Within minutes she was at Royal Terrace.

The demolition tractors had withdrawn to the end of the row, farthest from No. 15. Only Raymond Bigsby and Billy Wellbrow were there now, standing by Wellbrow's blue BMW.

'What's going on?' Bethany demanded.

'The Legal Department's checking. For some reason some old girl's been left in possession of this house and she won't come out.'

'Some old girl?' she echoed. 'Who? Who is she?'

'We don't know yet.'

'But that's impossible! The property belongs to the council; it was officially emptied in March—'

'Miss Dayton, we've been through all that already. She ought to be gone, whoever she is, but she isn't. I've asked the Legal Department to get a warrant and there's a bailiff coming from the magistrate's court to serve it. Can we just leave it at that for the moment?' Bigsby enquired crossly.

'You go and talk to her, miss,' suggested Ernie the foreman, sauntering up to join them. 'She might talk a bit of sense to a woman.'

Bethany was well known among the contractors for having a way of sorting out difficulties. Things might be going wrong, weather might be hostile, supplies might be delayed, men might be mutinous – if Bethany appeared on the scene, somehow good humour was restored within minutes. Perhaps it was because the workmen felt they couldn't swear and throw things about in front of her, perhaps it was that she made them feel foolish for acting childishly . . .

Certainly it was worth a try to send her to speak to the old witch inside No. 15.

She went up the three steps, looked at the knocker, but decided instead to tap on the door. Knockers were noisy things, and her instinct was to try a quiet approach.

The inhabitant had clearly witnessed her approach through her starched lace curtains. 'Yes?' she said through the wood.

'Could you open the door, please? I'd like to have a word if you could spare the time.'

'Oh, time . . . Plenty of that.' A pause. 'If I open the door, you're going to grab me.'

'Not at all!' cried Bethany, shocked. 'I just want to talk.'

'Who are you? Welfare? I don't want any Welfare, thank you, I manage fine on my own.'

'My name's Bethany Dayton, I'm an architect—'

'A what?'

'Architect. I design buildings.'

'Oh, you're one of *them*! I've nowt to say to thee.'

'Please don't say that. I'd like to understand how it is you're still here, when all the other tenants have gone.'

'Ha!' It was a snort of triumph. 'That's where you're all wrong, the lot of you. I'm not a tenant, never was. I own this house.'

'*What?*'

'Own it, lock, stock and barrel and everything else! So there you are, Miss Architect, what d'you have to say to that, eh?'

'But that's impossible!'

Once again the little triumphant sound. 'I've got the title deeds in the drawer of my desk, under safe lock and key. And that's where they're staying.'

'Mrs . . . ? May I know your name?'

'What for, so you can put it on the warrant yon legal feller was talking about? No, thank you. You're all so clever, you ought to know who I am and what I own, but no – you come storming up here with a great machine enough to scare the life out of anybody, and tell me you're going to knock down my house where I've lived ever since I got wed. I'm telling you nowt, so put that in your building machine and grind it!'

'Please . . . Don't get annoyed with me. I'm just trying to find out where we went wrong,' Bethany said in a worried tone. 'We had no idea you owned this house. Are you sure that's right?' For old ladies, she knew, could sometimes get odd ideas into their heads.

'What is it now, trying to make out I'm barmy? I tell you I've got the papers safe and sound.'

'Could I see them?'

'You don't believe me?' said the old voice, shrill with anger.

43

'Of course I believe you. But the others . . .' She paused, to let the ill-will be psychologically shifted to the men on the roadway, the workmen in their jeans and wind-cheaters, the lawyer in his dark suit. 'If I could tell them you've showed me the title deeds it would make a difference.'

'They'd go away?'

'Yes.' For what else could they do, if this fierce old girl really owned the house?

'I'm not opening the door,' came the determined statement. 'I don't know you, you could be trying to play a trick on me.'

'I'd never do that,' said Bethany. 'If you really are the owner of this house we'd have no power to do anything.' For the moment, she added internally.

'Tell you what – I'll bring them to the window of the office.'

'The office?'

'Where the plant's standing, that was my husband's office. The deeds are in the desk there. I'll get them out and hold them up in the window for you to see.'

'It would be better if you brought them to the door.'

'I'll show you through the window pane.' There was no arguing with that tone.

'Very well,' said Bethany.

'Wait there.' There was the faint sound of receding footsteps.

Bethany turned to wave at Mr Bigsby. 'Yes?' he called. She beckoned. With a frown he came to join her.

'She's going to open up?'

'No, she's going to bring the title deeds of the property to the bay window so we can see them.'

'She's not claiming she *owns* this house?'

'Yes, she is. It's probably just a fantasy of hers; she'll show us some old document . . .'

'Most likely a knitting pattern,' scoffed Bigsby.

At that moment the curtain in the window of the bay nearest the entrance stirred. Then it was pulled aside. An arm appeared, clad in a knitted sleeve belonging to a cardigan of which many were sold in chain stores. The arm held back the lace curtain, another joined it and two hands waved an envelope at them. An old envelope, of a quality not often see these days. The hands opened it, took out stiff folded papers. They were unfolded, straightened, then held up against the glass.

In typeface from a very venerable typewriter the document proclaimed: *This agreement between the Yallington Estate and Mrs Arabella Bedells of Barhampton is a continuation of the agreement made in the year One Thousand Seven Hundred and Eighty-two of Our Lord, pursuant to the wishes of the said Yallington Estate who shall hereinafter be regarded as the First Party and of William Bedells who now shall hereinafter be regarded as the Second Party. This continuation is made and delivered on this day, the 22nd July 1947, in consideration of the fact that the original agreement and documents made between the First and Second of the original, the said Arabella Bedells, were destroyed by enemy action on the 16th May 1941, but on the statements of witnesses known and proved to be present at the time of the said destruction the First Party willingly accedes to the request for this duplicate and continuation of the original agreement of Sale as now being verified between Yallington Estate and the Second Party.*

At that point it would have been necessary to turn over to the next sheet of parchment, but the papers were withdrawn and folded up. The lace curtain dropped.

'Oh *Lord*,' groaned Raymond Bigsby.

'Yes indeed,' agreed Bethany. For if that parchment wasn't genuine, she wasn't standing here on the doorstep of 15 Royal Terrace with a very worried legal gentleman.

She tapped on the door again, and kept on tapping until the footsteps sounded behind the door. 'Mrs Bedells?' she said. 'Mrs Bedells?'

'So now you know my name. Clever you!'

'Mrs Bedells, did you have any visits from representatives of the Town Planning Department in the last year or so?'

'Ne'er a one.'

'Did you know your neighbours had been served with notices saying they had to quit their premises?'

'Oh yes, full of it, they were.'

'Didn't it occur to you as strange that no one had approached you?'

'Why should it? They were only leasing. I *own* this house.'

'But Mrs Bedells, if you knew the rest of the Terrace was going to come down, didn't you worry about what would happen to your house?'

'Not at all. The council's done daft things before and as far as I could see it was going to do something daft again. But they don't affect me, with all their nonsense.'

'But you surely didn't think you were going to go on living here with everything else demolished all around you?'

'Of course I'm going to live here. I've lived here all my married life and I'm not intending to go anywhere else at my age!'

'Excuse me, madam,' interrupted Bigsby, 'but what you intend is quite impossible. The rebuilding plans for the Town Centre necessitate your vacating these premises at once.'

'That's that silly legal man again, isn't it? Go away, you interfering idiot. I told you the first time: you've no right here making a racket like a line of goods trains outside my door, and if you and your underlings don't move off I'll call the police!'

With that they heard the sound of footsteps receding into the house. Bigsby began banging on the door with his fist. Bethany caught his elbow. Didn't the man recognise finality when he heard it? Mrs Bedells had said all she intended to say for the moment, and no amount of hammering on her door would bring her back – quite the reverse. By the sound of her she was a doughty fighter. Raymond Bigsby with all his legal phrases wouldn't cow her.

In the marbled foyer of the Town Hall, a reporter from the *Barhampton Gazette* was speaking on his mobile to his editor at the newspaper office.

'I tell you, summat's up,' he insisted. 'Bigsby darted out of that tribunal like a startled rabbit. And it's quite an important case – a wrongful dismissal by the council. He just rushed out and left his assistant to handle it.'

'Hang on a minute and I'll look at the computer,' said the editor. A pause. 'Not much showing. There's been nothing dramatic such as a bank hold-up, and no big traffic accident because the hospital would be logged as "In Action". And if there'd been a fire, we'd have the Fire Service logged.'

'It's not that sort of thing, Mac. It's something legal. Why else should they call out one of their legal chiefs?'

'Where's he gone?'

'Not far – he didn't take his car. It's still in the parking lot.'

'I wonder what he's been called to?'

'Couldn't you get one of your moles at the council offices to tell you?'

'Right,' said Mac. 'Stay there, I'll call back.'

The reporter sat down on one of the carved benches in the hall. The concierge eyed him with suspicion. Devils, these reporters, always out to give you the slip, trying to get into confidential meetings and things like that. But the reporter did nothing until his mobile phone chirped at him. He put it to his ear.

'Yes? Ah-ha . . . Ah-ha . . . *No!* Who? Never heard of her. Okay, I'm on my way, Mac. I say – what a *story!*'

And the concierge watched him dash out with the mobile still to his ear.

The last thing Mr Bigsby wanted was to have the press on the scene. He knew from experience that the *Barhampton Gazette* liked to get stories that reflected badly on the Town Council. The situation was tricky enough without having bad publicity. When he saw the reporter hurry round the corner with his notebook at the ready, he let himself be drawn away from the door of No. 15 by Bethany.

'Now what should we do?' he groaned.

'Call off the rigs,' Bethany said.

'No way!' said Wellbrow. 'We've wasted enough time this morning. They can start at the other end of the Terrace.'

'Oh, fine – and when the photographer turns up and starts taking pictures of your machinery knocking down the neighbouring houses, what will you say in defence of your action?'

'I'll tell 'em time's money and we're already nearly two hours over schedule on this site.'

'Mr Wellbrow, you can't take that attitude.'

'No, no, Wellbrow, this is a tricky situation.'

'The other houses are due for demolition, aren't they? Give me one good reason why I shouldn't start.'

The reporter supplied the reason. 'Morning, folks,' he said cheerily, joining them. 'What's all this I hear about trying to turn an old lady out of her home by force?'

'Force?' squeaked Bigsby. 'There is absolutely no intention of using force of any kind!'

'No, but there'll be a bailiff here any minute, I gather, ready to throw her out.'

'Nothing of the sort, nothing of the sort! Where did you get that idea!'

'Isn't it right that you applied for a warrant to remove her and asked for a bailiff to come at once?'

'No, no, that's a misapprehension.'

'What are you saying?' cried Wellbrow. 'You told me you'd applied for a warrant!'

'But for heaven's sake, Wellbrow, that was before we discovered she *owns* the house.'

'She owns it?' crowed the reporter. 'You mean to say this old girl hasn't sold out to the Planning Department?'

'We . . . er . . . there seems to have been an omission . . .'

'Oh, great, marvellous! The geniuses who planned our magnificent new Town Centre were so inefficient they didn't buy up the property?' The reporter was delighted. It was the best story he'd had in months. He was scribbling eagerly in his notebook as he talked.

'You're from the *Gazette*?' Bethany enquired, moving up to him and laying a hand on his sleeve. 'I don't think I've met you. What's your name?'

'Jeff Jones. And you're the *& Daughter* in *Dayton & Daughter.*'

'I'm Bethany Dayton.'

'The Female Architect.'

'Oh, come on now, Jeff, don't call me names!' she laughed.

He eyed her. His instinct was to make her a target for the mistake that had occurred, but she was smiling at him with evident goodwill and moreover was rather good-looking even in her cotton shirt and dusty slacks. 'So what's the story here? Are you going to eject this old girl so as to get on with the job of tearing down her home?'

'No, we're not going to eject her or tear down her home,' Bethany said, shaking her head at him. 'Don't start writing a story that will only have to be corrected in the next edition. Mrs Bedells—'

47

'That's her name? Bedells? How do you spell that?'

Bigsby was making grimaces at her that meant, Don't tell him. But to her mind that was foolish. Within an hour he could find out who she was, and the story was going to appear so it might as well be accurate as far as it went.

'Her name is Bedells, she has the title deeds to number fifteen, and apparently through some oversight the property has never been acquired by the council.'

'Ho ho! So you're stuck, are you?' He was writing headlines in his mind: DEAR OLD LADY DEFIES DIGGERS, or whatever they were, these great machines lining up like tanks against her. It was going to look great when they published the pix. Where was the photographer Mac had promised?

'We are at a standstill, yes,' Bigsby agreed with dignity. 'However, the council will apply for and serve a Compulsory Purchase Order and everything will go on as planned, even though there may be a delay of a week or so.'

'And in the meantime,' Bethany put in, with a meaningful nod at Wellbrow, 'the rigs will back off and work elsewhere.'

'Now wait a minute—'

'Mr Wellbrow, I'm sure you can alter your schedule and start on another site today,' she cut in, before he could say anything silly in front of the reporter. 'We all of us want to save Mrs Bedells any discomfort or anxiety, now don't we?'

'Of course we do,' agreed Bigsby, picking up his cue. 'Mrs Bedells is legally entitled to enjoy safety and comfort within her own home, and although the council is also legally entitled to have its contractors continue with work on sites legally acquired for that purpose, we shall of course intermit the continuation of the work.' Pleased with this recital, Bigsby looked expectantly at the reporter.

Jeff Jones was unimpressed. 'What's that mean? You won't throw her out today but you'll do it tomorrow or the day after?'

'Nobody's going to throw her out,' Bethany intervened before Bigsby could get launched again. 'There's no question of that, so please don't imply anything of the sort when you write it up.'

'You're not going to move her out?'

'Not at present,' Bigsby said. He was determined not to let this foolish female make promises that the Town Planning Department wouldn't be able to keep. 'Certainly not until we've sorted out the purchase of her property.'

'But when you've done that? You'll kick her out?'

'Mr Jones, I wish you wouldn't use these emotive words. The Legal Department of the Town Council will guide the Planning Department in its future course, and when Mrs Bedells has to leave it will be with all dignity and goodwill on both sides.'

'I hear you,' said Jones. 'You're saying "when", not "if". She's going to have to go?'

'Look around you, man,' grunted Wellbrow. 'The place is going to be a desert in a week or so. Everything'll be flattened. She won't *want* to stay.'

'You mean you're going to come back again and start work even if she's still in the house?' said the reporter, scribbling in his notebook.

'Mr Wellbrow is naturally anxious to fulfil his contract. But there will be a delay, that cannot be doubted,' Bigsby said, frowning furiously at Wellbrow to tell him to keep his mouth shut.

'How long a delay?'

Luckily the roar of a motorbike saved Bigsby from the need to reply to this very moot point. The photographer from the *Gazette* had arrived. 'Well,' he cried as he was heaving his machine on to its stand, 'where's the little old lady?' He extracted gear from his saddlebags, the camera almost immediately at the ready.

'She's in the house, Dickie.'

Dickie surveyed the scene. The demolition tractors were backing away in obedience to frantic signals from Wellbrow and what was on view was a row of Georgian houses, some in not very good repair, with a group of people standing outside No. 15. Not the most dramatic picture for a cameraman.

'When's she coming out?' he enquired.

'She's not,' Bethany informed him. 'All we've seen of her so far is a pair of hands at the window.'

'What are you waiting for?' Dickie said to Jeff Jones. 'Get her out – no point in a picture without her.'

Truth to tell, the event hadn't proved as dramatic as Jones had imagined. The word from the mole in the Town Planning Department had been that an old lady was about to be turned out of her home under threat of having it bulldozed down around her. All that he had to offer the photographer were the anxious looks of one contractor, one legal eagle, and the architect of the new Town Centre.

So he mounted the front steps of No. 15 to knock on the door. He waited, knocked again, and after some delay a voice said, 'Go away.'

'Mrs Bedells? I'm from the *Barhampton Gazette* – you know, your local friendly newspaper. My name's Jones, I'm on *your* side. Would you like to make a statement for the press?'

'A statement?'

'Tell me about yourself. You're a widow, yes? All on your own, fighting bureaucracy gone mad. And your husband was . . . ?'

'Mind your own business! And get off my front steps.'

'But Mrs Bedells, you're going to need all the help you can get! Just give me some background so I can do a nice story. And if you'd open the door so my photographer can get a picture—'

49

'You want to put my picture in the papers?' cried the old voice from behind the sturdy door.

'Yes, holding the title deeds of the house, if you would.'

'Take yourself off!' she ordered. 'Put my picture in the papers, would you? You think I want to make a poppy-show of myself for the folk of Barhampton? Get out of here, you impudent man!'

And with that he heard the sound of footsteps receding on linoleum, then silence.

He stood for a long moment knocking and calling to her, but nothing came of it. Crestfallen, he retreated down the shallow steps to the pavement. Wellbrow had gone to brief his drivers where to move their vehicles for a start elsewhere on the day's work, but Bigsby watched the reporter's retreat with unconcealed triumph.

'Got a flea in your ear, did you?' he enquired.

Jones muttered that she wasn't easy to deal with. Visions of headlines featuring the words 'dear little old lady' faded. Mrs Bedells was anything but 'dear' – she was sharp and stubborn and suspicious-minded.

No sense in wasting any more time here. He could probably do better in the newspaper files at the office. The *Gazette* made a point of its strong interest in local news; somewhere in the morgue there must be some mention of Mrs Bedells and her dead husband, even if it was only the notice of their marriage and his funeral. He took the photographer aside to confer. They huddled together, a shabby enough pair, Jones in his leather jacket now somewhat scratched and worn and the corpulent Dickie in stone-washed blue denim that would have looked better on a teenager. 'I'm going back to the office, Dickie. She's not going to come out so what'll you do?'

'I'll hang around a bit, unless Mac sends me on something else. She's got to come out some time, even if it's just to buy a bottle of milk – you can see the milkman doesn't deliver here any more!'

'But that might not be today, Dickie.'

'Well, I'll give it an hour or two and if all else fails I'll try for a shot through the window – the lace curtains don't quite meet, I notice.'

'Best of British. I'll tell Mac what you're doing, he'll probably be in touch.'

With that Jeff Jones walked off to retrieve his car from the Town Hall car park, and seeing him quit the field Mr Bigsby breathed easier. He knew, as did every Town Hall official, that the press were only too keen to get something with which to belabour them. He too decided to go back to the office to find out the truth about Mrs Bedells's ownership of the house and why it hadn't been requisitioned. He accepted a lift back to his own car in Bethany's Suzuki. Bethany herself, by now very anxious, went to the site office to ring her father.

'It's true then?' he demanded as soon as she announced herself and began to speak. 'There's some madwoman in a house in Royal Terrace refusing to get out?'

'Who told you that? It's a bit inaccurate.'

'I got it from Ossie Fielden; he phoned me about an hour ago. And where have *you* been? I've been trying to get in touch ever since I first heard!'

'I've been in Royal Terrace. I forgot to take my mobile with me. Dad, it's no use trying to write her off as a madwoman. She's as sane as you or me. She owns number fifteen and she intends to stay there.'

'Owns it?'

'Yes, and she has the papers to prove it.' She gave him a description of the moment Mrs Bedells held up the deeds. She could see it again in her mind's eye – those two frail, bony wrists emerging from the worn knitted sleeves. Writing her off as a madwoman was a mistake; she was old, she wasn't well off, but she was the owner of her property and would stand fast in its defence. Because, perhaps, that was all she had.

'Are you telling me that it wasn't a council leasehold?'

'Yes. It seems only numbers one to fourteen were council property.'

'And she's been there all the time, living in that house, and nobody thought to check?'

'Seems not,' she said with a sigh.

'My God, heads are going to roll in the Town Planning Department over this! And the survey—' her father broke off, and she could hear him slam his desk with his free hand. 'The survey! What the devil was Alan Singleton thinking of, passing the terrain as being ready for demolition and excavation?'

This was a question that had occurred to Bethany early on, from the moment Mrs Bedells held up the documents in her bay window. How could Alan have failed to notice that the property was still occupied? The well-swept front steps, the immaculately starched lace curtains, the flourishing aspidistra in its well-polished pot – all these should have told him that this wasn't an abandoned house.

'We need to have a meeting to sort things out,' she said. 'It's going to be a serious hold-up, the press are on to it and of course it makes a lovely story—'

'Don't tell me,' groaned her father. 'She's a white-haired old lady in a dress with a lace collar and a cat in her arms.'

'Well, she's got a cat, but . . . as to the white hair . . . We never saw her. She wouldn't open the door and showed us the papers through a window pane.'

'Oh, ten to one they're false, then.'

'No, Dad, they're not. I could only see them from the front steps, but everything about them breathes authenticity. It seems an ancestor bought the property from the Yallington Estate in the eighteenth century.'

51

'The eighteenth century!'

'And if I remember rightly, the Yallington Estate was sold up on account of death duties a good few years ago.'

'Ah . . . the present Lord Yallington went abroad . . . California, was it?'

'It's not his whereabouts that matters, it's what happened to all the estate documents. Not that I'd expect them to say anything different. Mrs Bedells owns the property, probably left to her by her husband.'

'We'll get the legal boys to look up the will—'

'Oh yes, we have to go through all the motions, Dad, but the outcome is going to be the same. Mrs Bedells owns that house she's living in, and no work can go on in Royal Terrace until the council buy her out.'

'Splendid,' said her father sarcastically. 'Whose was that site? Well-brow's?'

'Yes, and he's hopping mad and tactless with it. Bigsby had to keep shutting him up in front of the reporter.'

'Oh, Bigsby was there, was he? Well, at least it means the council will see it's got to be dealt with. Now, come on, get in your car, I need you here for a conference.'

When she got to the offices in York, the solicitor for *Dayton & Daughter* had been called into attendance, along with the unhappy Alan Singleton. Daniel was in the midst of a lecture when she entered.

'. . . Utter incompetence! How could you *not* notice the house was occupied?'

'That wasn't my brief,' Alan countered. 'I had copies of the plans and the legal quittance, and the houses owned by the council were verified as cleared and ready for—'

'But for Pete's sake, there's clean lace curtains in the windows and a healthy plant! Isn't that so, Beth? You must have *seen* them—'

'No, I didn't. As far as I was concerned my job was to check the terrain for service piping and cables—'

'Dad,' Bethany intervened. 'Dad, let's leave the post-mortem until later. The press are on to this now. Has anyone thought to alert Iris Weston?'

Oddly enough, no one had. Daniel had his secretary get her on the phone. When the connection was made he picked up his receiver and barked: 'We're in the devil of a mess here, Iris. Can you come up here fast and deal with reporters?' The others in the room were unable to hear her response but from Daniel's side of the conversation they gleaned that at first she didn't think it very important.

But then Daniel mentioned the 'little old lady' aspect. A moment later he yelped: 'The national tabloids?'

The solicitor muttered to Bethany, 'Has it only just occurred to him this is just the sort of story they love?'

'Ssh,' said Bethany, trying to keep track of what was being said.

52

A moment later Daniel glared across his desk at Alan. 'She wants to talk to you,' he growled, and handed over the instrument.

'Yes?' Alan said, colouring up at having to talk to Iris in front of others. 'Yes ... Well, of course I don't accept ... No, the council's Legal Department had certified the property as belonging to the council, and the Town Planning Department had certified it as vacated ... No, I surveyed ... No, I'd no reason to ... Right. Right, I'll tell him.' He glanced at Daniel. 'She's catching the next train.'

He handed back the receiver but by the time Daniel got it to his ear, Iris had hung up. Bethany guessed that Iris was already on her way to King's Cross to rescue her lover from the mess he'd landed himself in.

The discussion resumed. It grew less accusatory on Daniel's side, because he heard words of comfort from his solicitor. The solicitor was of the opinion that the error could be blamed on the council's Legal Department, who surely must have known they didn't own No. 15 Royal Terrace and should have started negotiations to buy out the owner at least a year ago.

Phone calls began to flood in. Some, as Iris had foretold, were from national newspapers. Daniel barked at his secretary to tell these callers he was in a meeting. But other callers were put through – Wellbrow, other contractors, council officials, a worker for Age Concern who'd been alerted to the jeopardy in which Mrs Bedells was placed, the Mayor, the vicar of St Mary's who regarded her as a parishioner ...

In the end, the need for a meeting of Steerco was evident and urgent. Daniel snarled at his secretary, Madge, to tell the Committee Chairman to get everybody to the Town Hall at five o'clock. That gave them only three hours' notice, for by now it was long past lunch-time and Iris had arrived.

'I did as much as I could on my mobile while I was en route,' she began as soon as she came in. 'I've got friends among the tabloid journalists. But they all say they've got to use the story because if they don't the others will – you know how it is, none of them can afford to look as if they missed it.'

'How can it be so important to anybody? She's just some stubborn old hag who won't listen to reason.'

'She's the embodiment of defiance to council bureaucracy,' she corrected. 'For the time being, at any rate. OLD LADY DEFIES COUNCIL – it's just what everybody wants to read because everybody's crossed swords with a council official of some sort at one time in their lives.'

'But the people of Barhampton *want* the new Town Centre,' protested Alan.

'You keep your mouth shut,' Daniel roared. 'You can't seem to use the eyes God gave you to notice an occupied house, so button your lip—'

'Dad!' Bethany cried, horrified at his manner. 'That's not fair! You know as well as I do that when you're out with a surveying team your eyes are on the instruments and—'

'Getting angry isn't going to help,' Iris put in. She didn't want Bethany rushing to Alan's defence. If there had been something between those two she didn't want it revived by any sense of gratitude on Alan's part. 'What we've got to do is play this very cool, Daniel.'

'Cool? Have you any idea how much money this setback's already cost us?' Daniel was in too much of a rage to remember that he quite fancied this young woman with the smooth black hair and the smart London clothes. 'Let me tell you, this is a first-class, grade A foul-up, and desks are going to be suddenly cleared because of it. I'd imagine somebody in the council's Legal Department has already got his marching orders, and somebody *here'* – with a glare at Alan – 'ought to have the guts to accept blame and offer his resignation!'

'No!' cried Bethany. She owed Alan a lot for his support while she was getting her entry ready for the design competition; without that, she might not have done it in time for the deadline and would never have won the contract for *Dayton's*. So now that he was in trouble, she had to stand by him.

'No!' cried Iris at the same moment. 'That would be very bad public relations! *Dayton's* isn't in any way to blame, the Town Council got it wrong – no one here is to be viewed as under disfavour – that's our angle, don't you see?'

'Although that's not quite true,' Alan said with a deep sigh. His thin, rather intellectual features seemed to have sunk in upon themselves. He looked in the depths of misery, full of self-doubt and self-reproach. 'I *ought* to have—'

'No, no! The newspapers and the general public will be more happy to blame it all on the council. No harm should come to *Dayton's* reputation if we just play it cool.'

'But everybody on Steerco will be saying—' began Daniel.

'We have to show a united front to Steerco, and to the rest of the world. We emphasise the good points. Remember what Alan said. Everybody in Barhampton wanted the new Town Centre; they won't sympathise with this crazy old girl for long.'

There she was wrong. There were many people in Barhampton who had never wanted the new Town Centre. At public meetings held while the architectural competition was being advertised, various groups had protested at the vandalism of pulling down the old buildings. Industrial archaeologists wanted the derelict mills and warehouses retained because of their value as historical monuments to Barhampton's past. Small shopkeepers, forced out of premises where they'd made a living for years – perhaps generations – resented the fact that in the new Town Centre there would be less room for them, that chainstores and office HQs would take up so much space and ruin them by competition. The local History Society wanted to preserve as many of Barhampton's Georgian and Victorian buildings as possible. Tradesmen whose workshops were due to be demolished were as antagonistic to the bulldozers as Mrs Bedells.

The morning after she triumphed over the wrecking crew outside her door, her story appeared not only in the *Barhampton Gazette* but in the nationals. Without her summoning them, groups of supporters and well-wishers formed. They wrote and telephoned to the newspapers. They sent bouquets of flowers which she grudgingly took in through a crack in the door. The postman, who had seldom had anything except advertising material for her in the past few years, now had a bundle of letters that threatened to burst the elastic band.

For all those responsible for the 'insult', 'attack', or 'blunder' (depending upon which newspaper you read), it was a horrendous week. Steerco met every day, including Sunday. Cyril Ollerton, the Committee's Chairman and Deputy Head of Town Planning, managed to unravel the tangle of mistakes which ended in the stand-off outside the Bedells house.

'What it boils down to is this,' he reported at last on Sunday morning at a gathering in Daniel's home. 'The original list of houses to be vacated was typed on several sheets of foolscap. During the preliminaries in the Legal Department the list was transferred to computer. Somehow the last address, number fifteen, slipped off the end of the list. Don't ask me how or when, it seems somebody accidentally deleted the last item so that it looked as if the Legal Department had acquired the properties known as numbers one to fourteen Royal Terrace and that that was the whole parcel.'

'Computer error,' groaned Daniel. 'I might have known it.'

'But the survey plans must have shown fifteen houses,' said Billy Wellbrow. 'How come you didn't report the error, Singleton?'

'As far as I was concerned there was no error,' Alan replied, in a voice he tried to make firm and resonant. Iris had been giving him pep talks all week, to bolster up his morale and do away with his sense of failure. 'The legal papers certified "all" properties had been obtained and, again, certified as ready for demolition. As far as I was concerned that meant all fifteen.'

'But confound it, man, couldn't you see that one of them was still being lived in?'

'I was there soon after the Terrace was emptied.' Iris had coached him in this, forcing him to conjure up a scene he no longer clearly recalled. 'There were curtains or blinds in other windows too, still looking quite respectable. There was a window-box outside one window with plants in it, still growing as far as I remember, but then . . . they may have been plastic . . .' Alan sighed, but hearing Iris draw in a breath ready to leap to his defence, resumed on a stronger note: 'My job was to look at the terrain in general but in particular to ascertain that the service lines were mapped so that the bulldozer wouldn't damage them. If you recall, the council doesn't want to spend money on re-laying gas and water—'

'But starched lace curtains and a polished brass pot!' protested Ollerton. 'Surely you must have seen that they hadn't been abandoned by some previous tenant—'

'It's not fair to blame Alan on that point,' Iris broke in, unable to stay silent any longer. 'It's not his job to be an expert on housekeeping! If the Legal Department hadn't made a hash of it—'

'The Legal Department is not to blame,' Bigsby explained. 'The documentation was complete when it went to the Clerical Department for transfer to computer—'

'This is exactly what the public hate about us,' cried Bethany, sick of the buck-passing that had been going on for days. 'We're all trying to make ourselves invisible so as not to have to apologise. But we *have* to apologise, and make it sincere, because we've committed a terrible mistake.'

'A complete muck-up,' agreed Emmett Foyle, whose firm was to lay new roadways, one of which would run across Royal Terrace if they ever succeeded in demolishing the old houses.

'Well . . . who's going to apologise? How about you, Bigsby?'

'The Mayor would prefer it to be someone from the construction side of the affair.' Strictly speaking, the Mayor would prefer it to be someone in Ultima Thule – he wanted the blame to rest as far away as possible. And Bigsby was in complete agreement. The Legal Department was not to blame, not in any way.

'Oh, would he!' roared Wellbrow. 'If you think I'm going to let newsmen stick microphones down my throat you've got another think coming!' Wellbrow knew he was favourite for the task because it was his machines that had scared the old lady. The television boys especially wanted a scene where he would stand in front of those menacing contraptions, cap in hand, apologising for their bad behaviour.

'Ideally it should be a woman,' said Iris.

'Why should it be a woman?'

'Because that will to some extent disarm the opposition. I'd do it, but nobody knows who I am or what I do so it wouldn't have the same effect. It would look as if you're putting up a smoke-screen.'

All eyes turned to Bethany.

'Oh no,' she said.

'I think it ought to be you, Bethany,' said Iris in her most persuasive tones. 'You got some nice publicity when you won the contract, so that means you're known to the public to some extent and they think well of you. So that's good groundwork for a favourable reception.'

'Aye, lass, I think you're elected,' grunted her father. There she was, going into the limelight again, this daughter of his who somehow seemed to be at the forefront of things these days.

'But what would I say?' she protested. 'I can't go into a long spiel about how the Legal Department did this and the Clerical Department did that. The reporters would howl me down.'

'Exactly. So what you have to say is that your heart goes out to this poor lonely old lady whose home has been threatened.'

'Iris, I'm not getting up in public and saying my heart goes out to anybody,' Bethany said. 'Besides, she's not that kind of old lady. She's quite snappish and tart in her manner. And ready to knock us on the head if she gets a chance.'

'The public don't know that. She's hardly put her nose out of the door since last Monday.' Wily old thing, Iris was thinking. If she herself were running a campaign to put the Town Council in the wrong, this was just how she'd go about it. Make yourself out to be timid, wounded, too shy to speak in public . . .

'She must go out sometimes,' objected Foyle. 'How does she get her groceries, her cat food, stuff like that?'

'She's a sly old bird,' said Iris. 'She knows the photographers are trying to get a pic, so she goes out after dark when they've packed up and gone. I bet she slips off to some all-night store – a garage-shop or something like that. When the reporters try to interview her she talks through the door. She says she's afraid the council will send someone to grab her and drag her away. It all adds to the idea of her being in danger.'

'She must know we'd never try a thing like that,' Mr Bigsby cried in indignation.

'I don't think she does know,' Bethany said. 'She thought I was a welfare worker trying to take her away to sheltered housing or something. I tell you, she's determined not to leave her home and although we have to do it, no amount of apologising will make her go.'

'No, but it'll make us look better in the press,' said her father. 'And that might help us to get some urgency into the granting of the Compulsory Purchase Order.'

After much urging, Bethany agreed to meet the press on Monday to state the heartfelt regret of the contractors who had alarmed Mrs Bedells, and the sincere wish of the council to amend the situation. Iris wrote a statement for her, Bethany rewrote it, the others tried to put in important things about the complete innocence of officials, tractor-drivers, surveyors, the Mayor, Uncle Tom Cobbleigh and all. It was all the fault of the computers, they declared.

The final press statement wasn't a masterpiece of statesmanship but Bethany managed to keep some of her genuine regret in its wording. All the while it was being composed she kept reminding herself of those worn old hands in the window, that frail high voice telling her to go away. This was a real person they were dealing with, not some cardboard cut-out who had happened to get in their way.

She read it over in front of her mirror that evening, trying to make it sound less stilted.

All her rehearsing was wasted. She'd gone home from the work-site to change into more feminine clothes about nine-thirty on Monday morning, when the phone rang in her flat.

'Bethany, please come to the Town Hall for an emergency Steerco,' said her father's secretary.

'But, Madge, I've got to make this statement to the media in about half an hour—'

'That's been postponed in view of what's just happened.'

'What has happened?'

'Some lawyer's been on the phone asking for an urgent conference.'

'About what?'

'He says he represents the Royal Terrace Protection Group.'

'What on earth's that?'

'None of us have any idea but the legal eagles are taking it seriously so you'd better come.'

Bethany drove to the Town Hall at once. The concierge, who by now recognised her as a regular attender, nodded her through. She ran up the stairs rather than wait for the ponderous lift. Steerco was more or less gathered already. Sitting at the conference table was a man whose face was somewhat familiar to her.

'Haven't we met?' she asked as he rose at her entrance.

'Yes, at the party for the awarding of the Town Centre design contract. My name's Peter Lambot of *Pesh, Samuels & Company* and I'm here on behalf of the Royal Terrace Protection—'

'Yes, so I heard,' she intervened, raising her eyebrows. 'And who, exactly, are they?'

'They're a collection of concerned citizens who've been brought together by the events of the last week, Ms Dayton. And they've asked me to obtain a Protection Order to prevent you from demolishing Royal Terrace.'

Chapter Five

Iris Weston was the only one in the room who didn't understand the awfulness of Peter Lambot's announcement.

'What's he talking about?' she demanded.

'A Protection Order,' Bigsby said. 'It would prevent any work being done on the site and could well be followed by a Preservation Order.'

'But why?'

'The Ministry of the Environment can issue an order to protect a site of great architectural interest.'

Iris looked around at the others. 'Is that row of houses so special?'

'Not at all,' Bigsby said. 'It was probably put up by some local builder in the eighteenth century in the style of the time – copying the fine houses of the nobility but scaling them down.'

'Yes, a plainer, less grandiose style.' Daniel took it up. 'Royal Terrace is quite nice – but come on, Lambot, you're not going to say it's a supreme example of Georgian building.'

The solicitor had been sitting quietly while they cross-talked around him. He had watched them with an amused glint in his greenish eyes. Invited to speak, he took up a paper that had been lying in front of him.

'Royal Terrace has more to its credit than being a nice example of Georgian domestic,' he said. 'You know of course that the present inhabitant of number fifteen is Mrs Bedells – Mrs Nancy Bedells.'

'To our cost,' muttered Wellbrow.

'Mrs Bedells is the widow of William Bedells, who is a descendant of Arabella Bedells—'

'And who's *she*?' demanded Daniel.

'Wait, Dad, wait . . . That was the name on the document that old Mrs Bedells held up at the window. Mrs Arabella Bedells – in . . . it was all written out. One thousand seventeen hundred and eighty-something . . .'

'The year was 1782. Mrs Arabella Bedells was a well-known actress and playwright of her day.'

'Well-known? I've never heard of her,' cried Bigsby.

'You will,' remarked Peter Lambot with a momentary grin. 'The President of the Barhampton Local History Society took notice of that name when it was reported in the newspapers and did some research.' He opened a folder that lay in front of him, and selected a typed sheet.

59

He read: ' "Arabella Bedells was famous in her time, a great beauty, a comedy actress of some ability, a writer of plays thought of as racy by her contemporaries, a battler for the rights of women—" '

'Oh Lord,' moaned Daniel Dayton.

To his credit, Peter Lambot didn't laugh at the utter misery in that cry. He knew Daniel had just seen what might be the strength of the opposition. Women's Rights! He had only to utter a word of resistance to that claim and women's organisations would be down on him like a ton of bricks.

' "Arabella Bedells," ' Peter resumed, ' "was the heroine of a real-life eighteenth-century romance. The Duke of Brunswick saw her perform in London while on a visit to the court of George III. He carried her off to Brunswick—" '

'Brunswick, Brunswick . . .' muttered Bigsby. 'That's in the poem . . . about the Pied Piper . . .'

' "Hamelin Town's in Brunswick, By famous Hanover city," ' quoted Bethany.

'Mr Tallant tells me that it was part of the kingdom of Hanover at that time. I imagine there was some family connection between the Duke of Brunswick and George III, hence the visit to the court. Anyway . . .' He resumed reading. ' "The Duke whisked her off to his homeland and there she had two children, Frederick and Nicholas. He was married to someone else, of course, so by and by the Duchess arranged to have Arabella and her sons packed off back to England. But Arabella put up a good fight, got a large sum of money from Karl Friedrich, so that on her return to her home-town of Barhampton she was able to buy number fifteen Royal Terrace when that row was built, but moreover to put quite a lot towards the building of Barhampton's first theatre, the Naiad—" '

'The *Naiad*?' Bethany echoed in astonishment.

'It was on the banks of the River Barr,' Peter explained.

'Oh, I see – water nymphs—'

'Exactly. She seems to have been a lady of some imagination.'

'She seems to have been a woman of loose morals!' Wellbrow declared, throwing himself back in his chair in annoyance.

'Perhaps . . . Mr Tallant of the Local History Society can only get glimpses of her in the periodicals of the times, but her initials figure quite a lot in the scandal columns. Initials seem to have been the favourite way of hinting at naughtiness, I gather. "Mrs A.B. whose theatrical events among the wilderness of the Yorkshire moors—" that sort of thing.'

'Are you telling me,' cried Wellbrow, 'that you're going to get a Preservation Order on a house that was lived in by the local trollop?'

'Come, come, Mr Wellbrow. Arabella Bedells was an admired actress, a playwright, mistress to a royal duke—'

'Brunswick? Never heard of *him* until now either!'

'His only claim to fame, so Mr Tallant tells me, is that he threatened to reduce Paris to rubble if the revolutionaries harmed Marie Antoinette – but you see, that's quite romantic too – he's likely to come over as quite a sympathetic character when this tale is told in the press.'

'Who's going to tell the press?' yelled Wellbrow.

'Mr Wellbrow,' Bigsby reproved him, directing a severe glance to reinforce his tone.

'I am, of course,' said the representative of the Royal Terrace Protection Group. 'I've promised a press announcement for later this morning. It's my business to rally all the support I can so as to preserve Royal Terrace.'

'The Minister will never grant a Preservation Order,' Bigsby countered. 'Those buildings have got to come down.'

'Not if the Royal Terrace Protection Group have anything to do with it.'

Iris Weston had been listening to the exchanges with serious attention. From her point of view, things were going from bad to worse. Until today she'd never heard of a Preservation Order, and had no idea if it was a serious obstacle or not. Moreover, Billy Wellbrow was *not* being diplomatic about it, whatever it was. It was time for a distraction so that she could catch up with what it all meant. She said now, 'I wonder if we could take a break? A cup of coffee would be welcome, I imagine.'

Steerco's Chairman took the hint. On the house phone he called the staff cafeteria. People rose and began to form groups. Iris made for Wellbrow to coax him into a better frame of mind. Bethany threaded her way to the side of Peter Lambot. 'How does it come about that you're representing this new-born group?' she asked. 'Are you interested in Barhampton's literary past?'

'Well, I'm not *un*interested,' he replied, with an apologetic shrug. 'But if the truth be told I'm here because Mrs Crowther – you remember her?'

'Oh yes, you had to escort her to the design award party.'

'Mrs Crowther rang my firm and said it was their civic duty to lend someone to the Royal Terrace Protection Group, and because she's an important client they had to take notice, and I got elected to the job.'

'You don't sound as if you're delighted with the assignment?'

'Well . . .' He sighed. 'I can't help thinking it's wrong to pander to Mrs Crowther's whims . . .'

'So you don't really care one way or the other about Arabella Bedells and her chequered history?'

'Perhaps not.' He became more serious. 'But I do care quite a bit about Mrs Nancy Bedells, who seems to be in a very bad situation. You can't really be thinking of buying her house out from under her and putting her in the street?'

'Certainly not! You know better, Mr Lambot.'

'Well, I didn't *know* but I had the feeling you weren't the sort to take part in anything like that. The press does like to make a drama out of things, doesn't it?'

'A drama? It's a nightmare,' she said. 'I was supposed to give an interview this morning, trying to explain how sorry we all were and how we'd be putting it all right as soon as ever we can—'

'By putting it right, you mean what?'

'Buying the house from her at a fair price and giving her a flat elsewhere.'

'And if she doesn't want to go?'

'She's got to go, Mr Lambot. But not immediately, not in a great rush that makes her seem insignificant. We'll give her time to get used to the idea, we'll talk it through with her if only we can get her to come out and discuss things.'

'Good luck,' he returned. 'I tried to get her to open the door yesterday, after the Protection Group had told me their story and instructed me about the Preservation Order. Let me tell you, even though I came with the news that a whole group of people were rallying to help her, she was furious!'

'Furious?' Bethany echoed, surprised.

'When she discovered we were going to use the story of Arabella. She regards Arabella as a dissolute woman, doesn't want her mentioned at all. When I tried to say it was a good way to save her house from being knocked down she told me she was doing that by herself and didn't need any help from busybodies like me, thank you very much.'

'My word!'

'I went away much chastened. When I reported back to the Protection Group they were a bit taken aback, but that doesn't stop them from wanting to preserve the Terrace.'

Bethany faced him squarely. Tall as she was, she could gaze almost directly into his dark greenish eyes, where she tried to read the truth of the matter.

'They can't really believe this bit of local history is so important—' she began.

'Miss Dayton, the group is a motley collection. There are members who don't really give a brass farthing about Royal Terrace or Arabella Bedells – they have reasons of their own, they're really protesting about losing their business premises, seeing old landmarks go. They want to delay the work so as to have a chance to alter the plans—'

'That's not possible, Mr Lambot. I think you must tell your clients that they'll be wasting their time. But thank you for putting me in the picture. It seems it's much more complex that we'd guessed. I hadn't quite understood the psychology of the thing.' She'd got what she wanted from him – a frank assessment of the situation as he saw it.

'I'm glad you understand the seriousness of it. And please call me

Peter. I think we'll be seeing quite a lot of each other in the course of this battle. I'm only sorry we have to be on opposite sides . . .'

The coffee arrived. Her father, invited *ex officio*, joined them as they filed to get their cups and a biscuit. 'You don't really think you're going to get this Preservation Order, do you?' he enquired of Peter. 'The council went through all that when they were applying for Planning Permission.'

'We're certainly going to apply to National Heritage for a listing. We've got new grounds, after all. We didn't know until this week that the house had belonged to Arabella Bedells.'

'Arabella Bedells! If you ask me she's nothing to be proud of! I don't think the Minister is going to want to preserve the house where she entertained her gentlemen friends!'

'You're forgetting her literary attainments,' Peter remarked, with a suppressed smile. 'Barhampton's got very few famous names connected with the arts. We can't afford to disregard this one.'

'Utter nonsense! Besides, Barhampton folk wouldn't give you the skin off a spud for her literary attainments. What were they, anyhow? Name one play she wrote,' challenged Daniel.

'Well, as a matter of fact, I can do that. Her last play was put on at the Naiad with considerable success. It was called *Women, Hide Your Lovers.*'

'It wasn't!' protested Bethany, bursting out laughing.

'I regret to tell you that it was. Mr Tallant found it in old copies of the *Barhampton Bugle*, which was a weekly local paper of the day. They've got the newspaper on file in the Barhampton Archive, held in the public library, where you can look at it for yourselves. Arabella is listed among the cast and her performance is described as "giving full value to every fanciful invention".'

'Sounds like what used to be called a Whitehall farce.'

'It probably *was* like a Whitehall farce, Bethany. As I told you, her work was regarded as "saucy".'

'And you're asking us to hold up construction of the new Town Centre for the sake of a woman who wrote dirty plays?' demanded Daniel.

'It's being held up anyhow,' Peter pointed out. 'There's not a thing you can do until you can get ownership of Mrs Bedells's house.'

'Ladies and gentlemen, can we resume?' Cyril Ollerton called. 'I'm told there are reporters downstairs waiting for us to make a statement – we had promised them one before this new circumstance arose and we ought to decide what we're going to say to them now.'

Cups were set down, people drifted back to their chairs. 'Now then,' Ollerton began, 'what we have on the table is the information that Mr Lambot is applying to National Heritage to have a Preservation Order put on number fifteen Royal Terrace. The Royal Terrace Protection

Group – have I got that right? – have hired him to do so. Do we wish to make any public response to this action?'

'What can we say?' muttered Bigsby. 'Only that we acknowledge the information and will await the outcome of his application.'

'In the meantime,' declared Billy Wellbrow, 'the council is applying for a Compulsory Order to buy the house, and as soon as we get that we'll be inviting this woman to transfer to another address.' Although his tone was less strident, Iris hadn't been able to moderate his feelings of anger towards Mrs Bedells.

'You're not going to announce it in those terms,' she protested. 'We say that when the council obtains this Compulsory Order, we'll ensure that Mrs Bedells is provided with living accommodation of an equal value, only more up-to-date and comfortable.'

They haggled for a time over the wording of the announcement. Peter Lambot, sitting by, took little part. He understood the council had to respond to his intervention but he wasn't going to help them or hinder them.

The reporters downstairs were getting impatient. Steerco settled its view, Peter's assent was invited and they wrote out a short, joint report, which Cyril Ollerton and Peter Lambot took down to read to the crows in the lobby. Bethany after all wasn't called on to make her public apology with its insincere statement of concern for Mrs Bedells, for which she was grateful.

Ollerton came upstairs again alone, having left Peter answering questions from the press about the newly formed Royal Terrace Protection Group. He found the rest of Steerco in the midst of a wrangle. Wellbrow was saying that he wouldn't stand for any financial penalties caused by the delay but on the contrary wanted compensation for the time his men had been forced to hang about. Bigsby was saying he'd have to consult the legal documents to see what provision had been made for such problems.

Ollerton plunged in at once. As Construction Manager it was his job to see that hold-ups didn't occur or, if they occurred, to see that they cost as little as possible. So far he'd escaped blame in this débâcle, but by rights he should have ensured that Royal Terrace had been safely boarded off before the demolition vehicles arrived. Had that been done according to schedule it would have been the fencing erectors who noticed No. 15 was still occupied – and that would have averted the bad publicity of putting the house under siege by huge menacing machines.

Under cover of the argument Iris said to Bethany, 'That was a good move, to wheedle your way into Lambot's confidence. What did you get out of him?'

'What?' Bethany said, startled.

'Well, you were heads together for a good while and it was clear he was doing most of the talking. Did you learn anything we can use?'

'I had a conversation with him,' Bethany said. 'I wasn't trying to wheedle anything.'

'But you must have got something,' said Iris, giving her a nudge. 'Anybody could see he fancies you, you'd have been a fool not to make some use of that.'

Bethany edged away. 'Listen,' she said, choosing her words with care, 'I think he was just being friendly. I don't have this adversarial view of the situation that you do. I just had a normal conversation—'

'We're never going to get anywhere if you don't see that good PR depends on taking advantage of every opening,' Iris interrupted. 'Of course it's adversarial! The press wants to make us look bad and we want to make ourselves look good. This man Lambot has come on the scene because these history buffs want to put another barrier in the way – well, we need to know all we can about them and what they're up to. It's a case of them or us, Bethany.'

' "Two legs bad, four legs good"?'

'Beg your pardon?'

'It's from *Animal Farm*. I'm just trying to say that we shouldn't think of it as a conflict.'

'That's where you're wrong! Getting a good press is one of the hardest battles any company has to fight. And in this particular case, we're off on the wrong foot from the start – harrying a poor old lady, it looks like, whereas the fact is that *we've* done nothing wrong and *she's* being absolutely absurd.'

'No, she isn't!'

'Oh, come on, Bethany! She knew the Town Centre was being rebuilt, she saw her neighbours moving out, and she just sat there being bloody-minded about it.'

'Bloody-minded? Yet you want us to speak about her to the press as if she was our dear old granny.'

'Well, of course! We'd do ourselves no good if we said she was an old nuisance.'

Bethany shook her head. 'It's just dishonest.'

Iris gave her a look as much as to say, 'You're not serious.' At that moment the argument about construction delays was settled and the meeting began to break up. Alan Singleton joined them as they made for the door.

'It's a real mess,' he sighed.

'Well, there's a certain amount of damage-limitation in the arrival of the Protection Group or whatever it's called. It takes the attention off the rest of us for the time being.'

'I don't see how, Iris, but I expect you know best.'

'Are we likely to get this Compulsory Purchase Order soon? I mean, before the Protection Group can get its Preservation Order?'

'Who knows. Government departments . . .'

'Only it would be good to get her out of there and into something rather nice before—'

'I'd get her out of there soon enough,' growled Daniel, as they went downstairs. 'I'd cut off her water supply and the electricity—'

'You wouldn't!' cried Bethany in horror.

'Don't even think of it,' added Iris at once. 'It would be the worst possible publicity.'

'Oh, easy enough to have an accident with a pickaxe,' said Daniel. 'Happens all the time.'

'I'd have a man there within the hour to repair the damage,' Bethany said. 'Don't do it, Dad.'

'Whose side are you on, then?' he demanded, going red with annoyance. 'She's more important to you than the success of our business?'

'I don't want her victimised,' she insisted. 'She's an old lady all on her own.'

'I though you said you didn't like her?'

'What's liking or disliking her got to do with it? She's trying to defend her home and she has a right to, since *we* seem to have made a hash of preparing for the work.'

'So you'd rather think of us as being to blame, is that it? What about loyalty?'

'I was trying to explain a minute ago,' Iris put in, seeing she must divert Daniel's anger because the reporters were looking round as they came down the last few stairs. 'We've got to put up a united front for the press, saying we regret all the upset and of course want to look after poor Mrs Bedells. Honestly, Daniel, it would do us a lot of harm if we started to sound angry with her.'

'Humph,' he grunted, but put on an affable expression to greet the press.

Peter Lambot was still trapped in the big foyer. A group of perhaps twenty men and women were thrusting microphones at him, while photographers held up their cameras to take flash pictures over the heads of the little throng.

Reporters aren't easily fooled. They could tell that the members of Steerco were very unhappy despite the polite statement previously read out by Ollerton. They sensed that the hero of the hour was the lawyer acting for the Royal Terrace Protection Group, so they were determined to get something quotable out of him.

'This is a triumph for the people of Barhampton, isn't it?' Bethany heard one girl demand. 'You're saving an important monument for—'

'I wouldn't call it an important monument.'

'When will you put in your application to National Heritage?'

'I've already done that, so in the meantime the site will remain—'

66

'What if Mrs Bedells decided to sell out? She must be under considerable pressure—'

'I'm not aware that pressure has been put—'

'Can you get us an interview with her, Mr Lambot?'

'I'm afraid not – Mrs Bedells isn't—'

'She won't answer the door. Since you're acting for her, it would be a good idea to persuade her to agree.'

'I'm not acting for Mrs Bedells,' Peter said. 'My client is the Royal Terrace Protection Group. Now, if you'll excuse me, I've got work waiting for me at the office—'

They cut him off with further questions and were still pursuing him as he got into his car in the car park. Since half a dozen people had been asking questions at cross purposes and never allowing him to finish a sentence it was inevitable that the reports eventually laid before the public were full of inaccuracies.

Iris asked Bethany to take her to Royal Terrace. So far, she'd never seen the place where the drama had started.

'It isn't far,' said Bethany. 'We may as well go on foot.'

Truth to tell, Iris wasn't well shod for walking about among demolition sites, and even Bethany would have preferred her work clothes of slacks and desert boots rather than the formal clothes she'd changed into. But there were still public roads and pavements; access had to be maintained to the traffic bridge over the River Barr, and ancient rights of way to the riverbank had to be respected. So they picked their way along, a disparate couple, one tall and fair-headed, the other dark and more delicate of frame. If a spectator had been asked which of the two was the more likely to be ready for a fight, he would probably have chosen the tall girl with her Viking look.

Compared with the dust and rubble of the path round the hoarding of Market Square, Royal Terrace looked smart – neat, with crisply defined buildings still showing signs of good paintwork and its little private garden offering shrubs in the leafage of late May. There were no reporters hanging around. The press corps had gone en masse to the Town Hall in expectation of the statement by the newly formed Royal Terrace Protection Group.

As they approached, the door of No. 15 opened a crack, and a tabby cat slipped out. It trotted down the shallow steps, paused, sniffed the air, then headed across the road towards the garden.

Bethany changed direction so as to intercept it. 'Hello, kitty,' she said to it. 'Where are you off to? Going to catch a sparrow for your lunch, eh? Who's a lovely pussy-cat then?' She held out her hand. The tabby sniffed it, seemed to accept her, pressed her chin against the hand and lowered her head into it, asking to be stroked.

'That's clever,' remarked Iris, joining them. 'Making friends with the cat so we can make friends with its owner.'

'But she's nowhere around to see us being friends with her cat,' Bethany rejoined. 'I bet she's gone back to her kitchen. She stays away from the front, because of the reporters.'

'Well, let's get her to the door and tell her we're cat-lovers.' Iris went up the steps and plied the knocker. But she had as little success as anyone else, because no one came to the door.

Bethany meanwhile continued her conversation with the cat, who was now sitting with her head against Bethany's leg, enjoying having her ears rubbed. By and by it seemed to Bethany that there was a flicker of movement in the bay window to the left of the entrance. She straightened a little and tried to focus. Yes, there was a figure behind the immaculate lace curtains.

She stood erect, smiled, and gave a little wave. After all, why not? Behind the curtains was a fellow human being having a hard time, an old lady with whom she'd had a conversation once. Why not give a little wave of acknowledgement?

The hidden watcher made no response. Iris was still knocking on the door. Bored with her lack of success, she came to rejoin Bethany. 'No luck,' she said.

'She's at the window,' murmured Bethany.

'Really?' The other girl turned to look. 'Right, then let's take action. Let's find her cat for her.' With that she stooped to pick up the tabby.

The tabby wasn't pleased at being snatched away from the friendly hand stroking her head. She let out a cry and wriggled violently. Iris grabbed her round her middle. The door of No. 15 flew open. In the doorway stood a little woman in a black skirt and pink cardigan, who called out, 'What are you doing to my cat!'

Iris began to say, 'We thought it was lost,' but the words were cut off by a scream of pain as the cat's claws raked her left hand. She let go, the cat bounded away towards its home, streaked in, and the door slammed shut.

'Gotcha!' cried a voice behind them.

Bethany turned. 'Dickie!' It was the photographer from the *Gazette*.

'Just arrived at the right moment, eh?' he said with satisfaction. He pointed his lens at Iris, who was sucking her wounded hand and uttering muted curses.

'No, don't!' begged Bethany, but too late. The camera had clicked and Iris was recorded as she stood outside No. 15 scowling and licking the back of her hand.

This was a great coup for Dickie. His paper, the *Gazette*, not only used the picture of Mrs Bedells on the front page next day, but sold it on to the nationals. One of the tabloids used it, together with the picture of Iris over a headline: CATNAPPING?

The Gazette took the opportunity to do a little editorialising. *A lone old lady is holding her own against the council and its inept collaborators.*

68

The Royal Terrace Protection Group rightly wishes to come to this lady's aid and is investigating the possibility of a Restraining Order to prevent outsiders from intervening in any way upon the site. Royal Terrace, the home of Mrs Bedells's famous ancestress Arabella Bedells, certainly deserves to be safeguarded, and if at the same time Mrs Bedells can be given some sense of security, every Northerner would heartily approve.

The report itself included statements from both Iris and Bethany that there had never been any intention to harass Mrs Bedells. *'I was just going to return the cat to Mrs Bedells's door – I thought it was straying,'* said Iris. Bethany was quoted as supporting this. *'Perhaps Iris shouldn't have picked up the cat so suddenly. Cats have a mind of their own about things like that, don't they?'*

Daniel Dayton was furious about the whole thing. 'Is this what we pay you for?' he demanded of his PR expert. 'Weren't you the one who said we shouldn't appear to be bothering the old besom?'

If Daniel was angry, so was Iris. To be so cutely caught out was bad enough, but she felt Bethany had handled the mistake better than she had. The remark about cats having minds of their own struck her as very clever – just the kind of thing to put the cat-loving public on her side.

That evening the local radio ran a phone-in on the subject of Barhampton's new Town Centre plan and the snags that would now hold it up. 'Are you a supporter of the new Town Centre and its modern buildings? Or do you think more of old Barhampton should be preserved? What's your view of this new group that's sprung up to stop the demolition men getting at Royal Terrace? Call Mick Struther and share your feelings. Let's hear from you, folks,' urged the radio front-man.

Calls flooded in. Many, particularly the younger section of the community, were all for having a bright modern centre. 'The place has been dead after six o'clock for years. When we get the new multi-screen cinema and the cafés, there'll be somewhere to go, somewhere to meet friends. It'll be grand!'

On the other hand, there were many strong reservations. 'Of course we had town meetings about the proposed development . . . But it's only when you see Market Square all empty and boarded up that you realise . . .' And the industrial archaeologists had plenty to say. 'Those old warehouses by the river should never have been pulled down. They were a symbol of Barhampton's greatness as a wool town . . .'

Opinions on Royal Terrace were varied. 'I worked in an office in one of those converted houses . . . Draughty and inconvenient . . . And Arabella Bedells, who's she?'

There came a moment when the interviewer made a pause. 'Our next caller has something important to say. Are you there . . . *Mrs Bedells?'*

A thin old voice responded. 'I wanted to say what I thought about that piece in the *Gazette* this morning. But it's no use writing to them to tell them off because they wouldn't print the letter, would they?'

'Well, they might. You're a very important lady, Mrs Bedells.'

'Huh! I could do with being less important, thank you very much. And as for linking me with Arabella Bedells, let me tell you she's no ancestress of mine, it was my husband's family she belonged to, and a right hussy she seems to have been. He never approved of her and nor do I!'

'You don't approve of her, Mrs Bedells?' repeated Struther, delighted.

'She's all in the past, and what I'm concerned with is the here and now. It's all very well for the *Gazette* to talk about those two young women and harassment, but who's the worst at that game?' asked Nancy Bedells. 'It's all those reporters and photographers who ought to be stopped from crowding up to my house. And they've no right to take my photo and plaster it all over the newspapers.'

'But I'm afraid they have, Mrs Bedells. Freedom of the press, you know.'

'What about my freedom?' demanded the doughty old lady. 'It's got so I can't even put my head outside the door without somebody leaping at me like a pack of monkeys, asking me daft questions.'

'But your opinion on—'

'My opinion, since you're so keen on it, is that people should mind their own business! Thirty years or more me and my husband lived in that house and never bothered anybody, and what I want to know is why should a bunch of busybodies bother *me* now that William's gone. So now I've said what I wanted to say and you can tell your other phoners that fifteen Royal Terrace isn't draughty or inconvenient, and even if it was nobody can knock it down and that's that.'

There was a decisive click. The caller had gone off the line.

'Well,' crowed Mick Struther, 'there you are, folks! We got what the door-steppers couldn't get, an exclusive with Mrs Bedells! Remember, you heard it first on Radio Barhampton on the *Mick Struther Show*.'

The next caller was a lady with a prepared piece about community values that she wanted to read, but after her came a man who was a regular with the phone-in. 'Come on now, Mick,' he said when he was called up. 'That were a hoax, now warn't it?'

'Not at all, Don, that was the regular article! We had the line checked out while she was speaking and it was Mrs Bedells's phone.'

'Garn! She'd 'a made more use of it to get her point across if it had really been her.'

'I think that's where you're wrong, Don. Mrs Bedells doesn't plot and plan for media attention – I think she genuinely wants to be left alone.'

'Who she think she is? Greta Garbo?'

'Well, she may not be a film star, but she's quite a character, our Mrs Bedells. Bye for now, Don. Now our next caller is . . .'

The exchange between Mrs Bedells and Mick Struther was replayed on national radio later in the evening and reported on the TV news. Iris, in Alan's flat in York, listened to it with great attention. 'You know, we might be able to turn public opinion against her,' she mused. 'She really doesn't sound a very likeable sort, does she?'

Alan shook his head at her. 'Yorkshiremen are always going to admire one of their own who sticks up for their rights,' he said. 'If she's a bit crusty, they'll like her all the better.'

'But look at her,' she replied, holding out the newspaper with the photograph. 'Is she "one of their own"? Is she a Yorkshirewoman? She looks foreign to me!'

The picture showed Nancy Bedells leaning forward in the half-open doorway to scoop up her cat. She was glaring up towards the outer world with an expression of outrage. Her black hair was parted in the centre and two coils sat at her ears like earphones. Her face was small, thin, and wrinkled, and because this was a colour photograph her skin was shown as very dark, almost Mediterranean. Bony shoulders were hunched in a stridently pink cardigan over a bright blue blouse and a black skirt. The hands reaching out for the cat were skinny and unadorned except for a plain gold wedding band.

'Well, she's certainly not Greta Garbo,' Alan said.

'But don't you think she looks foreign? Italian, perhaps?'

'Now you know she doesn't speak with an Italian accent, Iris!'

'Well, if she and her husband were married over thirty years ago, she's probably lost her accent.'

'That's true enough, I suppose, but even if it is, so what? She's still a little old lady on her own in a house we can't get her out of.'

'But if we could say she was an outsider, support might drop away—'

'Darling, I wouldn't go down that road if I were you. We've got enough on our hands without digging into the old girl's past. As she herself said, it's the here and now that matters and I'd have thought your first priority would be to mend the damage caused by that confounded cat.'

'Honestly, Alan, that was an accident.'

'Of course, love. I know you'd never try to make use of the old girl's pet to get at her.'

No, thought Iris. Not now, at any rate. But there were other things one could use. The Local History Society wasn't going to be best pleased at Mrs Bedells's views on Arabella; the press in general were going to be annoyed at her calling them monkeys, and a tone of self-centred annoyance didn't make her remark any the more attractive.

Iris was building up a great store of resentment against Mrs Bedells. If that pigheaded woman hadn't insisted on staying on at No. 15 when she could *see* that her neighbours were packing up, Alan wouldn't now be in such disfavour with his employers. It just showed what a stupid old fool she was – she could have bargained a tremendous price out of the council for that house if she'd played her cards right.

And then there was the way she carried on about that cat. If she hadn't yelled at them, the cat would have been quite happy to stay in Iris's grasp – or at least so she told herself now. Those scratches had really hurt. She'd be entitled to sue Nancy Bedells for the wounds she'd received . . . Well, no, perhaps not, because Mrs Bedells would say she shouldn't have picked up the cat in the first place. And it would be bad publicity to cause a fuss . . . might make her look rather foolish . . .

But then of course there had been the embarrassment of having her picture taken in such a wrong-footed moment. Her boss at *Seymour PR* hadn't been pleased. She'd received a very irate phone call from him. He'd been on the verge of summoning her back to London and sending someone else in her place. Talked out of that, his attitude was: I want better results or else.

As if that weren't enough, Bethany had insisted on acting Ministering Angel over the cat scratches. She'd carried Iris off to the first aid post at the building-site office and of course – wouldn't you know – she was a trained first-aider and put disinfectant on the scratches which had stung like the devil. Then she followed that with sticking plaster which looked most unbecoming on the back of her hand. But of course Iris had had to say thank you while her real feeling was that Bethany was showing off.

And all this over some crackpot old woman who wouldn't even give so much as the time of day to people who tried to help her.

Well, thought Iris, recalling the words and more especially the tone of Mrs Bedells during her phone-in, your days as a local heroine are numbered, old girl. I can use the telephone too. A few calls to some friends of mine in the newspaper world and we'll see if they keep on thinking of you as dear old Whistler's mother.

Bethany too had listened to the recording of the phone-in on the national news while she waited for her newly installed spin-drier to finish its cycle. Her heart sank as she heard the crotchety old voice berating the radio link-man. While of course the old lady had a right to say whatever she liked, she certainly didn't seem to care about making friends or influencing people.

She was deep in thought, sorting the dried clothes into piles and feeling ruefully that they'd need a lot of ironing, when her phone rang. It was Peter Lambot.

'Did you happen to hear Mrs Bedells on the radio?' he enquired.

'Yes, I did,' sighed Bethany.

'I think the appropriate phrase is, she's her own worst enemy.'

'Very apt.'

'I tried to ring her after the broadcast – to offer a bit of legal advice, you know? – but she's taken the jack out of the wall, I think.'

'Poor old soul,' she said, picturing her. 'All alone at night in that row of empty houses with reporters besieging her and no one to turn to but her cat.'

'Well, strictly speaking, I don't think the reporters are there at night—'

'They are tonight,' she broke in. 'You can bet on it. After that broadcast, she'll be in the headlines tomorrow.'

'Yes, I think you're right there. I've had the President of the Local History Society on the phone, not best pleased at being classed with "a bunch of busybodies", nor the unkind remarks about Arabella.'

'And the press isn't going to like being ticked off for bad behaviour.'

'Bethany, she talked to you on that first day. I wonder . . . couldn't you try again? It really would be a help if someone could persuade her—'

'I don't think so, Peter. She thinks I was trying to steal her cat. She's not even going to come to the door if I knock.'

'That fool Iris Weston! Doesn't she know better than to—'

'It's no use blaming Iris,' Bethany said. 'The fault lies with the Town Council for not checking the title deeds of the land properly. And next after that our surveyor. Iris is very keen to absolve him, but . . .'

'You mean she's keen to absolve the construction people in general.'

'Well, yes, she's hired to do that, of course, but she's got a special interest in Alan.'

'Has she indeed?'

'Forget I said that, Peter. I ought not to be poking my nose into other people's affairs.'

'Now,' he said with a laugh, 'you sound like Mrs Bedells!'

'That's not a compliment!'

'No. I apologise. But you don't think there's a chance that she'd speak to you if you went to the door?'

'I don't think our publicity consultant would like me to try, even. Anything to do with Mrs Bedells seems to end in disaster.'

They said good night with mutual good wishes. They had a feeling that they had a lot in common, a wish to get out of this quandary in which they were trapped without harming old Mrs Bedells despite her crusty manners.

During the next few days an expert on press matters might have sensed a change in the attitude to the Royal Terrace story. By the time the heavy Sundays addressed the matter, they were saying gravely that, after all, nothing could be solved unless there was consultation. *While we agree that Barhampton Town Council has been much at fault, the next step must be a relaxation in Mrs Bedells's outlook*, commented the *Sunday Wire*. The tabloids were more outspoken. *Come on, old girl, give it a rest!* exhorted the *Sunday Banner*.

In the first days of the following week the story seemed to fade out. But on Wednesday night, about midnight, Peter Lambot's bedside phone rang. He dragged himself awake to pick it up.

'Mr Lambot?' cried a thin old voice he recognised through the haze of his first sleep.

'Yes?'

'Are you that lawyer who put his card through my door?'

'Yes, what's the matter?' He sat up in bed, alarmed. Mrs Bedells wouldn't ring him over a small thing.

'There's a gang of yobs in the Terrace, that's what, and they're throwing stones at my windows!'

Chapter Six

'Stay away from the glass!' Peter commanded. 'I'll be there in ten minutes.' He put down the phone, reconnected, dialled 999 and asked for the police to go at once to Royal Terrace.

When he got there he saw no delinquents. A patrol car had already arrived, its lights revolving in the dark Terrace, the driver speaking into his mike. Peter drew up behind it. The driver's partner came to speak to him.

'You the one that called it in?'

'Yes, Peter Lambot.'

'Can you come and speak to her? All she'll say to me is that she's all right and I'm to clear off.'

That sounds like her, thought Peter, and went up the shallow steps to the front door. He noted two or three half-bricks lying there. The window of the left bay angled towards the steps was broken, edges of glass glinting in the patrol car's light.

'Mrs Bedells?'

No reply.

'Mrs Bedells, it's Peter Lambot.'

'Oh, it's you, is it? What you want to call the police for?'

'But Mrs Bedells, you said they were breaking your windows—'

'So they were, but it only needed a man to give a good shout at 'em—'

The policeman had joined Peter at the door. 'Come on now, madam, open the door and let's have a look—'

'What do you think you're going to look at? All you'll see is some broken glass—'

'But Mrs Bedells, I need to see that *you're* all right.'

'Why shouldn't I be all right? I can stand to hear a bit of glass breaking.'

'But if you're upset or shaky—'

'Oh, go away, you silly young man! It's past midnight and I want to get back to my bed!'

'I can't go away, Mrs Bedells, I've got to write up a report—'

'Well, write it. Two panes broken and half a dozen boys got away – daft idiots, roaring up here with a siren going, how'd you expect to catch anybody if you do that?'

'But we heard they were attacking your house, Mrs Bedells. We wanted to scare them away so you wouldn't get hurt.'

'Mrs Bedells,' Peter intervened, 'I was the one who called the police so if you've got any complaint you should make it to me, not to the officer. But now he's here, he's got to report the situation, you must see that. Just answer his questions.' He gave a little laugh so that she could hear he was joking. 'It's the quickest way to get rid of him.'

'Huh,' she said. A pause. 'Well then.'

'Could you open the door, Mrs Bedells? Just so I can see you're all right, not cut by glass, don't need an ambulance?'

'I'm not opening this door for anybody.'

'But don't you understand, madam—'

'Could you come to the window?' Peter suggested. 'And put on the room light so we can see you?'

Another pause, longer. Then: 'Oh, all right.' A moment later the light went on in the room with the broken bay window and the owner of the house, in a woollen dressing-gown and with her black hair down her back in a plait, appeared.

'Well?'

'You didn't get hurt?' asked the policeman.

'No.'

'Do you feel unsteady, upset?'

'I feel angry, if you want to know!' One skinny hand came up, clenched in a fist.

'Would you like me to call a doctor?'

'Of course not. I want you to pack up and go.'

'The boys who carried out the attack – can you describe them?'

'Are you daft? It was black as pitch out there except for their car headlights.'

'They came in a car?'

'Musta done.'

'What kind of car?'

'One with four wheels, what d'you think?' She shrugged her shoulders and pulled the collar of her dressing-gown closer, to signify it was draughty at the window and she wanted this over with.

'Mrs Bedells,' begged Peter, 'be nice to the officer. He's trying to find these lads so he can warn them off. Do you want them to come back and break some more windows?'

For a moment the adamant expression weakened, and she appeared vulnerable, apprehensive. The policeman, quick to seize advantage, asked: 'Did you get a glimpse of any of them in the car headlights? What were they wearing?'

'Umm . . . One of 'em had a football top – you know, the kind footballers wear for training. I think it was maroon with strips of white. And they had those caps with peaks – you know – like they wear—'

'Baseball caps?'

'Yes. One of them had a baseball cap with a lot of yellow on it.'

'How many of them were there?'

'Five, I made it.'

'Tall, short, fat, thin?'

'Oh . . .' She waved a hand. 'I dunno – they were moving about, stooping to pick up stones, running, shouting . . . The one with the yellowish baseball cap, he was short – not much more than five foot. But then I moved away from the windows because they were breaking the glass and so I didn't see any more.'

'Thank you, madam.' He returned to the patrol car to confer with his partner. Mrs Bedells made as if to turn away but Peter spoke to prevent her.

'Mrs Bedells, perhaps it would be better for your safety if you moved out—'

'*Oh* no, *oh* no! Is that what this was, a scheme to get me scared so that I'd run away? Nobody's going to make me go even if they send a tank!'

At that moment another car roared into the Terrace and Jeff Jones of the *Gazette* leapt out. He ran towards No. 15 and its lighted window. The old lady withdrew at once, and a moment later the light clicked off.

'What's the story?' he shouted as he dashed up the steps to join Peter.

'Some louts were breaking her windows.'

'She all right?'

'All she wants is to get back to bed, she says.'

'Tough old bird.' Jeff peered at the house. 'Some damage, I see. Any idea who?'

'The patrolman got a sort of description. I think he may be radioing it in now. How did you find out about it?'

'Listen in to the police channel, don't I? I'd have been here sooner but I was at a do at the University, heard it driving back.' He swooped down towards the police car, seeing that it was about to drive off. Peter hesitated a moment by the door, then followed him. Only a short exchange had occurred between the reporter and the patrolman. The car drove off. Jones stood on the pavement shrugging in regret.

'Wish I'd got here sooner, might have been a good human interest piece if I could have had a word with the old girl. What did she say?'

'She wasn't co-operative,' Peter said. He had no intention of repeating any of the old lady's conversation to a pressman. One of his aims was to build up some sort of rapport with her but nothing would bring up her defences faster than to talk about her to Jeff Jones.

He was uncertain what to do next. The patrolmen had done their duty and with no other clues to gather they had gone on to some other incident. Jeff Jones was interested in the event only for its news value.

But could one simply drive away after the old lady had been subjected to such harassment? On the other hand, could he spend the night on guard in his car outside the house? Should he?

He was debating this when yet another car drove in.

He recognised it at once, Bethany Dayton's Suzuki.

Bethany had been summoned by Jones. She wasn't his first choice as female participant in the drama – he had tried to get hold of Iris Weston. But Iris was no longer at the hotel whose number she had given him some weeks ago. In fact, she was now staying at Alan Singleton's flat on her trips to York.

Finding he couldn't reach Iris, Jones decided on Bethany. He wanted a woman on the scene, so as to be able to get some quotes: 'Women aren't safe these days in their own homes . . .' That sort of thing.

Bethany hadn't stopped to ask herself why he'd called with the information that Mrs Bedells was beset by a gang of juvenile delinquents. Working on an architectural drawing for a project unconnected with the Town Centre, she had given her entire mind to it. It had taken a few seconds for the news to penetrate when she picked up her phone. Then, filled with alarm on behalf of the embattled owner of No. 15, she'd leapt up from her draft table and driven off for the Terrace.

All she saw was a dark row of houses, two cars drawn up, and two men in conversation. Jones had said the police were on the scene but there was no sign of them.

'Bethany!'

'What's happening? Jeff said—'

'Seems it's all died down,' Jones said in a tone of disgust. 'Kids ran off when the cops turned up; seems the cops couldn't get much out of the old girl, it's a washout.'

Without more ado Bethany went to the door and knocked. 'Mrs Bedells? Mrs Bedells, it's Bethany Dayton. Would you come to the door, please, Mrs Bedells?'

'She won't come,' called Peter. 'She's as mad as a hatter about the whole thing. The police could hardly get two words out of her.'

'Mrs Bedells?' persisted Bethany. 'I see your front room window is broken. Would you like me to get it boarded up?'

'Go away!'

'But Mrs Bedells, dear, you can't leave your window like that, now can you? It's not safe and it's draughty.'

'Mind your own business.'

'I'll just get a man to come and put a piece of wood for tonight, shall I?'

'Do what you like.'

Taking that for assent, Bethany summoned up on her mobile phone a carpenter who had done some work at her own flat. Not best pleased at being woken at one in the morning, he nevertheless turned out when he found he was going to do some work at the home of the famous Nancy Bedells who'd been in the papers last week. By two o'clock the window pane was boarded up and No. 15 was secure for the present.

It was this that made her father angriest when he summoned her to the office in Aldwark next morning.

'I don't know what the devil you think you're up to!' he raged. 'There she is, made to feel for the first time that she'd be better off out of it, and you seal up the damage and make her feel secure again.'

'You're not suggesting we should have left her with one of her windows gaping open?'

'Why should we rush to her aid if her windows get broken? Quite the contrary, let's see a few more get smashed.'

'Dad!'

'Bethany, see sense! Anything that shakes that old hag's defences is to our advantage. I don't want you shoring up the place for her!'

Bethany stared at him. He was disproportionately angry, as if he were grappling with a big let-down.

'Did you . . . Did you have anything to do with it?' she asked on a faint thread of voice.

'What? What did you say?'

'You didn't . . . set that up? That attack on the house?'

'What are you talking about, girl? Do you think I know any juvenile gangs?' He was shouting at her now.

'No, of course not . . . I'm sorry . . . It was just when you said it was to our advantage—'

'Of course it was to our advantage! And now you've thrown it away!'

'I thought it was the best thing to do. I couldn't just—'

'I don't know what you were doing there in the first place! Why can't you keep your nose out of things that don't concern you?'

'Dad, if you got me here just to give me a lecture about how to handle Nancy Bedells, let's not waste any more of our time. I'm not going to go along with any view of her that turns her into a target. She's an old lady on her own, and to stand by and let thugs frighten her is shabby.'

'Shabby, is it? What about the way *she's* behaving? Selfish and wrong-headed!'

'She's not an angel, that's for sure, but two wrongs don't make a right.'

'She's a confounded old witch and I'll have her out of there and get on with the demolition if it's the last thing I do!'

Bethany walked out. There was no arguing with her father when he was in this mood.

Before returning to Barhampton she went into a bistro for coffee. There she glanced through the newspapers on their wooden holders. The story had broken too late for the morning editions but she knew it was all over the local radio. The television news would pick it up for the midday bulletins and by the evening it would be back in the headlines again – the Royal Terrace story, the little old lady story.

When she got back to the site office in Barhampton the Chairman of Steerco rang her. 'I hear you were there last night,' he began. 'What did you think? Is she in danger?'

'I don't really know, Mr Ollerton. It might just have been a passing bunch of hooligans. On the other hand, it might have been caused by a certain feeling of animosity that was in the newspapers just before they dropped the story. I mean, if you're told that there's an old lady living on her own who's being a pain in the neck to everybody, it might tempt you to go and chuck a few stones at her. And if it didn't work the first time, you might be tempted to go and do it again.'

'The police say they'll look in on her when they pass. But of course they don't pass all that often.'

'Particularly now that the Town Centre is largely empty.'

'Exactly.' She heard Ollerton sigh. 'I wish I'd got that wrap-around hoarding up before all this happened.'

'Can't do it now. It would look as if you're putting her in prison.'

'I thought of hiring a security firm. But the cost . . .'

'Shall I go and try to talk to her again?'

'Did she talk to you last night?'

'No.'

'I don't see the point then. Really, Miss Dayton, I don't see what we can do. And yet if she gets hurt . . . It would be *such* a black mark against us.'

Not to mention a disaster for Mrs Bedells, thought Bethany to herself.

When she put the phone down it rang again. It was her mother. 'Bethany, are you awfully busy?'

'Yes, I am, as a matter of fact, but let's disregard that,' she answered with a laugh. 'Why do you ask?'

'I thought it would be nice if we could meet for a bite at lunch-time.'

'Yes, lovely, what day do you have in mind?' she asked, reaching for her organiser.

'Today, dear.'

'Today?'

'Yes, it just so happens I'm coming to Barhampton for an event so I thought it would be nice if we could meet. Just a sandwich and a drink, dear.'

The chances that her mother would be coming to Barhampton for any reason except to see her were a thousand to one, so something had happened. 'All right then, I'll see you at one,' she agreed. 'Where?'

'Well, you know the town better than I do . . .'

'Why not come to the flat, Mother? I'll lay on some sandwiches, and make some coffee.'

'Oh no, I don't want to put you to any trouble.'

'No trouble. I'll buy the sandwiches on the way home. One o'clock?'

'I'll be there, dear.'

Mary Dayton was a careful driver and always set off too early. She was therefore waiting by the kerb when her daughter drove up. The garden of the old house was bright with late tulips and a florid lilac, which she regarded with a flower-arranger's eye.

'Who does the garden?' she enquired.

'The people who have the ground floor. I'm going to have window-boxes.'

'Good for you.' Mary had brought a bottle of peach-flavoured mineral water to enhance the meal. She opened it while Bethany brewed the coffee. The sandwiches she'd bought from one of the caterers who brought a van to the building sites – good, hearty sandwiches bursting with commonplace fillings.

Mary chatted nervously as she helped get out mugs and plates. Bethany gave her news of her work, which always interested her mother although she sometimes didn't understand the details. At length, when the wall clock was showing half past one, Bethany asked: 'What's this about, Mother?'

'I wanted to have a word . . . about . . . you know.. what's been on the radio this morning . . . about that thing in Royal Terrace last night.'

'Yes?'

'I heard it was some boys . . .'

'Yes, about five of them in a gang, I gather.'

'Yes, well . . . You know Vera Ickstone's husband runs our church youth club?'

'I didn't know that. Who's Vera Ickstone?'

'She and I do the flowers for St Martin's – you must remember her – she always wears those cloppety shoes that are so fashionable now and she puts bits of wood in the flower arrangements. Trendy.'

Bethany had no recollection of the woman but said encouragingly, 'Yes?'

'She was on the phone to me this morning, very excited – her husband – David – was knocked up by the police just as they were going to bed to ask if he'd seen Terry Hobsgroom that evening.'

'Who's Terry Hobsgroom?'

'He's a lad that comes to the youth club. I don't know why, because all he does is cause trouble and steal things. Anyway, the police wanted to know if he'd been there last night.'

'And had he?'

'No.'

'And?'

'Terry Hobsgroom wears a yellow and black satin baseball cap. He's very proud of it. He got it when they went to Florida last year.'

'I'm not getting this, Mother,' Bethany said in perplexity.

'One of the boys who were throwing stones at the windows in Royal Terrace last night was wearing a baseball cap with yellow satin on it.'

Now the visit from her mother began to make partial sense. 'Do the police know this?' she enquired gently, for she sensed this was a very delicate moment. Someone at the church youth club might be a participant in the hooliganism of last night. The church youth club was one of her mother's charity projects. Feeling she was too elderly to lead debates or play table-tennis with the youngsters, Mary Dayton baked cakes for them, hemmed curtains for the windows of the prefabricated hut, ran table-top sales to raise funds.

'Oh yes,' she sighed, 'they suspected Terry Hobsgroom the minute they heard the description of the baseball cap. They went looking for him straight off, but they couldn't find him so they wanted to know if he'd been seen in York last night. Vera says David says they caught up with him this morning at the house of a friend and the pair of them say they went to Harrogate last night. They vouch for each other.'

'Hm.' Bethany got up to remove their plates. 'What I hear in your voice is that you don't believe them.'

'No. Neither do the police. But there's nothing they can do about it.'

'I suppose not. So that's that.' She scraped the remains of the sandwiches into a polythene bag and dropped it in the waste-bin. 'Would you like any more of this mineral water or shall I put it in the fridge?'

'Beth,' said her mother.

Bethany turned. Her mother's plump face was crumpling into an expression of utter misery. 'Beth, Terry Hobsgroom's father is a dump-truck driver.'

'He is?'

'And he works for Billy Wellbrow.'

Now the conversation began to make sense. 'Are you saying that you think . . . Billy Wellbrow put the boys up to . . . attacking Mrs Bedells's house?'

'Well, not directly. I mean, I don't suppose Billy ever spoke to the boys, but he knows for a fact that Terry's been in trouble with the police before now – he's had to give Hobsgroom time off to go to the magistrate's court.'

'So are you saying that Billy spoke to his dump-truck driver . . .?'

'I don't know. I think he may well have. You know Billy – he's always one to want to take action, to take a stick to somebody. He came to dinner about ten days ago, he was hopping mad about Mrs Bedells and all the trouble she was causing . . .'

Bethany knew only too well that there were Action Man types in the construction industry. Billy Wellbrow was fond of saying he 'came up the hard way', which seemed to mean he'd used his fists a lot and

82

dropped five-pound notes in places where they would do him the most good.

But to hire a gang of boys to go and harass an old lady?

And yet, done indirectly . . .? Billy Wellbrow didn't need to say to Hobsgroom, 'Send your lad and his pals to give her a scare.' Over a pint in a pub, the conversation might drift towards the desirability of getting Mrs Bedells out. 'Pity somebody can't make her less fond of the place.'

'Oh, it's a bit of a tip there already – all the other houses empty, rubbish lying about. Vandals will start on it soon.'

'Wouldn't be a bad thing if they did . . .'

As easy as that.

Bethany's heart sank. 'I don't see there's anything we can do about it. There's no proof it was Terry Hobsgroom and, in any case, it didn't have the desired effect. Mrs Bedells is still there and likely to stay until the crack of doom.'

Mary's eyes filled with tears. 'You haven't heard the worst bit yet,' she faltered.

'What? Mother, what?'

'I think your father knew.'

Bethany felt a thrill of conviction. She recalled her own instinct this morning, that he was too angry about the matter. 'What makes you say that?' she countered, hoping to argue against her mother's view.

'Well, he and Billy go a long way back. And then . . . last night he was pleased about something; he had that little smile about him. And this morning, when he heard on the radio how things had gone – that Mrs Bedells was still there and that somebody had made a temporary repair to her window, he was furious, really furious. He jumped up from the breakfast table so hard he upset the teapot.' Mary wiped her eyes with her knuckles. 'I just know he was in on it, Beth.'

To hide her thoughts, Bethany turned to pick the coffee pot off the workbench. 'Come on now, Mother, don't be upset. Dry your eyes and have another cup of coffee.'

'Thank you, dear.' Mary held out her mug for a refill. 'I don't know why I'm crying about it. It's not as if it's the first time your father has used a bit of sleight of hand over a business problem.'

'No, I'm sure it isn't.'

'And all of them are under a lot of strain, about the delays that are facing them.'

'I know that, Mother. I sympathise with them because it involves me too. All the same . . .'

'All the same, they shouldn't threaten old ladies.'

'No. I told Dad this morning that I thought it was shabby to do that. No wonder he was so angry.'

'Because he feels guilty.'

'I suppose guilt comes into it. It's frustration mostly, I think. And being made to look foolish. There they all are, in charge of a hundred million of public money, supposed to be putting up a new Town Centre, and one old lady with a closed door has got them flummoxed.'

'You've spoken to her, haven't you, Beth? Couldn't you persuade her to leave? It would really be best for her.'

Listening to her mother's plaintive voice, Bethany marvelled at the difference between the two women. Mary Dayton had spent most of her life keeping the peace in her family, placating her husband and diminishing the effects of his demanding nature. Mrs Bedells was made of different stuff. Her instinct was to fight back – openly, straightforwardly, reacting with sharpness to any offer of truce.

'Mrs Bedells isn't going to leave, Mother, unless the council can get a Compulsory Purchase Order and remove her by legal injunction.'

'But if her house has been attacked once, it could happen again!'

Bethany was only too aware of that, as were Cyril Ollerton and other members of the Town Council. Copycat attacks weren't out of the question – show a bad lad a target and he'll throw something at it.

The problem was solved for them that evening. As the early summer dusk closed in, a sense of something happening drew citizens to Royal Terrace. Newspapermen, a TV van with masses of cables and equipment, photographers with flashes at the ready . . . Someone had alerted them.

Lights were on in Mrs Bedells's house. But, more remarkably, there were lights in other houses too. A radio or tape player was belting out a loud version of 'When the Saints Come Marching In'. People were bustling about. From the upper windows of two adjoining houses a long banner was being suspended.

The crowd watched with interest as it was unfurled. It flapped about boisterously in the evening breeze. At length cords were led in from its lower edge to be tethered within the ground-floor rooms. The banner, thick black letters on white, read: SUPPORT NANCY BEDELLS. SAFEGUARD ROYAL TERRACE.

Bethany stood with the rest to read the message. Well, Dad, she thought to herself, I don't think this was the result you were trying to achieve.

Chapter Seven

Either by calculation or good fortune, the occupation of Royal Terrace obtained maximum publicity, for the 'invasion' took place on Friday night. TV cameras had plenty of good scenes to run for the late-night news. Local radio reported the 'invasion' as a live broadcast. Newspapers gave the story front-page coverage next morning with excellent pictures showing the banner unfurling from the Terrace windows. There were plenty of quotes from the group who had mounted the occupation: 'We're defending a lady who has been left defenceless by the authorities!' 'Nancy Bedells is an example to us all!' 'Stone-throwing thugs don't frighten us, nor do petty bureaucrats!'

The one thing reporters failed to get was a quote from the leading lady. Mrs Bedells remained hidden behind her locked front door, refusing to speak to anyone.

Naturally the Steering Committee held a crisis meeting on Saturday. Tempers were very frayed, not only at the impasse now facing them but at the thought of missing football and rugby matches. Iris Weston, who had been up practically all night dealing with the press, bore the brunt of some very cruel remarks. Bethany came to her aid, which didn't by any means please her.

'Just let things be,' she said under her breath to Bethany. 'Let them snipe at me – it gets their anger off their chests.'

'But it's so unfair – the media were bound to make a big thing of it.'

'Let's get down to business,' commanded Cyril Ollerton. 'Let's begin by saying that things were bad before, what with Mrs Bedells being a nuisance, but they're a hundred times worse now.'

'Aye, getting one old lady out would have been tricky but we coulda done it,' agreed Emmett Foyle. 'But there must be at least thirty of 'em in there now.'

'We'll get a court order,' Wellbrow said tightly. 'Those houses are council property – we'll get an eviction order, won't we, Bigsby?'

The lawyer sighed. He ought to have been on the links playing eighteen holes with an important business colleague. Instead here he was in the Council Room of the Town Hall, feeling out of place in his slacks and tweed jacket under the disapproving eyes of the portraits – all of whom were in black suits and some of them in hard high collars. He was dreading the wrangle he could foresee.

'Let's not do anything hasty,' he began. 'We'd be perfectly within our rights to apply to the courts, but if the Royal Terrace Protection Group contest the application we might have a hard time getting the order.'

'That can't be correct, Bigsby! The council has a right to keep people out of property it owns and schedules for redevelopment.'

'In law, yes. But look at the feelings aroused by this situation. Councillors might not want to instruct me to apply for an eviction order—'

'Are you saying,' shouted Wellbrow, 'that that bunch of lily-livered vote-counters won't support us?'

'Calm down, Billy, calm down . . .' Ollerton made pacifying motions with his hands.

'Calm down, he says! *You're* not losing money every minute that ticks away!'

And so it went on for an hour. They broke for lunch, but stood around in little groups and partnerships, muttering to each other. Bethany said to Ollerton: 'Would it be a good idea to get Mr Lambot to come this afternoon? We need to get some idea what this Protection Group intends to do next.'

'Ah . . . well thought of . . . Yes, let's ring him and ask if he can drop in. Bigsby, would you see to that? And Beth, why not ring your dad? We'd like him to sit in again – his views are always useful.'

What he meant, she was sure, was that he wanted someone more important than herself to represent *Dayton's*. She sighed inwardly but didn't demur. Her private opinion was that her father would only exacerbate the discussion. The new Town Centre was a *Dayton & Daughter* project, the first really big operation since her name was joined to his, and he could see it turning into a fiasco. Last night after the television news he'd been on the phone to her, giving her instructions about what to say at Steerco.

But she agreed that he ought to be here to make his own statements. If any important decisions were taken without his participation he'd be even more furious than he was at present.

The meeting resumed at half-past two. Peter Lambot had arrived and had asked permission to bring Mr Tallant, the President of the Local History Society and prime mover in the plot to save Royal Terrace. He proved to be a plump, late-middle-aged man with a double chin and bright blue eyes, slow to speak but with a very weighty manner when he did so.

Once again Mr Ollerton called the meeting to order. 'Thank you all for coming back to the committee so promptly, and an extra thank you to Mr Lambot, Mr Tallant, and Mr Dayton for giving up their Saturday afternoon at such short notice.' The three guests nodded in acceptance of the greeting. 'Now, as you can imagine, we've had a long discussion already about this matter, Mr Lambot. We're anxious to solve this problem as quickly and as tactfully as possible. What we'd like to hear from you and Mr Tallant is what the Royal Terrace Protection Group intend to do.'

Mr Tallant cleared his throat. 'I'd like to make it clear from the outset that the Royal Terrace Protection Group did not instigate the occupation of those houses.'

'You mean you disapprove?' Mr Bigsby said almost joyously.

'No, now that it has occurred I do not disapprove. In fact, the people who took that action have solved a problem that I myself could not. You'll understand, ladies and gentlemen, that I and my fellow-members of the Protection Group want to do just that – protect Royal Terrace, both for its architectural value and more especially for its heritage aspect. I confess that after the attack by vandals on Mrs Bedells's house the other night I was at a loss. These conservationists—'

'Conservationists!' snorted Daniel Dayton. 'Squatters, that's what they are! And you know what squatters do to property!'

'I am assured by a spokesman for the occupiers that they intend to look after the property,' Mr Tallant intoned.

'Oh, do they! They're not going to be there long enough to do anything if I have my way. I'll have the police round there before you can say Mother Skipton!'

'The police will not intervene, Mr Dayton,' Peter said. 'It isn't a crime to be a squatter—'

'Aw, come on, that's a quibble! You know the law only protects them so long as they don't do damage. But we all know what squatters are. They'll light fires in the middle of the floor and paint graffiti over the walls – and that's not mentioning the pot-smoking and the—'

'I am assured by spokesmen for the group that they intend to look after the property,' reiterated Mr Tallant. 'And as to pot-smoking, I have no reason to think anything of that kind goes on and mere accusations will get you nowhere, Mr Dayton.'

'We'll have that court order soon enough. We've special grounds for applying – the common good, the general intention on the part of the council to improve the environment—'

'How does it improve the environment to knock down a row of handsome Georgian houses?'

'How does it improve the environment to preserve it at the expense of a building scheme that's been agreed to by the majority of the towns-folk? The people of Barhampton *voted* for it.'

'But that was before they knew it was a historic site!'

'Historic site!' barked Wellbrow. 'A hussy's house, you mean!'

'Mr Wellbrow, your narrow-minded view of Arabella Bedells—'

'Gentlemen, gentlemen,' intervened Mr Ollerton. 'We're here to try to solve the problem, not lose our tempers with each other.'

'I never lose my temper,' said Mr Tallant with calm superiority. He had been a schoolmaster and had a regrettable tendency to treat people who disagreed with him as if they were primary-school pupils.

'These people you called in to occupy the houses—'

'I did not call them in, Miss Weston,' he corrected her. 'But I approve of what they did.'

'Did they ask Mrs Bedells if she wanted their support?'

'I have no information on that point.'

'Did *you* ask Mrs Bedells?'

'Er . . . no. I was unable to speak to her.'

'Knocked on the door and were told to clear off, eh?'

Mr Tallant made a little shrugging movement of the shoulders which clearly let them know that whatever had passed between him and Mrs Bedells, he wasn't going to tell them.

'What's your point, Iris?' demanded Emmett Foyle.

'We ought to put out a statement saying that Mrs Bedells has said a dozen times she wants to be left in peace and that these 'activists' aren't there by her invitation.'

'That's pretty weak, isn't it?' snorted Foyle.

'No, wait,' said Bethany. 'I agree it wouldn't carry too much conviction if we put it out just as our opinion, but what if we could get Mrs Bedells to say it?'

'Oh yes,' Iris agreed with irony, annoyed because she herself hadn't thought of it. 'I can just see Mrs Bedells agreeing to make any kind of statement that would help *us*. You know she's angry with us over that stupid cat.'

'Well . . . yes . . . But she weakens now and then, doesn't she?'

'How d'you mean, Beth?' asked Alan Singleton.

'As far as I understood the matter – about the boys throwing stones – she called *you*, Peter.'

'She called the police,' Wellbrow put in.

'No, she called me and *I* called the police,' Peter said. 'They got there ahead of me but she wouldn't speak to them—'

'There you are! She won't speak to anybody—'

'But she did speak to me, just a few words. She told me off for calling the police, said she only wanted a man on the scene to scare the kids away.'

Wellbrow growled below his breath, 'Showed more sense than you did, then . . .' He'd had a fright over the stone-throwing: he'd never expected the police to be involved.

'What I'm saying is, she actually telephoned Peter—' Bethany insisted.

'Only because I put my card with my address and telephone number through her letterbox.'

'What's your point, Beth?' her father demanded.

'I was wondering if she'd speak to Peter if he went and asked her about these squatters.'

'Don't be daft! We're not going to send *him*! He's their lawyer—'

'No, no, Mr Dayton, please – clear your mind of that misapprehension,' said Mr Tallant. 'Mr Lambot is acting for the Royal Terrace Protection Group, not for the activists. Although I do not disapprove of their actions, I would prefer not to have the Local History Society's name associated with them.'

'Well, all right, he's acting for your lot – we'd be stupid to send him to talk to Mrs Bedells.'

'Not at all,' countered Mr Tallant with great dignity. 'I should on the contrary be glad to have Mrs Bedells's opinion of the occupation of the Terrace. Don't you agree, Lambot? The Protection Group ought to be guided by her wishes to some extent. If she approves of the support from these young people, so much the better. If she disapproves, perhaps the Protection Group should be wary of being too involved with them.'

'Look here,' said Wellbrow, 'I'm not having *their* lawyer hobnobbing with the old girl.'

'I don't see how you could prevent me, Mr Wellbrow,' Peter observed quietly.

'No . . . well . . . what I mean is, I'm not having you go there and saying you represent *us* in any way—'

'Perhaps if Bethany came with me?'

'Bethany?'

'Yes, Billy,' her father put in with some eagerness. 'She's not on such bad terms with Mrs Bedells. After all, it was Beth who got her window boarded up for her the other night—'

'And a lot of thanks I got for it,' she remarked, with a rueful smile. 'But all the same . . . if you think it would do any good, I'll go with Peter to see if we can talk to her.'

They spent another half-hour wrangling about what they should say to her, supposing she would answer the door. It was going on for four o'clock when they set off from the Town Hall on their errand, on foot because it was a short walk. But before they reached Royal Terrace, they could hear that something was going on there.

There was a hubbub, shouting and catcalls with a background of pounding music from a tape player. In discord with that people were singing 'We shall overcome' to the muffled accompaniment of a guitar.

Bethany and Peter looked at each other in alarm. They quickened their step. They came round the hoarding of the Market Square to a view of the Terrace. A large group – some fifty people of all shapes, sizes and ages – were marching along the gritty roadway holding up makeshift placards on poles. The slogans voiced support for the new Town Centre scheme: *RENEW BARHAMPTON! AWAY WITH OLD RUBBISH! OUT! OUT! OUT!*

They were marching in time to the rhythm of an old Fred Astaire number played much too loud on a tape-recorder. Each time the tune reached the point where the words were 'Dust yourself off, Start all over again,' the crowd broke out into loud song. The guitar music and its accompanying chant was from a group of conservationists, who had linked hands and taken a stand in front of the houses they occupied. It was a strange performance: 'We shall overco-o-ome – START ALL OVER AGAIN!'

Reporters with mikes, photographers with cameras, and television apparatus were greedily recording the whole affair. Bethany and Peter came to a halt. 'We ought to get out of here before they spot us,' Peter said.

'Right.'

They were turning back when Jeff Jones sprang up out of nowhere. 'Hello, come to pour oil on troubled waters?'

'We came to have a word with Mrs Bedells,' Bethany said. 'But now is clearly not the time.'

'What were you going to say to her? If you were going to offer to move her out, seems to me you've chosen exactly the right moment.'

Peter was shaking his head. Bethany, however, frowned and hesitated. What could the poor old soul be going through, trapped in her home with this rumpus all around her.

'Have you been to the door?' she asked Jones.

'Yes, me, and all the rest of the world and his wife. But she's saying nowt.' He gave Bethany a pat on the arm. 'Go on, have a go. If you can get her to move, you'll be doing her a favour. This kind of thing could easily turn ugly.'

'What do you think, Peter?'

'I'm not supposed to urge her to move, Bethany. I'm supposed to help keep Arabella's house safe.'

'Well, don't say anything about moving out, then. I'll talk about that, if we can get her to the door. But I think we ought to speak to her. This—' she gestured to the scene around them in the Terrace – 'this could be scaring her half to death.'

He nodded agreement. They walked forward. Jeff Jones came with them.

'Oh no you don't,' said Bethany. 'She won't co-operate if you're there. She probably hates you for putting that picture in the paper.'

'I've a perfect right to come with you.'

'That's true but it wouldn't make sense. She won't talk if you're there.'

He struggled with the logic for a moment. 'All right,' he said at last with reluctance, 'but I get first shot at anything you get from her – okay?'

'Right,' Peter said, 'stay here.'

As they made their way forward Bethany protested, 'You shouldn't have agreed to that.'

'All I said was "Right, stay here." That's not an agreement.'

'Oh,' said Bethany. It wasn't her way to examine every dot and comma of a statement. She reminded herself that Peter was after all a lawyer and that she'd better bear that in mind if they spoke to the old lady.

The little crowd in the Terrace paid scant attention to them as they mounted the steps of the house on the end of the row. Peter knocked on the door. 'Mrs Bedells? Mrs Bedells, it's Peter Lambot. Remember me? You telephoned me the other night and I came.'

No response.

'She probably can't hear you for this racket outside,' Bethany said.

'I can hear you all right,' said a tart voice from behind the door. 'I'm not deaf!'

Her callers were so taken aback that for a moment they couldn't think of a word to say.

'Well, what do you want?'

'Er . . . we wanted to make sure you were all right, Mrs Bedells, dear,' said Bethany.

'I'm as all right as I can be expected to be with all this hullabaloo! They're scaring my poor little cat half to death. If you had anything to do with them coming here I'd be obliged if you'd tell them to clear off.'

'It's nothing to do with us, Mrs Bedells. We're as upset about it as you are—'

'Disgraceful! They play loud music all hours of the day and night and gallop about in the street talking at the top of their voices and their children are always shouting and screaming—'

'Their children? They've got children with them?'

'You'd know it if you lived here, my girl! And they were hammering away last night well past midnight, putting up boards where the windows had been broken on numbers eleven and eight. And they must know they've no right to do it, because that property isn't theirs, as I know very well because my William and me, we were the only freeholders in the Terrace by the time he passed on.'

This was the longest speech Bethany had ever heard from her. She guessed it sprang from a need for companionship in the midst of this mob of noisy strangers. She said, in an attempt at reassurance, 'I think they mean well.'

'Mean well! They put bits of paper through my letterbox telling me they're protecting me! Who asked them to? What right have they to be here? Squatters, that's what they are! Won't pay rent, break into decent property and leave it a pig-sty. Oh, I've seen 'em on telly, I know what they're like.'

'But I think these people are different, Mrs Bedells,' Peter explained.

'They want to save the Terrace from being knocked down and they'll prevent any vandals from doing damage—'

'They're vandals themselves! Moving in and settling down as if those houses belonged to them! And let me tell you, most of those places were fixed up as offices. It's no place to bring children, and what they're going to do about bathrooms and doing the laundry, I can't imagine!'

Some of this tirade was lost in the increase of noise around them. Bethany glanced over her shoulder. Jeff Jones was at the foot of the front-door steps, watching the mêlée and speaking into his tape-recorder. 'What's going on?' she asked.

'Reinforcements,' he replied. 'I think some of the folk who were inside the houses have come out to help.' He said into the recorder: 'New placards have appeared – SAVE NANCY'S HOME – that's a good move, personalise the row . . .'

Bethany addressed herself once more to the defender behind the door. 'You can hear how noisy it's getting,' she said. 'There are a lot of people milling around out here. Don't you think, really, it would be better if we moved you out?'

'Move me out? Like a piece of furniture? Go away!'

'No – wait—' said Peter. 'I know you don't want to move.' He frowned and shook his head at Bethany, and she made a little grimace of apology.

'No, I'm sorry, Mrs Bedells, I spoke without thinking. But you see, by staying put, you've brought all these other people here.'

'*I* didn't bring 'em! They're nothing to do with me. Putting letters in my door, calling me Nancy – who gave them the right to call me by my first name? The impudence!'

'If you would say a few words to the reporter – that you don't want help from the conservationists—'

'I'm not saying a word to any reporter and that's flat. But *you* can tell 'em from me to clear off, and here—' pieces of paper began to peep out of the letterbox and then fall to the ground – 'give 'em back their rubbish and tell 'em to stick it in their pipes and smoke it!'

As they stooped to retrieve the sheets of paper they could hear her shoes clatter on the linoleum of the hall as she withdrew. Jones, ever watchful, leapt up the steps to catch up one of the letters.

Someone in the crowd behind them saw the paper. 'They're serving an eviction order!' There was an eddy of protesters towards them. Placards on broomsticks and pieces of clothes-pole were waved; some said: PROTECT OUR NANCY and some OUT! OUT! OUT! Both sides were demanding to know what was going on.

Jeff Jones was keeling over in the face of the pressure of bodies. 'Clear off, clear off,' he yelped. 'You'll damage my recorder!'

'What have they been saying to her? What's that you've got?'

'I dunno – She pushed it through her letterbox – it's a statement maybe. Hey! Mind what you're at – you'll have me over.' He elbowed a space so that he could look at the writing. Mystified, he read it out: ' *"Dear Nancy, You can rely on us to protect your rights and react against any—"* '

The paper was snatched out of his hand. A very pretty girl with a mane of artistically tangled black hair held it aloft in one hand while with the other she waved a placard on a stick. The placard proclaimed: WE STAND BY NANCY! 'Here you are, comrades,' she called, and passed the paper back to friends at the rear.

'That was mine,' protested Jones. 'Give it back!'

'She's got another!' someone shouted. 'Her that was calling through the door at her!'

'Give that to me,' demanded the dark-haired girl, leaning past Jones to get at Bethany.

'Now hold hard there,' Peter said. 'It's only the letters you put in her door – she wants you to have them back.'

'Hand them over – you're trying to put a summons on her—'

'No, no,' Bethany protested. 'We're here to help her—'

'She's that woman from the building firm, I saw her picture in the paper—' came a cry from the crowd.

'Help her?' screamed the girl with the placard. 'You're here to harass her! We could see you telling her off—'

'No, no, I was only talking to her. And in fact she was saying she didn't want you here making a racket.'

'That's a lie!'

'So move away and let her have some peace and—'

'We're her friends! You're the one should move away! Come on, shift yourself—' And the girl stretched out a hand to grab Bethany's shirt collar.

'Don't do that!' cried Bethany, putting up her arm to fend her off.

The girl in reaction brought down her left hand, the one holding the placard on a stick. With her right hand she held on to Bethany's collar. They swayed.

Peter dived forward to catch at Bethany. On the steps they lost their footing. They went down together in a tangle, knocking against others crowded on the steps. For a moment they were protected from the ground by the press of people, other bodies holding them up. But the crowd fell back, the trio fell to the stones, there was a gasp of dismay.

Bethany hit the pavement on her side. The girl protester rolled over on top of her, the placard flailing. It descended out of control.

Bethany felt a sharp blow to her temple. Then there was blackness.

Chapter Eight

When she opened her eyes, Bethany found she was in the Casualty Room of Barhampton Hospital. Someone she couldn't see very well was bathing her forehead with tepid water. She put up a hand to prevent this and a voice said, 'Lie still now, dear.'

She let her hand drop. A trickle of water went into her eyes. She tried to sit up. The voice said, 'No, now, luv, you've got a nasty gash there, keep still.'

The voice came to her rather faintly, through a tremendous pounding that was going on in her head. Someone had an old tin bath in there and was hitting it with a hammer.

She lay back. After a moment she said through unsteady lips, 'How did I get here?'

'In an ambulance, of course, what else?'

'How . . . how long have I been lying here?'

'About twenty minutes. Couldn't get to you at first, there were lads from a football match before you. How did you get this cut?'

'I . . . er . . . fell . . . I think . . . down some steps . . .'

'There's wood fibres in the cut. Were you on a building site or something?'

Bethany thought about it. 'Someone hit me . . . with a billboard.'

'A billboard?'

'On a stick, you know? *SAVE NANCY.*'

'Oh, like *SAVE THE WHALES*?'

'Yes.'

'Just you lie there a minute, pet, and I'll fetch Doctor to look at you. You're not making too much sense.'

Bethany lay in a curtained alcove, with a buzz of activity going on beyond. 'Doctor', when he came, proved to be an Asian, young, pale, and exhausted. He took her wrist in thin cool fingers. 'Pulse quite normal,' he remarked. He held his hand before her eyes. 'How many fingers am I holding up?' When she gave the correct reply, though faintly, he set about taking her blood pressure, went through the routine of tests for a new arrival, and pronounced her likely to live. 'I think we'll just have an X-ray to make sure your skull is all right,' he said.

'It feels as if I've got ten blacksmiths in there,' she muttered.

94

While she was waiting to go up to X-ray, her father came stamping in. 'My God!' he cried when he saw the dressing applied to her temple. 'I couldn't believe it when I was told you were attacked—'

'Dad,' she begged, 'don't shout.'

'Shout? I'll roar the place down. Who did this to you?'

'I'm . . . not too sure. Someone with a banner on a stick.'

'One of those damned activists! I'll have him in manacles with spikes on!'

'As a matter of fact . . .'

'What?'

'I think it was a girl.'

'A girl clouted you?'

'With the corner of her placard.'

'Bethie, she'll be in jail in the morning if I have owt to do with it! I told the police—'

'Oh Dad, please . . . Stop shouting.'

'When I had to ring your mother and tell her—'

'Don't let her be worried. I'm all right, really.'

'All right? They say they're going to do an X-ray. How can you be all right?'

'It's just to make sure, I think. Honestly, Dad . . . I don't think there's anything wrong . . .'

The hospital porter came at that moment to take her to the X-ray department. She called faintly as she was rolled away, 'Tell Mother not to worry.'

The X-ray found nothing wrong but Dr Patel decided to keep her in until next morning, just to be on the safe side. The wound was sutured, she was given painkillers which she immediately brought up in a bout of sickness, then after a tidy-up she was taken to the ward. The next thing she knew it was morning and the headache was still as bad.

'Good morning,' said the nurse who came bearing an early morning cup of tea. 'Feel like a drink?'

'Oh, my head,' groaned Bethany.

'Nine stitches,' said the nurse. 'I'll give you something for the pain. I'm to tell you your mother came to see you but you were asleep and she's coming back again today.'

'Today? But . . . don't I remember I was just being kept in overnight?'

'Quite right. But we'd like you to stay until lunch-time. Your mother's bringing you clean clothes; the things you were wearing got grubby from being on the ground.'

'Yes,' agreed Bethany, remembering the sensation of that roll down the steps – painful, bruising . . .

Breakfast was brought about eight, but she couldn't face the scrambled eggs and thick white toast. She was perpetually thirsty, though, and drank the weak tea eagerly. She was allowed up to wash and brush her teeth, but the toothbrush seemed to jar her headache into more thunderous activity. She found she had bruises on her shoulders and arms which were now turning a beautiful shade of greenish blue. She stood at the washbasin, remembering last night's events in flashes and feeling shaky. She was quite glad to return to her bed.

At about nine her mother came. Pale with anxiety, she broke into a tremulous smile when she saw Bethany giving her a little wave of welcome.

'Darling, I was so worried! Last night you looked so . . . defence-less . . . like a little girl again . . . Your father says you were attacked?'

'I'm still piecing it together. I think it was an accident.'

'He's so angry! He was on to the police first thing this morning, demanding to know if they'd got the criminal.'

'Mother, she wasn't any sort of . . . well, never mind. Did you bring me clean clothes?'

Her mother held up the little overnight bag she'd brought. 'I'll take the other things and put them in the car. They tell me you can go at lunch-time. You'd better come home with us overnight, don't you think, luv?'

'What will you do until lunch-time?'

'Oh, there's morning service at St Mary's – good heavens, you shouldn't be worrying about what I'll be doing, you should be worrying about yourself!'

Bethany put her hand up to the dressing on her temple. 'It's just a gash,' she said. 'They tell me it won't leave a scar. Please stop worrying about it, Mother. And please tell Dad to stop making a fuss.'

'But he's furious, Beth. I don't know if I can.'

'Tell him it isn't going to do us any good to have a lot of publicity about "violence" in Royal Terrace. Telephone him and tell him to cool it.'

'I can't phone him, luv, he came with me this morning, he went to see the Superintendent at the police station – I think they know each other or something. He wants to make sure they're going all out to find this girl who—'

'It would be far better if they just forgot about her—'

'But Bethie, she can't go round bashing people on the head.'

'It was an *accident*, Mother. She got carried away. And she was only a kid. Don't you see, Dad isn't going to look good in the press if he pursues some idealistic little lass who never meant any harm? Tell him to talk to Iris about it. I'm sure Iris will agree with me.'

'As a matter of fact Iris was busy for hours last night trying to damp things down in the press. Luckily there were no pictures taken.'

Bethany nodded her head in agreement, then regretted it because it still ached. 'The TV cameras were all at the other end of the Terrace,' she recalled. 'But that snooper Jeff Jones was right at our elbows.'

'Yes, he seems to have sent word around to the big Sundays but it's

96

only a line or two. Mostly the report's about the squatters and the singing and the banners – there's only a few words saying something like "Miss Dayton, architect of the new Town Centre scheme, was hurt during the demonstration".'

'Let's try to keep it at that. Try to make Dad drop it, Mother.'

Mary promised to do her best. 'I'd better go,' she said. 'There's a policewoman waiting outside to interview you.'

'Oh Lord,' said Bethany.

'I'll be back at lunch-time. They say you can either eat lunch here or leave – which would you prefer?'

'Is that a genuine question?' said Bethany, and waved her away.

The policewoman who succeeded her was about Bethany's age, very prim and official. She asked her to go over the events leading to her injury. Bethany said that a young girl had got her feet tangled up as they came down the steps at the front of the house; they had fallen in a heap, and as a result the placard had hit her.

'You're saying it was an accident?'

'Yes.'

'Did you know this girl?'

'No.'

'Can you give a description?'

'About fifteen or sixteen. Tall, slender, lots of long dark brown hair, a loose white cambric or poplin top, jeans.'

'Any distinguishing marks? Jewellery – like earrings or St Christopher medals?'

'I don't recall,' said Bethany, picturing the big silver hoops swinging from the girl's ears.

'We'd really like to get a good description,' said the officer with a frown of encouragement. 'We're going to have to question the people in those houses, and you know it's always difficult handling squatters.'

'But it's not important, really,' she returned. 'It was an accident, really it was.'

'My superiors are treating it seriously, I'm afraid,' said the policewoman, with a faint sigh that told Bethany she agreed it was all a storm in a teacup.

Don't worry, thought Bethany as the WPC shut up her notebook and left. If I have anything to do with it, by this afternoon your superiors will have decided not to bother any more.

Surprisingly tired by these conversations, she lay back and closed her eyes. When she opened them again, Peter Lambot was hovering by the bed, a bunch of Parma violets in his hand.

'Peter!'

'They said it was all right to come in. I didn't realise you'd be asleep.' He moved in embarrassment from foot to foot, the rather severe features softened by anxiety.

'Just a nap,' she said. 'Sit down, how nice of you to come.'

'I rang last night. They said you'd only be kept in overnight and then this morning they said you'd be going at lunch-time so I thought I'd just drop by with these.'

'They're lovely,' she said, burying her nose in the scent of the violets. 'I'll take them with me when I go.'

He cleared his throat. 'Have . . . er . . . the police interviewed you?'

'Yes, about half an hour ago, I think.'

'Bethany, they asked me what happened and . . . you may disagree with this but . . . I said I thought it was an accident.'

'Oh, thank heaven!' She gave a great sigh of relief. 'That's what I'm saying. We don't want a fuss, Peter.'

'No, the last thing the Royal Terrace Protection Group wants is to be linked with any kind of violence.'

'The same goes for us – the developers – we don't want to look like a bunch of ogres taking stern measures against a silly little girl. I told the policewoman as little as I could, and to tell the truth I think she was only going through the motions because someone – probably my father – is harrying her boss about it.'

'Could you get Mr Dayton to play it down, do you think? I quite understand that he's upset that you got hurt – and so am I, of course. I got a real scare when I saw the blood on your face.'

'Scalp wounds always bleed a lot,' she soothed, from past experience of wounds on building sites.

He blew out a breath. 'You take it so calmly!'

'You must realise, Peter, I've tripped over buckets and fallen off scaffolding in my time. But generally the first aid post on the site deals with it – I'm not used to waking up in hospital.'

'We were all so worried! That reporter chap dashed for his car and followed the ambulance when it drove off – I think he thought you were about to expire.'

'Would have made a better story for him if I had. But it's all small beer, really. Don't worry about the police inquiry, it'll all die down, I'm sure.'

Clatterings and rattlings of trolley wheels let them know that lunch was being brought up to the ward. 'I'd better be off,' he said. 'Are you going home later? Can I drive you?'

'My mother and father are here, they're going to take me back to York for overnight – you know what parents are like,' she said with a smile.

'Quite right in this case. Anybody needs a spot of TLC after a bang on the head.' He took her hand momentarily. 'See you around,' he said.

'Right.'

After the ward doors swung shut behind him she held the posy of violets to her nose. She would pin them to her jacket when she left.

She still felt surprisingly unsteady as she dressed but the headache was decidedly better. She said goodbye to the few patients in the ward – for most had of course managed to get themselves sent home by the weekend – then went with her mother down to the car. Her father was waiting there, passenger door open, looking anxiously for her arrival.

'How're you feeling?'

'Better all the time.'

'You're still pale.'

'I'm all right, Dad, truly.'

She was going to get in the back but he beckoned her to the front passenger seat. Clearly he had something to say to her. He deferred it until they were leaving Barhampton on the York road.

'Bethie, the police tell me they've got nothing by way of a clue about this girl who whacked you.'

She said nothing.

'They're talking about making a foray among the squatters this afternoon, but Nelson – that's the Superintendent at the local cop-shop – he was a bit unwilling on that point.'

'I see his point.'

'You do?'

'Of course. I think they're mostly genuine about saving Royal Terrace, but some of them are probably out for a bit of a confrontation with authority – and if the police turned up on their doorsteps that would be an ideal opportunity. "Police provocation", that kind of thing.'

Daniel nodded. 'That's just what Nelson was saying.'

She let a moment go by. Then she said: 'Even if they find this girl, what's the point? She didn't mean to hit me. I certainly wouldn't want to bring any charges against her.'

'You wouldn't?'

'No, I'd rather see this all die away quietly.'

'That's what Iris has been saying.'

'Iris is clued up about this sort of thing.'

Mary Dayton, from the back seat, remarked that Iris should be listened to.

'Happen you're right,' said her husband. 'I know Nelson would be glad if I let it drop.'

'Give him a ring when we get home, Dad. Tell him I think it's all a fuss about nothing.'

'If you're sure? After all, you were the one that got hurt . . .'

At home there was a delicious scent of cooking. Mary had prepared a casserole before leaving for Barhampton that morning. Daniel busied himself pouring pre-lunch drinks. Bethany asked for one of the fruit-flavoured mineral waters; she still had a tremendous thirst, but food didn't appeal to her much. With a Scotch in his hand, Daniel went to telephone Superintendent Nelson with the opinion that it would be best if the injury to his daughter were written off as an accident.

Bethany set the table for the meal. Her mother brought in the hors d'oeuvres. 'That was a nice little bunch of violets on your jacket,' she said. 'Boyfriend?'

'Oh no, it was just Peter Lambot. He dropped in just before lunch.'

'He's not a boyfriend?'

'He's the solicitor acting for the opposition,' Bethany said with a laugh. 'Please don't complicate matters!'

'I see what you mean.'

A bread roll and a little smoked salmon were quite enough by way of lunch. Afterwards she went up to her old room and, lying down on the bed, fell into a deep sleep. When she awoke it was mid-afternoon, the headache was gone, and she celebrated by taking a long refreshing shower – protecting the dressing, as she'd been told, by wearing one of her mother's shower caps. It made her look like an illustration to a nursery rhyme.

Bethany felt like a new woman when she came downstairs. On the half-landing she paused, surprised to hear angry voices from the living room.

The voices belonged to her father and Josh Pembury, Head of Landscaping for Barhampton and a member of the Steering Committee. To hear him speaking up in such loud tones was a great surprise, for he was a man who seldom raised his voice. Seldom spoke at all, unless he had something important to say.

Josh belonged in the outdoors rather than in a committee room. Tall, broad-shouldered, his brown hair was lightened by exposure to sun and wind. He had rather sleepy brown eyes whose gaze generally dwelt on the sky that could be seen out of the boardroom window. Most of the other men on Steerco disregarded him, but he was an ally to Bethany: he shared her views on the importance of trees and flowers in the townscape, and spent time with her trying to find room in the budget for more greenery.

Both men turned as she came in, breaking off the conversation. 'You're really all right?' Josh said, taking one long step towards her to look in her face.

'Yes, thanks, I think I'm quite recovered.' She looked questioningly at him.

'This damn fool,' said her father, 'has come to plead for his daughter.'

'His daughter?'

'Alison – Allie – I don't think you've met her. She—'

'She was the one who knocked you out last night,' snorted Daniel. 'Would you *believe* it? Head of a department in Barhampton Town Council, and he lets his daughter join a band of protesters obstructing the council's work!'

'Daniel,' murmured his wife. 'Calm down.'

'Calm down! Dammit, this man's daughter whacked Beth over the head with a panel of wood—'

Bethany sat down. 'Please,' she said, 'could we be a bit quieter? I said I was quite recovered but that doesn't mean I want a shouting match.'

'I'm sorry,' Josh said, although it wasn't he who had been making the most noise. 'Perhaps I shouldn't have come, but Allie was in such a state – she thought she'd more or less killed you and then one of her friends in the squat rang her about midday to say the police were asking about her . . .'

'I called them off,' Daniel growled. 'Bethie said she didn't want it pursued any further.'

'Thank you, Bethany,' Josh said with fervour. 'It'll make all the difference in the world when I tell her. She hardly slept last night and she's been half-hysterical all morning . . .'

Mary Dayton raised her eyebrows at this. 'Couldn't her mother calm her down?'

'My wife died about eight years ago, Mrs Dayton,' he explained. Mary made an encouraging sound so he continued: 'Allie took it very badly. A sister of my wife's came to live with us but didn't seem to understand that my little girl was still grieving for her mother, so that broke up. Then I had a housekeeper who didn't handle her very well and after she left . . . Allie would be about eleven then . . . we decided we could manage on our own. But,' he sighed, 'it isn't easy being a single parent.'

'It isn't easy being a parent of any kind,' Mary said gently, thinking of her own family problems. 'If I could ever be of any help?'

'Thank you,' he said. But Bethany could tell he wouldn't take Mary up on her offer. And she knew just why. She couldn't imagine that fiery young girl of last night ever listening to advice from a conventional woman like Mary Dayton.

'You can tell Allie she's got nothing to worry about,' she said encouragingly to Josh. 'We want to keep this as quiet as we can. Just think of it! COUNCIL OFFICER'S DAUGHTER WHACKS COUNCIL'S ARCHI-TECT. Luckily it's too long for a headline but if Jeff Jones got wind of it he'd have a lovely time.'

'God forbid,' groaned Daniel. He was sorely put out. His Saturday had been ruined by having to attend Steerco and now his Sunday too with all the aftermath of the demonstration. Monday, which he never looked forward to anyhow, looked like being more of the same. And this idiot – this weak-kneed moron who couldn't control his own daughter – was standing there looking sorry for himself and getting sympathy from both Mary and Bethany.

Mary sensed his discomfiture. 'How about tea?' she suggested. 'And scones – I just took them out of the oven – and there's home-made ham too, although I didn't make it myself, I bought it at the Easter church bazaar.' Thus chatting, she spread goodwill through the room as she so often had in the past. She even managed to get her husband out to the kitchen, supposedly to take the jam down from a storage shelf, but in fact to separate him from Josh and let him simmer down.

'I'm not required to help,' Bethany said laughing. 'I'm an invalid in Mother's eyes.'

'I can't tell you how sorry I am about Allie's behaviour—'

'Believe me, it was an accident.'

'Your father is saying she shouldn't have been there in the first place, and of course he's right. But she's such an impressionable lass, she takes things terribly to heart, and so she went rushing to the aid of Mrs Bedells—'

Bethany couldn't help thinking that Allie Pembury would be offended if she knew how Mrs Bedells felt about her intervention, but it wouldn't be kind to say so. 'Allie's how old?' she enquired.

'She's just sixteen. Supposed to be working for her GCSEs, but she's not really academic.'

'She's at Barhampton High School, I suppose.'

'Yes, and can't wait to leave. She wants to go into acting, she's quite a star of the school's drama club, but you know how precarious that is . . .'

'Never mind about her acting ability,' Daniel interrupted, marching back into the room, having escaped the dire fate of helping get the tea things. 'I hope you gave her a good talking to and stopped her pocket money.'

'Oh goodness . . . I haven't got to that point yet . . . She was so distressed at hitting Bethany, and so my first priority was to calm her down—'

'So she should be,' grunted Daniel. Privately he was thinking that in days gone by she'd have got a good spanking, but these days you couldn't lift a hand against a girlchild.

'Well, you know, what with all the blood, and Bethany being rushed off in an ambulance – she was almost hysterical when she first got in last night, and then this friend rang to say a police officer had been asking for anyone answering her description. Really, she's been in tears all morning and too upset to have any punishment meted out.'

'Tell her to dry her tears,' Bethany said gently. 'Nothing more is going to happen.'

'Thank you, it's so generous of you.'

Too generous, thought her father. Bethany was being very forgiving, but Daniel had points he wanted to make as soon as possible to Cyril Ollerton, the Chairman of Steerco and Deputy Head of Town Planning on Barhampton council. This nitwit who couldn't control his own child – who let her rush off to befriend that old witch in Royal Terrace – and him an employee of Barhampton Town Council, a head of a department no less . . . He ought to be taken to task, at least, and Ollerton would have to be prompted to do it.

Mary arrived with the tea things. In the little to-do of handing out plates and scones and jam and cups, the mood of the afternoon improved. The scones were delicious, as Mary's scones always were. But Daniel's temper received a further trial when the doorbell rang and, opening the door, he found his old crony Ossie Fielden on the doorstep. Ossie often dropped in for afternoon tea of a Sunday.

'Oh, it's you,' he said.

Ossie's bushy grey eyebrows climbed up towards his hairline. 'You're in a good mood, I gather.' And then, regretting his tone, 'The lass is all right, isn't she? I heard she'd been allowed home.'

'Trust you to be well up with the gossip,' Daniel said. 'Come in then. I suppose you want some of Mary's baking.'

Ossie trod on his heels into the living room. 'How do, how do,' he called out, hurrying to give a peck on the cheek to Mary and a warm clasp of the hand to Bethany. 'Oh, look at our wounded soldier,' he remarked, studying the dressing on her temple. 'Ten stitches, I heard.'

'Nine,' laughed Bethany.

'Jeff Jones tells me it was a girl that biffed you. I hope you biffed her back.'

'I don't go in for unarmed combat, Ossie.'

'But I hear she was armed. With a cudgel or something.'

'Nothing of the kind,' said Josh sharply.

Ossie turned to look at him. 'Oh,' he said. 'So it were that lass of yours that did it, eh?' He knew Josh only slightly, yet knew he had a teenage daughter who was considered a handful.

'Ossie, hold your tongue,' Daniel commanded.

'Can't a man ask a question?'

'Have some tea, Ossie,' Mary said, picking up the teapot.

'You been worried about Bethie?' he enquired as he came to take the cup from her.

'I got a bit of a scare,' she said, with a sigh. Daniel had not enquired about her feelings.

'No wonder. This thing in Barhampton is causing a lot of trouble to a lot of people.' He picked up a buttered scone from the plate, popped it into his mouth, and immediately picked up another. 'Best scones in Yorkshire,' he observed. Then, with a sudden change of tack, 'I hear the council's in a dilemma over these squatters.'

'You'd know as much about that as I do,' growled Daniel. 'Never met anybody like you for rumours.'

'Jones tells me the council are slacking off over the assault on Beth. I can see why—' with an arch glance at Josh Pembury – 'never do to go into court with a charge against the daughter of one of its own employees. So the Barhampton police want to keep clear of the problems in Royal Terrace, and who can blame 'em? But what're the council going to do about getting that lot out, eh?'

103

'You tell me,' said Daniel.

'As far as I can tell, nowt,' reported Ossie. 'The Mayor doesn't want bad publicity. Jones tells me the press are taking the attitude that the squatters have arrived on the scene to support poor brave Mrs Bedells. Who wants to have his picture taken dragging 'em out and throwing 'em into cop-wagons?'

'Did you come here just to depress me, Ossie?'

'Nay, I came for thi wife's scones, lad. But let me tip you the wink – you don't want to wheel out any legal big guns for the moment. All the Town Councillors are very nervous about losing votes if they seem to be persecuting that conservation bunch. All of a sudden the council has got keen on Arabella Bedells and her house; they don't want to seem a collection of Philistines, even though they are and never heard of the woman until a couple of weeks ago. So think on, lad, think on.'

'We *are* thinking on,' replied Daniel snappishly. 'All you're doing is telling me we have a problem. We know that. What we want is some hint from the council how they're going to resolve it – because bear in mind, Ossie, it's the council that owns those houses the squatters have taken over. If anybody's going to call up the legal big guns, it ought to be the council. However—' he wagged a finger – 'tell your pals on the Barhampton council that if we're involved in long delays over this Royal Terrace thing, there's one or two of the construction firms will sue—'

'Because it will mean they can't move their machines on to other contracted work and they'll be in difficulties . . . Aye, the repercussions could be serious. Don't think the Mayor has forgotten things like that.'

'So what's his solution?' Bethany enquired, thinking of Jim McGuire who'd been so worried about late payment. For small firms such as his, to finish one job on time and move on to another was essential.

'He hasn't got one. Have you?' Ossie said to her with a teasing smile.

'We-ell . . .'

'What?' said both Daniel and Josh Pembury with immediate eagerness.

'It's not exactly a solution. But it's an obvious way to minimise delays. We'll have to re-schedule the order of work.'

'You're joking!' groaned Daniel.

'It would be an enormous job.'

'Can you think of anything else, Josh? I know it would be a big job, but not as big as it once was because we've got computers now. And when you think about it, what's the alternative? To stand around waiting to start on Royal Terrace while the council argues with the squatters and the courts dilly-dally about issuing eviction orders?'

'Are you going to tell Cyril Ollerton he has to re-schedule? He'll go straight and jump off Barhampton Bridge!' cried her father.

'We'll have to do it as a collaboration. I can help because I've got the whole plan of the Town Centre permanently in my head and of course on my computer. You could come in on it too, Josh – you know the terrain better than practically anyone in the town, you could contribute by showing us new traffic paths for the machines – for of course we meant to move the tractors straight across Royal Terrace after demolition but now we'll have to go round it, and we were going to use the private garden as a park for the Cats but we can't do that now . . .'

In her enthusiasm she had snatched up one of the Sunday newspapers and was scribbling notes to herself on its borders. Josh produced an envelope from his pocket and did likewise. 'Mr Ollerton must go to the council first thing tomorrow and persuade them to let us re-schedule. It will mean some hiccups in the work and some re-negotiation of existing contracts—'

'And there goes the budget,' Daniel put it.

'But, Mr Dayton, there's the contingency allotment. That's what it's there for, surely – to cover unexpected costs,' Josh put in.

'You can bet money's already flowing out of the contingency allowance,' Daniel replied. He knew for a fact that this was so, mostly because of specialist legal advice sought by Bigsby. The fees of specialist lawyers were always high.

Ossie Fielden nodded agreement. 'All the same, lad,' he said to his old friend, 'your girl's put forward a way to get things going again. I imagine there's a good sum still available in the contingency fund, and if some has to be advanced from next year's budget, well, that's what the Finance Department is for – balancing budgets.'

'Hmm . . .' muttered Daniel. 'Where are you going when you leave here, Ossie?'

'I'd planned to go to a thing at the Railway Museum. But happen I'll give it a miss. I might drive back to Barhampton and see if I can find Cyril Ollerton – of a Sunday he generally goes to a folk group that sings and twangs guitars at the old Victoria Hotel.'

'Aye,' agreed Daniel, 'go and sing a few folk songs, Ossie.'

Cheerfully Ossie took the hint, made his farewells, and left. Mary saw him to the door. 'You're a good friend, Ossie,' she said, and gave him the traditional peck on the cheek.

'Aye, lass,' he agreed, and hurried out to his car.

Josh was also taking his leave. 'I want to thank you for being so forgiving to Allie,' he said, shaking hands warmly with Bethany as he made his way out of the living room. 'When I get home I'll tell her how nice you were about it, and perhaps she'll get a good night's sleep tonight after all.'

'I hope so. Please tell her she should put it all behind her.'

'Bethany, don't be so soft,' her father intervened. 'The kid hit you and she should make some sort of amends, surely – at least she ought to apologise, shouldn't she?'

Josh gave an exclamation of agreement. 'Of course, Mr Dayton! I ought to have thought of that. Bethany, would you let me bring Allie to see you tomorrow after school to say she's sorry?'

'What time does "after school" mean? You and I might still be locked in the Council Room.'

'That's true . . . Well, I'll tell Allie about it when I get home and tomorrow perhaps you and I could fix a time and place – how about that?'

'That would be fine.'

'You're sure you're going to feel all right about work tomorrow?' Mary put in as they joined her at the front door.

'Mary, she's got a job to do,' her husband said. 'Don't try to mollycoddle her, we need her at the Steering Committee.'

'So long until tomorrow, then,' said Josh, and with a wave went out to his car.

'Don't be too forgiving to that kid,' Daniel growled to his daughter. 'You can tell by the way he talks about her that he's got her on too slack a rein.'

'Daniel, Allie Pembury isn't our Bethany's problem,' said his wife, making a start on clearing away the tea things.

But there she was quite wrong.

Chapter Nine

Bethany was late next morning at Barhampton Town Hall. Although she still had clothes in her room at the family home, she asked her father to drive her to her flat, where she changed at leisure. She had a feeling this was going to be a long and tiring day, so she wanted to be clad in something in which she could feel comfortable.

Daniel for his part hurried to the meeting of the Steering Committee. He wanted to know what Cyril Ollerton had decided about the idea of re-scheduling the work on the Town Centre. He was pleased to discover that Ollerton was now promulgating the idea as if he'd thought of it himself, and had already designated the sub-committee who would undertake it.

According to Ollerton, this would be himself, Alan Singleton, and Bethany. No one had any objection to this plan, since Ollerton was in fact the Construction Manager for the project and Alan was the Project Manager. They were the logical choices.

When Bethany arrived, she accepted the membership of the committee but suggested that Josh Pembury should be included.

'Is there any reason why you want a fourth committee member?' Ollerton enquired with a degree of frost in his voice. Josh was very much out of favour this morning, since the news had spread about Allie and her activities.

'I think if you ask Josh he'll tell you he's already had some thoughts on how to set about the re-scheduling. My opinion is that his knowledge of terrain is so thorough—'

'Singleton's knowledge is very thorough. After all, he's the chartered surveyor.'

'Of course. But Josh has specialised knowledge of existing walkways and footpaths on the site. It's been his job for years to keep them in good order and to clothe the territory with plants and trees.' She paused. 'It's not essential to have him, of course. I just thought we might perhaps be glad of his thoughts.'

All that was true. But she had two further reasons. First, she wanted to minimise the antagonism against Josh caused by his wayward daughter. Second, she was privately of the opinion that Cyril Ollerton wouldn't have as much time for the sub-committee as he thought he would. He was by no means inefficient but heading up a steering committee for a new Town Centre was a job he hadn't had to cope with before and he wasn't having an easy ride.

'Well, happen it's not a bad idea,' said Ollerton. 'I daresay you're not feeling quite on form this morning, after all, Bethany.' The others chimed in with belated enquiries after her health, which she dealt with as briefly as possible. 'Right, then,' resumed Ollerton, 'all those in favour of Josh Pembury as a member of the temporary re-scheduling committee?'

A show of hands settled it. Although everyone understood its necessity and importance, the hope was that the life of the sub-committee would be very short. The main committee needed to concentrate its mind on the vexed problem of Mrs Bedells and her supporters squatting in the houses of Royal Terrace.

Ollerton deputed Bigsby to act as Chairman of Steerco in his absence. The sub-committee excused itself and went out. The first thing to do was find a corner in the Town Hall where they could work. Next they had to have a computer link so that they could have simultaneous access to architects' drawings, engineering plans, construction schedules, financial obligations, and every other element in the building scheme; they all recognised that the work wouldn't end when they left the Town Hall for the day; most of them would want to call up plans and figures from home.

While the computer expert set this up for them they had a break to drink coffee and exchange ideas. As Bethany had foreseen, Ollerton was called away almost at once to deal with an argument down the hall – Bigsby couldn't control the Steering Committee.

'So much for that,' said Alan Singleton with a shrug. 'I don't think we'll get much from him until they've sorted out their intentions about the squat.' He sipped from his styrofoam cup. 'And what are your intentions about your daughter and the protesters, Josh?'

'Intentions? I don't know what you mean, intentions. Allie went on that protest before I really understood what she was up to, and now of course that I've explained how awkward it is for me, she won't do it again.'

'I should hope not. Luckily only us on Steerco are in the know but it would look bad if it got out – a department head of Barhampton council and yet his own daughter—'

'Give it a rest, Alan,' Josh said with weary resignation. 'I've had it already from Ollerton and from Bethany's dad, and from Ossie Fielden, and no doubt I'll get it from the Mayor and anybody else who thinks they've got a right to tell me off.'

'Well, you can't deny it isn't helpful. Iris has enough to contend with, let alone teenage girls who ought to know better. What was she thinking about, getting mixed up with that lot? She must have known they were making things difficult for the council!'

'Alan,' said Bethany, 'can we stop examining Josh's family life and get back to business? One of the things we have to think about is the existence of the electricity cables and gas mains. You have that on schematic?'

'Yes, but not on computer—'

'Could you fetch the plans so we can transfer them on to disk? And while you're at it, can we have the geological survey? We had suitable routes worked out but now we're changing them. Those caterpillar tractors are heavy machines – we don't want them going into any underground streams or channels.'

'Right you are,' said Alan, setting down his coffee and hurrying off to the council offices for the plans.

Josh gave her a glance of gratitude from his sleepy brown eyes. 'That was good of you. Alan can say what he likes about not many people being in the know, but everybody I've come across at the Town Hall this morning has given me a fishy glance.'

'They'll soon have other things to think about,' she comforted. 'Allie will fade out of their minds by tomorrow.'

'And speaking of Allie, we were saying that it would be good if she could meet you and apologise.'

'But not today, Josh. And not for a couple of days, I think. We're going to be up to our necks in work.'

'You're right. What would you say if I suggested . . . let's say . . . Friday evening? That would be good for Allie too – end of the school week, you know, when she's always more relaxed and happy.'

Bethany reflected that Allie was supposed to feel remorseful and apologetic, but kept the thought to herself. 'Friday should be fine,' she agreed. 'If we haven't broken the back of this job and got the machines working elsewhere on site by then, we might as well give up.'

Their task wasn't to re-schedule all the work on the entire Town Centre site. There was excavating and foundation-laying in progress elsewhere in the area. But all the work at Royal Terrace and anything adjacent to it had to be timetabled anew. The three main members of the committee – that's to say, Bethany, Alan and Josh – slaved away at lists and plans, 'undoing' and 'redoing' on computer until at last they ended up with a schedule that looked as if it would work.

For the first three days Bethany found her powers of concentration weren't as good as she would have liked. The bang on the head seemed to have made her slower in putting facts together. Moreover, she had a great need for sleep; instead of staying up past midnight working on new ideas, she found she needed to totter off to bed.

By and by, however, things got back to normal; her thought processes speeded up.

As the new timetable emerged, contractors had to be persuaded that they could fit themselves into it. The Legal Department was called up to soothe away contractual problems, the Finance Department grudgingly agreed to part with some money by way of inducements, claims for unfair discrimination as regards priority were dealt with, and in the end an All Clear was given for the Royal Terrace contractors to start elsewhere on the Monday.

'TGIF,' groaned Alan as they switched off the printer after it delivered the last sheet of work schedule at four o'clock.

'And so say all of us. I hope we've foreseen all the problems . . .'

'It's amazing to me how much you carry in your mind, Bethany,' said Josh in admiration. 'If anything's been left out, I'll be very surprised.'

Privately she felt that there had been times when her mind had gone blank. But today she felt confident again. 'Well, of course, it's my baby,' she said. 'Any time we talk about starting on footings here or back-hoeing there, I see it in my mind's eye, as I did when I was drawing the design.' And thank goodness for that, she said inwardly.

As they gathered up their belongings to leave the drab little office, Josh said, 'Are we still on for this evening?'

'Of course.' She would really rather have gone home, taken a long bath, and then curled up on the sofa to watch something undemanding on television. But she had promised to meet Allie, and felt it to be her duty.

She wanted to make it clear that she bore no grudge against the girl, yet had to tell her that it was wrong to let emotion take over. Bethany hadn't been badly hurt – but that was good luck, both for herself and for her assailant. Because Allie *had* grabbed her, *had* caused her to tumble down the steps, *had* hit her with a wildly flourished board on a pole. Had the injury been a fractured skull instead of a slight concussion, Allie would have been in very serious trouble.

She took some trouble with her appearance – not to impress either Josh or his daughter, but because the padded dressing on her temple had been replaced with a small piece of tape, so that she felt for the first time in days that she could do her hair and put on make-up with enthusiasm. She wore a soft poplin blouse the colour of forget-me-nots, a linen skirt in dove grey with new sandals of matching suede. She brushed her short fair hair into a gloss, applied pale lipstick, surveyed the effect and decided it would do.

Josh had already suggested that, to ease the embarrassment of the encounter, they should meet in one of the chain restaurants of Barhampton. It was a steak-house on the road that meandered along the northern perimeter of the town; when she got there at the appointed hour of eight, it was busy – diners at the tables set out under umbrellas among the flowers of the June garden, the car park already quite full.

Josh was waiting for her at the tiny bar. With him was the dark-haired girl of last Saturday – but what a change! No more long wild tangled

110

brown locks, but a neat French plait. No dangly earrings – instead maidenly pearl studs. No tattered jeans and loose top – no, tonight she was wearing a dark blue pleated skirt and a lightweight knitted top that might almost have been a school sports shirt.

Her father, in cords and a cream linen shirt, was equally sedate. He rose at Bethany's entrance. 'I booked a table for inside but if you'd rather be in the garden they tell me there's still a table free out there.'

'Let's do that, then.' She felt that if conversation proved difficult, they could talk about the flowers and trees, which were after all part of Josh's occupation.

'This is Allie,' he said. 'Allie, say hello to Miss Dayton.'

'We've met,' Bethany said with a teasing smile and offering her hand, to do away with any tension.

'So we have,' agreed Allie. 'But not under the right circumstances, eh? I'm terribly sorry for what I did, Miss Dayton.'

'I gather you've paid for it in anxiety and apprehension,' said Bethany.

'Oh, rather! That weekend—' the girl threw up her hands and rolled her expressive brown eyes – 'I never want to go through anything like that again.'

'Let's hope you don't. All you have to do is keep away from banner-carrying.'

A faint colour came up on Allie's pale cheeks. 'I'm sorry that I hit you,' she said, 'but I have to stand by what I believe. I think what happened to Mrs Bedells is wrong.'

'Oh, so do I.'

'You do?' The tone was pure astonishment.

'Of course. It's a problem that has to be solved. But not by staging incidents that get media attention and scare the poor old lady to death.'

'But it's for her sake—'

Josh had been to tell the waiter they would take the outdoors table. They were now ushered out into the garden, seated, handed menus, and fussed over so that the difficult conversation of a few minutes before could be dropped.

Josh and Bethany ordered turkey steaks. It turned out that Allie was a vegetarian but the restaurant was well-known for its enormous salads. Wine was ordered, with Diet Coke for Allie. Bethany started a new line of talk.

'I hear you're interested in dramatics,' she commented.

'In drama, yes,' said Allie.

Oh, thanks for the correction, thought Bethany, but smiled politely. 'You've been in school plays?'

'Yes, the usual things, *Much Ado* and *The Importance*.'

'*The Importance* . . . ? Oh, *of Being Earnest*! Did you play Lady Bracknell?' she enquired with a laugh.

111

'Oh, they wouldn't bury her under all that make-up for an old woman,' Josh said. 'With Allie's looks, she always plays the young lead.'

'It was a joke, Daddy,' said Allie, giving him a playful slap. She turned back to Bethany. 'But much more important, I'm a member of the Barhampton Thespians. There we do really interesting plays instead of what's on the school curriculum.'

'Such as what?'

'Oh, Bertolt Brecht and Alan Ayckbourn . . .'

'And do you play the young leads in those?' teased Bethany.

'Goodness, no – there are some marvellously experienced people in the Thespians – I only get walk-on parts or I do the props – but it's marvellous to be part of it in even the smallest way, and of course by and by, when I've had more experience, they'll let me do bigger things. *Next year,*' she sighed dreamily, 'they're going to do *The Constant Nymph* but I don't suppose I'll get the lead . . .'

'I don't know the play,' Bethany confessed.

'You're not interested in the theatre?'

'I'm afraid I get most of my plays via television.'

'Oh, television!' cried Allie, her eyes lighting up. 'That's the way in, if only you can get on telly! There are ever so many actors and actresses who made it after being in just a commercial! And of course if you can get into a *soap!*'

'Wouldn't that be a bit of a come-down after Shakespeare and Brecht?' Bethany quipped.

'Oh, of course, you'd do it just to earn a living, but you'd do the serious things for love, in little experimental theatres, and that's of course where you meet the young directors who can take you with them when they go up in the world . . .'

'Too bad you were at Mrs Bedells's door last Saturday,' Bethany rejoined, still joking. 'All the TV cameras were at the other end of the Terrace.'

'Now we don't want to talk about that,' said Allie's father with an anxious glance at his daughter. 'It still upsets you to think of it, doesn't it, luv?'

But Allie's thought had gone off on another tack. 'It's true the TV people were very interested in that protest last Saturday . . .'

'Of course. I often think TV news is what they have pictures for. If something seems to be *happening*, cameras will cover it, but if it's only thoughts or opinions they're not interested.'

'That's true,' said Josh. 'And if they have to give thoughts and opinions they always produce graphs—'

'Or "library pictures"—'

'Anything to fill up the screen so that we won't look away and miss the next advertisement.'

'You say that as if it's wrong,' Allie put in, 'but don't you see, that just proves the power of TV. I mean, politicians take lessons these days in how to make a good impression before the cameras. Ye-es, if you think about it, TV can make all the difference . . . Some actors sneer at it, but you have to admit it's the way to get parts in the theatre. You know yourself, Daddy, when we go to see a play in York, the advertisements almost always say "Joyce Thingummy from *Tiddlywink Street*" or "Tom Whatsit from *Tramway Lines*".'

This long analysis of the state of touring companies was brought to an end by the waiter bringing the dessert menu. Bethany was glad to see that Allie, despite her seriousness over acting, had a normal teenage interest in ice cream and Black Forest gateau.

Bethany found herself sympathetic towards the girl, despite the fact that she seemed to have very little sense of humour and was clearly accustomed to being first in her father's life. Here was a girl who, like herself, was something of an odd one out. Bethany had been thought 'weird' by her school-fellows because she alone knew what she wanted to do with her life. She too had wanted to take up a career her father thought unsuitable.

Yet in one respect she'd been so much luckier – she had always had her mother. Without Mary Dayton, life would have been very different for Bethany. Allie, poor child, was motherless. Perhaps there were things Bethany could do for Allie – listen to her if she had feminine problems, hear about her youthful romances . . .

In this kindly mood she gave heed to all her conversation throughout the rest of the meal and, when it was time to part, murmured that they 'must do it again some time'.

'We certainly will,' Josh agreed with enthusiasm. 'I don't know when I've enjoyed an evening more! I often think it must be dull for you, luv,' he said to his daughter, 'having only me at home to talk to.'

'Oh, you're great, Dad,' Allie said fondly. 'Even if you do go on about trees and bushes most of the time.'

'There, you see?' he said to Bethany. 'I probably bore her to death!'

The evening, although not particularly enjoyable, had gone off quite well, Bethany told herself with satisfaction as she dropped off to sleep that night.

The following week was the beginning of the re-scheduled timetable. Bethany was here and there around the building sites, sometimes coming across mix-ups that needed sorting out but more often finding that the machines and men were efficiently at work. Her two colleagues of the re-scheduling committee reported the same: a few hiccups but on the whole all was well.

When she ran across Josh, she would always ask after Allie. She was somewhat surprised to hear that Allie was still connecting herself with the squatters at Royal Terrace.

'But I thought you warned her off?'

'Oh, but Bethany, what she's doing is really good. She and her friends are re-planting the shrubs and bushes those bad boys pulled up in the Terrace garden! Isn't that a grand idea? And they've replaced the glass in the windows the boys broke – in fact, I think you could say Allie is taking part in real conservation work.'

'But Josh,' Bethany protested, 'I thought you had told her it would be best if she took no part? Because, after all, your bosses don't *want* anyone preserving Royal Terrace—'

'But just while the litigation is going on, don't you think it's better if the place is kept looking nice?'

'It's better for the TV cameras,' Bethany acknowledged. 'Is that what it's for? Get the place all spruced up and then invite the media to see it?'

'Oh, I don't think it's anything like that. It's for Mrs Bedells, to make her feel comfortable and looked after. I mean, think of it – she didn't want the light blocked by the boards at those broken panes, surely. It's much better for her to have them properly mended.'

Privately Bethany thought Mrs Bedells would rather be left alone. And as to the provision of photo opportunities, she was proved right – the local paper and TV channel featured the 'revival of Royal Terrace'.

'Confound 'em!' shouted Daniel Dayton when he saw it on his TV news. 'They've no right to do that!'

'Now, Daniel, it's not against the law to plant a few bushes and put in a pane of glass,' said his wife.

'That's just the trouble! We can't do a thing without looking like Scrooge! And there's that lass of Pembury's again – standing by that rose bush, smiling into the camera – hasn't that man got any sense?'

Bethany, seeing it at home on her own set, was remembering: 'Some actors sneer at it but it's the way to get parts . . .' Allie, it seemed, had taken heed of her own words and put the idea into action. But no, that was ungenerous. Allie was doing it for the sake of Mrs Bedells.

All the same, Bethany thought, she ought to consider the trouble her actions might cause her father.

There was a fuss at the next meeting of the Steering Committee. Josh said he was sorry but he didn't think there was much wrong in making the Terrace look decent even if it was only for a few weeks while the lawyers sorted things out. Iris Weston made soothing noises and pointed out that if the council took any stern action against Allie or her father, it would look bad in the press. As to reversing the work the protesters had done – well, of course, that was out of the question.

'In fact,' she said, 'it would be a good idea to do something ourselves – put a few pots of flowers in among the bushes. What can you get in pots – something showy?'

'Lilies,' said Josh. 'And hydrangeas.'

'Have the council got any in the plant nursery?'

'Oh, sure.'

'Then I think that's what we should do.'

'Good Lord,' groaned Ollerton, 'it's like *Alice in Wonderland*! His daughter's chums make us look bad by tarting up Royal Terrace for that old nuisance, and now we're going to help them by supplying pot plants.'

'Well, why should the opposition get all the good publicity?' Iris asked, and went off to alert her media friends that Barhampton council were about to do something kind and friendly for Mrs Bedells.

Mrs Bedells, interviewed through her door by a very persistent reporter, announced that she didn't want anyone's plants and bushes, and she'd already ordered a glazier to come and mend her windows when those busybodies from along the road came and did it without ever being asked to. If something needed doing to her property she could see to it herself, thank you – she'd been doing so for years. What she wanted was everyone to go away and let her live her life in peace and quiet.

'Is that what you call good publicity?' Ollerton asked Iris.

'It's as good for us as it is for the activists,' Alan Singleton pointed out. 'She doesn't want their help any more than she wants our potted plants.'

'She's a bad-tempered old troll,' groaned Billy Wellbrow.

And it was difficult to disagree with him – although it had to be admitted they'd never have had to worry about Mrs Bedells's bad temper if the Planning Department had bought her house in the proper manner in the first place.

On the following Saturday Josh invited Bethany to his home for afternoon tea. 'I'd like you to see where I live – it's an old cottage right out on the edge of the moors. We can sit under a cherry tree that's at least a hundred years old, and have scones – but they'll be bought scones because Allie isn't much of a cook.'

It wasn't really all that convenient, as Bethany had accepted an invitation from Peter Lambot to go to a show that evening in York. However, she thought perhaps Josh wanted to enlist her help over Allie, so she accepted.

The cottage proved to be one of a row of very ordinary labourers' cottages, facing straight on to a traffic road going north to the moors. The taxi-driver deposited her at the appointed hour, three o'clock; she had a moment or two to assess the place with her architect's eye. Its only advantage was its position at the outermost end of the row, so it had a garage – in regrettably new brick. In front, each house had a really tiny garden which most of the householders had filled up with a hedge and a few rose bushes.

She went to the door and knocked. She heard Allie's voice: 'Oh, she's here already!' There was a muffled flurry, then Josh opened the door.

'Sorry, we didn't hear you drive up—'

'That's all right.'

'We were just in the midst of trying to take the tea-set off the dresser shelves,' he laughed, ushering her in. 'Normally we never use it.'

'But you shouldn't have bothered—'

'Oh, we felt we must put on a bit of a show! We almost never have visitors except Allie's school chums. Come in, come in. Let me take your jacket – or would you rather keep it on? We'll be outside.'

She let him relieve her of it and the cardboard box she carried. It was a cream sponge bought from one of the family bakers near her flat. 'My contribution to the tea,' she said.

'Well, look, Allie,' he said, offering it to his daughter. 'Miss Dayton's brought a cake—'

'That's awfully kind of you,' said Allie, accepting it less gently than he had taken it from Bethany. She flounced off with it towards the back of the house while Bethany was led into the sitting room. Her jacket was laid across a chair-back.

The sitting room was comfortable, with some good pieces of furniture, clearly brought from a larger house – probably from the home of Josh and his late wife. The room at the other side of the narrow passage was the dining room, glimpsed as containing a table, two chairs, a dresser with a display of rather nice china. There was room for little else.

Basically the house was a Victorian two-up-and-two-down. An extension had been built on to the back by the same unfriendly hand that had erected the garage, so as to give a small kitchen and, presumably, an equally small bathroom above it.

Josh explained: 'We moved here when Allie was about eleven. We'd stayed on in our big house at first because of having to have someone to live in and look after my wife, you know, but when we got rid of the housekeeper we decided to make a clean break. I got the offer of a job in Barhampton so we bought this cottage . . .' He gave a stifled sigh. 'It seemed big enough at the time, but now . . .'

'Do you have some ground at the back? I see you're right up against a grove of trees.'

'Yes, that's partly the reason why I bought the place. I do a bit of experimental growing in the wood – try out imported trees. Come and look.' He led the way through the kitchen where his daughter was pouring boiling water into a handsome china teapot. Her clothing today was less demure than for the date at the steak-house. She was clad in jeans almost white with wash and wear, and a skimpy tank top of jade green. The beautiful hair was tied back with artless care in a ribbon that matched the tank top.

Outside the kitchen door was a glassed-in veranda full of plants in pots. Beyond lay a tiny garden dominated by the promised cherry tree, now in green leaf and shading a garden table and three uncomfortable wrought-iron chairs. A path led past them, to the grove. It proved to be small, hardly larger than the area in many gardens where the household grows a few vegetables or a row or two of soft fruit. But in this area the trees were mostly young, and carefully labelled.

Bethany had a passing acquaintance with some of the names, for as an architect she always felt it her duty to clothe the outlines of her buildings with suitable plantings. They chatted for a few minutes about a new variety of Norwegian whitebeam he was growing, then returned to the cherry tree to find Allie setting the teapot on the table. 'Here we are, we're all ready,' she announced. 'Would you like to sit there, Miss Dayton.'

'Oh, please, call me Bethany.'

'Of course. Yes – well, sit there, I hope you'll find it comfortable, and can I just pour you a cup? Milk before or after?'

'Doesn't matter,' said Bethany. 'When you've drunk as many mugs of tea as I have with building workers, you take it in any shade, strength, and degree of sweetness.'

Allie applied herself to the task of hostess. She did it fluently, and Bethany found herself wondering if it was a variation of her role as Gwendolen in the school production of *The Importance of Being Earnest*. But that was unkind, so she chatted instead about the house. 'Do you enjoy being on the edge of the moor? You must have lovely walks nearby.'

'Oh yes, it's great for picnicking – the river's not far off. Daddy and I used to go there in summer to feed the Canada geese. And of course when I'm learning a part, I can go up on the moor and talk to myself for as long as I like and nobody hears me.'

'Are you learning something at the moment?' Bethany sipped the tea, which was a good deal weaker than she was used to.

'As a matter of fact, we're going to do an outdoors production of some of the work of Arabella Bedells.'

'Arabella Bedells? But I thought none of her plays had survived?'

'None of them are complete – but Mr Tallant found some bits and pieces, and one of the Thespians has a friend in London who's a theatrical historian so he's doing some research, so we'll probably have enough to do an hour's reading – just a few excerpts that were printed at the time for people who wanted to do amateur theatricals – though not much of it the racy stuff because of course it had to be suitable for young ladies to read aloud at home in those days and we couldn't have them talking about naughty things, now could we?'

This was rather an alarming spate of information. It struck Bethany that Allie was in a state of suppressed excitement. She glanced at Josh, but he was smiling and nodding in acceptance of his daughter's words.

'That sounds very enterprising,' she remarked. 'Did you say it was to be an open-air performance?'

'Yes, if we can get it together while there's good weather.'

'So where will you be performing?'

'Well . . . in Royal Terrace,' said Allie, with a glance of determination towards her father.

'Allie!' he exclaimed. 'You never told me that.'

'Well, you never asked.'

'I thought you'd be doing it in the school grounds.'

'It's not a school production, Dad – I told you – it's the Thespians.'

'From the way you spoke . . . I thought it was a school history project.'

'Dad, with GCSEs just coming up, school isn't starting on unnecessary history projects, now is it?'

'I wonder if you'll be allowed to put on a show in Royal Terrace?' Bethany said in a neutral tone.

'Who's going to stop us?'

'It is council property, luv,' Josh reminded her.

'So it is. Can you imagine them sending for the police to throw us out?'

'Allie, have the Barhampton Thespians thought about the problems that might arise?'

'Problems? Why should there be any problems? All we're going to do is put together a few scenes written by Barhampton's famous woman playwright and read them in public.'

'But in a venue that isn't available to them – it's council property, most of it. The council won't give permission.'

'Perhaps we won't ask for permission.'

'Allie, whose idea is this?'

'If you want to know, it's mine.'

Bethany shook her head. 'I think when the director or producer or whoever it is at the Thespians finds out what they're getting into, they'll drop the idea.'

'No, they won't! It's a great idea – they'd make a lot more money with that than with another dreary production of *An Inspector Calls*.'

'I really don't think they ought to, dearie,' admonished Josh, shaking his shaggy head. 'It sounds a bit dodgy—'

'Josh, it's more than dodgy. I bet the Thespians have no idea that they might run into big trouble. The council would do all it could to prevent it—'

'Call the police, you mean,' sneered Allie. 'That seems to be their first thought—'

'They wouldn't have to do that. Royal Terrace isn't licensed for public performances – I bet there's a by-law that forbids it. And how could you advertise and sell tickets? The minute posters started to appear, the council's solicitor would tell the Barhampton Thespians to stop – and of course I don't know any of them, but I doubt if they're willing to go against the council and be part of the Royal Terrace protest.'

'Oh, right! So you mean you're going to tell some rotten council lawyer and spoil everything!'

The girl jumped up from her seat at the tea-table, threw down her napkin, and stalked off into the house. Josh had to set down his cup and his plate of scones before he could follow her. Bethany was left staring at the tea-things and thinking that she wouldn't care to be Allie Pembury's mother for all the tea in China.

The minutes stretched on. She debated whether to get up and join the pair. She could hear argument in the kitchen, and then at last loud footsteps running up a wooden stair and the slamming of doors. Josh returned.

'I'm sorry about that,' he said, slowly sitting down in his chair and picking up his cup. 'Artistic temperament, you know. She gets a bit carried away.'

Bethany was surprised. She hadn't expected to hear the outburst waved away with such a simple excuse.

'Josh, it seemed to me that she hadn't told you what she was intending.'

'Oh no, that was probably my fault. I don't always catch on to what she's saying – she's always so full of enthusiasm, you see. I find it hard to keep up with her because I'm a bit of a slow-coach.'

'But you do see now that she mustn't get this acting group involved in a public performance in Royal Terrace?'

'Oh, certainly not. I can't imagine what made them think of it in the first place.'

'But didn't Allie say,' Bethany said gently, 'that it was her idea?'

'No, no – well, at least – well, she *is* very keen to help old Mrs Bedells, and she may have thought this was a good way to get publicity for her—'

'Josh, old Mrs Bedells doesn't want publicity. You ought to tell Allie she's not helping the poor old soul if she draws crowds around her house.'

'You see it that way because you're thinking like a member of the Steering Committee. And of course I agree it would be nice if everything had gone completely smoothly over the Town Centre scheme. But as Allie says, Mrs Bedells has rights and if her friends want to uphold them for her—'

'Her friends? Josh, these are people she doesn't even know.'

'But they *want* to be friends to her. You think she's cranky, but they'll win her round, you'll see.'

'To what? To giving support to the squat? That's just what we don't want, Josh. That would only make matters worse.'

'Not at all. When the old lady has to move – and I quite see she'll have to, one day – she'll have a big group of friends who'll visit her in her new home and—'

'But you don't seem to understand! She doesn't want that!'

'I don't see how you can be so sure of that, Bethany. You've spoken to her less than half a dozen times, now haven't you? Can't you agree it's just possible that she's a lonely old lady who needs friends?'

Unwillingly she murmured that perhaps she didn't know Mrs Bedells so very well that she could predict her reaction to future offers of friendship. They drank their tea, Josh loaded the tea-things on a tray, and they left the shade of the cherry tree for indoors. He set the tray on a kitchen work-top, muttering that he'd just see if Allie felt like rejoining them. Bethany, left to her own devices, decided to be useful and so set about doing the washing-up.

The cottage was so small that it was impossible not to overhear at least Josh's side of the conversation.

'But, sweetie, we've got a guest . . . But, luv, you can't just sit up here . . . Well, it's hardly good manners . . . Well, I know, she didn't approve of what you – no, I'm not saying she has a right to . . . But Allie, the whole point was that I wanted you to get to know her . . . Now don't be difficult, dear . . . Oh . . . Oh . . . All right.'

He came slowly downstairs to the kitchen. 'She's feeling depressed,' he said. 'I don't think she's up to being good company.'

'That's all right.' She remembered her own adolescence – days when she felt totally at odds with all the rest of the world. 'Where should I put this cake?'

'Oh, you've washed up. Now that's all wrong, you're a guest.'

'It's okay, Josh.'

There was a flurry of footsteps on the staircase, the front door opened and closed.

'She's gone out!' exclaimed her father. 'Oh now, that *is* too bad! I'll get her—'

He was plunging off in pursuit. Bethany caught his shirt sleeve. 'Leave her be,' she advised. 'Perhaps she'll go for a walk on the moor and recite something from a play. Anyway, she'll probably feel better by and by.'

'Well . . . I suppose . . . I don't even know where she's headed so I suppose it's silly to – and in any case I can't leave you here doing the washing-up—'

'It's all right, Josh, really. She's just in a mood, I expect.'

He sighed. 'It's not easy. I don't pretend to understand her.'

Bethany put the cream sponge back in its cardboard box, found a plastic container for the bought scones, and decided she'd done enough of the housework. Josh put the crockery back on the shelves of the dresser in the dining room.

'Shall we go outside again? It's nice under the tree . . . and I must admit I always feel happier out of doors.'

She nodded agreement, but as she settled herself once more on the wrought-iron chair she was wishing inwardly for a comfortable arm-chair.

'You see the garage?' Josh enquired.

'What? Oh . . . yes.' She looked towards the house.

'Allie's room is the one above the dining room, with that little window looking out over the garage. What I was wondering, Bethany . . . You see, Allie goes to these acting classes run by an ex-dancer who has a school for movement and drama – out by North Barrgate.'

'Oh yes?' she said, wondering what on earth this was about.

'She does exercises every day – or at least she tries to – and in summer it's not so bad because she can do a bit of leaping about in the garden. But in the winter . . .'

'Yes?'

'Well, of course, she does the exercises indoors. And keeps banging into the furniture. It's terribly frustrating for her.'

'Isn't there a gym at school?'

'Of course, and she sometimes gets the use of it, but then, you know how it is these days, schools are hard put to it to find room for all the activities they have to do and so the gym is occupied a lot of the time and what I was wondering was . . . I thought perhaps we could extend Allie's bedroom by knocking down the wall and extending it over the garage. What do you think?'

So that's why I'm here, thought Bethany. To be asked about con-structing an exercise studio for Allie . . .

For a moment she was irritated. Invited to afternoon tea, subjected to a tirade about Royal Terrace, walked-out-on and now a request for unpaid architectural advice.

But then her sense of humour took over. Really, Josh was so hapless! She shaded her eyes to take a good look at the cottage wall and the garage. 'It'll cost you a pretty penny. You'd want to have that wall thoroughly examined – I mean the bit at ground level. You don't know whether it would bear the load.'

'I could get Alan to take a look.'

'I suppose you could. How old is the garage?'

'Dunno. It was here when we came. If I remember, the estate agent said it had been built two years previously.'

'So it's, say, seven years old. The bricks look good quality. All the same, I think you want a proper survey to make sure it could take the weight of another storey.'

'But assuming it's strong enough, you see nothing against extending the bedroom?'

'Have to see if there's any kind of Preservation Order on the cottages first, Josh.'

'Oh Lord!' he cried. 'Don't mention those words! I've had enough of Preservation Orders to last me the rest of my life!'

A glance at her watch told Bethany that Peter Lambot would be arriving soon to take her to York for dinner and the theatre. She got to her feet. 'Well, it's been lovely to see your little house, Josh, and thanks for the tea—'

'You're not going?'

'Well, yes, I am—'

'But I thought we'd have dinner later – there's an awfully nice old pub on the moor—'

'I'm sorry, Josh, I really can't. I've already got an engagement for this evening.'

'Oh. I hadn't thought of that. I just took it . . . Of course, silly of me – Saturday night, of course you'd have a date . . . I just thought that you and I and Allie would spend the afternoon and evening together . . . get to know each other . . .'

'I'm sorry, Josh, we've got tickets for the theatre.'

'Oh yes, of course . . . that nice dress and jacket . . .'

'Yes, I'm all dressed up,' she agreed, very embarrassed at how things had turned out. Hapless? He was clueless, she said to herself. Surely he knew better than to expect a colleague to give up almost the whole of a precious Saturday to helping with his naughty little daughter?

Glad to get away, she went indoors to wash her hands and tidy her hair. When she came downstairs tucking her make-up away in her handbag, Josh was holding the loose jacket of knitted silk that went with the dress. 'Where are you parked?' he enquired.

'I came in a taxi. I'm being picked up at five – any moment now.'

He opened the house-door for her. A car was already parked alongside the narrow pavement outside. Peter got out to open the passenger door for her.

'Oh, it's Lambot,' Josh said in surprise.

'So it is,' she agreed, smiling.

'Oh . . . well . . . have a nice time.'

'Thank you, Josh. And thanks for a nice afternoon.' She walked away quickly, to end the moment which Josh seemed to find baffling. Peter gave Josh a friendly wave as he closed the car door and went round to the driver's seat. In the rear mirror she could see Josh standing on the threshold, gazing after them, dejected and disappointed.

'Did you have a nice tea-party?' Peter enquired as they set off.

'To tell the truth, no,' she replied, laughing a little yet uncomfortable. 'Josh's daughter, Allie, she's a great supporter of yours.'

'Haven't met her but I saw her on the television—'

'Well, she went up in the air over being told not to do a production of a play or something—'

'Oh yes, I heard she's into amateur theatricals—'

'I don't think she'd like you to call it that. She's very serious about it, wants to make a career . . . Anyhow, this play was to be done in Royal Terrace.'

'What?'

'You hadn't heard about it?'

'No, and I can foresee difficulties.'

'Exactly. Josh was trying to tell her that he could be in trouble again – you weren't there, but he got quite a telling-off from Ollerton over Allie's prowess with a placard.'

'Poor Josh! So his daughter wasn't a very good hostess?'

'She just walked out.'

'Walked out?'

'Got up and left. She went up to her room first, and he tried to coax her down, but she wouldn't come and next thing was, she'd gone out.'

'My word. Quite a temperament,' said Peter, with a little shake of the head.

'Ye-es . . . Perhaps I'm being cynical, but I can't help wondering if she acts it up a bit – to . . . to sort of *manage* her father.'

He made no response to this, and after a moment she said, 'Was that unfair?'

'I've no way of knowing, Bethany. And in any case you're the last person I'd suspect of unfairness. I was wondering, though . . .'

'What?'

'Well, no . . . it's a bit far-fetched . . .'

'Come on, tell me – you've got me really hooked!'

'I was wondering if she saw you as a prospective stepmother?'

'Peter!'

'Well, it is possible, isn't it? You work alongside Josh, and you're friends with him, and I'm right in thinking today wasn't the first time he'd brought you together with Allie . . . ?'

'Yes, but the first time was just so she could apologise.'

'Yes, and that being accomplished, perhaps she's asking herself why he invited you again. And has put two and two together . . .'

'Well, her arithmetic is poor,' said Bethany. 'Nothing would induce me to get mixed up in a situation like that.'

'I'm happy to hear it,' Peter said, giving her a glance of satisfaction.

The conversation turned to their plans for the evening, which were to have a leisurely meal and then attend a one-man show at the Theatre Royal. At the end of the evening he drove her home to her flat in Barhampton. By the gate to the old house they stood together, the street quiet around them and the scent of mock orange filling the air.

Bethany was asking herself whether she would invite him up for a night-cap. If she did, how would he understand the invitation? And how did she want him to understand it?

As she hesitated, he solved the problem for her. 'Well, good night,' he said. 'Thanks for a lovely evening.' He kissed her on the mouth, a gentle kiss that lasted a long time and became less gentle the longer it lasted.

It was she who moved away first. Better not to rush things. But the time was coming . . .

She went up to her flat with all memory of the vexatious afternoon with Josh banished from her mind. She took off the jacket and dress of knitted silk and hung them up. She began preparations for bed but was too restless to think of sleep as yet. Putting on a dressing-gown, she poured herself some mineral water, curled up on the sofa, and switched on the television for a little amusement.

The midnight bulletin came on. The national news was full of political problems and scandal as usual. Then came the local items.

And there, almost at once, was Allie Pembury.

She was dressed in a long white gown of some historical period, vaguely Victorian perhaps. With her was a man of about middle age, wearing breeches and knee-boots and a loose-sleeved shirt of the kind the film star Errol Flynn wore for his sword fights.

They were standing on some sort of dais in the little private garden of Royal Terrace, an attentive group around them. As the camera opened on them, the man was saying: ' . . . You cannot long resist my power!'

'Nay, sir,' declaimed Allie, 'not all your riches can command my heart, for it is warded by the truest love. One that is dear to me defends it still, though absent by the cruel force of Fate . . .'

'This scene is one of several,' said the TV link-man as her voice faded out, 'which Barhampton actors hope to put on later in the summer. The words are by Arabella Bedells, the woman playwright whose house is just behind me in Royal Terrace. The house is a matter of dispute between the Town Council and a group of protesters here. Mr Tallant, you are the President of the Local History Society, am I right?'

'Yes, and as you can tell from the scene just played here, I have been able to find some very attractive pieces of Arabella's work. We're here tonight to give the townsfolk a taste of the production we intend to put on, and to ask them to support us in preserving the home of Barhampton's eighteenth-century heroine.'

Bethany's phone was ringing even before the news ended. 'That blasted girl!' cried Daniel Dayton. 'Did you see it?'

'Yes, I did.' She was saying inwardly, You wicked imp, you *knew* it would cause trouble.

'I'm going to get Ollerton to have that chap fired! I'm not having that girl of his making fools of us every five minutes!'

'Dad, you can't fire a man for what his daughter does . . . be reasonable. And think how bad it would look in the papers—'

'Oh, the papers, the papers – Iris Weston's supposed to deal with all that but somehow we never come out on top, do we? It's time to *do* something—'

124

'I don't see what we *can* do, Dad. We could prevent them from putting on a proper show, but I don't see how she's done anything wrong in standing in a garden and reciting a few bits of dialogue.'

'I'll see to her,' her father snarled. 'She thinks she's such a clever little minx, but I'll settle her hash for her. Just you wait.'

'Now, Dad, simmer down. There's nothing you can do except put a good face on it.'

He grunted what might have been 'Good night' and hung up. Bethany was a little worried, because when Daniel Dayton decided to take the gloves off, things could get quite alarming. But although others rang her next day to mourn yet another publicity coup on the part of the protesters she heard no more from Daniel about plans to deal with Allie Pembury.

And indeed, Allie was busy elsewhere. It was the week of GCSE exams, and she was sitting in a classroom wrestling with questions she couldn't answer because she'd done almost no revision.

Daniel, however, had consulted with Iris Weston and concocted a plan. Or, more exactly, they laid a trap.

And Allison Pembury fell right into it.

Chapter Ten

Like all those who sat their GCSEs, Allie was delighted to be set free. In her case, even more than the rest, because she knew she'd done badly and in any case thought them a waste of time.

The *Barhampton Gazette* ran several features in the week that followed the exams. They were headed *Changing Outlooks*, were accompanied by good photography, and showed Barhampton in the throes of the rebuilding of the Town Centre.

Naturally Royal Terrace received several mentions: *The Terrace that houses the historic residence of Arabella Bedells is surrounded now by building equipment ... Barhampton Town Council is negotiating with the National Heritage Department to prevent a Preservation Order on this pretty little row of houses. The protesters who took over the empty homes can still see the little private garden in front, but from the back, monster wrecking machines frown down. These great caterpillar tractors cost a fortune and are a big investment on the part of the building contractors. Necessary equipment for demolition ...*

The photographs that accompanied this last article showed a track excavator parked on the lot that ran along the back of Royal Terrace. Its long neck was angled – by chance, perhaps – so that it peered like a threatening dinosaur into the back windows of the Terrace houses. The article and its photograph appeared in the Thursday morning edition of the *Gazette*.

That night, after dark, television crews arrived outside the parking area of the building machines. Passers-by going home from cinemas and snooker clubs paused to ask, 'What's up?'

'Dunno. We got a tip something was going off tonight.'

If the TV crews were willing to wait, so were the home-going public – for nothing is so fascinating as a film crew in action. Around eleven o'clock, a group came with a ladder, clambered over the wooden hoarding that protected the parking lot of the machinery and, chanting 'Out, out, out!' formed a semicircle round the track excavator that overlooked Royal Terrace.

The TV crew became alert. They too produced ladders, lightweight aluminium ones often used in pursuit of news. Before many minutes had gone by cameras and lights were pointing over the wooden hoarding at the group round the Cat.

After a brief pause, a banging noise could be heard. The cameras focused. Someone was wielding a sledgehammer against the windshield of the Cat. Bang, bang, bang – to no effect. The wielder of the hammer didn't know that the windscreen was made of safety glass, shatter-proof up to a high level of impact.

A young man joined the hammerer. There was a short consultation. The youth, who perhaps knew more than he ought to about opening the locked doors of vehicles, opened the door of the excavator's cab.

The slight figure with the heavy hammer clambered aboard. The TV lights weren't quite strong enough at that distance to illuminate the assailant but it could be seen that it was a girl, long-haired, slender, clad in jeans and a loose white top.

More banging. This time there was a little cry of triumph. The hammer blows were directed at the controls of the Cat. Undoubtedly they were doing damage. The semicircle of supporters began to sing: 'We shall overco-o-ome . . .'

Journalists with cameras took flash photographs. The girl with the hammer decided she'd done enough smashing up inside the cab, threw down the hammer, which was undoubtedly heavy and more difficult to wield than she'd expected, and instead accepted a placard on a stick from a colleague.

She leaned out of the open door of the cab, holding aloft the placard. TV cameras zoomed in on it. *MONSTERS OUT! SAVE THE TERRACE!* it appealed.

'Give us a wave, luv!' called the reporters.

Obligingly she waved her banner. Boadicea, Warrior Queen!

In the distance police sirens could be heard. The semicircle of singers broke up, dashed for their ladders, and clambered over the fence. The girl in the excavator cab had to climb down, and in doing so got her placard caught so that she was delayed. By the time she'd given up wrestling with it and had run to the fence, the police had commandeered the escape ladders.

The cameras dwelt on her, small, alone, looking up at the police constable now climbing down to arrest her. Joan of Arc!

It was marvellous cinema. If a script had been written, it couldn't have brought more attention from the audience. A cheer went up, opposed by some booing from those who disapproved of attacking machinery with hammers. The girl was taken by the shoulder, cautioned, and ushered towards the fence.

She climbed up demurely. When she got to the top, before stepping over to go down the other side, she struck a pose – arms out, head back. 'Save the Terrace! Support our Nancy!' she called.

Then she disappeared from view as uniformed arms pulled her down the ladder and off to the police car.

She was all over the TV news that night and on the front page of almost every newspaper on Friday morning. *Allie Pembury, heroine of the Protest Group!* Some reportage: *Sixteen-year-old Allie has been a member of the group from the outset . . . Teenage beauty with high ideals . . . 'We must stay faithful to our pledge to help Nancy Bedells,' says young firebrand . . .*

The tag-line was that she had been charged with wilful damage and was due to appear at the Barhampton Magistrates Court. Once again there was a grand turn-out of newsmen and women. The culprit pleaded Guilty, the Chairman of the Bench looked severe and said that he thought he would like a social worker's report before deciding on a sentence. There were others involved in this act of vandalism, he noted, who ought to be brought to account. He conferred with his fellow magistrates on the subject of bail.

In the body of the court two people got to their feet. 'I am prepared to offer bail on behalf of the accused,' said one.

'And you are?'

'Peter Lambot, Your Worship, acting on behalf of the Royal Terrace Protection Group.'

'I'm . . . I'm Allie's . . . I mean, the accused . . . I'm the accused's father, sir,' faltered the other.

'I see.' The magistrates put their heads together. After a moment's discussion the chairman said, 'We are of a mind to release your daughter into your custody. Will you accept responsibility for her good behaviour and ensure she appears to answer the summons in due course?'

'Yes, of course, Your Honour . . . Sir . . .'

'Very well. The prisoner may go, but must be ready to return to the court when called.'

'Yes, sir,' said Allie, meek but determined. This morning she was playing Cordelia from *King Lear*.

The moment she stepped out of the court she was mobbed by reporters. Josh could scarcely keep hold of her arm. 'What are your plans now, Allie? Any more hammer-blows for freedom? Who was the lad with you? Was that your boyfriend?'

'No, no, I haven't got a boyfriend . . .'

'A pretty girl like you? Come on!'

'Allie, we'd better not say anything,' urged her father, a hand at her elbow. 'Come along now, dear.'

'No, wait a minute – Allie, Allie look this way!'

Shouting and tussling for vantage points, the reporters surged around them until Josh got her into his car and drove away. Peter Lambot, watching the scene, thought that probably their phone would ring off the hook for the next twenty-four hours.

The follow-up story in the *Gazette* next day, Saturday, was that Allie had been suspended from school.

Everyone connected with the new Town Centre followed the story. When Bethany went to visit one of Jim McGuire's excavations on Saturday, she found him sitting on an upturned bucket reading the paper.

'Dunno what all the fuss is about,' he remarked to her as she joined him. 'That was an old Cat of mine – due for the scrapheap.'

'Yours?' she said in surprise. 'What was it doing in that lot next to the Terrace, then? You've no work in that area, have you?' She asked merely out of politeness. She knew very well that McGuire's excavators were busy here, knocking a hole where the old Bingo Hall used to stand.

'Like I said, luv, that old rig's got a lot of defects, not safe to use. I'd nowhere to put it – you know my yard isn't one of the biggest – but Bill Wellbrow said I could park it with some of his on that lot. Surprised me a bit – Wellbrow isn't usually that kind-hearted to the likes of me.'

'Billy told you you could use his parking space?'

'Yeh.'

She frowned. As McGuire said, Billy wasn't noted for generosity. 'When was this?'

'Oh, last week some time – Tuesday, Wednesday.'

'You went to him and asked?'

'Nay, lass, no use asking a favour from Billy. No, he came to me and said he'd heard I were going to scrap the Cat and said while I waited to have it collected, it could stand with those of his by the Terrace, where there's a bit of space.'

'I see.'

'Bothered by that?' the contractor asked, looking at her with interest.

She summoned a laugh. 'Surprised. As you say, Billy's not one to do any favours.'

But Billy was one of her father's cronies. And Billy – or at least one of his drivers – had been involved in the attack on Mrs Bedells's house.

She recalled Daniel's anger: 'She's such a clever minx! I'll settle her hash for her!'

Had he arranged for that track excavator to be there for Allie Pembury to vandalise? And the boy who had been with her – the one who with his head carefully averted from the TV cameras had opened the door of the cab so that Allie could smash up the controls . . . Might that by any chance have been Terry Hobsgroom again?

She got into her Suzuki to drive to Josh Pembury's cottage. Since it was Saturday Josh wasn't at work. He kept normal council-office hours, unlike those involved in the actual construction, which had a time schedule to keep.

Though it was well past ten in the morning, the curtains of the front windows were drawn, no doubt as a defence against prying cameras.

Cars were parked along the road. One or two reporters got out to question her as she went to the door. When she knocked Josh asked: 'Who is it?' before opening to admit her.

'Sorry about that. The press have been here – one or two hung about until past midnight and some turned up again around six. I don't know what they think they're going to get by it.'

'How's Allie?'

'Bearing up surprisingly well. She's got a lot of inner strength, you know.'

And a big appetite for publicity, thought Bethany, but kept it to herself. 'Can I speak to her?'

'What about?' asked Allie, coming from the kitchen with a piece of toast in her hand. 'If you've come to read me a lecture, don't bother.'

'I'm not in the lecture business,' said Bethany. 'I just hoped to get a bit of information from you.'

'About what?'

'About that lad who helped you over the fence and opened the Cat's door for you.'

'What about him?'

'He wasn't your boyfriend?'

'The reporters asked me that. I don't have a boyfriend. All the boys around here are so . . . immature and uncultured.'

'So who was he, then?'

'Just someone who turned up to support the protest.'

'You didn't know him?'

'No.'

'Are you just saying that to protect him, Allie, or was he a stranger?'

'I told you, I didn't know him,' said Allie with irritation. 'I don't know all the people at the squat. People drift in and out of a thing like that.'

'So whose idea was it that you should attack that machine?'

'Mine, of course.'

'No, come on, Allie.' Bethany went close to her, looking her full in the eyes. 'Was it *his* idea?'

'Well . . . we talked about it . . . he showed me the pix in the *Gazette*. I forget which of us had the idea first.'

'Oh, Allie,' groaned her father. 'You're so trusting!'

'This boy turned up out of nowhere and suggested you should smash up one of the excavation vehicles?'

'Well,' the girl said, indignant now, 'it was peeking over the fence at us in Royal Terrace – it was *insulting*! So he said wouldn't it be a good idea to hit it where it hurt, make it lower its head. Of course to do that you had to get at the controls, but he said it wouldn't be difficult, and it wasn't, was it!'

'And what happened to him? You got arrested – where did he get to?'

'He was quicker than I was when we heard the sirens. Besides,' said Allie, throwing up her head in an attitude suitable for a heroic saboteur, 'I didn't mind getting arrested – there's no point in a protest if you don't go all the way with it.'

'Oh, Allie,' Josh groaned again.

'So how long had this boy been coming to the squat?'

'I don't know, about a week or so.'

'And what was his name?'

'I don't know.'

'Come on, Allie. This boy had been hanging about for a week and persuaded you into vandalising an excavator – and you never had a name to call him by?'

'I'm not going to tell you.'

'Oh, I see. He runs off and leaves you to face the music alone but you're going to protect him?'

'You bet I am!' cried Allie, in a defiant tone that she'd used many times these last few days. 'He's a comrade!'

'He's an agent provocateur! He stayed around long enough to talk you into foolishness and then vanished. What was his name, Allie?'

She hesitated, taken aback by Bethany's accusation. 'Well . . . he said to call him Clint . . .'

'Oh right.' His name, Bethany was thinking, is Terry Hobsgroom. But how are we going to prove it?

'Did he say anything to give you a clue about where he lived, anything like that?'

'Why are you asking all these questions?' Allie countered, recovering her composure. 'What's it got to do with you, anyhow?'

'Now, sweetie, that's no way to speak to a friend—'

'A friend? She comes here poking her nose in, trying to get Clint into trouble – you've got a funny taste in friends, Daddy!'

With that she turned on her heel and strode away towards the back of the cottage. They heard the back door slam.

'She doesn't really mean it,' her father said in apology. 'She's upset.'

'Do you think so?' asked Bethany. Her impression was that Allie was enjoying it all – the drama of the night attack on the machine, the limelight of the arrest and the court appearance, the confrontation about loyalty to a 'comrade'.

'Well, of course she's upset. Being treated as if she were a criminal—'

'But what she did was wrong, Josh.'

'Yes, of course, but she did it for a good reason—'

'What she *thought* was a good reason—'

'Yes, she thought so. This boy Clint got her into it.'

'Yes, and what she doesn't seem to understand is that it won't be easy to get out of it. She was caught red-handed, she pleaded Guilty, and she'll probably be fined quite a lot. Are you ready to pay up, Josh? And to accept the fact that she'll then be on police files?'

'But the magistrates will see . . . they'll understand . . . it was just a mistake, idealism gone wrong . . .'

'They may understand all that. But they have to think about the owner of the machine.'

'The owner? Some well-off contractor, like Billy Wellbrow.'

'As it happens it's a man called McGuire, just starting out. He hasn't got a lot of money and I'd be surprised if he's got much in the way of insurance.' And probably the insurance is invalidated, she thought to herself, because it wasn't parked in his own yard.

'I never thought of that,' said Josh.

'But on second thoughts the machine was due to go to the scrapyard—' and as Josh looked relieved she added, 'but Allie didn't know that!'

'This boy Clint—'

'He's why I'm here, asking questions—'

'But I can't see it's going to do any good, Bethany. He's vanished, and if he's got any sense he'll stay vanished – and even if we knew where to find him, what good does it do? It only means two young people would be in court because of mistaken idealism.'

'Idealism?' Bethany echoed, anger growing at every word. How could her father do such a thing – take advantage of a silly young girl, send in a traitor to trap her?

She had to speak to Daniel Dayton. And she knew just where to find him mid-morning on Saturday.

She drove towards York, threading her way through Saturday shopping traffic. The golf club lay to the south-west of the city, the former estate of a magnate and now a very exclusive domain for businessmen at weekends.

Bethany was known to the receptionist at the desk because she had been to social events here with her parents. He smiled a welcome. 'Morning, Ms Dayton. Your father's just come off the green, I think. He'll be in the bar with Mr Wellbrow.'

'Thank you, Reggie.' She walked past on the well-known route to the former morning room of the big old house, and there among ash-wood panelling and glass cases of golf trophies, she found the two men enjoying a pre-lunch gin. Others were engaged in the same pleasant pastime. The scene was tranquil, somewhat smug.

'Hello, luv!' cried her father on espying her. He smiled, then seeing her serious expression looked alarmed. 'Not something else gone wrong on the site?'

'No, I just want a word with you.'

'About what?'

'About Allison Pembury.'

Billy Wellbrow gave her a wink over the rim of his glass. 'Cut short her career as a protester, didn't we?'

'Then you admit you cooked all that up to trap her?'

'Cooked what up?' her father intervened before Wellbrow could say any more. 'I don't know what you're talking about.'

'Yes, you do. You arranged for that track excavator to be where it was so that she could get at it and be caught—'

'Absolute nonsense!'

'Then why was it parked in Billy's vehicle park? And why were all the media alerted.'

'*She* did that,' said Billy. 'She rang up the TV crowd and told them there was going to be summat worth watching—'

'How do you know that?'

''Cos Iris Weston told me, that's how.'

'Yes, and it was Iris who planted those stories about the machinery and how expensive it is and all that – tempting her to have a go at it.'

'Nay, lass, that's just your opinion. You don't like Iris, I've noticed that, so you want to think the worst—'

'I want to find out the truth! You sent that boy – Hobsgroom – the same one who threw bricks at Mrs Bedells's windows.'

'Me?' Wellbrow said, throwing up his hands. 'Whatever makes you think such a thing?'

A waiter approached, looking questioningly at the trio – the two men with their drinks left untouched and the angry young woman. 'Mr Wellbrow,' he said with some anxiety, 'you know the club rules – no business talk in the bar.'

'Right you are, Eddie,' agreed Wellbrow, smiling and shrugging as if to say, Just a silly woman causing trouble.

'Now see what you've done,' Daniel said with a grin. 'You'll get us in trouble with the club secretary. They don't like business talk and they don't like lady visitors who cause a fuss.'

His daughter gave him a glance of ice. 'How can you sit there and chuckle when you've got a kid in big trouble?'

'*I* have? Any trouble that girl is in is of her own making, Beth.'

'She was set up, Dad!'

'Oh really? She saw some photographs of machinery in the papers and she decides to take a hammer to it—'

'Only because Terry Hobsgroom put it in her head!'

'Terry Hobsgroom? Who's Terry Hobsgroom?'

'He's the son of one of Billy's drivers.'

'And you can prove he even knows Allison Pembury?'

'Excuse me,' said the waiter, who had only retreated a step or two. 'I'll have to fetch Mr Inshall ... the other members are looking annoyed, Mr Dayton.'

'Come on outside,' Daniel said and, getting up, he took his

daughter by the elbow and led her out of the bar, out of the vestibule and into the fresh air of the front courtyard. 'Now then,' he said with annoyance, 'let's have no more of this bull in a china shop behaviour. What do you think you're up to, making me look a fool in front of my friends?'

'I'll tell you what I'm up to,' she retorted, flashing blue fire from angry eyes. 'I'm trying to get you to admit that you sent that juvenile delinquent to make Allie Pembury attack that excavator—'

'And I'm telling you you're wasting your time! So drop it—'

'She's going to get a police record, Dad—'

'She should have thought of that before she climbed over that fence.'

'He talked her into it – and then he ran away and left her—'

'And didn't she just love that? Interviews on TV, pictures in the papers—'

'Dad, she's a sixteen-year-old kid!'

'And should have been taught her manners long ago! So if her father won't see to it, what's the result?'

'You take it on yourself to teach her a lesson.'

'So you say. What *I* say is that if she weren't a silly vain little fool she wouldn't listen to what anybody else says, particularly when it comes to damaging valuable property—'

'Come on, McGuire tells me that Cat was a write-off—'

'Nowt o' t'sort! Even scrap metal's worth something—'

'You got Billy Wellbrow to offer McGuire free parking space and arranged for Iris to get pictures in the papers.'

'That's what *you* say.'

'And sent Terry Hobsgroom to chat her up, just so she'd be tempted.'

'If she hadn't *wanted* to do it, no amount of chatting up—'

'And what it amounts to is you've plotted and schemed like a sneak to blacken the name of a silly schoolgirl!'

At the word 'sneak' her father frowned at her with so much ferocity that for a moment she thought he might strike her. But then he drew a great gulping breath of air, and drew back.

'Right,' he said. 'We have to stick together for the duration of this task in Barhampton but once that's done, we're finished!'

'Fine with me.'

'We'll get this Town Centre sorted because it would look damn funny if we split up while—'

'You never wanted me as a partner in the first place.'

'No, I didn't, and I was right, wasn't I?'

'I always knew you used dodgy methods when it suited you.'

'That's right, just like a woman! Get on your high horse—'

'If speaking up against cheating and dirty tricks—'

'Dirty tricks! Dirty tricks! That stupid little girl dashes into the limelight every chance she gets but *she's* not in the wrong, oh no. You come here and call me names—'

'Are you really going to tell me you think it's right to drag that kid into court, get her a police record, involve Josh in paying a heavy fine—'

'Oh, him! If you weren't so soft on him, we wouldn't be standing here now—'

'I'm not soft on Josh Pembury – it's nothing to do with him – it's *you.* You don't seem to feel a bit of remorse.'

'No, I don't, and if I can get him thrown out of his job I'll consider it a good result, for of all the daft, silly men—'

'If you so much as raise a finger to lose him his job, I'll tell him what you've done and he'll bring a case for wrongful dismissal.'

'Go on then, go on! Pick up your banner and go and join that crowd who want to ruin your Town Centre – for you certainly don't seem to belong with us who're trying to put it up.'

She gave an angry laugh. 'You'd love that, wouldn't you – to get me to withdraw from the construction team, but I won't, it's my design and I'm going to see it through!'

'Not if you're going to spend all your time defending—'

'I wouldn't have to defend anybody if you would stop conniving.'

A car had driven into the courtyard and drew up, to discharge a quartet of men in golfing gear. As they approached the entrance they looked with curiosity at the two opponents on the threshold. 'Excuse me,' they said as they passed, and to Daniel, 'How do, Dayton?'

The spate of words died away with their going by. Father and daughter stared at each other in silence, shocked at the things they had said to each other.

It was Bethany who recovered first. 'You'd better get back to your pal Wellbrow. Tell him if he pays Hobsgroom or his lad to play any more tricks, I'll—'

'You'll what? There's nothing you can do and you know it. If you want to play with the big boys, learn to stick by their rules.'

She shook her head, turning away to her jeep. 'Tell Mother I won't be home for Sunday lunch tomorrow.'

Her father scowled, taking a step after her. 'Hey-up! She'll want to know why.'

'Oh, you'll think of something,' she said, walking off. 'You're very inventive, Dad.'

She drove in the general direction of Barhampton, hardly knowing where she was going, her thoughts busy with what had just gone by. It was useless to hope that her father would change his ways; he had been master of the house and of the business for too long. She'd never expected to change his mind about what had happened to Allie Pembury – in fact, now she thought it over, she'd expected nothing except verification when she went to see him. But now she knew – Allie Pembury was the victim of a plot hatched by Daniel Dayton, Billy Wellbrow, and Iris Weston.

The problem now was, what ought she to do? *Should* she do anything? Allie had in fact smashed up the controls of the excavator. True, the vehicle wasn't ever going to be used again but, as her father had said, Allie didn't know that. She'd intended real damage to someone else's property. If Bethany went to the police, this was likely to be their view – and besides, she could produce no proof that the girl had been tricked into her 'demonstration'.

Bethany knew beyond a shadow of doubt that there had been a plot. But neither Wellbrow nor her father had made any actual admissions, and if questioned were sure to deny any responsibility.

As to Iris, in fairness Bethany had to suppose that she was largely in the dark about Daniel's intentions. He might have called her and said: 'How about some newspaper coverage of how the job's going – some nice pix of the machines in action and that sort of thing?' It sounded very reasonable. Iris, using her friendly contacts, would have set to work and happily achieved what was asked for. She might have had no idea Terry Hobsgroom was flourishing the newspaper under Allie's nose and urging her to take action.

So going to the police would achieve nothing, because she could produce no plotters to mitigate what Allie had done.

Peter Lambot had appeared in court ready to act for the Royal Terrace Protection Group. Perhaps he would be able to point her in the right direction. She drew into the side of the road, picked up her mobile phone, looked up Peter's home number in her notebook, and dialled.

No reply. Of course not. It was a fine Saturday. Peter was probably out enjoying it, as was the rest of the population.

She was about to drive on when it occurred to her to try the offices of *Pesh, Samuels & Co.* Foolish, of course – he wouldn't be there.

The phone at the other end was picked up. 'Hello?' said a surprised voice.

'Peter!'

'Hello? Who's . . . ? That's you, Bethany, isn't it?'

'Yes, it's me. I never really expected you to be there.'

'I'm nearly not here. I was just going to close up and go out to lunch when the phone rang.'

'What are you doing in the office at noon on a fine Saturday?'

'Catching up. I spent a lot of time yesterday phoning around, trying to find out what was likely to happen on the Protest Group thing, so office work got left unfinished. I though I'd do an hour or two of catching up—' He broke off. 'You don't want to hear all that. What can I do for you?'

'It's about the Protest Group that I'm ringing you. We need to talk, Peter.'

There was a tiny silence. Then he said, 'Are you upset about something?'

'A bit.'

'Had lunch yet?'

'No.'

'Neither have I. How about if we meet for a bite?'

'I'd like that. Where?'

'Where are you? At home?'

'No, I'm driving back to Barhampton on Barrbridge Road.'

'Okay, let's meet at the Nether Ford – do you know it? It's an old coaching inn off on the right.'

'Peter, I was born in the neighbourhood! Of course I know the old Netherfy.'

'Meet you there in, say, half an hour.'

'Right you are.'

She arrived first, ordered a glass of wine, and took it out to one of the benches that were spread along the riverbank. One or two others, local people mostly, were enjoying a quiet pint while they gazed at the brown water rippling softly over the stones. Here the heavy old stage-coaches used to ford the river on their way to the Great North Road, rocking against the stony bed while the shallow water washed halfway up the yellow-varnished wheels. A peaceful spot now, with all the traffic drained off to the motorway, the old Netherfy was a favourite with those who knew it.

Peter appeared bearing a mug of beer and a menu. 'They told me you'd arrived. What would you like to eat?'

'I'm not very hungry. Just the ploughman's, Peter.'

'Okay, but I think I'll go for the home-made lasagne. Shan't be a minute.' He went back to order the food, then settled himself beside her.

'Now, tell me what's bothering you.'

'How do you know I'm bothered?' she countered, smiling a little.

'I could hear it in your voice when you rang. And since you mentioned the Protest Group, I take it it's about Allie Pembury and the grand sabotage attempt.'

'Yes.'

'What's troubling you?'

'Do you know if the police are making any further enquiries?'

'Well, I know they went to the Terrace to try to find the lad who was with Allie.'

'But they didn't.'

'No. And "nobody knows nowt about him".'

'That's what I expected.'

'Well, you know . . . solidarity. And of course Allie refused to tell them anything about him.'

'I think I know who it was.'

Peter, about to raise the beer mug, set it down with a thump on the trestle table. 'You do?'

'You know that lad who was throwing stones at Mrs Bedells's windows?'

'Er . . . yes . . . If I remember rightly, the police thought it was Terry . . . Hobsworth?'

'Hobsgroom. I think it was him.'

'With Allie? Smashing up the Cat?'

'Yes.'

'That can't be, Bethany. The boy the police suspected of the stone-throwing was a well-known tearaway, as far as I could gather. The boy with Allie on Friday night was one of the protesters.'

'No.'

'I beg your pardon?'

'I don't think he was a protester. I think he was somebody hired to drop in on the group, befriend Allie, and get her to climb that fence and hit that vehicle.'

Peter accepted this with a moment's silence. Then he said, 'Hired by whom?'

She didn't reply.

When he understood she was going to say nothing, he went on, 'With what object?'

'To catch Allie doing something wrong. To spoil the image the papers had built up – they'd made her look like a sort of noble creature, like that princess in the long white gown in *Star Wars*. If they were to catch her out smashing up something . . . it would make her look bad and get her out of the action.'

He picked up the beer mug again to take a sip or two. 'That's rather subtle,' he observed.

'Oh yes. It's not only the Foreign Office who go in for subtlety.'

'Are you saying that someone on Barhampton council cooked this up. Cyril Ollerton, for instance? If he did, I'll have his head on a plate—'

'No, not Cyril. Not someone on the council.'

'But it's someone you know.'

She nodded.

The barmaid came with the food. They were silent except to say thank you. When she had gone Peter said, 'It's your father, isn't it?'

She unwrapped the napkin from around the cutlery. It took all her attention.

As if she had assented, he asked, 'Are you sure?'

'As sure as I need to be.'

'You've spoken to him about it, haven't you? That's why you're so upset.'

'I spoke to him, yes.'

'And he admitted it?'

'Peter, my father's much too canny to admit anything. And if you question him till Doomsday you'll never get anything out of him. But he and his followers set that trap for Allie.'

'I see.' He took a moment to consider it. 'Eat your lunch,' he commanded.

Obediently she spread some butter on a piece of the crusty bread. She said, 'I don't think he stopped to consider that it would have repercussions on other people. For instance, if the magistrates impose a fine, Josh will have to pay – and it might be quite a lot, mightn't it?'

'Might be. And old Mrs Crowther won't pay it. You know she got me into this affair, rushing in to support the Royal Terrace Protection Group. But she telephoned on Friday morning to tell me emphatically she was having nothing to do with people who took sledgehammers to things. So there's no more money coming from *that* side.'

'I could speak to Jim McGuire. He owns that track excavator but he's going to sell it for scrap. I bet he wouldn't press charges if we spoke to him about it.'

'That would be great. But there's the matter of the social worker's report. If she – it's a she, Mrs Delamott – if she says Allie has destructive tendencies or whatever they call it—'

'Peter, she was enticed into it! I haven't got evidence that would convince the police, but surely a social worker ought to look at things more sympathetically?'

'Well, I could certainly talk to her. After all, that lad has made himself noticeably scarce since the event . . . If Allie will drop her "I and I Alone" attitude . . .'

'Oh, she's such an idiot! She sees herself as the heroine of a melodrama whereas if the truth were known she's been played for a sucker!'

'Inelegant but accurate,' Peter said, and she laughed. 'That's better,' he went on, 'don't be so concerned. We'll save this sacrificial lamb, even if she's determined to offer herself for the barbecue.'

She nodded. He picked up his glass and held it as if for a toast. 'There are a lot of campaigns being run in Barhampton at the moment. Here's to the "Save Allie" campaign!'

'Yes, here's to it.' She touched his beer mug with her wine glass.

They were sealing a partnership.

Chapter Eleven

When the day came for Allie's reappearance in court, the press were disappointed. The Chairman of the Bench said in neutral tones that the report by the social worker had been studied. The magistrates were satisfied that the accused had acted out of misplaced idealism, the owner of the machine said its value – which was only as scrap – hadn't been altered by the damage and declined to press charges. Therefore the Bench felt that a caution was in order and with this admonition Allie was dismissed from the court.

Well done, Peter, thought Bethany when she heard the news on her car radio.

The schemers were perhaps less satisfied, because the media still regarded Allie as a heroine. But so long as Allie was kept in order by her father from now on, they were prepared to accept the result.

'Aren't we going to use the chance to get Pembury sacked?' Wellbrow demanded of his friend Daniel Dayton.

'My lass will kick up a row if we try it,' said Daniel.

'Your lass is a bit on the impractical side,' sighed Wellbrow. 'Let's at least get him off the Steering Committee.'

'Nay,' said Daniel, foreseeing all kinds of trouble with Bethany if they tried that, 'let it be. When you think it over, it makes no matter if he stays on. He doesn't say much—'

'But he always votes for anything that puts up the cost by needing bushes and trees.'

'Now, Billy, you can't argue that out of the specifications at this stage. Those were laid down in the original Town Centre plan, so they *don't* put up the cost. I know what you mean, mind,' he added. 'He's not much of a help getting the work kept to schedule. But Bethie says she'll rush to the rescue if we try to get rid of him.'

Iris Weston, who was of the party as they stood chatting in the car park of the old Town Hall, looked vexed. 'I don't like it that Bethany's so friendly with him.'

'She likes him because he's "green",' laughed Daniel.

'Hmm. I've got a feeling she interfered to save Allie Pembury from something a lot more serious than a caution.'

Daniel made no reply. He had no intention of letting anyone know how serious a quarrel he'd had with his daughter outside the golf club. 'I grant you she's too good-hearted,' he acknowledged.

'And you can see by the way Josh looks at her that he thinks she's his good angel.'

'Ah, you ladies . . . You can see things us men can't see. Intuition, that's what it's called.'

'I'm serious, Daniel,' Iris insisted. 'I think Josh sees Bethany as a kind-hearted stepmother for his daughter.'

It gave him a start. He himself had accused his daughter of being 'soft' about Josh. Might it really be that these two were attracted to each other?

Iris, who could read him like a book, was pleased. From now on Daniel was likely to take note of everything Josh said and did. In his sleepy, rather unworldly way, Josh was a nuisance, and his daughter Allie even more so. She needed to be kept under control – a control her father seemed incapable of exerting. Perhaps if Daniel kept an eye on Josh, Josh might keep an eye on Allie. Of course, if truth were known, Allie's recent misbehaviour had been deftly engineered by others – but all the same she was a problem.

At home that evening with Alan in his flat in York, she mused about the future. 'The press aren't going to leave it alone, you know,' she said as they sat over supper in the soft June twilight. 'They feel they've got a pretty young heroine sticking up for something with a lot of human appeal . . .'

'But if Pembury keeps her locked up for a bit . . .?'

'Well, I hope he will – or can! But she got off very easily over hacking that machine.'

'That was only fair, dear,' said Alan Singleton, prodding at his salad with distaste. He didn't really care for salad, but Iris said it was good for him. 'That track excavator only had scrap value. Lucky, really – if she'd had a go at something valuable, it would have been a different matter.'

'Alan, with a girl like that you never know what she'll do next. I've seen her type often – in public relations you meet a lot of them, mad keen to get into the public eye, ready to do almost anything to be a "star" – bunjie-jumping, roller-blading round China, lying in a tank full of snakes – anything!'

'Well, I've never met the lass, but Beth says it's only because she's young—'

'Well, "Beth" is wrong, as she so often is—'

'Do you think so?' he said, startled. 'That's strange. On the whole I think Beth is pretty clear-headed—'

'She likes to think she is,' Iris broke in, struck by an instant pang of jealousy. The easy friendship that remained between her man and Bethany Dayton still had the power to make her uneasy. 'But she's wrong to rush to the aid of someone like Pembury.'

141

'I don't think she did.'

'Oh yes, she did. Her father and some of the other members of Steerco would have been glad to give him the push after all the trouble Allie has caused, but Bethany argued them out of it—'

'What makes you say so?'

'Alan, it's my business to know who's doing what! I expected them to jump at the chance to get rid of him, but Daniel has been damping it all down – and you can bet it's because of that daughter of his!'

'Well, that's all to the good, Iris, if you come to think of it. Josh might have sued for wrongful dismissal—'

'I didn't mean they ought to sack him, Alan. But there are ways of getting rid of someone who's a nuisance – you can move him to another department—'

'Where would you move Josh? He's an expert on landscaping – you couldn't very well transfer him to the Accounts Department.' By spreading some lettuce leaves over the chopped-up vegetables he managed to make it look as if he'd eaten most of the salad. 'Anyway, moving Josh might not stop Allie.'

'No, but the threat that her father might lose his job if she didn't behave . . .?'

'That's too complicated for me, sweetheart. Is there any pudding?'

'There's strawberries—'

'And cream?'

'Darling, you know I never eat cream, but there's yoghurt.'

He sighed. During Iris's visits, it was really better to go out to a restaurant, where they could order separately. Sometimes he longed for the treacly richness of Bakewell tart . . . He went to fetch the strawberries. He augmented his portion with a large helping of ice cream.

Alan had lived on his own for so long now that he was adept at catering to his own tastes. He had organised his flat to suit his lifestyle – comfortable, casual, with big cupboards for his walking gear and his surveying equipment. Now that Iris shared the place with him when she came North, little femininities had crept in – suede cushions in fashionable colours, a Chagall lithograph on the wall of the living room, lingerie draped over the shower rail to dry.

He liked it – except for the food. Iris was on a permanent diet and so, when she was in York, was Alan.

Iris cleared away the plates of the first course; she wasn't a good housekeeper but she liked tidiness. When they were settled at the table again Alan resumed the topic that had interested him. 'For all you say about Beth and Josh . . . I think she's more likely to take up with Peter Lambot.'

'Peter Lambot? The lawyer who acts for the Protest Group?'

'Yes, him.'

'What on earth makes you say that, Alan?'

142

'A friend of mine saw them together at the theatre here one evening.'

'Really?'

'Yes, and if you remember, they were together at Royal Terrace when Beth got bopped on the head by the Pembury lass.'

'But that was a chance meeting—'

'No, he asked for her to go along with him – the lawyer—'

'Did he? Yes, I believe he did. But that only proves *he* thinks something of her, not the other way round.' For Iris, in her heart, always had the anxiety that Bethany might still be thinking of Alan.

'Well, he's right to think of her – she's a lovely girl, is Beth.'

Iris busied herself with spooning yoghurt over her strawberries. She didn't want to enter into any song of praise for Bethany Dayton. She determined to warn Daniel Dayton that his daughter had been seen out and about with the lawyer for the opposition.

Really, these provincial circles, with their relationships and nuances . . . London was so much easier. In London you knew who was 'in' and who was 'out'. One day she was going to arrange for a good job for Alan in London, and then they would shake the dust of Yorkshire from their feet for ever.

Daniel Dayton wasn't best pleased when Iris spoke to him about Peter Lambot. 'You're saying Bethie is keen on him?'

'I'm told they were seen out together.'

'Who? Who told you that?'

'Never mind. If it's true, it means she's getting too friendly with the opposition.'

He looked glum. 'Don't expect me to do owt about it,' he remarked. 'My daughter doesn't take advice from me.'

'But she's a partner in your firm! She's got to listen to what you say.'

'Iris, luv, you don't understand. Bethany and I have never seen eye to eye.'

She dropped the matter. The seed had been planted.

Daniel knew better than to address his daughter on the subject of her love life, if any. It would never be a good idea, and less still after their big quarrel. So he decided to get his wife to do the job for him.

He and Mary often spent Sunday afternoons working in the garden. For Mary Dayton her garden was an important source of material for flower arranging. Daniel, on the other hand, loved the machinery; to sit up on the big lawnmower and make a stately progress across the quarter acre of lawn was very enjoyable. Then there would be the pleasure of afternoon tea, to which friends often came.

This Sunday they had tea out on the lawn. Ossie Fielden arrived bearing a gift for Mary, a new container for flowers bought at a Japanese store in Manchester. After suitable exclamations of delight on Mary's part and the consumption of three scones by Ossie, Daniel made his opening move.

'Well, what's the gossip around Barhampton these days, Ossie?'

'Nothing you probably haven't heard yourself, lad. You're the centre of a lot of chat these days, what with the trouble over the Town Centre and that lass of Pembury's getting herself arrested. A lot of folk expected him to get the sack over that, y'know.'

'Well, it were on the cards, Ossie. But we decided it would look bad.'

'Oh, that was the reason, was it? Bob Egram said it were because your Beth took his part.'

'Well, she did.'

'And quite right too,' Mary put in with weight behind the words. 'You can't fire a man because of what his children do.'

'Quite right, luv, so Josh Pembury lives to fight another day – though he's not a chap with much fight in him, is he?'

'Don't know him well,' Ossie said, sipping tea. 'Some of the lads who work alongside him at the Town Hall say he's on the look-out for a nice new mother for that girl Allie.'

There was a pause. Daniel looked at Ossie. Ossie realised this was an invitation to go further.

'He's keen on your Beth,' he said, 'or so I hear.'

'I hear it too,' Daniel acknowledged. 'But my view is that when she got in a state about him losing his job and all that, it was simply a matter of principle.'

'No romance?'

'You'd know more about that kind of thing than me, Mary,' said Daniel, looking at his wife expectantly.

Mary Dayton knew very well when her husband was trying to manipulate her. She had had long experience of it. Sometimes she went along with his moves, and sometimes she quietly evaded them. This afternoon she was interested enough to respond to his opening because there was something going on that she didn't quite understand.

A couple of weeks previously her husband had come home from his golf game in a very bad mood. Daniel was often out of sorts after golf, but this time there were none of the usual excuses about the wind taking his ball, or the bad mowing of the green. This was a sharper anger, nor did it wear off as it usually did by evening.

At dinner that Sunday she'd mentioned she was preparing one of Bethany's favourite dishes for Sunday lunch.

'Beth says she can't make it tomorrow,' growled her husband.

'Says she can't? When was this?'

'This morning.'

Mary looked as she felt – perplexed. 'But you were playing golf with Billy this morning.'

'Aye.'

'So how did you come to speak to Beth?'

'She happened along.'

144

The golf club was nowhere near anywhere that was likely to interest Bethany. Mary let that pass. She at once understood that her daughter had sought Daniel out to say something to him, that it had put him in a terribly bad mood, and that as a consequence Bethany had decided not to come to the family Sunday lunch.

Mary had rung her daughter. Yes, quite true, Bethany wouldn't be coming to lunch on Sunday. 'Too much work to do,' she said.

Well, it was quite clear to Mary that her husband and her daughter had had a big row and that Bethany was avoiding her father. But that had happened many times in the stormy adolescence of Bethany Dayton. Experience told Mary that she must just wait it out.

Now here was Daniel making an opening for Mary to talk about Bethany. She was quite willing to do that. She'd had tea with her daughter in York last Wednesday and they'd talked about Josh Pembury. And there seemed no harm in relaying the conversation.

'Beth likes Josh because they're in sympathy with each other over the need for greenery in the new Town Centre. She once said to me he was a bit of a genius – a sort of a modern Capability Brown.'

'That's the chap who did the gardens at all those stately homes, isn't it? He'd better not be planning any open vistas with Greek temples in Barhampton,' Ossie laughed.

'He's keen on having the Barr as a key element,' Daniel said. 'Glimpses of trees and the river from lots of different angles – and that's what Beth's design offers, so the two of them are pretty much hand in glove.'

'But arm in arm – are they, Mary, luv?' Ossie enquired.

'I don't think so.'

'I *did* hear she and that lawyer chap went to the theatre together a couple of weeks ago,' Daniel mentioned.

Mary suppressed a smile. So that was what he was after? 'Yes, they went to see a one-man show – *George Orwell and Big Brother*. She said it was excellent.'

Ossie was a little taken aback. Well up on local politics, he missed out on personal matters – unless it was an affair between a councillor and a secretary. It was news to him that Bethany was friendly with the solicitor for the Royal Terrace Protection Group. After all, they were the opposition. If they succeeded in getting a Preservation Order, that would make life very, very difficult for the contractors building the new Town Centre – and most of those contractors were old friends of Ossie Fielden.

'I hear he's a very clever feller,' he remarked.

'George Orwell?'

'Nay, lass, Peter Lambot. That old Mrs Crowther thinks the world of him; she lets him handle all those doubloons Charlie Crowther left her. There was a rogue for you,' Ossie said with admiration, 'imported

145

washing machines by the thousand at twenty quid and installed them in council flats by contract for a hundred and twenty . . .'

Daniel didn't want to talk about Charlie Crowther, dead and gone for twenty-five years. He wanted to talk about Peter Lambot.

'Reckon he's aiming for a partnership at *Pesh, Samuels*?'

'I'd imagine so. Old Bernard Samuels should be retiring soon—'

'Wonder why he came to Barhampton, to a tiddly little firm like *Pesh, Samuels*?'

'Well, I hear he got tired of the London rat race. Besides, he's a Yorkshireman by birth, comes from Leeds originally if I remember rightly.'

'I've never thought to ask him, because of course we've only ever met to cross swords – but is there a Mrs Lambot?'

'Nay, that's a daft question, Daniel. Would your Bethie be going out with a married man?'

'But is she "going out" with him? wondered Daniel.

'I'll tell you who *is* going out wi' someone,' said Ossie, a fine scrap of gossip coming to mind. 'You remember that Lionel Chase that took over the Liddleworth Quarry? I hear he's taken up wi' a lass from Harrogate . . .'

Mary let the conversation drift on in the dreamy afternoon warmth. She understood what Daniel had been after. He wanted to know if there was anything serious between her daughter and Peter Lambot.

Well, so did she. She had no objection to carrying out his wishes on this point, although quite often she could prove deliberately obtuse in response to the hints he threw out.

There was no problem about getting together with Bethany. Mother and daughter met often, sometimes merely for a cup of tea, sometimes for an evening out at the cinema, or an afternoon's shopping. Mary rang Bethany. They decided to go out for a Chinese meal, an outing that needed at least two so as to deal with the huge array of little dishes. Mary had a fondness for Chinese food but since Daniel hated it, he never took her to a Chinese restaurant.

'Well,' Mary began, having made a start on her crispy duck pancakes, 'will you be coming to lunch next Sunday?'

'I don't think so, Mother.'

'Doing something nice?'

'I'm visiting one of my sheltered housing sites. You remember that place I designed out at Carfaxton? It's more than a year since it was completed and I want to find out if it's "functioning".'

This was one of Bethany's rules. When she put up a building, it was her duty to visit it two or three times over the following years if at all possible, to see if it was a good place to live. Her view had always been that those who designed huge tower blocks with concrete walkways around them should be forced to live in them for at least six months, to learn the drawbacks. Architects had responsibilities, not only to the organisation paying for the building, but to those who would have to live or work in it.

Mary knew all this. She also knew that there was nothing urgent about such a visit. If Bethany wanted to come home for Sunday lunch, she could do so. But clearly she didn't want to.

'Are you and your father at odds with each other again?' she enquired. 'Is that why you don't want to come home?'

Bethany pushed tofu and ginger about on her plate. Her head was turned away in embarrassment. In her sky-blue top and tan skirt, she looked very young – almost the schoolgirl over whose young years Mary had stood guard.

'You know how it is,' she murmured. 'We don't really get on.'

'I'm used to that. I'm used to your getting hurt and having to come to terms with it. But this time it seems more serious. Your father's feeling guilty – and that's been going on now for a couple of weeks at least. Usually he convinces himself he was right and gets over it. This time he seems . . . I don't know . . . fundamentally upset.'

'So he should be,' said Bethany, and captured a cashew nut between her chopsticks. She put it in her mouth and began to crunch it so as not to have to make any further reply.

'What's he done?' Mary enquired with a sigh.

'Now, Mother, don't expect me to tell tales on Dad. If he wants you to know, he'll tell you.'

'But it's something bad.'

'In my opinion – yes.'

'Is it to do with you and Josh Pembury? Ossie was saying last Sunday he hears you stood up for him in the Steering Committee.'

'Mother, if you're going to believe all you hear from Ossie, you'll think York Minster was intended as a super-cinema.'

'So you're not falling for Josh?'

'Falling for Josh?' Bethany echoed incredulously.

Her mother laughed. 'I see that's the wrong tack,' she observed. 'Well then, are you falling for Peter Lambot?'

Bethany stared at her. After a long moment she said, 'Was that another bit of Ossie's gossip?'

'Don't blame it all on Ossie,' said Mary. 'I'm interested in knowing, myself.'

'Honestly . . . !'

'Don't want to say, is that it?'

'Did you tempt me out to this feast of Chinese cookery just to question me about my love life?'

'No, it's because I love the Chinese lanterns and the statuettes of goddesses,' her mother laughed. 'Well, yes, if truth be told, I do want to know what you feel. It's important, dear. You know I try to keep up with what's going on, even though mostly I only hear your dad's side of things. But you do talk about Peter with a certain . . . warmth. And from what Ossie and your father were saying, it's going to cause a problem if you get involved – because he's what they call "the opposition".'

'I'm not responsible for what they call him,' Bethany said with distaste. 'Those men on the Steering Committee – they see things in terms of black and white, your side or my side. Peter's acting on behalf of the Royal Terrace Protection Group and, to some extent, for Mrs Bedells. That doesn't make him an enemy, now does it?'

'But if they think it does?'

'That's their problem.'

'Bethie, be reasonable. Things are complicated enough over this Town Centre. Don't make it worse by getting close to Peter – unless he's really important.'

Bethany said nothing.

'Oh,' said her mother. 'I see he is important.'

The waiter came with yet another set of small dishes. They responded to his enquiries about the food, asked for more tea. When they could return to their conversation Mary said: 'Am I being tactless by talking about this?'

'There's really nothing to talk about, Mother.'

'But you think I'm being tactless all the same.'

'I want to be left alone!' Bethany burst out. 'Dad tells me not to get mixed up with Josh Pembury and now it's Peter – he put you up to this, didn't he?'

'Darling, I'm concerned – you know I am. I don't want to pry, and I wouldn't be asking these questions except that I've got to know where I stand. Your dad's really bothered – I know him, I know when something's got him upset. *He* won't tell me what's at the back of it, and now *you're* acting as jumpy as a cat. Just let me know, Beth – am I to stand up for you and Peter Lambot or am I to let your father growl on about him as if he's an enemy?'

Bethany shook her head. 'Don't get involved, Mother.'

'It's no use saying that. I *am* involved. I want you to be happy. Just give me a clue where your happiness lies, that's all I'm asking.'

Mary reached out a hand across the table. Her daughter took it. 'Oh, Mother . . . You're always fighting my battles for me with Dad . . .'

They smiled at each other, remembering past times, difficult times. Mary pressed her daughter's hand.

They went back to their meal. 'It's serious, then, this thing with Peter?' Mary hazarded.

'Fairly serious.'

'Right. That's all I want to know. So are we going to have some Oriental fruit salad or have you had enough?'

148

'I've had enough,' Bethany said, and meant it to apply beyond the food on the table.

At home later, she considered their conversation. She hadn't wanted to talk about Peter. The relationship between them was still too young to be talked about. She had this superstition that if you talked too much about something important, you spoiled it, stunted it in some mysterious way.

She reflected that, after all, her mother's questions had been about how she felt over Peter. As yet, Bethany had no idea how Peter felt about her. She had intuitions, hopes . . . But so far, that was all.

Bethany Dayton wasn't the only one in Barhampton that evening to be feeling uncertain. In her bedroom at the cottage Allie Pembury was standing staring out at the moonlit trees that formed a boundary between the garden and the moors.

There was an element of Cathy in *Wuthering Heights* about her pose. She was barefoot, wearing a loose, long cotton nightdress, and one thin-boned hand rested on her breast.

She was considering her life. Life is short, art is long – that was a Latin quotation or something. So, if life is short, why was she wasting any of it cooped up in this boring little town? She was destined for great things – she sensed it, she knew it . . . A great actress, with all London at her feet, and a career opening up in world cinema – not Hollywood, of course, unless she could choose the script and the director . . .

First, she knew, she had to learn her craft – be the protégée of some star of the theatre, be taken up by a teacher who would show her how to harness the powers she felt dammed up within her . . .

But to be taken up, she had to be noticed. Over the last couple of months, that had been a real possibility. She had been in the public eye, and the public loved her.

But now . . . Now everything had died away. Daddy was being so difficult, always asking what she was doing, where she was going.

Even the freedom conferred by being suspended from school had turned sour. At school, though she wasn't a popular girl, she had status – the other girls thought her odd, laughed at her behind her back – oh, she knew that, of course – but they respected her. Now, with only herself for an audience, it seemed almost pointless to have been a heroine, a rebel. She might go up on the moors and recite towering passages from Marlowe or Webster, but what was the use? There was no one to hear, no one to applaud, no one to understand . . .

She was dwindling away. She felt it. From being important, an object of attention, she was becoming a nothing.

And time was passing. Art is long, life is short. If she didn't escape from Barhampton soon, get accepted by a drama school, begin her career, someone else would take up the space that should be hers. Some other pretty girl, with talent and ambition but with more luck.

She'd heard it said that you made your own luck. She threw up her arms to the clouded moon. Was that the message she was meant to hear? Not to stay cooped up in this pokey little cottage but to go out, to make things happen again, to be a star in this little firmament?

Allie had a native shrewdness that guided her thinking. She had to use the stage that was already prepared – impossible to start all over again with something new.

No, she was the champion of old Mrs Bedells, La Pasionaria of the fight to save Barhampton's literary heritage. It was in Barhampton that her career must be reignited – she must use the vast construction site for another act of rebellion against the inhuman machines.

But not in or around Royal Terrace. That was becoming a bit of a cliché. She must do something new, something on a bigger scale.

She went to bed at last, her restlessness allayed for the time being. During the next day or two she would think . . . think seriously. And when she had a good plan, she would act. She would act so that the whole of Barhampton, the whole of Yorkshire – *of Britain* – would be amazed. And this time she wouldn't seem to court publicity by alerting the press in advance: that would cheapen her action, which would be noble and bold.

Two nights later, when the moon was waning but still bright in the sky of early July, she acted.

And it ended in near tragedy.

Chapter Twelve

A security guard on his midnight round first sensed that something was afoot. Walking inside the perimeter of the fence that walled off the big site to the River Barr, he found a narrow opening where two pieces of hoarding met.

Too narrow for anyone except a kid, he thought. He reflected that kids liked to get on the site to treat it as an adventure playground. Yet that was only in daylight – this was the middle of a July night when kids would be home in bed.

All the same, better just to take a glance around.

He did so by putting his head and shoulders through the opening. He saw a bicycle propped against the fence.

Ruddy kids, he groaned to himself. You never knew what they'd get up to. Who was this one, and what did he want at this time of night? You had to bear in mind that pilfering was rife on any building site – hence the security patrol which he shared on this site with another man throughout the hours when construction wasn't taking place.

Pilfering . . . sometimes it amounted to outright theft. Forklift trucks were a favourite item – thieves would get on site and simply drive them away to some prearranged hiding-place. In a couple of days a forklift truck could be on a ship headed for the Far East.

Bricks, piping, sheet insulation, hoists, scaffolding – they simply walked off any section left unguarded. And you couldn't ignore the fact that kids were often sent to spy out the land for some would-be looter.

But whatever this one was here for, he had to be found, because the big area neighbouring the river was full of traps and hazards. The demolition of the old woollen mills was incomplete so there were a lot of pitfalls, especially in the dark.

The site was lit by lamps on forty-foot poles, giving quite good illumination for a quick look round. There were also security cameras, because after the attack on the track excavator by that daft lass, everybody had got a bit edgy and big vehicles like that were very valuable. Illumination and surveillance – but where there were lamps there were also shadows, so it might not be easy to find this rascal.

Sighing to himself, the guard spoke into his two-way radio. 'Barr Mill One to Control, over.'

151

'Control here. Something wrong, Joe?'

'Might not be much. There's a gap been pulled in the perimeter on Area 4, opposite the cement-mixer that was in use today – I think it's Wellbrow's.'

'You're there now?'

'Yeh, and there's a bike parked against the fence—'

'Motorbike?'

'Nay, a push-bike, so it's probably just some kid. Should I go and look for him myself or will you send somebody?'

'I'm just looking for you on the cameras . . .'

'I'm not in vision, I dare say – hang on, I'll move to my right. Can you see me now, Martin?'

'Gotcha. Wait on, I'll pan either way – nope, nothing to see – d'you reckon it's just one, or are there likely to be a lot of them?'

'Can't hear anything, Martin – if there were more than one they'd be calling each other mebbe—'

'Unless they're carrying off summat. What's nearby that they could take? Stop there, I'll look at the manifest. Nay, unless they're carting off sacks of cement there, I dunno what they could be after.'

'I'll go and take a look around, shall I?'

'Righto. Keep talking to me, Joe.'

'Will do.' Joe hefted his heavy torch, switched it on, and began a quiet walk between the piles of equipment and materials.

'I'm going north along the path that Wellbrow's gang was cementing this morning, towards the main demolition site. Nothing to see on the stack of cement bags. There's the cement-mixer. Nobody there. Two wheelbarrows . . . Gibson's dump-truck – hang on, I'll just check it's safely locked – yeh, locked, cab's empty.'

'I see you now, Joe,' Martin intoned, as he had been taught to do when learning the use of the surveillance equipment. 'You're on Camera 5, and you're lit up by the tungsten in Group 5 standards. Now you're going off-screen – heading north, I now have you on Camera 6 – hey up!'

'What?' barked Joe, scared by the sudden excitement in Control's tone. Control was supposed to be very calm and organised at all times.

'I see something – movement – something white, on the wall of Building 2.'

Building 2 was one of the old mills, partially demolished. Camera 6 was mounted on a pole almost alongside, because this was an area where keen fishermen tried to slip through to the riverbank. The River Barr was a good place for anglers now that the mills had ceased to pollute its waters, but for the time being access to it was limited by the construction sites for the new Town Centre.

The security men were quite used to catching a man with a rod and a folding stool as he tried to get to some favourite spot. But to have someone on the wall of the old building was much more serious. Because the wall was unsafe.

The old North Barr Mill had been famous in its day for thick checked woollens for gentlemen's overcoats. Designed and built in the 1860s by an ancestor of Daniel Dayton, it had been a grandiose structure with turrets at each of its four corners. Because of the rearrangement of building schedules caused by the hiatus at Royal Terrace, work had been called off on the old North Barr, now Building 2 on the work plans. The wrecking ball had done its work on three sides but the back-hoe had never started work on removing the rubble.

So for an intruder it was a relatively easy climb up the slopes of old brick towards the turret on the south-east corner – so long as he was light-footed and lightweight, so as not to disturb the shifting surface. The four-sided tower that graced the wall still had window apertures and in one of the openings part of the wooden window frame still survived.

As far as Joe could make out, it was towards this that the lad was heading. 'Hey, you! Stop there!' he shouted.

The figure continued on its way, although there had been a momentary pause at the sound of his voice. In his radio, Control was barking orders at Joe: 'Tell him to get off that – it's not safe. Get him down, Joe!' Then there was a break. 'I'm zooming in on him – oh! Oh, my God!'

'What?' demanded Joe, panicking. 'What?'

'It's never a lad, it's a lass!'

'What?'

'I can see her – long hair, dangly earrings . . .'

'But lads wear—'

'Joe, it's a lass – I'll send some help – we've got to get her off that wall.'

For the lass had reached the wall that was still standing, had climbed from the rubble to its top, and was tightrope-walking along its jagged surface towards the turret.

Allie's plan had taken her two days to think out. She had walked around the centre of Barhampton surveying the building sites for a good vantage point. This high wall of the old North Barr Mill had looked inviting, and the window frame that still existed was just the place for her banner.

She had concocted the banner by taking a white single-bed sheet from the linen cupboard. Spread on the garage floor, it had given her a big surface. With the tin of black paint and a wide paintbrush bought out of her pocket money, she had written her slogan on it in three rows of capitals: *SAVE BEDELLS HOUSE!*

She had tied lengths of strong cord, borrowed from Daddy's gardening materials, on each corner. She intended to tie it to what remained of the window frame of the turret.

But when she got on the demolition site she found it a spookier place than she'd expected. She knew by observation that the security lights on their tall poles came on at dusk, so she'd expected to find the site lit up like a football pitch for an evening game. But the illumination wasn't as strong as she'd thought, and there were shadowy vales between the mounds of material and equipment. Big vehicles loomed like dragons in the dimness.

She found herself faltering. Perhaps it would be a good idea to go back to the gap in the fence and just cycle home. But then she heard the immortal line from *Macbeth*, which she hoped one day to utter on stage, echo inside her head: 'Infirm of purpose! Give me the dagger!'

Her banner was folded and tied by its cords round her middle, under the loose muslin top. She pressed her hand against it for reassurance. Tomorrow at dawn it would be hanging from the turret, drawing the eyes of all the morning rush-hour travellers. Everyone would be amazed, asking each other who had dared do such a deed. She would let half the day go by while everyone wondered – and then she would step forward. 'I did it,' she would say, 'I want the people of Barhampton to remember their heritage!' Or no, perhaps she might say, 'I did it to remind you of a great actress,' because that way she could go on to say how she intended to follow in the footsteps of Arabella Bedells.

By this time she had stepped lightly along the jagged top of the wall and was at the turret. She hadn't considered how to get inside. It had a door, but the door was on the inner wall of the little square, where a stone staircase used to come up from what had been the top floor of the building. The staircase was gone and the door was out of reach.

She leaned against the tower. The light from the surveillance lamps cast gleams and shadows across the wrecked building. There was no way to get inside the turret to hang her banner from the window.

Unless she clambered up from the main wall on to the roof of the turret? There might be a hole in the roof; she might be able to drop down inside and get to the window. She didn't stop to consider that if the staircase to the turret was gone, so perhaps the floor might have fallen away.

Voices were calling to her. She paid no heed. She mustn't let them distract her. It was tricky here. To get up on the canopy of the turret she must pile a few bricks on the surface of the uneven wall so as to act as a staircase – two steps made of bricks, perhaps three, and then she'd be able to see if there was a hole in the roof.

'Come down, miss – it's not safe! Oy, d'ye hear me? Them bricks will cave in! Miss! The building's unsafe!'

Control had sent two men to help Joe. One had approached from the north, scrambling across piles of rubble and gaining some height in the process. The second had driven up in a skid steer, a little four-wheel vehicle with a scoop on an arm that could be elevated and lowered. The scoop's arm wasn't long enough to reach the turret but it was the nearest easily manipulated vehicle.

Allie had made her makeshift staircase. The roof of the turret was now at her eye level. She could see there was no hole in it. But since it was intact, she could clamber up on to it, drape her banner over the edge. She would weight it down with old bricks. True, it would flap in the wind, but that might be more dramatic. People would have to pause to read the message.

'Lass, get down off that turret!' yelled Joe, bursting his lungs to make her hear. 'You'll fall—'

'I'm coming to get you,' shouted the driver of the scoop, leaning out of his cab and waving at her.

On Joe's radio Control was begging: 'Get her down, for God's sake!'

'I'm trying, I'm trying!' groaned Joe. And, yelling, 'Come down, come down, it's all as weak as water!'

He saw the girl on the turret roof raise her hand in a brief gesture. In the slanted light, it was difficult to make out exactly what she was doing. Perhaps it meant she understood what they were shouting at her. Her banner was draped down from the roof now, but impossible to read.

A slithering, scraping sound. Stone and brick grating on each other. The girl screamed. The turret swayed. The man clambering up the pile of rubble gave a shout of alarm and felt himself slipping backwards.

'Help!' shouted Joe. Then, recalling that Control couldn't hear if he didn't switch to Send, he pressed the button and wailed, 'Call an ambulance, Martin—'

The words were drowned in the sound of the collapse. The turret tilted outwards, the one remaining wall of old North Barr Mill seemed to bulge and bend, then almost in one piece it keeled over, taking security lights and cameras with it.

Martin at the control panel didn't need to be told what had happened. He swung round in his swivel chair and pressed the button that connected him immediately with the Ambulance Service. 'Wall collapsed at Building 2 on Riverside Site, Area 4 on your plan – urgent request – someone was on the wall – quick, quick!'

'North Barr Mill, right, understood. Entrance point 2A – is that okay?'

'Hurry, hurry,' grunted Control, and switched off.

He grabbed up his phone to call the Emergency Team. On a big construction site, major accidents were not uncommon. Heavy vehicles could go out of control or overturn, piles of material could topple, scaffolding could collapse. At any time, four trained First Aiders were on call. The leader of the Emergency Team said he and his gang would be there in ten minutes.

By that time the ambulance had arrived at Entrance 2A. Its pulsing light glowed on the gates that had been thrown open to let the team through, but the vehicle could go no further; access was limited by lack of a wide enough pathway to the wall. The ambulance team dropped out of the vehicle, ran towards the sound of men's voices.

In the shaft of the scoop's headlights, Joe and the scoop-driver were tearing at the rubble with their hands. The Emergency Team, equipped with lighting equipment and a heat sensor, took over. They could hear nothing, but the sensor told them the girl was under a pile of wreckage. After a moment they uncovered a corner of the white sheet which had been her banner, and one white trainer. The ambulance men, stretcher and resuscitator at the ready, stood by.

The six men, working with exquisite care, soon uncovered the girl's head and shoulders. The leader of the First Aid team knelt over her, feeling her neck for a pulse.

'Yeh,' he said, 'she's still with us. But that's a bad position.' He turned to the ambulance team. 'Look at her foot – that leg must be broken.'

'Right, you work at getting the rest of her out. We'll take over resuscitation.'

The sirens of the ambulance and police had brought the newsmen. They were kept at the outer perimeter of the site, shouting for information, demanding to be let in. The flashing lights of the ambulance outlined their avid faces. Anything to do with the new Town Centre was big news in the district. They were determined to get a story.

By and by the police herded them aside. The ambulance men came out wheeling the stretcher. 'Who is it? Who is it?' shouted the reporters. One even tried to push forward to peer at the face of the patient.

'We don't know, she's got no identification.'

'She? It's a woman?'

'It's a little lass,' said one of the Emergency Team gruffly. 'And why her mother and father let her out at this time of night I'll never know.'

When the ambulance had gone the reporters cross-questioned the rescuers. Who was the girl? Describe her – oh, that sounded like . . . And within minutes Allie Pembury's name was being bandied about. When one of the policemen came out with the banner folded over his arm, some of the letters painted on it were visible – enough for the quick-witted to know that one of the words was *BEDELLS*. 'It's her all right,' the reporters agreed among themselves, and began to talk into their mobile phones.

Billy Wellbrow was alerted to the fact that there had been a bad accident on one of his sites. Swearing and fuming at being woken in the wee small hours, he telephoned the police for confirmation. Yes, a girl with a banner . . . Yes, it was Allison Pembury; they had rung her father to see if she was at home in bed and of course she wasn't. The father was at the hospital now, waiting to hear . . . Yes, serious injuries, so far as they knew . . .

Wellbrow said all the worst words he knew to relieve his feelings

156

about the Pemburys, father and daughter. Then he rang Daniel Dayton.

'I know,' said Daniel. 'I already got the news from the Barhampton police. I've got a friend or two on the force.'

'What are you going to do?'

'Do? Nothing. What is there to do?'

'Pray?' Wellbrow suggested. 'Pray she doesn't die.'

'Oh, shut up and go back to bed,' growled Daniel. 'It's after three in the morning.'

But he himself didn't do so. He went downstairs to make himself a cup of tea. By and by Mary came down looking for him. 'Was it that phone call, dear?' She looked at him, sitting hunched over a mug at the kitchen table. 'Something bad?'

'Couldn't be worse. That damned Pembury girl again.'

'At this time of night?' she gasped, astonished. 'What's she done now?'

'Brought a building down on top of herself, that's what.'

'Daniel!'

'Aye, you may well cry out! She's badly off, I hear – in surgery now and a long wait before we hear what's what.'

Mary sat down beside him. 'Poor lass,' she sighed.

'Poor lass? Idiot child! What the devil did she think she was at, clambering about on a demolition site at one o'clock in the morning? Well, in fact I know what – she was going to put up a banner.'

'A banner!'

'I tell you, lass, she's a great fool, alive or dead—'

'Daniel! There's no idea that she's going to die?'

'I don't know, Mary. I'm waiting to hear.'

'We'll go to the hospital,' Mary said, springing to her feet. 'We can be there in—'

'We'll do no such thing! If we go there and hover about, it looks as if we think we're in some way responsible. And we're *not*! There's a fence all round the site plastered with boards saying DANGER KEEP OUT! Round the North Barr Mill there are saw-horses with special warning notices and there are instructions to workmen to wear hard hats—'

'But in the dark, perhaps she couldn't see them.'

'Mary, the place is lit up like Blackpool in December! All-night lighting, security cameras – I tell you it's not our fault!'

His wife stood hesitating. Then, because she could see that he needed to talk, she set about pouring herself a cup of tea from the too-strong brew her husband had made. She sat down again, but this time opposite so that she could see his face. He was much paler than usual, and his sleep-tousled hair gave him the look of an unhappy but elderly schoolboy.

'What's worrying you,' she enquired, 'if all the security precautions were all right?'

157

'Anything to do with that girl is bad news,' he grunted. 'And even if we're as innocent as lambs, we're going to be blamed, somehow. *She'll* be praised for her courage and daring, and we'll be hauled over the coals for not doing enough to keep her from hurting herself.' Or killing herself, was his thought – but he didn't utter it.

'Have you rung Iris Weston?'

'She's not due in York again until Saturday.'

'Well, ring her in London, then. You know she can do all the contacting from there – better, perhaps, than from here. If it's going to turn out a problem for you, hadn't you better put her in the know?'

'I suppose so,' he groaned. He rose unwillingly. 'I'll kill Josh Pembury next time I see him,' he said between his teeth. 'What the devil does he mean, letting his daughter out at night to risk her life?'

Allie Pembury was on the critical list at Barhampton Hospital for almost a week. No one but her father was allowed to see her. He was besieged every time he left the hospital by reporters demanding to know the extent of her injuries, whether she had spoken to him, what she had said. A favourite question was: 'How do you feel about what's happened?' The correct answer would have been, 'Distraught,' but he always pushed past them in stunned silence.

Bewildered hospital personnel were badgered for information. Finally Allie's surgeon appeared on the front steps to make a prepared statement.

'Allie Pembury is now making progress and her condition is not life-threatening. She suffered a concussion but we are satisfied that the cranium is intact. Her injuries are considerable, consisting of fractures to the ribcage and extremities, which will need further surgery. However, in due course we believe that modern surgical processes will restore full use of her limbs.'

Which the newspapers interpreted as meaning Allie had severe fractures which might leave her walking with a stick.

Visiting was restricted. Only her father and a woman police officer were allowed at first and then, by arrangement, one television reporter who was to make his interview available to the rest of the media.

At the outset it looked promising – the room filled with flowers, the slight figure in the bed with the cage protecting broken ribs and limbs, the equipment ranged alongside in case of need. But it proved unrewarding. As a result of the concussion, Allie couldn't remember what had happened on the construction site.

The most poignant moment was when she was asked what she thought about her future. The TV camera dwelt on her eyes as they filled with tears. 'I wanted to be an actress,' she said brokenly, 'but if I can't walk . . .'

Guilt overwhelmed everyone who had been in any way connected with the series of events that had led to this hospital bed.

'I feel I didn't take her seriously enough,' Bethany told Peter Lambot. 'I kept thinking of her as a silly kid. I never understood how deeply she felt things.'

Peter sighed. 'I know what you mean. I think I probably encouraged her in some of her antics – because it was such good publicity on the side of the Protection Group. But if I'd ever thought it would lead to this . . .'

'And what makes it worse is that my father hardly seems to care. His only concern is that the contractors shouldn't be sued for negligence—'

'Well, that's being looked at now. The police are still questioning the security people. Of course it's terribly difficult – when the wall came down it changed everything – the look of the site, the placing of the warning notices, everything.'

'It's one of Billy Wellbrow's sites. He has the contract to move the rubble away from most of the sites. He would have been responsible for moving the remains of the three walls that had already been demolished. But when we had to re-schedule things so as to work around Royal Terrace, he had to call his men off the North Barr Mill – I wish I hadn't let that happen; we could just as easily have finished at the mill and gone on afterwards, but at the time . . .'

'None of us could have known that Allie would take it into her head to climb up that slope of rubble on to the wall that was still standing.'

'I know, I know, but I keep thinking . . . And McGuire is the same, he keeps saying that if only he'd used that old track demolition vehicle to knock down that last wall before he decided the machine should go for scrap . . .'

'The *Gazette* is being quite sympathetic to the contractors – I mean, it isn't suggesting they're to blame—'

'But that's the local paper, Peter. The editor doesn't want to be on bad terms with the local bigwigs. I hear the building magazines are going to run a series about safety on building sites . . . Almost as if they feel we weren't doing enough. My father's furious about it.'

'I don't understand why he's taking it so personally. He's not a contractor, *he's* not being blamed.'

'You don't know him, Peter. *Dayton's* is responsible for the whole scheme. He sees himself as . . . sort of Napoleon, directing everything from above. So if anything goes wrong he wants it sorted *immediately*. He's got Iris Weston at work on the phone almost twenty-four hours a day, trying to chat up her friends on the nationals to get sympathetic coverage.'

They were in the car park of the old Town Hall, after a particularly distressing meeting of the Steering Committee. Its Chairman, Cyril Ollerton, had been quite unable to keep control. Accusations and counter-accusations had been shouted across the table, little angry conversations had broken out between members without respect to the

159

Chair, Peter had been harangued about the damage done by the Royal Terrace Protection Group and threatened with a lawsuit. As an example of civilised discussion it would have been rated at zero.

They paused by Peter's ruby-red Volvo. It gleamed in the July sunlight, hot to the touch as he eased open the passenger door. 'Need a lift anywhere?' he asked.

'No, thanks, I've got the jeep. I'm going over to the old cinema site.'

'Bethany, it's Saturday. Can't you take some time off and relax?'

'But everything's been put at sixes and sevens by the accident – we're inspecting safety procedures on all sites—'

'Forget it all! That's what's wrong with us – we're all too close to the problem, pressed up against it like kids against an ice-cream van. Let's take the weekend off!'

'And do what?'

'It's a lovely day, it's going to be the same tomorrow – let's go up into the Dales and look at the scenery, fill our lungs with the scent of the gorse. Or we could go to the sea – somewhere quiet, watch the sea-birds, go for a sail in a hired boat . . . What do you say?'

She stood listening to his voice, now so well-known that she caught every nuance. Her gaze was on the other cars in the car park but she could imagine his narrow, rather serious face alight with the force of his words.

If she agreed, it meant more than a weekend of relaxation from the worries of Barhampton. If she agreed, it was a commitment.

They had been on the brink of this decision for weeks now, edging towards the moment when they would acknowledge they were in love. From what seemed to be opposite sides of a controversy they had met in a friendship growing deeper as they understood how much they had in common.

She admired him because he was quick and clever, and had integrity. She liked him because he wanted what she wanted, harmony between the warring cliques of Barhampton, good manners in negotiation, decency, the general good of the community. She was growing to love him because he pleased her, seemed to sense her thoughts, understood and cared for her.

And beyond that there was the sexual attraction, the wish to lie beside him in the first moments of intimacy, to learn his body and to share his passion. They had kissed from time to time – in leave-taking or greeting, briefly, almost in passing. Yet each time there had been that tremor of longing. She knew he felt it too.

A little silence had developed between them after his words. She said with a casual firmness that masked her real feelings: 'The Dales would be nice.'

'Ribblesdale? Scannsdale? There's a nice little inn at Scannsdale, by the river . . . I've stayed there for the fishing.'

'Think they could put us up at such short notice?'

'Soon find out,' he said, and took out his mobile phone and a pocket address book. Within seconds he was talking to the owner of the Waterside Inn. He smiled as he folded away the phone. 'All fixed. Dinner for two at eight tonight. Shall we use my car or yours?'

Their glance travelled to her mud-stained Suzuki. 'I think we'll take yours,' she laughed. 'We don't want to give the wrong impression.'

The impression they gave when they arrived that evening at the inn was of a couple very much in love. The owner had been prepared to greet Peter Lambot with information about the fishing, but curbed his tongue. The chambermaid showed them to their room; he sent up the menu so that they could consult about their meal, and while he waited to hear their choice he asked his wife to set them a table in an alcove by a window overlooking the stream.

'Candles, dear,' he told her, 'and one of your nice little flower arrangements.'

'Ah, like that, is it?' she said with a smile.

Very much like that. Dreamlike, softly touched with magic, the time went by. They could never afterwards remember what they ate. The murmur of voices from the few other diners scarcely reached them. The roses on the table spread a gentle perfume more heady to them than any of the precious essences of the Orient. At last, hand in hand, they went upstairs to the starlit room.

And to the glory that awaited them.

Chapter Thirteen

Allie Pembury lay in her hospital bed, very depressed.

Everyone was being very sweet to her. The hospital staff took a special interest in her, her father spent almost all his time with her, flowers and fruit arrived every day. In all her life she'd never had so much attention. Yet she was dispirited beyond words. At any moment her eyes would fill with tears, which spilled down her pale cheeks unchecked. Nurses would say kindly a 'tut-tut' and try to cheer her up.

What was there to be cheerful about? No matter that the doctors and surgeons spoke hopefully about orthopaedics and physiotherapy, she sensed that a long and painful programme of treatment lay ahead.

Months. Perhaps years. And during that time, what about her career? When the multiple fractures of her legs had mended, when she could walk again, what would she look like? Something from *The Hunchback of Notre Dame*?

When she was allowed to look in a mirror, she was horrified at her appearance. Her beautiful long hair had been hacked about so that dressings could be applied to her scalp wounds. She'd had blue and yellow bruises on her face. Her eyes seemed to have sunk back into her head.

After a couple of weeks her face wasn't so distressing to look at. The bruises faded, the dressings were removed and her hair was arranged so that the shaven portions weren't visible. The broken ribs began to mend, so that the pain in her chest was less severe.

But her legs . . . The first repairs had been attempted. Her legs were now supposedly mending, strapped up to equipment, the surgeons looking at X-rays and assuring her that in the end all would be well.

'I'll be able to walk?'

'Of course, of course!'

'I won't have a limp?' she asked again and again.

'The big thing is to get the bones to mend, my dear. It's not going to be quick, you've got fractures of the tibia and fibula of both legs. Then there's damage to the patella on the right leg. That's where the problems might emerge, Allie; a kneecap is a delicate piece of engineering. First let's get the long bones to heal, and we won't do that by worrying and fretting, now will we?'

In her low spirits she took that cheeriness to mean that she wouldn't walk perfectly. And who would want to hire an actress who walked with a stick?

At first, when questioned about the accident, she genuinely couldn't remember what had happened. But as the effects of the concussion receded, memory returned.

However, she didn't want to talk about it. It was enough to say tearfully, 'I don't remember . . .' Then, in the hours when the hospital room was dark and she was supposed to sleep, she went over it and over it in her mind.

She'd wanted to make a big gesture on behalf of old Mrs Bedells and her house. She filtered out of her mind the recollection that she'd also wanted to be in the newspapers again as the champion of Barhampton's literary heritage.

On the demolition site, there had been darkness, scary things in the shadows, scurryings, rats perhaps, but she had bravely carried on with her task. She had been resolute, like Joan of Arc. With the result that she now lay crippled on this bed, her hopes wrecked as well as her body – unless she got the very best treatment, and that would need money because it wasn't only her legs that had been harmed; her voice was weaker because of a deficiency in her breathing – though the doctors said that was temporary, yet who had ever heard of a good actress who couldn't control her voice?

Round and round went her thoughts, and the conclusion she came to was that she would need money to kick-start her life again. And the way to get money was to make Barhampton Town Council pay for what they had done to her, with their grandiose scheme for a Town Centre and the great piles of rubble where they'd knocked things down and huge machines that lurked in the shadows and tottering walls that buried you and broke your bones . . .

Peter Lambot had come to visit her, bringing flowers and a tape for her tape-player of Gielgud reading poetry. It was the mere fact that he was a lawyer that put the idea of a law suit into her mind. When he came again, this time with a basket of fruit from the Royal Terrace Protection Group, she broached the subject.

'Sue the council?' he said, astounded. 'On what grounds?'

'Well, I've got both legs fractured and I had four ribs broken and a concussion! I—'

'But Allie, you were trespassing!'

'But the council should have had proper precautions—'

'There's a great boarded fence all round the site, and notices everywhere saying KEEP OUT. The police went over the ground very thoroughly and are saying there was no negligence on the part of—'

'It was dark, you couldn't see the notices and anyhow where I went in, there weren't any—'

'But the security men were shouting to you that it wasn't safe—'

'No, they weren't—'

'Allie, there were three men from the security patrol and the man in charge of the radio – they all say they called to you to come down.'

'Well, they would say that, wouldn't they?'

Peter sat back on the uncomfortable stackable chair and drew a breath. 'Are you saying they didn't call to you?'

'That's what I'm saying. Or at least I didn't hear them.'

'I see. You were up on the wall, they were below you, one of them having followed your route from the gap in the fence. By the way, did you pull the fence apart?'

'Me?' said Allie. 'How could I pull an opening in a big fence? That gap was there already. I think some truck must have backed into it or something.'

'But you knew the gap was there?'

'Oh yes, of course, I planned it all, you know. I knew there were lights that were supposed to make it easy to walk about on the site after dark. If I'd known,' said Allie, looking sad, 'that the light would be so poor, I'd have taken a torch. But it was dark and spooky and I worked my way to the old mill and climbed up the rubble to the wall – that was quite easy, there was nothing to stop me—'

'No notices? There were notices saying it was a danger area and hard hats had to be worn.'

'If there were, it was too dark to see them, Peter. I just scrambled up the slope and on to the wall, and everything seemed fine until I'd put up my banner – but then everything just collapsed around me.'

'And you didn't hear the men shouting to you to come down?'

'What men? I never saw or heard anybody. The place was deserted.'

'But Allie, there's a regular security patrol—'

'Is that what they say? I bet the men sit in the hut playing cards and listening to pop music.'

'Allie!'

'Well, they're to blame and I want them to pay for it. I want you to sue them for the injuries I've suffered.'

Peter had listened with growing alarm to the tale she was telling. He listened to many people telling him tales of woe in the course of his work so he had learned to tell the truth-teller from the perjurer. He had no doubt Allie Pembury was lying.

And he found it unbearably sad.

'I don't think it would be a good idea, Allie. Cases like that can go on for years, and the wear and tear—'

'Wear and tear!' she cried. 'Don't talk to me about wear and tear! Look at me, trapped in this bed, everything I hoped for washed away in saline drips and blood transfusions, my career down the drain.'

'Your career – Allie – you're still at school—'

'But I was on the verge of big things, Peter – I was, I was! And now because the council was too mean to put up proper lights and notices and things, I've lost it all—'

'The council weren't responsible for the lighting and security, Allie, it was the building contractors—'

'Well, I want to sue them then. I want them to pay for the treatment I'm going to need, the lessons I'll have to take to get back to where I used to be before I was crushed under that wall. Do I have to sign some papers? Will you get started on it and bring me the forms or whatever next time you come?'

He studied her eager face, alight now with vigour and enthusiasm although still pale from ill health. He thought to himself that a law suit might be good medicine – but he couldn't go along with it.

'No, Allie, I don't think you should do it.'

'But I'm instructing you – isn't that what it's called? I'm hiring you, I want you to be my solicitor—'

'No, Allie.'

'What?'

'I refuse to act for you. In the first place a minor can't initiate an action of this sort. And when you think it over you'll know I'm right. You're letting yourself get run away with by your desire for some sort of . . . revenge, I suppose it is . . . I don't know how to give it a name. But you ought to forget the whole thing.'

'I'm not going to forget it! Someone's got to pay for what happened to me—'

'Is that what your father says? Does he agree with all this?'

'Oh, Daddy . . . well, Daddy's still too stunned to take things in . . . I haven't told him my plan yet, but he'll agree. He knows how much it means to me to be well again, to be what I used to be with a great future ahead of me.'

'Allie, the best advice I can give you is to drop this idea. I don't think you have any grounds, and the evidence—'

'Evidence? What evidence? It's only what those stupid men say – who are they, a bunch of uneducated idiots who can't get anything better to do for a living! It's my word against theirs – and of course they're not going to admit *they* were to blame—'

Peter had risen and was now moving towards the door. 'You're not thinking straight, Allie,' he said with regret. 'Speak to your father and I'm sure he'll tell you the same. Without his agreement you can't do anything, and I doubt very much if he'll agree. So concentrate on getting better and stop plotting things like this.'

When the nurse came to check routinely, she found her patient flushed and with a slightly raised temperature. 'Now, what's up?' she asked, kind and concerned. 'You're a bit unsettled – something bothering you?'

'Oh, people are so patronising!' cried Allie. 'They treat me as if I'm an imbecile child!'

'Who, one of your visitors?'

'That stupid solicitor – telling me to think it over – as if I don't know my own mind!'

'That man who was here?'

'Mr Lambot, yes. I was telling him I ought to get compensation for what happened – and he just passed it all off as if I was talking nonsense!'

To the nurse, who was young and to whom Allie was something of a heroine, this was a chance to be of use. 'There are plenty of other solicitors,' she suggested. 'In fact, there's one dealing with a case in Men's Surgical at the moment – road accident, I think he does a lot of that sort of thing.'

'What's his name? Could you ask him to come and see me?'

'We-ell . . .' It occurred to Nurse Wilson that she might be doing something wrong. 'I don't know . . . I mean . . . It's not my place . . .'

Allie quickly understood. A young nurse, in her first year of qualification – she didn't want to bring strangers to Allie's bedside. 'Tell you what,' she said, 'could you get his card from him next time he's here?'

'Oh, that's easy. Mr Spellman in Men's Surgical is sure to have one. I'll ask him for it, okay?'

'Thanks a million,' sighed Allie, and relaxed back among her pillows.

The card was procured that afternoon. Allie asked to have the telephone brought to her bedside so that she could ring the number. Mr Painswicke wasn't available, said his secretary at first, but on asking to leave a message Allie gave her name. The secretary had no difficulty in recognising it, often in the papers these days, and announced that Mr Painswicke had just walked in the door. An appointment for him to visit Allie was quickly arranged. 'I could come by at the evening visiting hour,' he suggested. 'Would that suit?'

'Oh yes, please – the sooner the better.'

So Walter Painswicke called at seven o'clock by arrangement, to meet Miss Pembury with a view to bringing a case of negligence against the contractors responsible for the site at North Barr Mill.

He had no idea what to expect. Allie was known to him through the newspapers and TV. He thought of her as something of a crackpot, and had only skimmed the news items. That she was still a schoolgirl never occurred to him. There was money to be made, and Walter Painswicke was never a man to turn his back on such a chance. Even if the evidence for a court case were slight or inconclusive, the nuisance value of threatening a suit usually brought an offer of settlement – and the sums could be quite substantial.

Allie's version of events soon convinced Painswicke they were on to a winner. He might not actually *believe* her, but that didn't matter.

166

'You deserve compensation, Miss Pembury. A young girl, losing months out of her life in a hospital room, and as for the future – who knows?'

'The doctors say—'

'Yes, yes, everything is going to be put right, of course that's true,' interrupted Painswicke, 'but how long will it take? And you know, your ambitions for the theatre – you'll need special coaching to make up lost ground – it all takes money, of course.'

'Yes, I know that . . . they said I'd have to come back more than once for further surgery, but if I could have a tutor – a voice coach, for instance—'

'Well, let's not go into such detail,' Mr Painswicke said, thinking that this girl was cuckoo. But it was his experience that people began to lose touch with reality where money was concerned. However, the chances of settling out of court were quite good: he'd persuade the contractors that to be mean to this popular girl would make them look very bad indeed, which would probably open the pocket books in short order.

Peter Lambot had imagined that he'd talked Allie Pembury out of her idea of suing the contractors. Not so. He learned on the legal grapevine about a week later that Allie had hired Walt Painswicke, a well-known ambulance-chaser, to handle the case.

'Is he a good lawyer?' asked Bethany when he told her.

'Good? Well, he gets a lot of cases, causes a lot of disturbance, and generally settles out of court for . . . well, not very large sums, in some cases, but he makes money. Accidents and industrial injury are his field.'

'I suppose you could say this is a case of industrial injury,' mused Bethany. 'But Allie isn't an employee, that's the difference. If you look at it realistically, she was a trespasser – but of course the contractor has a duty to make the site safe even for a trespasser.'

'Yes.'

'And the site *was* safe, Peter. We tightened up security after that business of the attack on the track excavator.'

'Yes.'

'What's the matter?' She was studying his frowning features.

'She tried to hire me to take the case,' he said. 'Because I was the only solicitor she knew at the time, of course. I said no, naturally.'

'Because it would have been so awkward?'

'Because she's prepared to lie her head off if it comes to court,' he said. 'She says the lighting was poor, she couldn't see any warning signs, the men didn't call to her to come down, and if they say they did they're lying.'

'Oh, Peter!'

'And what makes it worse is that when the wall collapsed, it brought down the security cameras and lights nearest the spot, so there's no way to disprove what she says.'

167

They were in Peter's flat, where she spent a lot of time these days. It was more spacious than hers, in a modern building about ten minutes' drive out of the town. In the course of the three weeks that had passed since they went to Scannsdale, she'd transferred some of her belongings so that if she stayed overnight, it was easy to dress and be ready for work next morning.

By unspoken consent they had told no one of the change in their relationship. But they weren't treating it as a guilty secret; in time they knew it could become common knowledge. There would be problems, that was undeniable. They would face them when they must, but in the meantime they wanted to enjoy the first pleasures of being in love without the reproaches of their colleagues.

They were sitting now in Peter's living room, an airy room with some furniture that Bethany recognised as by a contemporary Danish designer. Charlie Parker was discoursing sweet music from the stereo system. It was a thundery Sunday morning in early August and they were waiting for the weather to clear so they could go for a walk on the moors, followed by brunch at a recommended hotel. Bethany reflected that if things had been as they used to, she'd have been driving to York now for Sunday lunch with her parents. It was a relief not to think about her father – he would be so furious when he heard of the claim for damages.

Thinking about her own father made her think about Allie's. 'Does Josh go along with all this?' she enquired.

Peter shrugged. 'I don't know. I suggested to her that she ought to talk to him about her plan to sue, but she's so unpredictable.'

'Perhaps he doesn't even know.'

'Oh, I doubt that. Painswicke wouldn't take on a client who's under age and has a legal guardian . . . or would he? Or does he even know she's only sixteen?'

The weather cleared up, they went out for their walk and put all thoughts of Allie Pembury and her litigation behind them. But Iris Weston had no such luck. The gossip about Painswicke had reached her by means of Bigsby, the solicitor who was head of Barhampton council's Legal Department. At first Bigsby thought nothing of the story, but mentioned it almost jokingly in passing to the Publicity Officer. To his surprise Iris was immediately alarmed.

'Oh Lord! That's *all* we need!'

'What? Are you alarmed by it? I assure you, it must be a joke. Painswicke is a scavenger when it comes to finding clients; he could never have come into contact with the child. I'm sure it's all nonsense.'

'You don't know that kid,' moaned Iris. 'She's caused us more trouble than any hundred other people put together! I'll tell you this – if it's true and that idiot Pembury has let her begin a suit against us, I want him sacked!'

'What good would that do?' Bigsby enquired, moved by her alarm to take it seriously. 'Besides, she can't do anything unless her father lets her. She's a minor, she can't sign legal papers.'

'Right. *He's* got to be told to tell *her* to drop it. You must speak to him at once.'

'I'll have to consult the council.'

'Don't waste time on that. You're empowered to act on their behalf, surely? I tell you, Raymond, if this gets out, we're in trouble. She's got to be stopped before she starts.'

She was too late. Jeff Jones of the *Barhampton Gazette* had heard the tale and had hurried to Painswicke for verification. From him he got a cautious, 'Well, we are discussing the matter with a view to taking action.' The *Gazette* had it in print on Tuesday morning.

Josh Pembury was called before the Steering Committee. He'd taken compassionate leave when his daughter's condition was so critical, and in addition some unpaid leave. But now when she seemed to be taking more interest in life he was reassured enough to return to work – and to face the questions about her actions.

'What was she doing out at that hour of night?' demanded Cyril Ollerton, Chairman of Steerco. 'A sixteen-year-old girl, roaming about—'

'Excuse me, Mr Chairman,' intervened Alan Singleton, anxious to be fair. 'Most sixteen-year-old girls can be out and about after midnight, at parties and discos and—'

'But this lass weren't at a party,' growled Billy Wellbrow, 'unless you think of a wrecking party!'

'Now, gentlemen, let's be reasonable about this,' Mr Bigsby the lawyer said. 'We must agree that Miss Pembury had no intention of wrecking anything when she set out. Her only ambition was to drape her banner from a high point. Am I right, Mr Pembury?'

'Yes, of course, and that's hardly a criminal offence—'

'It may not be criminal but it's highly embarrassing when the papers make a field day out of the fact that her father's a council employee,' Iris Weston said tartly.

'Embarrassing! Is that the main emotion you feel?' Josh cried, stung by her tone. 'My daughter could have been killed!'

'Yes, she could,' Wellbrow rejoined, 'and if she had, it would have been her own fault—'

'Don't you dare say that! If the site had had proper notices posted—'

'That site was stuck with notices like postage stamps on a parcel,' shouted Wellbrow. 'Anyone working on it will bear witness—'

'My daughter said it was too dark to see them—'

'And that's a lie too, because the place is lit up at night—'

'My daughter doesn't lie,' cried Josh. 'Allie is incapable of telling a lie.'

'Josh, calm down,' said Bethany. 'Please – everybody – calm down. We'll get nowhere if we—'

'Where exactly do we want to get to?' enquired her father, who these days attended all Steerco meetings as if invited. 'Is there a resolution before the Committee? If not, I move that Joshua Pembury be suspended from membership of the Steering Committee.'

'On what grounds?' Bethany asked. 'Are you saying that because his daughter trespassed on one of our demolition sites we're going to—'

'Josh is a continual source of embarrassment to this Committee because of Allie's actions,' Iris cut in. 'Every time she goes public, there's work for me to do repairing the damage.'

'But suspending Josh from the Committee isn't going to stop Allie.'

'Nay, come on,' said the Chairman, 'the lass is in hospital. She won't be doing us any harm for the foreseeable—'

'On no? So what about this rumour that she's preparing to sue the demolition contractors?'

'Oh, that was only a wild rumour in the *Gazette*,' said Ollerton.

'It was, was it? Then who's this Painswicke she's been talking to?'

'Well, he's a lawyer, of course, we know that—'

'And she's saying she'll bring an action for half a million in damages—'

'That's not true,' Josh intervened. 'No reporter from the *Gazette* has spoken to Allie – they made that up.'

'But she has been speaking to Painswicke?'

'Well, yes.'

'And she's going to bring a suit against us?'

'Billy,' sighed Bethany, 'use your brains. A sixteen-year-old girl can't bring a suit. Allie Pembury is a minor. Unless her father takes action on her behalf, Mr Painswicke is talking nonsense. And Josh—' she turned coaxingly to her friend – 'you're not going to sign anything that would cause trouble to the contractors, now are you?'

'But she's been injured – perhaps crippled – through negligence.'

'Now we'll have no more of that!' declared Daniel Dayton, much too loud. 'There's no negligence on any of our sites! I won't have you talking like that – it's disloyal—'

'I have to be loyal to my little girl,' Josh said in stubborn support to Allie. 'She may have been misguided but she had a good intention – she wanted to hang up a banner – and as a result she's lying in a hospital bed with her legs smashed up.'

'Mr Pembury,' said Raymond Bigsby with quiet formality, 'I think the Steering Committee has a right to your loyalty too. We must ask you to make a statement saying that Mr Painswicke has *not* been retained by you on behalf of your daughter to bring an action against the demolition firms.' He paused. 'I must underline how important this is. I do not see how Barhampton could continue to employ a council officer who was suing its contractors on behalf of his child. The conflict of interest would be impossible.'

There was a long silence. Everyone round the mahogany table stared at Josh, with some enmity, some with disdain, and, on Bethany's part, with pity.

Josh said at length, 'You'll fire me if I go along with Painswicke – is that it?'

Cyril Ollerton cleared his throat. 'I think the council would take a serious view if you decided to sue the contractors. A very serious view.'

'Perhaps we could break for coffee now,' suggested Bigsby, anxious to get Josh aside and have a word with him.

'Nay, I want a yes or no from him now!' shouted Wellbrow. 'I'm not going to stand around drinking coffee with a man who's prepared to blacken my name!'

Everyone sat rigid, shocked by the unbridled rage in Wellbrow's voice.

Josh moved uneasily in his chair. His shoulders sagged. He needed his job; he'd moved to Barhampton to start afresh for Allie's sake, and the money from the sale of his old house had been used up buying the cottage and renovating it. His savings weren't large – he spent a lot on his hobby of raising sapling trees, and Allie herself got through a lot in clothes and lessons at acting class and voice production and so on.

So at lengthy he said, 'All right. I'll tell Painswicke it's all off.'

'You'll make a statement?' insisted Iris Weston.

'I'll tell Jeff Jones he got it wrong.'

'That won't be quite enough. I'd like a retraction of the charge that there were ever any grounds for a case against—'

'Come on, Iris,' Alan Singleton broke in, 'don't be so hard on Josh. Surely it's enough if he just sends Painswicke packing.'

'I'm certainly not going to make any statement that implies my daughter's been telling lies!'

'No, of course not, Josh. Come on, Iris – come on, everybody – it's surely enough if he just says Painswicke got a bit carried away and he isn't hiring him.' Alan was making soothing motions with his hands, and after a moment's consideration Iris began to nod. Experience had taught her that it was better not to press too hard. She would get Josh to write a few words; she would edit them, and when she issued the statement she would by her own manner tell her friends on the newspapers that Allie had been quite in the wrong.

Slowly the tension round the table relaxed. The meeting took its coffee break. Mr Bigsby, ever vigilant, stayed at Josh Pembury's elbow. 'Perhaps it would be a good idea to telephone Mr Painswicke now,' he suggested. 'So that when we resume, the Steering Committee can be told the matter is behind us.'

'Well . . . all right . . .' Josh searched in his pockets for the card with the lawyer's telephone number and, having found it, went to a wall phone in the Council Chamber. Bigsby hovered near enough to hear Josh's end of the conversation. He was nodding in satisfaction as Josh hung up.

But he had reckoned without Walter Painswicke's instinct for publicity. He too decided to make a statement to the press, and did so by telephoning an acquaintance on one of the tabloids.

'Yes, it's true Pembury has decided not to go on . . . Well, that's what I'd like to know . . . You have to remember he's *employed* by the council who hired those contractors. "Intimidated" . . . well, that's a word I wouldn't care to use for fear of being charged with slander but . . . yes, I think it's odd . . . more than odd.'

'Let's get this clear, Walter,' said his acquaintance. 'Off the record. Are you saying the council has put the screws on Pembury?'

'I'm just wondering what kind of a deal has been done behind the scenes,' Painswicke said, lowering his voice so that it conveyed both suspicion and sorrow. 'That poor child is being deprived of her rights. Her life has been ruined – doesn't anybody care?'

The journalist cared – he had a good sob story and his editor decided to run with it. He actually used Painswicke's question as a headline: DOESN'T ANYBODY CARE?

The month was August and there were no Parliamentary rows or big crimes to amuse the newspapers. They caught up the story of Allie Pembury and the injuries she'd undergone during her valorous attempt to help preserve Barhampton's claims to literary fame. The hospital refused to let her be interviewed so of course they went after her father.

Josh, ever unhandy with words and feeling aggrieved at his treatment, was trapped on the steps of the hospital as he came out from a visit with his daughter. Allie had been weepy and vexed at hearing he had sent Mr Painswicke away. He couldn't help himself – he had to lash out at somebody.

'Of course the Steering Committee persuaded me to change my mind,' he said. 'You wouldn't believe what goes on there! They'd persuade you black was white!' He blundered on. 'It's nothing but bickering and wrangling and trying to pinch pennies so that Bethany has to fight for her plans—'

'Bethany – that's Bethany Dayton, of *Dayton & Daughter*?'

'Yes, the architect – she's the only one who really cares about people – she cares about Allie and she cares about the people of Barhampton – she wants them to have a beautiful Town Centre. The rest are only interested in doing well out of it.'

'But her father, Daniel Dayton – he's a well-known architect too – surely he—'

'She has to fight him every inch of the way, I can tell you! Concrete towers – that's what *he* thinks of as town planning! And the contractors would go along with anything that would save them money.'

'But surely not to the detriment of good construction, good safety practice?'

Josh was brought up short. He tried to recall what he had been saying. The previous day in order to save his job he had agreed to give up hiring Painswicke. Was he now endangering it by his unguarded remarks?

'No,' he said slowly. 'I believe the work on the new Town Centre is being carried out to a high standard because Bethany Dayton is supervising it day by day. I think the new Town Centre will be a credit to Barhampton when it's finished. But,' he added bitterly, 'it will have cost a lot in suffering to my poor little girl.'

The reporters loved it. 'MY POOR LITTLE GIRL,' cried the headlines.

'Right,' said Daniel Dayton to Cyril Ollerton. 'He's fired.'

Chapter Fourteen

Iris Weston had learned in the course of her successful career that knowledge was power. One of her problems with the situation in Barhampton was that she didn't know enough. She'd never had to deal with a committee before, only with boards of directors who could take decisions that resulted in immediate action. Such things as applications for Preservation Orders or Compulsory Purchase were foreign to her.

Alan Singleton was little help over such matters. He was a qualified surveyor but legal aspects of his work had always been turned over to the Legal Department. 'Still, there's no doubt the chief stumbling block is the house that Mrs Bedells is living in,' he observed when Iris asked for his help. 'So long as she owns it and refuses to sell, we're stuck. And of course, the press is on her side.'

'There must be some way to handle her,' mused Iris, shaking her black hair and resting her head against the sofa cushions.

'I don't see how. She's in the right, after all.'

'Oh, Alan . . .' So far she hadn't been able to make him see that right or wrong had little to do with her work, which was to put her clients in a good light. She considered the matter. 'What we need is a way to put her in the wrong.'

'I beg your pardon?' Alan said, startled.

'Look at it this way. As you say, the press are on her side – feisty little old lady defies council – but what if we could turn them against her?'

'What good would that do – even if you could do it?'

'Well . . . it might hurry up that Compulsory Purchase Order. That's stalled because National Heritage doesn't want to make itself unpopular by seeming to victimise the Bedells woman. But if we could get people to look at her as she really is – a stubborn old nuisance – we might get things moving.'

Mrs Bedells had faded out of the headlines in the past couple of months. Her cause, however, had been kept in the public eye through the actions of Allie Pembury, and it was one of Iris's ambitions to make young Allie seem less of a heroine too.

But this wasn't an auspicious moment for trying to deal with Allie. With the help of his professional association her father was in negotiation over taking voluntary redundancy. The council had decided, at

Daniel Dayton's urging, they didn't want to employ him after what they termed his disloyalty; but they didn't want to make him a martyr by firing him so he was being asked to resign. That was a subject best kept in low key.

So, since she had to steer clear of the Pemburys, father and daughter, Iris was focusing her attention on Nancy Bedells. In her London office she called in her secretary, dictated a list of things to be done, and thus a couple of researchers were hired for a short-term investigation.

What they turned up with was surprising. Mrs Bedells *wasn't* Mrs Bedells.

There was no record of a marriage between William Bedells and any woman called Nancy. The late William Bedells had been married, true – but his wife had been Rose Anne Forbes, and she had pre-deceased him by some thirty years. There was no record of a certificate for a marriage between William and any other woman.

So when William died at the age of sixty-two, he had been living for some twenty-five years with a woman who wasn't his wife. Her name was really Nancy Bedells; she'd changed it by deed poll. William's will, leaving his estate to Nancy Bedells, was therefore perfectly legal.

But she was not the legal wife of the late William Bedells and never had been. To use a phrase that had gone largely out of fashion, Nancy Alice Bedells had been his mistress.

Iris was staggered by the news. 'You're sure about this?' she demanded of the researcher, a university student earning some cash during the summer vac.

'Absolutely.' Social history was his subject. He was quite offended that anyone should doubt him. 'I've been through the records back to front and upside down. Unless they were married abroad . . . But there's no record that Nancy Bedells was ever issued a passport so she couldn't have been abroad. There's very little in the way of information about her. Her maiden name was Lee, her birth was registered in the County of Cumberland. Her father was Roland and her mother was Ellen, they seem to have been working on a farm which no longer exists, it's a housing estate now.'

Iris made a motion as if pushing aside this tide of information with her hands. 'Nancy Bedells isn't actually Mrs William Bedells – that's the main thing. Right?'

'Right.'

'We-ell . . .'

What was she to do with this material? It seemed to make no difference to the legal situation: William had left his house to Nancy Alice Bedells and Nancy Alice Bedells was the rightful owner. But the moral aspect . . .?

The moral aspect. Would anyone care that the old couple had not been legally married? Might it even increase sympathy for Nancy? She could imagine the headlines – FAITHFUL LOVERS FOR A LIFETIME! Or even worse: LEGACY OF LOVE.

She rang Alan in York to tell him what she'd learned. 'Would you speak to Raymond Bigsby? See if it makes any difference on the legal front?'

'I imagine he must know all this, Iris. He'd have had to verify the facts about the house's ownership when he sent in the application for Compulsory Purchase.'

'You think he knows all this?' she cried, astounded. 'And never told me?'

'Well, you know lawyers . . .' Alan felt he had to defend Bigsby for not thinking of passing on information to Iris. He himself, though he loved and admired her, hadn't quite come to grips with her job. 'They've got this thing about confidentiality, and anyhow I expect he couldn't see that it matters,' he explained.

'Of course it matters! It puts that old pest in a totally different light—'

'Not where the law's concerned, perhaps.'

'Well, will you tell him anyhow? I can't seem to get hold of him.'

'He's on holiday, Iris. After all, it's August.'

So it was, and Iris herself should have been in Tuscany, in a holiday house her firm made available to their staff. The temperature in London was over ninety, it hadn't rained for weeks, she felt dried out and weary to the bone.

She sighed so loudly that he could hear it over the phone. He felt a protective sympathy for her. Poor darling, she worked so hard, but everything seemed to go against her. 'Tell you what,' he suggested, 'let's get away from it all for a few days, eh? How about a long weekend somewhere peaceful and cool? Oslo, perhaps. Or Stockholm.'

'Places in the north are full of gnats in August, darling. Let's go to Geneva or the Pyrenees.'

So they turned away from the problem of Nancy Bedells and took themselves off from Thursday to Monday. But before he left, Alan stopped by Daniel's desk at the offices of *Dayton & Daughter* to mention a few routine matters – telephone calls returned, instructions for invoices sent to the computers, and so on. When they turned to general conversation, it occurred to him to tell the head of the firm of Iris's discoveries.

Daniel was transfixed by the news. 'Not married?'

'No, seems not.'

'Never were married?'

'No, no record of any marriage, ever.'

'Living in sin for twenty-five years?' He laughed in delight. 'So what about all that holier-than-thou stuff, disapproving of Arabella Bedells for being an abandoned hussy and telling the squatters in the Terrace to clear off because they were an immoral bunch?'

Alan was taken aback. As usual, he had adopted Iris's view. 'It's a bit awkward though, Daniel. I mean, we can't make any use of it.'

'Can't make any use of it? You're off your rocker! Nay, lad, this is great! I'm not quite sure what's best to do, but I'll think on.'

Alan had a plane to catch. In the ensuing rush he let the chat with Daniel slip from his mind. He didn't even think of mentioning it to Iris during their stay in Perpignan – after all, they had other things to occupy them.

Daniel went home from his office in Aldwark that evening in high good humour. He even went so far as to open a particularly fine white Burgundy without even consulting Mary as to the main course of the meal.

'Oh, what's this in honour of?' she asked when she saw the label on the opened bottle. Daniel rarely opened anything special when they were dining alone.

'I'm having a little private celebration, my love. I think I've at last got the Bedells woman where I want her.'

'You have?' She set down the last dish, and returning to the kitchen to take off her apron, said over her shoulder, 'There's a herb sauce to go with the lamb, dear – Celia Dawson got it at her cookery class.'

'Aye, right,' said her husband, pouring it lavishly over the meat. He helped himself to vegetables, then raised his glass in salute. 'Here's to Iris,' he said.

'Iris Weston?'

'Aye, her – smart lass. I thought so from the start, though I began to have doubts when she got so smitten with Singleton. But she's turned up trumps this time, bless her.'

Mary didn't really want to talk about Iris Weston. She'd never quite trusted her and, at first, had been worried by the way she seemed able to handle Daniel. She herself was very glad that Iris was 'smitten' with Alan and, that being so, she felt she ought to show an interest in Daniel's toast. 'What's she done that's so marvellous, then?' she enquired as she took her place at table.

'Oh, nothing very much – she's only turned up information that's going to spike the guns of the opposition.'

'That's good. Which particular opposition is this?' For there were so many in the wrangle over the new Town Centre: the Protection Group, Mrs Bedells, National Heritage who were stalling on the Compulsory Purchase Order, Peter Lambot, Allie Pembury, Allie Pembury's father, the association representing him in his redundancy negotiations, the press which seemed to side with Allie, old Uncle Tom Cobbleigh and all.

'Iris has unearthed some stuff that will turn everybody against Mrs Bedells,' Daniel announced.

'Really?' Mary doubted that very much, but preferred not to say so.

'Yes, wait till you hear. What d'you think? That old harridan was never married to William Bedells!'

'Who?'

'Who what?'

'Was never married to – oh, William Bedells, the man who used to live in that house.' Mary at last caught up with her husband's train of thought. 'Wait a moment, Daniel. Are you saying that Mrs Bedells isn't Mrs Bedells?'

'Well, she is and she isn't,' said Daniel, relishing every minute of it. 'She calls herself Mrs Bedells and she's entitled to call herself anything she likes – the Grand Cham of China, if she likes. But *legally* she's never been married to William Bedells. William Bedells was only married once, to a woman called Rose Anne Something, who died six years later, I think it was . . . Well, anyhow, he was a widower and he took this Nancy to live with him—'

'Daniel!'

'Good, isn't it?' he gloated, and took an appreciative sip of the Burgundy. 'She changed her name to his, by deed poll, quite legal, but you have to wonder why they never got wed and *my* opinion is she was married to someone else – no, maybe that's wrong because she changed her name from Nancy Lee and that was the name on her birth certificate so it seems like she wasn't married to anybody else – no, but it's absolutely certain that there's no marriage registered between her and William so there you are. Nigh on forty years she's called herself Mrs Bedells and it was an illicit relationship.'

His wife set down her knife and fork. She sat back a little in her chair. 'Are you sure of all this?'

'Oh, aye. Iris had researchers on it in London – Public Record Office, all that sort of thing – there's no doubt about it, Mrs Nancy Bedells isn't a married woman.'

'But the house?'

Daniel sighed. 'She owns that – no getting away from it. It was deeded to her as Nancy Alice Bedells and since she changed her name to that legally, the inheritance is unassailable. But that's not the point, Mary! Think back – think how she told us all off for wanting to make a heroine out of Arabella Bedells. She called her a hussy because she was an actress and had children by the Prussian duke or whatever he was. And being outraged by the behaviour of the squatters – good heavens, who is *she* to look down her nose at them, considering what she is!'

'And what is she, Daniel?'

'She's a wicked old woman who's tricked us into thinking she's better than the rest of us, whereas the truth is she's been living a lie all her life.'

'Daniel,' said Mary, 'she's an old lady of about eighty living on her

178

own in a house that's cut off from the rest of the town, scared to step outside her door for fear reporters will set upon her, in danger of losing the home she's had for – what – forty years, probably existing on a pittance—'

'And whose fault is that?' Daniel broke in. 'Once we get the Purchase Order we'll give her a fair price, and she's been offered a flat in a sheltered housing set-up—'

'But she wants to stay where she is—'

'Well, she can't, and I'm going to get her out of there in the next week or so or my name's not—'

'And how are you going to do that?'

'I've already got it going. Once the press start on this story about her being old Bedells's fancy woman—'

'Fancy woman?' cried Mary. 'They lived together as man and wife for thirty years! That's a marriage, Daniel—'

'No, it isn't, it's a lie, a façade they put up—'

'How can you say that? They lived happily together—'

'We don't know that they were happy. She may have had some hold over him—'

'Daniel, stop that! You're trying to make her into a villainess. She's a solitary little old lady—'

'Don't be so soft! You're such a pillar of the Church, Mary, are you going to say you approve of what she's done?'

'No, I don't approve. You know I uphold the Church's views on wedlock. But the rest of the world has different ideas these days and let me tell you, Daniel, I don't think you'll find many people are shocked by what Iris has found out.'

'Shocked? Maybe they won't be *shocked*. But it'll change their attitude towards her – she's a schemer, a liar, so they won't admire her any more—'

'Even if that's the result, what good does it do you?' Mary cried. 'You'll have made her a talking point again, but the legal situation—'

'It's not so much the legal situation, it's the politics,' Daniel interrupted. 'The Minister's been pussyfooting about the Compulsory Purchase Order because he thought it would make him unpopular to grant it. But if Mrs Bedells isn't a heroine any more, he'll likely say yes and we'll get her out of that house—'

'Daniel, you can't do that—'

'I damn well can! In fact I already have. The *Gazette* will feature it tomorrow and I bet the nationals will have it too – Jeff Jones's editor will have sold it on as an exclusive for a good price.'

'Oh, no, Daniel,' said Mary in real distress. 'You can't mean you've blabbed all this to the press? You've snitched on her? How could you? How *could* you!'

Daniel stared at his wife as if she had gone demented. 'What d'you

179

mean, how could I? It's a chance to get the upper hand at last! She's caused us all kinds of problem and now it's time to turn the tables. She's going to be out of that house and we'll get the demolition done and construction started before the winter weather sets in.'

'Is that all you ever think of?' she demanded. 'Getting your construction done, being the boss of everything?'

'Mary, of course I think about it! This is a big scheme, with architects and town planners all over the Continent watching us. What kind of fools do we look like, held up for months by some lying old hag—'

'When has she lied to you? She told you she owned the house, and so she does. She wants to stay there and it's the council's fault, not hers, that you can't get her out. You absolutely must not attack her as if she were a criminal—'

'She's a selfish old toad! Does she care if Barhampton doesn't get its new Town Centre? No, she doesn't! Does she care even that the house was once lived in by somebody famous? No, she doesn't. All she thinks about is herself. I can't begin to imagine why you're defending her—'

'I'm defending her because she's old and alone and poor. If you can't understand that, you've got no heart at all.'

'Well, talking of heart, that old bat hasn't got one if you ask me. She's cost us thousands, what with the delay and the re-scheduling. The council's Social Services have tried to help her, so has the Housing Department, the Legal Department; all those stupid squatters have tried to be friends with her, even our Beth – and what happens? She tells 'em all to shove off. Why you feel any sympathy for her, I'll never—'

'You'll never understand,' Mary broke in. 'You don't have to tell me. You never understand anything—'

'What? I do too, I understand you're getting all soppy about this old bag—'

'There you go, belittling her – just because she's old and difficult. Mrs Crowther is old and difficult but I notice you never call *her* an old bag.'

'Mrs Crowther isn't standing in the way of the most important development that Barhampton has ever—'

'Buildings, money, sticks and stones – that's all you care about!' she flashed. 'People always come a long second best with you, Daniel Dayton—'

'Buildings, money, sticks and stones – don't say it in that tone of voice!' he retorted, his voice rising in indignation. 'They're what keeps the roof of this house over your head, they pay for your food and your car and the plants you buy for your garden—'

'And for your precious bottles of wine and your cigars and your Savile Row suits – that's not what I'm talking about, man! I'm trying to tell you that over the years you've grown more and more obsessed with *things* – with the business, with getting the contract to put up yet another pile of concrete blocks—'

'Concrete blocks?' he shouted. 'Since when did you become an architectural critic? It's our Bethany, she's been getting at you – her and her silly designs with fancy bricks and tiling—'

'You've always had a down on her,' Mary cried. 'You just don't want to admit that she has talent – more than *you* have.'

Daniel threw down his napkin and rose from his chair. 'I've had enough of this!' he snarled. 'Can't a man come home after a hard day and have some peace and quiet? I tell you some good news and you attack me as if I've committed some sort of crime. Well, I don't have to stop and listen to you.'

'No, you don't want to hear the truth—'

But he had stamped out. She heard the front door slam and a moment later his car zoomed down the short drive to the road.

Mary got to her feet more slowly. She was trembling – partly with anger and partly with shock. In all her life she'd never spoken like that to her husband. Her way had always been the gentle word, the patient wait, the hint of reproach – until in the end she might get her way, or else resign herself to failure. But to berate Daniel as she had done this evening . . . !

But she didn't regret it. She had been right, she felt it strongly. And to her what was so distressing was that Daniel saw nothing wrong in his action. Either that, or he'd persuaded himself it didn't matter.

That was the problem. The things that mattered were not the same to husband and wife. Daniel had always been strong, demanding, deter-mined to succeed. As the years went by he'd become *hard*, so impercep-tibly that she'd failed to see it. She tried to look back on their early days, and it seemed to her that he would never then have been so cruel as to hold up an old woman to public scorn.

I should have been more aware, she told herself. She felt a sob rising in her throat and stifled it. I won't cry, she said inwardly, clenching her fists against it.

Activity was the best remedy for foolishness. She set about clearing the dinner table. When she took the food into the kitchen she had a momentary impulse to tip it all into the waste disposal but, as always, good sense prevailed. She put it all in containers and into the freezer. She stacked the dishes in the dishwasher. She folded the tablecloth. She corked the open bottle of Burgundy and set it on the drinks tray.

That done, she went into the garden and by the late evening light studied flowers for the church next Sunday. She didn't cut them yet, for it was only Thursday, but she noted them in her flower notebook, thinking about lily Stargazer and canna Firefly and dark leaves from the rhododendron for the altar steps . . .

181

Around ten o'clock she made herself a cup of hot chocolate and went to bed. She didn't sleep, nor did she expect to. Even the long session with the flowers in her garden hadn't soothed her. Her mind was going over and over the scene at dinner.

At something after midnight Daniel arrived home. She heard the garage doors go up, heard him backing the car in and the slam of the car door as he got out. There seemed a long delay before he opened the front door, and she knew he was probably more than a little drunk, unable to concentrate on getting his key in the lock.

He stumbled into the bedroom at last. The bathroom light went on, he floundered about for a while and then he fell into the twin bed on the other side of the night table. In a moment or two he was snoring.

And now at last tears began to trickle from her eyes, running down her cheekbones to the pillow.

In the morning he failed to hear his alarm so she had to rouse him. Quite clearly he had a terrible hangover. He made a bad job of shaving, came down to breakfast looking like Goliath after David had felled him. She had brought in the papers from the doormat as usual – the *Financial Times* and the *Gazette*.

Daniel looked first at the *Times* as he always did. Mary had already seen the headline on the Barhampton paper and had no wish to read further. They sat in silence, Daniel drinking his coffee but making no attempt to touch the food on his breakfast plate.

At eight-thirty, as usual, he went out to the hall, collected his car keys from the dish where they lay, and opened the front door. 'Don't forget the Marryatts are coming to dinner tonight,' he said over his shoulder as he went out of the front door.

Mary cleared the breakfast table, put the dishes in the dishwasher, and set it going. At nine the daily help arrived. Mary left her vacuuming the living room. She used the telephone in the kitchen, the dishwasher humming in the background.

Bethany answered almost at once. 'Hello, Mother, I'd have rung you if you hadn't called. You've seen this awful thing about Mrs Bedells in the *Gazette*?'

'Yes, Bethany, of course.'

'It's rotten, isn't it? I wonder if it's true?'

'I think it is, dear.'

There were overtones in the reply that Bethany was quick to catch. 'Is anything wrong, Mother?'

Mary sighed. She didn't want to unload her marital problems on her daughter. 'Where are you at the moment, love?'

'I'm at the riverside site – there's a problem about the pilings – never mind about that. Why d'you want to know where I am?'

'Could you go home to your flat? I'd like to meet you there in a little while.'

'Well . . . yes . . . of course. But if it's a coffee date, we could meet at—'

'No, dear, I'd like to come to your flat and bring a suitcase.'

'A *suitcase*?'

'And Bethany – could I stay with you for a bit?'

Chapter Fifteen

Bethany knew there was something wrong. But all she said was, 'Of course, Mother. Are you going to drive in or shall I come and fetch you?'

'I'll be at your flat in about an hour, dear – is that all right?'

'No problem!'

But of course there was a problem: for one thing, Bethany had site visits to make. She hastily cancelled them, using her mobile. Then she rushed into the nearest furniture store to buy a single bed, a set of curtains, and a curtain pole, which she loaded into her Suzuki.

There was a little room in her flat with which she'd done nothing – her suitcases were still standing in the middle of the floor. She hurried home to turn it into a spare room, glad to remember that it had a big cupboard that would do as a wardrobe.

She hung the curtains, pulled the polythene off the bed and mattress, made it up with spare sheets, dragged a small table and a lamp to its side, filled a vase with water and was putting a welcoming bunch of alstroemeria into it when she heard her mother's car draw up outside. She dashed to the kitchen, started the coffee-maker, and was at the door just as Mary rang the bell.

'Well, there you are!' she said inanely as she let her in. 'Let me take your case.'

'Thank you,' said Mary, and followed her into the spare room. Bethany put the case by the wardrobe door while her mother looked about. 'I'm being a nuisance,' she said, her tone uncertain as she took in the hasty arrangements.

'Not a bit of it. The coffee's on, come along and we'll have a cup while the microwave defrosts the Danish pastries.'

'That would be nice,' said Mary.

It was clear something world-shattering had occurred. Bethany immediately thought: Another woman! And her next thought was: Iris Weston? But no. Although Iris had been somewhat seductive in her attitude at first, now her attention was taken up first of all with her work and secondly with Alan Singleton. So was it some other girl? Yet in the past her mother had weathered Daniel's little adventures without walking out on him. What was so different now?

184

Bethany had better sense than to ask questions. Mary Dayton was a reticent woman. If and when she wanted to talk about what had happened, she would do so. Bethany must wait for clues. However, not to ask anything at all would seem odd so she said, 'Lovely to have you, Mother, but I haven't done any catering for the weekend.' In fact, she'd been planning to go away with Peter over Saturday night and Sunday.

'I'm sorry! Did you have plans?'

'No, no, nothing important.'

'I just thought I'd like a little break, Beth . . . you know?'

A little break in Barhampton? At the best of times the town had little going for it, but now with its shopping centre dead, it was no holiday attraction.

'And . . . er . . . I suppose Dad is off somewhere too?'

'No,' remarked Mary with satisfaction. 'He's got the Marryatts coming for dinner tonight, as a matter of fact.'

'But, Mother!'

'I left him a note. He'll have time to book a table somewhere and telephone them to meet him at the restaurant.' She gave a smile in which there was a grim triumph. 'He'll probably tell them I've got a virus or something.'

'Whereas the truth is?' asked Bethany, seizing the opportunity she was offered.

'I've left him.'

Bethany, appalled, could think of nothing to say. Luckily the coffee-maker gurgled that it had finished its task. She turned to pour into thick mugs. At length she said: 'Does he know you're here?'

'Of course, dear. It would have been silly not to tell him.'

'Then he'll be round here like a raging bull—'

'Not until after he's taken the Marryatts to dinner. First things first,' she said with a grim smile. 'He wouldn't offend an important client like Marryatt by cancelling at the last minute. But I'd imagine he'll be here around midnight.' She sighed. 'If you've any sense you'll be out with your young man or in bed and asleep – or perhaps both.' And she gave a little nod of understanding as she ended.

'Do you want me to be here?' her daughter asked.

'I haven't thought about it, love. I'm just taking one step at a time.' Her plump features were oddly calm, considering the emotional turmoil she must be going through.

'Perhaps that's best.' Bethany scarcely knew whether it was best or worst, so took refuge in practical matters. 'I'll have to do some shopping or we're going to starve.'

'I'll do that, dear. I'll just unpack and then I'll go out to the shops. You go and get on with your job.'

'Well . . . there *are* things to deal with. There's a problem at the riverside site and I ought to – well, you don't want to hear all that but perhaps I'd better get on.'

'Shall you be back for dinner? Not that it matters, love,' Mary added quickly. 'If you've got a date I can easily—'

'I'll be back,' said Bethany, suddenly realising she couldn't leave her mother alone on the first night of separation from a husband of thirty-five years.

As soon as she was in the Suzuki she called Peter on her mobile phone. 'Can we meet?' she asked. 'Something important has come up—'

'If it's about this news of Mrs Bedells in the paper—'

'Mrs Bedells!' In the drama of the last couple of hours, she'd completely forgotten the woman. 'No, it's not that, it's more personal. I've got to talk to you but not on the phone.'

'Had lunch?'

'Not yet.'

'The Packhorse in fifteen minutes,' said Peter and hung up.

He was there first, in the garden which made the old town pub attractive. He was addressing a bap filled with ham and lettuce. Bethany had bought a ploughman's and a glass of wine on her route through the bar. He got up to relieve her of her burdens and kiss her. 'What's wrong?' he asked, alarmed at the tension he could feel running through her.

She sat down, accepted her wine glass from him, and took a heartening sip. 'Something very strange has happened—'

'About Mrs Bedells? No, you said not—'

'My mother has come to stay with me.'

'Oh?' He listened to the tone of her voice more than the words. 'That's unexpected?'

'Very. At a moment's notice.'

'And for how long?'

'That's unspecified. She says she's left my father.'

'Sorry?' He genuinely thought he had misheard her.

'Mother has left Dad. So she says.'

He sat in silence, absorbing this. To tell the truth, he thought any woman who could live with Daniel Dayton must have something of the angelic about her. To leave him seemed good sense to Peter.

'This is permanent?'

'Who knows?' Bethany sighed.

'Have you asked her about it? Why she's done it? I mean, is it "another woman"?'

'I don't know. I don't think so. I can't ask. Mother's . . . not apt to confide in anybody. And she's very upset. She conceals it well but I know her . . . I think they've had a big row.'

Peter, who had had his share of clients with marriage problems, asked gently: 'Has it happened before?'

186

'That she's left him? Good God, no! It's as if the world's turned upside down!' Bethany put her palms to her cheeks, feeling them colour up at having to discuss her family's affairs. 'All through my childhood, Mother was the rock on which our happiness was founded. I think she put up with an awful lot – because it was her duty. She soothed and placated, she went along with behaviour that at first us kids didn't recognise as selfish – we just thought that . . . well, that's what Dad is like. But Mother wanted us to have a stable, happy childhood. And we did.'

'They never had rows?'

'We-ell . . . Not that we knew of. Later, when I got into my teens, I could see there'd been upsets, but Mother somehow seemed to smooth them over. When I was at university and began to have ideas about . . . you know . . . women's rights, all that sort of thing . . . I used to ask her why she put up with it. She'd smile and say, "All marriages have their ups and downs. This marriage has just had one of the downs." And that was that. In the end she often got her own way . . . persuaded Dad to do something or not to do it. Patience and Perseverance, that seemed to be her motto.'

'But now her patience is exhausted, is that it?'

'It seems so. The point is, Peter . . . There she was on my doorstep with her suitcase . . . a bit like a refugee . . . I feel . . . I feel I can't leave her on her own, you know?'

'You mean about this weekend?' he asked, understanding at once. 'Never mind, there will be other weekends.' He took her hand and pressed it. 'Eat your food.'

'I'm not hungry.'

'Nevertheless, eat. You'll be rushing around building sites all afternoon, you can't do it on a couple of sips of wine.'

In obedience she picked at the garnish of the ploughman's plate.

'Perhaps I shouldn't ask,' Peter remarked, 'but have you any idea what the row was about – if there was a row?'

She shook her head.

'Could it have been Iris Weston?'

'Oh, you'd noticed that, had you?'

'I can see he thinks she's attractive. But on her part . . .'

'She isn't interested. Although she uses her wiles to handle him.'

'Yes.'

'I really don't think it's that famous "other woman" syndrome. There have been some in the past but she . . . she turned a blind eye because she knew they didn't really matter.'

'So this was something she felt really mattered.'

'Seems so.'

'Could it be something to do with the Barhampton Town Centre? Royal Terrace?'

187

'What?' she said, startled. 'I don't see how.'

'I only ask because that thing about Mrs Bedells is all over the *Gazette* this morning. The two things coming together . . .'

'Perhaps Dad got too triumphant about the "scandal". He can sometimes get awfully gleeful about his enemy's misfortunes.' But she shook her head. 'I don't think that would be enough to cause a break-up. It must be something more than that.' She sighed deeply. 'Whatever the cause, I have to stand by her – you understand that, Peter, don't you?'

'Of course I do. But how is he going to take it, Bethany?'

'Like the Towering Inferno, I should think. At the moment he doesn't even know.' She shook her head at the thought. 'Oh Lord, how he'd hate it! To think that we're sitting here discussing something in his life that he doesn't even know about.'

'How is he going to find out?'

'She says she left him a note. Oh,' she said, putting a hand over her eyes to hide sudden tears, 'I . . . I'm sorry. It's just . . . it sounded so *trite* – but she's so unhappy, and it's going to cause so much trouble because when Dad gets upset, everybody suffers.'

'Don't, darling.' He put an arm round her shoulders, leaning forward to shield her from other people. 'It's all right. He'll have to get over it. He's a grown man, after all. He can't lash out at you, because you and your mother are out of his reach, with a door you can close on him.'

'But on the business side – I have to deal with him every day—'

'But it's not *your* fault.'

'As if that makes any difference.' But she wiped her eyes with her knuckles, sought for a tissue, and blew her nose. 'No, you're right, I've dealt with his bad tempers before and I'll have to do it again – but this time is going to be much worse than usual.'

'That's the spirit!' He patted her shoulder in approval. 'Now, to the strictly practical. What are we going to do about the immediate future? It's clear you don't want to leave your mother, so the Scannsdale trip is indefinitely postponed—'

'Oh Peter – thank you for being so understanding.'

'What about this evening? You'll be wanting to stay home with her in case?'

'Nothing's likely to happen until late. He was expecting Mother to prepare dinner for him and some guests – I think it's Mr and Mrs Marryatt – and as Mother rightly said, he won't offend Marryatt by cancelling at the last moment because he's a bigwig in machinery sales. So he'll take them out to a restaurant and then I imagine he'll come tearing out to Barhampton to drag her home.'

'But she won't go.'

'I don't know. She might. Perhaps she's only teaching him a lesson.'

'Do you think it's that?'

'I don't know, Peter. I really don't know.'

'Would you like me to be there? Moral support?'

'Oh no! No, for heaven's sake! That would make you his mortal enemy for ever! What, let you see him pleading with his wife? No, Peter, you're marvellous to suggest it but it really isn't a good idea.'

Peter looked unwilling and very troubled. He only knew Daniel through business acquaintance but he could always sense in him a tendency to ruthlessness. Physical violence? Surely not – yet if pushed to it, Daniel was the kind of man who might use his fists.

'I don't like to think of you and your mother having to deal with him if he's in a state.'

'We'll manage.'

'But suppose he—'

'We'll manage, Peter. We have to – it's the only way.'

He gave a sigh of anxiety and resignation. 'But you'll ring me to let me know what's happened?'

'Yes.'

'No matter how late it is? Promise you'll ring.'

'I promise.' To turn his attention away from the prospect she made a determined attempt to eat some of her lunch. After a mouthful or two she asked, 'What's happening about this thing with Mrs Bedells?'

Peter shrugged. 'It's a mess. You'll have seen that the Chairman of the Royal Terrace Protection Group was asked for his view.'

'No, I didn't have time to read that far.'

'Oh. Well, Tallant said that the report was an unwarranted intrusion on Mrs Bedells's privacy – which it is – and that it made no difference to their determination to preserve the Terrace – which it doesn't. He and some of his fellow members went to the house first thing this morning in an attempt to tell the poor old soul that they still supported her—'

'Oh, good heavens, can't the poor woman be left in peace?'

'They meant well, Bethany . . . Well, she wouldn't come to the door so they put a letter under it, saying more or less the same thing, and then they came to *Pesh, Samuels* asking me to make a complaint to the Press Commission.'

'And are you going to?'

'I'm looking into it. There are guidelines. I'm trying to find out if what was published amounts to harassment—'

'But even if there are grounds for a complaint, Peter – the apology usually comes weeks later. What use is that to Mrs Bedells?'

'Not much. But it might keep the reporters away from her door. And of course it's good publicity – the Protection Group wants its aims to be kept in front of the public.'

'But that's more or less *using* her too, isn't it?'

'Oh, Bethany . . . if only things were straightforward . . . I'm hired to advise and represent the Protection Group. If they want advice on making a complaint to the Press Commission, they have a right to my best efforts.'

'And what about Mrs Bedells's rights?'

'Don't quarrel with me about it, Bethany. I want Mrs Bedells to be looked after just as much as you do.'

She was ashamed. 'I know, I'm sorry. It's just . . . I'm all raw edges at the moment.'

He reached out to take her hand again. The forthcoming encounter with Daniel Dayton was enough to make anyone tense.

They chatted about unimportant matters for a few more minutes, then as they parted Peter extracted a firm promise that she would telephone that night after her father had gone.

But in fact Daniel never appeared at her flat that night. At about one in the morning the two women, wan and exhausted, decided to go to bed. Bethany rang Peter, who snatched up the phone at the first ring.

'He didn't come, Peter.'

'What?'

'Mother's worn out with anxiety. She's gone to bed, but whether she's going to sleep in another matter.'

There was a momentary pause while he considered the news. 'Is this good or bad, Bethany?'

'I've no idea. Usually Dad rushes straight in to the attack. Mother was sure he'd be here as soon as he'd said good night to the Marryatts – and she knows him so well, I took it for granted she was right.'

'Scare tactics.'

'What?'

'He's leaving her in a state of apprehension so as to weaken her resolve.'

'Do you think so?'

'Do you? You know him better than I do.'

Her long sigh came to him across the phone. 'I'm so tired I can't think. I've got to get some sleep, Peter. I just felt I had to ring and let you know the state of play.'

'Yes, and thanks for that – if I hadn't heard from you in about another ten minutes I was going to drive round and see what was going on.'

'Nothing's going on. It's weird. I'm going to bed, love. Good night.'

'Good night.'

At first Bethany lay awake, going over and over the events of the day. But towards four she fell into a heavy sleep. She was roused from it by repeated rings on her doorbell at six-thirty in the morning. When she failed to answer the caller began knocking loudly on the door.

Stumbling across her room, pulling on a cotton wrap and worrying what her downstairs neighbours would say to the racket, she got to her front door. When she opened it she found her father on the threshold.

'Good morning, Bethany,' he said.

He was freshly shaved and well turned out, as always at the beginning of the day. Since it was Saturday he was wearing leisure clothes, a thin cotton shirt with a faint blue check, dark blue chinos and a golfing jacket with his club's emblem on the front.

Bethany, with her dressing-gown half-on, half-off, and her hair on end, felt at a total disadvantage. She stammered, 'What . . . what are you doing here?'

'I've come to breakfast,' he said. 'May I?' And he shouldered his way past her into the living room.

Following, Bethany saw that her mother had come from the spare room to find out what was happening. She at least had her silk dressing-gown buttoned up and, though pale, looked wide awake. She'd even had the foresight to run a comb through her grey hair.

'Good morning, Daniel,' she said. 'This is an early call?'

'You know me,' he said. 'Always up with the lark.'

'Couldn't you have chosen a more civilised hour?'

'Afraid not. I've got engagements for the rest of the day. I thought I'd drop in on you first.'

'Dad,' said Bethany, at last coming to grips with the situation, 'will you please go away?'

'Now is that any way to treat your father? Aren't you going to at least offer me a cup of coffee?'

'No, I'm not.'

'That's very undaughterly. Is this how you brought her up, Mary?'

His wife gave him a thoughtful gaze. 'I'll make you a cup of coffee, Daniel,' she said. 'And then you can get off on your list of engagements.' She nodded at Bethany, as if to say: Go and get yourself together, lass.

Bethany retreated to the bathroom, where she showered hastily. As she went from there to her room, she heard their voices in the kitchen – apparently a perfectly normal conversation. She pulled on jeans and T-shirt, ran a comb through her wet hair, and hurried to the kitchen.

'Not a bad little place you've got here, Bethie,' Daniel remarked as she came in. It was his first visit, although she'd been there for almost six months. 'Not much room for a lodger, though, I'd imagine.'

'Mother's welcome to stay as long as she wishes.'

'But she's got more sense than to wish to stay another day, haven't you, love?'

'Thank you for having a good opinion of my sense. However, I've decided to take a break from the ups and downs of married life so I'll be here with Beth for the foreseeable future.'

'Come on, now, lass, don't be difficult. Whatever it is that's upset you, I apologise. There now, I can't say fairer than that, can I?'

'And you think that sorts it, do you? An apology will undo all the harm you've done?'

'Me?' cried Daniel. 'What harm have *I* done?'

191

'You've set the press baying around poor Mrs Bedells again, that's what you've done! And what's worse, you don't even seem to care.'

'*He* did it?' Beth broke in. And turning to her father: 'You were the one who told the papers about the marriage?'

'The lack of a marriage – yes, I told them and I think it'll have a good result—'

'A good result? By what standards?' Mary demanded. 'That poor old soul has suffered enough at your hands—'

'Oh, for heaven's sake, stop sentimentalising her. She's a bad-tempered old crone who's making a lot of problems that should never have arisen and it's costing—'

'That's it, that's it, profit and loss.'

'Mary, we went through all that before. The delays and difficulties are wasting time and money and before long, if things don't sort themselves out, there'll be penalty clauses to consider. If you think I won't use any weapon I can to get rid of Mrs Bedells, you're living in a dream world.'

'Dad, did you actually give the information to the papers?'

'Yes, I did.'

'How did you get hold of it?' And then, after a second's thought, 'Did Iris Weston find out and put you up to it?'

'She found out, yes. As to "putting me up to it", I don't need anybody to prompt me when I see a good move.'

'You really think it's a good move to hold that poor woman up to public display? To drag out secrets in her private life?'

'What I did was bring out the truth—'

'How would you like it if someone did that to you?'

'Huh!' snorted Daniel. 'There's nothing in *my* marriage to be ashamed of! Your mother and I have had thirty-five years of happiness together.'

'Oh, Daniel!' cried Mary, and began to laugh, with something like hysteria in its peals.

Her husband stared at her. 'What? What? What are you laughing at?'

Bethany hurried to put her arms round her mother and hold her tight. 'It's all right, Mother,' she soothed. 'Don't, don't, it's all right.'

Daniel was sitting with amazement on his blunt features. 'What's got into you, lass?' he demanded. 'Why are you taking on so?'

'There, there,' Bethany was saying. 'I'll get you a glass of water—'

'I'm all right, Beth. Thank you, dear. It was just – so unexpected . . . so *funny*!'

'Funny?' Daniel echoed, bewildered. 'What did I say that was funny?'

Mary was wiping her eyes with her fingertips. She sighed. 'No, perhaps it was sad. And the saddest thing about it is that you believe it's true.'

'Well, it *is* true. Oh, I admit we've had our bad times . . . When

192

Dennis died . . . it took me a while to get over that, I agree. And of course it was a disappointment when Robert decided to take up medicine . . . We had our arguments over that . . . But on the whole we've made a good go at it, Mary, and when you compare us to other couples who rush off to the divorce courts—'

'What you see is couples who've been honest enough to admit they've made a mistake,' she broke in.

'What?'

'I've been a coward, Daniel. I took refuge in the idea that the Church wants marriage to last a lifetime, and I told myself I mustn't do anything that would harm the children – that was another excuse I used. I agree it's a bit late in the day to find the courage of my convictions, but it's happened—'

'What's happened? What are you talking about?'

'I've realised I don't want to live with you any more.'

'*What?*' He was horror-stricken. For a moment the self-confidence left his face and he looked almost frightened. 'What are you saying, Mary?'

'I can't respect a man who victimises an old lady. I can't sit in silence any more while he goes on doing things I think are contemptible.'

'Contemptible?'

'Ever since this hold-up over Mrs Bedells's house—'

'But why on earth should that mean so much to you? For God's sake, lass, what can she matter to you? You don't even—'

'There you are – you're not even aware that what you've done is wrong! You're so bound up in your own self-regard that you think you can do anything – *anything* – and it's justified.' She shook her head in weariness. 'And I've got to the stage where I can't bear it any more. The silly affairs with other women, the business weekends where you come home smelling of someone else's perfume – I accepted all that because some men have to keep on proving themselves in that way. But when you sink to being an informer—'

Daniel, scarlet with mortification, jumped to his feet. 'This is no way to go on, Mary! In front of our Beth—'

'Don't worry, Dad,' Bethany put in. 'I always knew about Celia Ormerod and Joan Manders.'

'What?'

'The girls at school used to gossip about it – oh, not only you, Dad, they knew about almost all the goings-on among the parents.'

'Now that's enough!' shouted her father. 'You hold your tongue, young lady! I won't be spoken to like that.'

'No, perhaps it was cruel,' she agreed, already regretting it. 'But you ask for it, trying to take the moral high ground. All the same, I apologise for naming names.'

'It's not true, Mary! This is just fairy-tales from her schooldays—'

'No, it's true, Daniel, and I could add some names to the list if I wanted to. But it's not important, because it's past and I've put it behind me. What's important is the present, and for the present I need to get away from you.'

'Get *away* from me?'

'I can't go on watching you digging yourself deeper into a pit of malice and self-deception. What you're doing is wrong – wrong, cruel, callous – do you understand me?'

'Mary!' Never in his life had she spoken to him like that. He felt as if the earth had opened under his feet. None of the usual words came to his tongue; he couldn't brush it off as some womanish trifle, some foolish qualm of conscience such as she was prone to. He heard judgement in her voice, and he was totally unaccustomed to being judged. And so he was stricken to silence.

His wife studied him with secret pity. It must be hard for him, after a lifetime of imagining himself invincible, to be brought low. 'I think you'd better leave, Daniel,' she murmured. 'You've got engagements for the rest of the day, you said.'

'But – but—'

'And I think it would be best not to say any more to each other at present.'

'But . . . what's to come next, Mary?'

'That remains to be seen.'

'But you're not seriously thinking . . . I mean, you mentioned divorce . . .'

'I haven't got that far, lad, so be easy on that score. At the moment all I want is to be away from you.'

'*Mary!*'

'A hard truth, eh? But it's true, and today is a day for speaking the truth. I don't like you at the moment, Daniel, so let me be by myself to think about it. We'll see what comes of it.'

Wordless, shocked, a beaten man for the first time in his life, he trudged out of the room. Bethany followed to see him out.

He paused as he passed the threshold. 'Try to talk her round, Beth.'

'To what?'

'To coming home, of course.'

She shook her head. 'You haven't understood what's just been said, Dad. You'd better stand back and take a good look at yourself before you think of asking her to come home to you.'

She gave him a gentle push to get him out and closed the door. She heard him standing outside, breathing hard, at a loss. She waited, afraid he might recover his strength and start pounding on the door. But after a moment or two she heard his footsteps going down the stairs.

Chapter Sixteen

Iris Weston arrived home at her London flat to find her answering machine blocked up with urgent messages about Barhampton. Her boss at *Seymour PR*, her secretary, Billy Wellbrow at *Wellbrow Construction*, Daniel Dayton at *Dayton & Daughter*, Jeff Jones at the *Barhampton Gazette*, and one or two journalistic friends from the tabloids – all were desperate to speak to her.

From hints and half-statements she learned that the news about Mrs Bedells's marital status had leaked out. Furious, she rang Alan, who had travelled home straight from Heathrow. He, however, hadn't yet reached journey's end and wasn't carrying a mobile so, since most of the other parties wouldn't be in their offices on Sunday night, she in desperation rang Jeff Jones.

'What's all this about Mrs Bedells?' she demanded without preamble.

'Don't tell me you don't know!'

'Never mind the cross-talk – what's been published?'

'She's a lady of loose morals, it appears, has been for years and years. William Bedells wasn't her husband.'

'Oh Lord,' she groaned.

'You didn't know?'

'Of course I knew, but I didn't want it given out to the press until I'd thought how to handle it. What idiot gave you the story?'

'I never reveal my sources,' Jones said with prim amusement.

'What's been the general reaction?'

'The Royal Terrace Protection Group have rallied round like heroes. Peter Lambot is trying to get an order preventing the press from harassing her. Daniel Dayton thinks it'll jerk the Heritage Secretary into refusing a Preservation Order, though why I'm not sure. It's not as if a Preservation Order depended on the purity of the property owner. I rather like that,' he added, listening to himself. 'Note the alliteration.'

'Never mind your literary genius,' she snorted. 'Who's picked it up?'

'The tabloids are interested but haven't made up their mind what to think about her. The broad-sheets gave the news a little mention on an inside page. Now, in return for this Deep-Throat information I'll expect first go at what the Steering Committee say about it.'

'I can't see that the Steering Committee will have anything to say about it, Jeff. That's the point. I didn't see how it got us any further . . .'

'You weren't thinking of keeping it to yourself, were you, luv?' he asked.

'Until I saw how to use it, yes, I was.'

'Well, it's good for a laugh, at any rate,' Jeff said, and signed off.

Instead of going to bed, Iris drove to her office, where she found the relevant tear-sheets already filed in the most recent folder labelled *Barhampton*. The results weren't as bad as she'd expected.

The tabloids didn't quite know how to handle the information about Mrs Bedells. Some had adopted a 'Well, what do you know!' attitude; one had decided on a headline: ALWAYS BEEN FEISTY! and went all out for approval by their women readers, implying that the old lady had been and still was a champion of women's rights. The broad-sheets merely supplied the information, adding in some cases that Mrs Bedells's marital status made no difference to the quandary in which Barhampton council found itself.

Her hand hovered over the telephone. Should she call a few of her friends so as to try for a slant favourable to her clients? But it was very late on Sunday night, the papers had probably been put to bed by now. She caught a glimpse of her reflection in a mirror advertising one of the firm's clients, and saw how pale her face looked under its fall of black hair. She decided to sleep on it.

Next morning she was at her desk early. A quick run through the newspapers told her that interest in the Bedells story had waned and was almost dead. Best to let well alone, she told herself. She rang Alan to ask what was happening in York.

'Not much,' he said innocently. 'The *Barhampton Gazette* got that information about Mrs Bedells—'

'I know that, Alan. My answering machine was chock-a-block when I got in. What I'd like to know is, *how* did it get hold of it? Did you tell them?'

'Me? Of course not.' His relationship with Iris had taught him to have a great reticence where the media were concerned. After a moment's thought he added, 'I told Daniel, though.'

'You what?'

'Well, he is my boss, you know, Iris.'

'That idiot,' she fumed. 'I bet he leaked it to Jones! Won't he ever learn that public relations is a specialty? But of course he thinks he's an expert at everything—'

'I don't see that it matters so very much, dear—'

'Perhaps not. We've been lucky, the press hasn't known how to treat the story and I hear national TV news hardly mentioned it. But what about the local boys? Did they go for it big?'

'Well, here in the office they've mentioned it and it seems the Protection Group people were interviewed; supported the old lady –

196

invasion of privacy, that kind of thing.'

'Yes . . .' She sighed. Working to get good publicity for your clients was hard enough. Controlling the client was even harder. She told herself firmly she mustn't tell Daniel Dayton what she thought of him.

After a quick glance at some routine matters and a worried word with her boss, she set off for York. It was necessary to be in the field, to get the feel of local attitudes. No meeting of the Steering Committee had been called but there was an informal gathering in the York offices of *Dayton & Daughter*.

To Iris's surprise, Daniel wasn't overflowing with triumphant glee. On the contrary, he seemed rather subdued. His usually strong features seemed to sag; there was a shadow behind the blue of his eyes. Bethany Dayton, after a few words regretting that Mrs Bedells had been targeted once again by the media, was quiet also: you might almost have said, thought Iris, that there had been a family upset.

Billy Wellbrow, expectedly, was disgruntled. 'You'd think folk would have more regard for Christian values! That woman was living with that man without benefit of clergy but nobody seems to think the worse of her!'

Iris gave a severe glance round the room. 'I did the research that uncovered the story but I hadn't decided whether it was to our benefit to release it. Please, in future, will you all discuss any material with me before letting it be known to the press?'

There were murmurs of assent. Bethany said, 'I expect you know that the Protection Group are going to complain to the Press Commission.'

Iris was irritated at the idea that Bethany could tell her anything. 'It's what I would do if I were representing Mrs Bedells. It's an obvious ploy.'

'A ploy?' said Bethany, in a vexed tone. 'Surely it's the *right* thing to do, for the good of Mrs Bedells?'

'Oh yes, if you like to think of it that way, but even if the PCC rule in favour of the complaint their ruling won't appear for weeks. I'm not worried about that.' She threw up a hand to emphasise her next point. 'What bothers me is that the squatters may get stirred up—'

'The squatters? What's it got to do with them?'

She suppressed her annoyance at the ignorance behind the question. Didn't this stupid lot understand that everything affected everything else? 'The squatters have been relatively quiet for the last few weeks but they're not there for fun – they like to get results, keep the action going. For a while now they haven't had much to use as fuel for a protest, but now they can claim that a slur has been cast on their heroine.'

'Huh! Some heroine!' snorted Wellbrow.

She ignored him pointedly. 'We should always bear in mind that if they mount any stunts, the reporters will be there like a shot. Cameras get good pix when protesters go into action.'

'Reporters! Photographers! I'm sick of the lot of them,' Daniel grunted, and called the conference to a halt. 'I need a drink,' he said.

Iris drifted towards Bethany. 'Is your father quite well?' she enquired. 'He seemed very quiet.'

'He's got a lot on his mind,' Bethany replied, and escaped to her car for the drive back to Barhampton.

She felt the need to be doing something – something restorative, something unconnected with this new anxiety about Royal Terrace. She decided it was time she paid a visit to Allie Pembury in hospital, so stopped at a boutique to buy a suitable gift.

She'd felt unable to champion Josh when his resignation was called for, but she still felt a great sympathy with him. They kept in touch by occasional telephone calls, so she understood the difficulties he was facing in the negotiations over his severance pay. His news about Allie was that she was improving: the fractures were healing well, and the damage to her right knee wasn't as severe as had been thought.

A brief visit with a pretty Japanese fan would salve her conscience about having ignored the girl for quite a while. Moreover, it would form a breathing space between the family row last night and the calls of today's work schedule.

To her surprise Allie was in the day room and what was more, on elbow crutches. 'My word! You *have* got on a lot since I last saw you,' Bethany exclaimed.

'You know what Nietzsche says,' Allie replied with a shrug.

'No, my knowledge of German philosophers is very limited,' Bethany said, suppressing a smile. 'What does he say?'

'He says the will is the most important thing about mankind. You have to *will* something to make it happen.'

'And you've *willed* that you should be up and about, is that it?'

'Up and about, and in six months' time walking without a limp. That's my target.'

'Well done,' said Bethany. 'And I see your hair is growing back in nicely . . .'

'Yes, but you see this scar at my temple?' Allie said, with total seriousness as if it was quite run of the mill to ask a visitor to undertake a minute inspection. 'They tell me I'll need plastic surgery to get rid of that—'

'But it scarcely shows, Allie – it'll get lost in your hairline, surely.'

'That's not quite good enough though, is it, especially if I get roles in TV things – the camera can be very cruel to any defects.'

'So you're still set on being an actress?'

'Of course.' Allie gave her a surprised glance. 'I know that's what I was intended to be.'

'I see. Well, that's a good ambition, it'll spur you on to get better fast, and once you've finished school—'

198

'Oh, I'm not going back to school! My GCSE results were awful, so Daddy agrees there's no point in me going back and wasting time trying them again.'

'So what will you do, then?' Bethany asked, although she guessed the answer.

'Try for RADA of course, once I can get around better.'

'RADA!' That was a surprise. Acting school she'd expected, but aiming so high at so early a stage in her training seemed a little presumptuous.

'Well, that or the equivalent. There are one or two good schools of Speech and Drama – not *here*, of course, but since Daddy's got the push from his job we're thinking about selling up and moving.'

'But, Allie, I thought he was going to work up a little consultancy about special trees, using that bit of ground—'

'But he can do that anywhere, can't he? Doesn't have to be here in Barhampton.'

'Well, that's true . . .'

'The only thing in, the property market is so unpredictable, Daddy says he might sell at a loss. A lot depends on how much he can get from Barhampton council for his "golden handshake".'

'I don't think it'll be very golden,' Bethany warned. 'More like silver, Allie.'

'Oh, Daddy's got it all in hand,' Allie replied, and took a step or two about the day room to celebrate the thought of leaving dull old Barhampton.

It was on the tip of Bethany's tongue to ask if she ever wondered whether her father wanted to quit Barhampton. But she hadn't come to start an argument, merely to show her continuing interest in the Pemburys. So she said, 'Do you think you'll be allowed home soon?'

'Any day now. I'll have to come back to attend the orthopaedic clinic pretty regularly, but Daddy's asked them to recommend a private specialist so I should soon make a lot of progress.'

'A private specialist? Won't that be pretty expensive?'

'I suppose so, but with the sale of the house and the golden handshake and all that—' She broke off, looking a little anxious and regretful. 'One thing though, being cooped up here in hospital . . . I've faded out of the limelight a bit, haven't I? I was sort of relying on drama school teachers recognising me and giving me a bit of favourable attention. You can't deny a bit of exposure on the box is good for getting attention!'

'That's certainly true,' Bethany agreed. 'But it's talent that really matters, I'm sure—'

'And I've got that! But there's no denying my voice has been affected by what's happened – there isn't the same depth of tone – but that'll come right once I start with a voice coach.'

'Voice coach, acting school – you're full of plans, that's for sure.

Mind you don't rush things too much, Allie. So long for now and all the best.'

As she drove away from the hospital, Bethany looked back on this conversation, and the more she thought about it the more it worried her. It seemed Josh's daughter expected far more in the way of funds than he was likely to raise. Did he understand how much Allie was counting on special medical attention and coaching by a voice teacher? Or, in his rather sleepy way, was he waiting to see how things turned out?

She made a note on her organiser to ring Josh as soon as she had a minute. But other matters took priority: she had a day's work to do, and then within forty-eight hours Mrs Bedells was back in the news.

One of the daily tabloids had decided to back Mrs Bedells despite the unfortunate revelations about her past – or rather, because of them. The features editor had for a long time made a point of backing the feminist movement, partly because she had a lot of sympathy with it and partly because, as she justified it to her editor, it always sparked controversy.

While the good weather lasted the newspaper had decided to organise what they'd entitled '*A Bedells Beano!*' They'd contacted a well-known champion of women's rights, a veteran of the old bra-burning days, with an invitation to support Mrs Bedells against the criticism of the conventional, by opening the party proceedings and making a speech.

The squatters, learning of this, were delighted. Things had gone very quiet to their way of thinking – no newsmen or cameramen, no excitement or banner-waving. The promise of free drinks and sand-wiches, of cake and crisps for the children, and lots of media attention for the speechmaking, thrilled them to the core. They promised their complete support. The Royal Terrace Protection Group, not entirely taken with the title *Beano* but keen to get public notice, offered to come with placards. The Barhampton Thespians, not to be outdone, declared they would put on a rehearsed performance of the scenes from Arabella Bedells's plays, in costume and with recorded music of the period.

Raymond Bigsby advised Barhampton council to go along with it. 'You could of course forbid it,' he sighed, 'since the Terrace belongs mostly to the council. But you'd get even more adverse publicity and earn the undying enmity of the *Comet* . . .'

'It might rain,' suggested the Mayor in forlorn tones.

'Let's hope for a deluge.'

But the September weather continued fine and very warm, with high pressure sitting over the British Isles.

'It's really awful,' Bethany said to Peter. 'Poor old soul – she never gets any peace.'

'Couldn't you do something about that, Bethany?'

'Such as what?'

'Well, we know she never answers the door or the telephone or comes to the window any more, not since the squatters moved in. But she talked to you a couple of times. Couldn't you go back and have another try? I mean before Saturday, before the shindig.'

'But what could I say, Peter? I can't *prevent* the party. The council's given tacit assent to it, and as for the newspaper – nothing would stop them from holding this event.'

'No, that's true, nothing can stop it, I'm afraid. But don't you think this is a moment when Mrs Bedells might actually agree to move out?'

Bethany was surprised, and her glance showed it. 'Isn't that rather a sneaky thing to do?' she enquired.

He understood at once. 'You think it's taking advantage of her, is that it? In my opinion the old lady's been through enough. Don't forget, I'm supposed to be acting in support of the Protection Group, and this shindig is actually being supported by the Group because they feel it keeps the issue before the public. But I'm worried about making her life even more miserable than it already is. I'm beginning to think she *ought* to move out, never mind what the Protection Group say.'

'Well . . . Of course I'd be glad if she vacated the place and agreed to sell.'

Peter touched her cheek with an admonishing finger. 'Not so fast, not so fast. She could leave the house but remain the owner.'

'That's true. But I bet she feels that the moment she leaves, the wrecking ball will knock it down.'

'We'd have to persuade her it would be safe. The Royal Terrace Protection Group could fight for the protection of the Terrace even if the house were empty, you know. We don't actually need her presence – although of course they feel she attracts sympathy to their case.'

They sat for a moment in thought. They were in Peter's flat, with the windows wide open to the warm evening air. Bethany was free of any feeling of guilt at leaving her mother on her own, for Mary was in fact out enjoying herself. Since the separation from Daniel, a new Mary Dayton seemed to be emerging, more lively, more inclined for pleasure. Bethany was pleased to see the change, for it released her from the sense of responsibility. Absurd, really, to feel a maternal responsibility for her own mother – yet it had troubled her at first.

But this evening she had come to Peter's flat with her mind at rest. A few days had gone by since last they had spent time together. They were eager for each other, quick to catch fire from kisses and little embraces. Their love-making now was a celebration of their growing knowledge of each other, how to please, how to tempt or thrill – the lore of shared passion, the joy of tumultuous surrender.

Afterwards they had lain together quietly, she with her head on his chest, he with his arm about her and his chin against the short crop of fair hair. For a time they had said little but by and by Peter went in search of a bottle of chilled wine. He donned a dressing-gown and

201

brought one for her, one that had become 'hers' in his mind. They sat now by the open window, sipping, glancing out at the slopes of the moors where the heather was still a veil of purple, and talking together in thoughtful tones.

'I agree this party is taking things right over the top,' Bethany mused. 'I suppose I could try to get her to talk. But you know what she's like – she'll probably stay at the back of the house no matter who comes to the door.'

'You could put a note in first – what about that? Say you're coming to speak to her at such and such a time with a view to being a help over the impending "party". I mean . . . what about this? Could you offer her temporary accommodation? So that she could be away while the *Beano* is going on?'

'Well, I *could* . . .'

'Then you know, if it was a nice place you were offering . . . you might persuade her to stay on. What d'you think?'

'It's worth a try, anyway.' She was surveying in her mind the property to which she had access. There was a retirement block in a village about four miles away; a ground-floor flat had become vacant only recently because its owner had gone to stay with relatives.

Their talk turned to other matters, and by and by they ceased to need words. As the night breeze began to blow, they closed the window and went back to their realm of delight until it was time for Bethany to leave.

Without consulting anyone else, she put Peter's suggestion into action. Very early on the morning of the Wednesday before the *Daily Comet*'s big event, she put a letter through the door of Mrs Bedells's house, marked in large red capitals URGENT – FROM BETHANY DAYTON – PLEASE OPEN!

The letter inside suggested that the Saturday party might prove very disagreeable for her, and that Bethany could offer a place to stay, even if only temporarily, if Mrs Bedells would like to leave. *I'll drop by later today to talk to you about this. If you're interested, please come to either the door or the window. With good wishes for your welfare, Bethany Dayton.*

Alas, when she got to the house that afternoon, the preparations for the *Beano* were going on apace. Mrs Bedells remained shut off behind her locked door and her net curtains. Sighing, Bethany realised she'd chosen a bad time. She scribbled a few words on a leaf of her notebook. *I quite understand you didn't want any of the others to see us talking. I'll come back after dark. It will have to be rather late but please let's talk.*

She got to the Terrace as soon as night began to fall but there was still a lot of activity. A platform was being put up, in part to accommodate the Barhampton Thespians but also for an impromptu karaoke on the day. The children of the squatters regarded this as an adventure playground. There was a great deal of shrieking and calling, a lot of hammering, sudden squeals from loudspeaker systems.

Better to leave it a while. She went in search of a cup of coffee or a glass of wine and found both in a bistro within about ten minutes' walk. Posters were pinned up on the bistro's notice board: *SATURDAY! ROYAL TERRACE! BEANO!* There were no indications of timing, which seemed to mean anyone could turn up at any time; the fun would start when enough people were present and end when the last merrymaker went home. For anyone who liked a quiet life, the outlook was poor.

At about eleven she left the bistro. Something like tranquillity had descended on Royal Terrace. There were still children running about, some of them dancing on stage to loud disco music from a tape-player, but that was at the far end. Bethany went up shallow steps to knock quietly on Mrs Bedells's door.

No answer. She knocked again, louder, realising that the sound had to compete with the music in the street. Still no answer. Only at the fourth attempt did she catch some indication of a presence on the other side.

'Mrs Bedells?'

'Is that Miss Dayton?'

'Yes, Mrs Bedells – do you remember me? I came that day your cat went for a walk across the road.'

'And scratched that other lady, yes, I remember.'

'How *is* your cat, Mrs Bedells?'

There was a momentary silence. Then a forlorn voice said, 'Tibbles has run away. She couldn't stand all the upset.'

'Oh! I *am* sorry.'

'Them squatters!' cried the old lady. 'They've turned this place into a madhouse! This used to be a lovely respectable road, everybody decent and earning an honest living. But *them* – living off the Welfare, squalling and playing loud music all hours of the day and night, they're nowt but rubbish, that's all they are!'

'I know it's been hard for you, Mrs Bedells. That's why I wanted to talk. Wouldn't it be better if you moved away?'

'No! Nobody's ever going to say as Nancy Bedells let herself be beaten!'

'But you've heard the racket they made today – it'll get worse until Saturday and then Saturday will be like bedlam—'

'I've been putting cotton wool in my ears. I'll just put more in, that's all.'

'Wouldn't you consider going away, even just for the weekend? From Friday, say, till Sunday?'

'And where would I go, tell me that? Some old people's home where

203

they'll declare me off my head and lock me up? You must think I came down with the last shower!'

'Mrs Bedells!' There was genuine shock in Bethany's voice. 'You don't really think I'd do a thing like that to you?'

'Well . . . I don't know you . . . how do I know what you're up to?'

'I'm trying to help. Really I am. And as to who I am, you read the papers, I know you do, so you know I'm the architect for the new Town Centre—'

'Yes, it's your fault the Terrace is being pulled down! Who gave you the right to knock down my house? You're no friend to me so don't pretend—'

'Listen, Mrs Bedells, don't let's waste time on quarrelling. I'll admit that a bad mistake's been made and that you're having a very bad time of it. This weekend it's going to be even worse. So why not get away to somewhere quiet? As to locking you up – Good Lord, I've got no powers of that kind, but I *have* got access to property – privately run property, nothing to do with the council or the Welfare, I guarantee it.'

'Yes, but when I get back home I'll find you've changed the locks so I won't be able to get in!'

'No, no! How *can* you! I never even thought of such a thing!'

There was a long pause. Then the old lady said, 'Mebbe you mean well. As to getting away – I don't know what to make of it. And I'm tired, it's late and it's been a tiring day. I can't think about it tonight.'

'Shall I come back in the morning?'

'Nay, there'll be folk here from eight o'clock on, hammering and shouting instructions at each other – a body gets no rest! Come back about this time tomorrow night.'

'But tomorrow's Thursday, Mrs Bedells. That's leaving it a bit tight if you're going on Friday.'

'I haven't said I'm going. I don't trust any of you after the tricks you've played on me.'

'I understand,' Bethany said, seeing it was no use arguing in the face of all the mistrust and bad faith that had gone before. 'I'll come back tomorrow.'

Peter was encouraging when she spoke to him on the phone next morning. 'She may say she doesn't trust you but I think she *wants* to. Cooped up alone in that house, only creeping out when she thinks no one will catch her at a disadvantage – it's like being in solitary confinement. She needs someone, and I think you've volunteered for the part, Bethany.'

'I hope you're right. I've telephoned the manager of the retirement flats and he's agreed to make the empty one available for the weekend, but he says it can't be permanent because he's got a waiting list of purchasers.'

'Let's hope the old girl agrees to take up your offer.'

'I've got some sales brochures showing the interior of one of the flats.

I thought I'd take one with me tonight – it might persuade her.'

'It's a good idea.' He hesitated. 'Does anyone know what you're doing?'

'No, of course not, only you! If it got out there'd be cameramen there – NANCY GIVES UP – can't you just see it?'

'Don't even think it! She'd dash right indoors again. The only reason I asked is that . . . well . . . you know, she is a very old lady. If she should slip and break a hip, or anything disastrous—'

'If I can persuade her to leave the house, I'll swaddle her in cotton wool from door to door, I promise, Peter.'

He laughed, and was satisfied that she understood the responsibility she was taking on – *if* she could persuade Mrs Bedells to trust her . . .

That night she was back at the door of No. 15. If possible there was even more activity than on the previous night – testing of sound systems and coloured disco lights, an electronic keyboard being tried out, pennants and banners being hung from the squatters' windows.

Mrs Bedells was on watch for Bethany behind the lace curtains of the side bay window, and preferred to speak to her from there – presumably so that she could see her face while they talked. The lamps from the works vehicle park next door gave light to make Bethany fairly visible, but Mrs Bedells remained a veiled presence in her front room.

'Have you thought about my suggestion?' Bethany asked.

'I've though about it, yes.'

'And have you decided to do it?'

'If I were to go . . . just for a couple of days . . . do you promise I'd not be held against my will in this place?'

'It's not a prison, Mrs Bedells. Look.' She held up the brochure, open, against the window pane. The old lady bent to look at it but the light was too poor. She shook her head, drew back.

'Open the window a little and I'll slip it through so you can take it away to your kitchen or somewhere, and look at it.'

Mrs Bedells shook her head again. 'If I open the window to take it you'll grab my wrist.'

'No, of *course* I won't! I'm trying to be a friend to you, believe me.'

'I don't see why you should be, that's the point.'

'Look, open the window just a crack and I'll slip it through.'

'Well . . . all right . . .' She unscrewed the safety catch on the sash, easing up the lower panes a fraction so that the brochure could just pass through. She took it, closed the window, refastened the catch, and walked away.

A long wait ensued before Bethany could catch the faint sound of her footsteps returning. 'Well, it *looks* quite nice.'

'It's one of a block of eight. That was the show flat – of course the furnishings won't be the same because the last tenant has taken his furniture with him to Torquay, so there'll only be borrowed things – a bed and a side table and so forth. But I'll make sure it's comfy.'

'What about food?'

'There's a kitchenette – did you see? All fitted out. You can take your own supplies if you want to, and cook what you like.'

'And how'd I get there?'

'I'll drive you there.'

'No! Once I get in your car, how do I know where you'll take me?'

'Here we go again,' Bethany said in exasperation. 'Once and for all, Mrs Bedells, I'm *not* a kidnapper, I'm not a member of some kind of Welfare Mafia. All I want is for you to have a weekend of peace and quiet.'

'And you hope that's going to change my mind about giving up my house so you can knock it down!'

'Mrs Bedells . . . !'

'What?'

'You know Peter Lambot? The lawyer you telephoned when the boys were throwing stones?'

'Yes?'

'You trust him, don't you? You believe he wants to preserve the Terrace?'

'Well, yes.'

'If I bring him with me when I come to drive you to the flat, will you believe I've got no ulterior motive?'

'I suppose so.'

'So are you going to accept my offer or not?'

'Don't get snappy with me, young woman! I need time to weigh it all up.'

'But time's getting short! If you want to go, it's got to be tomorrow night before the jollifications start.'

'Huh! That's all you know! There's so many folk want to put on their act on that stage they've set up, they're talking about Friday night for a send-off. The *Comet's* thrilled to bits with itself about it – all on about community spirit and how they've roused the people's emotions and everything.'

'I hadn't seen that,' mourned Bethany. 'I don't generally read the *Comet*. Well, so that makes it all the more urgent – perhaps we ought to go tonight.'

'No,' cried the old lady. 'I'm . . . I'm not wrought up to going tonight. Besides, I've got to pack . . . and water my plants . . .'

'Tomorrow, then. Shall I come for you tomorrow night?'

'Huh . . . Might as well,' agreed Mrs Bedells.

'What time? Shall we make it late, after the first-nighters have gone home?'

'Lord knows when that's likely to be. You don't know this crowd – they stay up till the small hours.'

'Well . . . shall we say eleven o'clock? It'll be quite dark then, and if we wait until something's going on on stage, we could probably slip away without being noticed.'

'We could try, I suppose.'

'Come on, Mrs Bedells, take a positive attitude!'

'What?'

'Look on the bright side.'

'I see what you mean. All right then, tomorrow – about elevenish.'

'I'll be here.'

'With that lawyer.'

'Yes, with Mr Lambot.'

'All right then.'

And with this grudging agreement Bethany had to be content.

Though it was past midnight, Peter picked up the phone at the first ring. 'How did it go?'

'She's agreed to leave.'

'You're a miracle worker!'

'Not at all. It was the promise that you'd be there too tomorrow that persuaded her to agree.'

'Me?'

'You will come, won't you?'

'Of course, love – anything to help the poor old thing out of her prison, even if it's only temporary. What time are we to—'

'Let's discuss that tomorrow, Peter. It's getting late and Mother will be wondering where on earth I am.'

'Yes, of course.' He kept his voice carefully neutral. Bethany's mother was proving quite a problem. Since she came to stay at the flat, Bethany always had to go home to her after she had spent a happy time with Peter. He was always careful not to say how much he missed having Bethany by his side in the night.

But when Bethany got home, her mother wasn't there. She'd had a dinner date with Ossie Fielden which ought to have ended long ago, so where on earth was she? Worried, and yet reproving herself for it, Bethany made herself a drink and sat up to await her return. Absurd – sitting up for your mother . . .

Mary Dayton came in soon after one in the morning, weary yet radiant. 'Beth! What are you doing, still up at this hour?'

'I'm waiting for you,' her daughter said with a rueful smile. 'I was worried – another few minutes and I'd have started ringing round the hospitals.'

'Oh, darling! I'm sorry! But I was having such a good time I never thought about how late it was getting.'

'But where have you *been*? That must have been a very long dinner menu!'

'Well . . . After we'd eaten, we went dancing.'

'Dancing?'

'Bethie, I haven't gone dancing in years. I mean, sometimes at those dreary conferences there's been after-dinner dancing, but it's so ... lifeless, and you have to accept all kinds of partners who feel it's their duty to ask you to keep in with the boss, and some of them can't dance worth a ha'penny ... I mean, young men want you to do this sort of wobbling about and waving your arms, but they don't know any steps ...'

'And Ossie does?'

'Oh yes, Ossie could have been a champion ballroom dancer if he'd wanted to, love.'

'Ossie?'

'Can't believe it, can you? You see him as an old man with his hair thinning out, but he was a lad in his time, was Ossie. And he goes to this Ballroom Dancing Club, where they have a proper band that plays proper music, and you can do a fox-trot or a waltz without bumping into people standing still wriggling on one spot. So that's where we went after dinner, and it was really lovely, I haven't enjoyed myself so much in years.' She yawned, stretched, and then winced. 'Mind you, I used muscles I haven't used in years ... I'll pay for it in the morning!' She moved towards her room, lilting a little tune and making dance steps as she went. 'Good night, love.'

'Good night,' Bethany returned, astounded at the playfulness she'd witnessed. This was a new Mary Dayton, one that took some getting used to.

During a convenient break next morning Bethany dropped in at *Pesh, Samuels* to speak to Peter. 'I said we'd be there about eleven. I don't know what the situation will be – last night there was a lot of activity, they were testing the sound system and so on.'

'From the way the *Comet* is going on, it looks like it's the biggest thing since the World Cup. They've got some girls' pop band to appear on Saturday night, so the poor old Thespians and their Arabella-Bedells-thing have been pushed forward to Friday.' He offered a copy of the newspaper folded to show photographs and headlines.

'Barhampton Thespians, *Women and Love* by Arabella Bedells – catchy title, at any rate!' she said. 'And *Local Talent – Do Your Thing*! I wonder what that means?'

'I suppose it'll be like those talent-spotting shows on television.'

'Perhaps that's a good thing. If they're all cheering and booing local wannabe's they won't spend any time looking at Mrs Bedells's house.'

'Let's hope we can sneak in and out without being noticed,' he sighed. 'One good thing – they seem so determined to have a good time, they've forgotten it was to show support for old Mrs Bedells.'

'Let's hope she'll come with us.'

'You think she might not?'

'She's very uncertain, Peter. Poor old soul, she's been through an awful lot in the last few months and had hardly a word with another human being—'

'You don't mean she's losing her marbles?' he said with sudden anxiety. 'Because if so, Bethany, ought we to meddle—'

'No, no, she's quite sensible, only very suspicious – and who can blame her.'

They agreed to meet for a meal and go on from there to the Terrace. Parking the car might be a problem, because access to the area was difficult due to building activity. But Bethany knew her way about the sites, and had a nook picked out, not far from No. 15.

About ten that evening they drove in Bethany's Suzuki to the parking space. From there they went on foot to the Terrace, and had they been uncertain of the way they would have been guided by the noise. Someone on stage was performing on an electronic keyboard, pop songs so that the audience could sing along. Bethany and Peter joined the crowd, swaying like the others to the strains of 'By the Rivers of Babylon'.

One song succeeded another, then a compère appeared. 'The next item is Stan Stellar, our favourite local DJ, who will give you some music to dance to. How's about that then, folks?' Applause. The compère, who knew events had to follow fast on one another if the evening was to be a success, waved for silence. 'And then, so you can all have a nice rest after that, we'll have the Arabella Bedells item, *Women and Love* – don't be misled by the fact she was a lady from long ago, friends. Talk about *raunchy*! Whe-e-ew!' He made movements as if mopping his brow.

This was greeted with cheers and laughter. The DJ walked on stage, followed by two couples who were going to dance to his music as an example to the audience. Spotlights lit up the pair, Stan Stellar gave a bouncy introduction to the disco sounds he was putting on his turntable, and through somewhat distorted speakers the music belted out.

'Now might be a good moment to filter towards number fifteen,' Peter said into Bethany's ear.

'Okay.' They threaded their way between gyrating figures with coloured lights flickering over them. They reached Mrs Bedells's house. Someone had strung a banner over the doorway – OUR NANCY – OUR STAR! but all the attention was centred on the platform and the sound systems further up the Terrace.

The house itself was in darkness, the door shut fast. 'I wonder if she'll even hear us when we knock?' murmured Peter.

'I expect she's standing behind those lace curtains watching us this very minute,' Bethany replied. She gave a little wave towards the window at which she'd spoken to Mrs Bedells last night, but the curtains didn't stir.

209

'We'd better wait for a lull,' she suggested. 'When the dancing stops and they're expecting the naughty play by Arabella . . .'

'Right.'

The music began to die away. Stan Stellar announced over its closing drumbeats and guitar riffs that while the audience took their last twirl and mopped their brows, the Barhampton Thespians would bring on a few props and the musicians would set up their music stands. 'Here's a different beat, friends – authentic eighteenth-century tunes for you to sing along with.'

Bethany knocked on the door of No. 15 as the crowd stopped dancing so as to move closer to the platform and not miss a word of the 'raunchy' dialogue. The door opened a crack.

'Are you ready, Mrs Bedells?' Bethany asked in a low tone.

'Well, I've got my case here . . . but I'm not so sure . . .'

'Come on now, Mrs Bedells,' Peter coaxed. 'You've had a taste of it this evening. What do you think it'll be like tomorrow, an all-day event with an even bigger crowd.'

'Well . . . all right . . . just let me make sure I've turned off the gas and the electric . . .'

At that moment a taxi drew up at the end of the Terrace that was still open to access. From it emerged first a young woman in a print dress, and then a slight figure in jeans and a loose white top. There was a moment's hiatus while something was handed about. It proved to be two elbow crutches. Then, moving with surprising swiftness, Allie Pembury limped along the few yards of pavement to reach the steps of Mrs Bedells's house. At her side was her friend Nurse Wilson from Barhampton Hospital and behind her came Jeff Jones and a cameraman from the *Gazette*.

'Friends!' called Allie. 'Friends, supporters of Nancy Bedells!'

Friends, Romans and countrymen, groaned Bethany inwardly. She grasped Peter's arm in warning. Allie Pembury was going to make a speech.

The crowd further along the Terrace, waiting impatiently for the Thespians to arrange themselves on stage, turned to see what was going on. 'Why, it's Allie!' they cried. 'Where's your banner, Allie!'

Laughing with pleasure and surprise, they surged along the roadway to greet her. She was their pet, their little heroine, who had risked her life to tie a banner on the cupola of the old mill. 'How are you, Allie? Fancy you being here!'

'I wouldn't miss this for anything,' she told them. She limped up two of the shallow steps to give herself a vantage point for her speech.

'Hello, everybody!' she began, waving one of her elbow crutches aloft to let them know the difficulties she'd overcome so as to be here. At her side the friendly nurse from Barhampton put out an arm to steady her, beaming with delight at being part of this heroic enterprise.

210

'You going to act for us, Allie?' called a man at the back of the crowd. 'Give us a bit of that Arabella stuff!'

'As a matter of fact, I have a few lines of Arabella Bedells's immortal verse to speak,' said Allie, taking a deep breath. 'You all know, friends and neighbours of Barhampton, that Arabella was an actress, a star of the stage and a free spirit even in those far-off days. She knew what it was like to be criticised and victimised for trying to live her own life! So here are the words that have survived from one of her marvellous plays.'

Allie gave her elbow crutches to her companion, threw out her arms, and began:

> *'What though they rage, they never can prevail*
> *For Heaven protects the right with front of finest mail!*
> *I laugh at checks and mankind's cruel laws*
> *For I am armed with complete steel –*
> *The justice of my cause!'*

The door of Mrs Bedells's house had re-opened as this recitation was in progress. Its owner stared aghast at the back of Allie Pembury and the crowd she'd collected.

'Oh, that dreadful, dreadful girl!' she gasped. 'What a trick to play on me, Miss Dayton!' She drew back and slammed her door shut.

Peter swore under his breath and raised his hand to knock. Bethany caught it, holding him back and shaking her head.

'It's no good. She won't come out now. Not while this circus is going on.'

The TV cameramen had hurried to find out why the main crowd had transported itself to the other end of the Terrace. Finding Allie Pembury on the steps of Mrs Bedells's house, they spotlighted her and trained their cameras. 'Tell us why you've come, Allie. Have you risen from a sickbed to be here?'

'I couldn't *not* be here,' she replied. 'You all know how much it means to me to support Nancy, our last link with the great Arabella Bedells!'

'How are you? Legs okay?' shouted one reporter.

'Mending fast. Barhampton Hospital has been so *wonderful . . .*'

Barhampton doctors praised by actress heroine, scribbled Jeff Jones on his notepad. 'They agreed to your coming here?' he enquired.

'I'm being allowed home tomorrow,' Allie explained. 'Of course they want me back at the Orthopaedics Clinic, but I wanted so much to be with my friends of the Barhampton Thespians tonight that I crept out.'

The Barhampton Thespians, in their eighteenth-century costumes and uncomfortable wigs, were standing on the platform looking sour at this upstaging by a minor member of the club. The reporters went on calling questions to her, the crowd cheered at her replies. Bethany and Peter, as

211

disappointed as the Thespians and with more reason, slipped away from the shadows behind the star of the evening and made for Bethany's car.

'What should we do?' Peter wondered. 'Wait, and come back later?'

But Bethany had read the expression on the old lady's face. 'It's no use, Peter. She doesn't trust me any more.'

Chapter Seventeen

Bethany drove Peter home to his flat, but didn't go in. It was late and though next day was Saturday, that for her was a working day. Moreover, she was depressed by the evening's events. Peter sensed her mood. As they were saying good night he murmured, 'Don't blame yourself. It was a good idea.'

'Was it?' she wondered. 'Were we kidding ourselves? What right have we to try to influence her in what she does?'

'Oh, come on, Bethany, all we wanted to do was give her a bit of peace and quiet—'

'But why should we do it by making Mrs Bedells into a refugee? We should have tried it from the other end – made the council forbid the show—'

'What, get Barhampton council to stand up against a newspaper like the *Daily Comet*? Be realistic, Bethany.'

'The *realistic* fact is that Mrs Bedells is convinced I set her up for that performance with Allie Pembury—'

'Nobody could have foreseen that Allie—'

'Nobody ought to be interfering in that woman's life! Just because she's old, that doesn't mean she needs to be shepherded about by people like us. We were wrong to think we knew what she ought to do.'

'You mean I was wrong. It was my idea in the first place.'

'Yes, you were wrong. And I was wrong to let you persuade me—'

'If I remember rightly, you didn't need much persuading—'

'No, I didn't, and if you want to know that makes me even angrier! Just because you suggested it, I fell in with the idea. I didn't even stop to consider whether just for once you might be wrong!'

'What are you saying? That I always think I'm right?'

'Well, lawyers have a tendency to think they're right!'

They were almost glaring at each other. They were on the verge of a quarrel. She recovered herself enough to say, 'We ought to call it a day. I don't know about you, but I've had more than enough.'

'Right you are.'

'Well, good night, then.'

'Good night.'

He got out of the Suzuki, closed its door, and stood back. She drove off without a wave or a backward glance. She was irritated and disappointed and miserable.

When she got home the scent of flowers reached her even before she had got her door open. Her mother could be heard pottering about in the bathroom though the door was open. Bethany called, 'It's me,' then went to the bathroom to find the bath full of flowers up to their necks in water.

'Oh, good Lord, Mother,' she groaned. She was longing for a hot bath and bed.

'You don't mind, darling, do you?' her mother asked with blithe confidence. 'It's my week for doing the church flowers.'

'But where did you—'

'I went to the house, of course – at a time I knew your father would be in the office.' Mary was tweaking a blossom here and there to make sure it stayed above the water level. 'These Michaelmas daisies have got rust . . . If I'd been at home I'd have sprayed them . . .' She sighed a little. 'Never mind, I'll clean them up before I do the arrangements and anyhow nobody'll be able to see the stalks once I've put them in the vases . . .' She rolled up a sleeve to keep it from getting wet. 'And I picked up my mail and guess what? There was a note from Robert.'

'Good heavens!' Bethany's brother Robert was still in Albania, and seldom heard from except by fragmented phone calls from some ill-equipped hospital at the back of beyond.

'How're things going for him?' Bethany enquired. She greatly admired Robert, whose example she had followed when standing firm about her choice of career.

'Up and down, as usual, but the great thing is, he's in Venice!'

'In Venice?'

'Yes, it's lovely, isn't it? Of course it's not really a holiday, it's to chase up some supplies that should have reached them but have gone missing, but guess what? I'm going to Venice to see him for a few days next week.'

'Well!' Bethany was really taken aback. It was years since her mother had gone abroad except as 'spouse or partner' for one of the many conferences arranged by architects' associations or town-planners. 'You're going on your own?'

'We-ell . . . as a matter of fact . . . I'm going with Ossie.'

Bethany, shocked despite herself, managed to check the protest that rose to her lips.

'Yes, with Ossie.' Mary studied her daughter and began to laugh. 'Good heavens, you look like a nineteenth-century schoolmarm! I'm going to Venice because I got a note from Robert to say he'd be there for a couple of weeks perhaps, and when I told Ossie he suggested he and I go there to see him. We'd hardly be spending a torrid weekend with Robert there at our side!'

'Oh!' Bethany sank down on the edge of the bath. Here eyes filled with tears. 'Oh, Mother, I'm so sorry! I don't know what's the matter with me. I've said and done everything wrong tonight.'

Mary led her into the living room, drew up a chair, and sat her down on it. 'What's happened? Had a row with Peter?'

'No – yes – not exactly. I don't know.' She got out a tissue to wipe her eyes. 'Everything's going wrong. The new Town Centre has caused all sorts of trouble, young Allie Pembury got injured on one of our sites, Josh has lost his job, you and Dad have split up because of it . . . It's awful! I wish I'd never entered that design in the competition!'

'Don't be silly, darling.' Mary put her arm round her daughter's shoulders. Here was this clever, capable woman, nearly thirty-three years old, and still beset with the insecurity that had plagued her through her teenage years – all because her father had disapproved of her. 'All right, so things have been going wrong. But isn't that always the case with a big construction? I'm sure I've had your father tell me a hundred times that the contractors have done something idiotic, or the ground's subsided, or the client's changed his mind . . .'

'Well . . . that's true . . .'

'And from what I've seen of the Town Centre as it's going up, it's beginning to look rather nice.'

'Do you think so?' She tried to read her mother's gaze through tear-filled eyes.

'I certainly do. When it's finished—'

'If it ever does get finished!'

'Come on, Beth, don't talk foolishness. You know it will be finished one day next year and you'll be proud of it.'

'Yes, but think what it's *costing* in human misery—'

'If you include me and your father in that, I'm not miserable,' Mary said stoutly. 'To tell you the truth, I'm enjoying myself.'

'But this thing with you and Ossie—'

'What "thing"? Robert wrote to say he's in Venice so I managed to get him on the telephone and suggested I should meet him there, spend a few days with him. I scarcely ever see him now,' she went on, sadness coming into her voice. 'If he gets time off, he almost never comes home . . .'

They let the thought die away. They both knew that if Robert came home it would only mean arguments with his father, who heartily disapproved of his son 'wasting himself' in charity work.

'It was Ossie's suggestion that I should go,' Mary resumed, 'and when he asked me if I'd like company, I jumped at the idea. I don't know if I'd be any good at travelling alone. And if you're worrying about my morals, don't – Ossie and I have booked separate rooms and, besides, there's nothing like that between us.' She gave a little laugh and added, 'Yet.'

'Mother!'

'Oh, is it such a scare to think I might take a lover?' her mother said. 'Children always seem to imagine that their parents are made of something entirely different from themselves! It's all right for you and Peter to get carried away, but poor old Mother must be a saint – is that it?'

'No-o – of course, if you feel something special for Ossie – I mean—'

'You'd give me your approval, would you? Listen to me, child. Ossie's one of the best men who ever stepped in leather, and if I were to divorce your father Ossie is probably the only man I'd ever think of as a replacement—'

'*Mother!*'

'It's all right, I'm not thinking about divorce. But I'm enjoying my freedom and I'm going to Venice next week with Ossie, and if I feel like going to Istanbul the week after with the manager of the dry-cleaner's, I'll do it and you'd better not throw up your hands in horror, my girl!'

Bethany began to laugh. All at once the events of the evening began to seem less of a disaster. 'All right, all right, I apologise. I'm sorry, I'm so used to . . . I don't know . . . thinking of you as a fixed constant . . . But you're right, it's time you enjoyed yourself a bit.'

'Come on then,' said Mary, 'let's have a nightcap and get to bed. *You* look drawn and weary, and *I've* got to be up early tomorrow. I'm going to Manchester for the day to get my hair done.'

Next morning, as Bethany made breakfast, she kept an eye on the television news. When the national bulletin was over, the local session came on, and there was the *Bedells Beano* in all its initial glory, with the revolving disco-lights and the would-be Frank Sinatras and Tina Turners. A short sound-bite of Allie Pembury was included: '*The justice of my cause!*' and some information about her plans for the future. 'So you'll be leaving Barhampton?' asked an unseen interviewer.

'Well, it's better that we do, after the way the council treated my father.'

'How do you mean?' was the instant question, catching at a new 'scandal'.

'Well, they've been so unjust . . . He's had to resign, you know . . . they left him no alternative.' The item concluded with a quote from a 'spokesperson' for Barhampton council: 'Mr Pembury left us by mutual agreement and there was no coercion.'

Ten seconds later Bethany's phone was ringing. Her mother, just emerging from her room, went to answer it. 'Oh . . . Hello, Daniel . . . Yes, quite well, thank you. And you?'

Bethany concentrated on making tea and setting out milk and sugar. After a few polite exchanges her mother called, 'Your father would like to speak to you.'

216

He plunged straight in when she took up the receiver. 'Did you see that on the TV?'

'Yes, but it's best to take no notice.'

'What does she think she's up to? She's implying there was something underhand about his resignation whereas we all know that he brought it on himself—'

'Calm down, calm down, Dad. Raymond Bigsby will deal with any innuendoes.'

'I'm going to tell Iris to issue a statement—'

'Leave it to Iris to decide what's best—'

'But we can't let that confounded girl say that we've done something wrong!'

'She's just attention-seeking, Dad. She's got no grounds for what she said and if we make any response we're only helping her get the limelight.'

'Hmm . . . You really think so?'

'I'm sure of it. If you'd seen the way she moved in on the show last night and hogged the stage—'

'You were there?'

'Yes, as it happens—'

'I don't think you should go to the Terrace while this daft thing of the *Comet*'s is going on. It looks as if we're giving it our support.'

'I shan't be going again.'

'No, well, that's all right then.' He hesitated. 'Your mother's well, I hear?'

'Oh yes, she seems to be enjoying life.'

'It's more than I am,' he muttered. 'Meals out of the freezer, no clean shirts . . .'

'Life is hard, Dad.'

'You think it's funny, do you?' She made no response and he went on after a moment, 'Get her to come home, Bethie.'

'No.'

'What? You don't care that she's making us a laughing stock?'

'I'm sure she isn't—'

'That's all you know! Joe Glossop was telling me yesterday, she's been seen gadding about at a dancing club. A dancing club! At her age! Next thing we know, she'll have taken up with a toy boy.'

'Don't be silly, Dad.'

'Does she . . . Does she confide in you?'

'If she does, I'm not going to tell you about it.'

'No, of course not . . . but does she . . . does she mention Ossie Fielden?'

'Frequently.'

'I thought he was a friend of mine,' groaned Daniel. 'I wouldn't believe it when I first heard . . .'

'It's too early in the morning for this, Dad,' Bethany said with a sigh.

'And the toast is burning. Goodbye.'

'No, wait—'

But she put the phone down.

Mary, in her dressing-gown, was drinking her first cup of tea. 'Is there trouble about Allie Pembury again?' she enquired.

'Oh, it's nothing.' Bethany sat down, picked up the cereal packet, then put it down. 'Some kind friend has told Dad about you and Ossie Fielden,' she said.

'Oh?'

'You know he's taking it badly, Mother.'

'I suppose he is.'

'Shouldn't you . . . say something? I mean, to reassure him?'

'I don't want to reassure him. I want him to know what it feels like when your partner takes off for a bit of fun with someone else. Heaven knows, Bethany, I've had that experience a dozen times in my married life. Now it's his turn.'

'What is it? Revenge? Pay-back time?' It surprised Bethany; her mother wasn't the 'own-back' type.

'Let's say it's a little educational exercise. And,' Mary said, 'to emphasise the lesson, I may send him a postcard from Venice.'

Part of Bethany's plan for the day was to visit the sheltered accommodation where Mrs Bedells would have spent the weekend. She'd rung last night to say briefly that the visitor wouldn't be coming, but felt she owed the warden a personal apology. Moreover, it gave her the opportunity to check how comfortable and suitable the complex was. She did this frequently, her view being that the architect's responsibility extended beyond designing a building; it was important to know how well the building suited its purpose when in use, whether those who used it or lived in it found it comfortable.

Mr Haverford accepted her apology without comment. He escorted her up staircases and down in the lift, but was soon bored. Since Bethany preferred to speak to tenants on their own, so as to get their true impressions of the facilities, she was glad when he withdrew.

At coffee-time she dropped in on the sun-room, where tenants could gather for a break and company if they felt the need of it. It was a conservatory with UV screening but plenty of light and warmth and, by design, a good view of the gardens and the distant moor.

There were only two occupants. 'What's the matter?' asked Bethany jokingly. 'Coffee no good here?'

'Oh, it's not that,' said one, a plump comfortable figure with well-dressed white hair. 'Saturday, you know. Always been shopping day, has Saturday – old habits die hard so most folk are off to York or Harrogate.'

'I've seen you here before, haven't I?' asked her companion, who was a little older, more careworn, and less well turned out. 'Visiting someone?'

'No, as a matter of fact, I'm Bethany Dayton. I designed this building.'

'Designed it? How do you mean, designed it? Did the curtains and furniture and that? Because if you did, I think these cane chairs—'

'No, I'm an architect, I design buildings. I drew up the plans for this one so I keep coming around to see if it's working all right.'

'Working all right?'

'If you like living in it.'

'It's not bad, is it, Jephthah?' said the plump one. 'I wish we didn't have cane chairs and sofas in this room because they catch your stockings something awful.'

'I'm sorry,' said Bethany. 'I didn't choose the furnishings, but I'll mention it to Mr Haverford.'

'Oh, him! We keep telling him. Did you say your name's Bethany? That's biblical, you know. Same as mine. I'm Jephthah, that's in Judges, if that means owt to you. It's a man's name, really, but my mother liked it anyway. Jephthah Barnes, how do you do.'

'And I'm Mabel Montgomery, how do you do. I've been thinking,' Mabel went on, 'weren't you in the papers a while ago? I seem to remember something.'

'Yes, our firm designed the new Town Centre in Barhampton.'

'Oh, that. Oh, now I remember! Didn't you all get involved in a hoo-ha with Nancy Bedells?'

'You could say that,' Bethany acknowledged ruefully. 'We still are, if it comes to that.'

'Lives in Royal Terrace, if I remember rightly. Used to think a lot of herself, still does, I wouldn't mind betting.'

'Mabel,' reproved her friend.

'Well, she did, Jephthah! Just because she landed a man who had his own business – and what was it, when you came right down to it? Sending out little books about etiquette and how to write posh letters if you were invited to a banquet – still, she felt that made him a "professional man", a writer – same as somebody in his family a hundred years agone – but all he did was write these little poppety booklets at a shilling a go.'

'Mabel,' said Jephthah in a reproachful tone. 'You know what it says in the Bible – "*The stroke of the tongue breaketh the bones*".'

'Oh, pooh,' Mabel retorted, with a sidelong grin at Bethany. 'I'm not saying anything that isn't true. Tell the truth, I thought he was a fine-looking man, William Bedells. Wouldn't have minded him myself, only Nancy got in first.'

'Now that's envy,' said Jephthah, 'and "*Envy and wrath shorten the life*".'

'I often wonder who this feller was that put all these sayings in the Bible for you! Upon my soul—'

But the rest of her rebuttal was lost in the arrival of some of the Saturday shoppers, with carrier bags full of interesting items they wanted to display. Bethany was rather sorry; she'd have liked to glean a little more about Mrs Bedells in her young days. It was difficult to learn much through the panels of a door or through window-glass.

When she got home to Barhampton at mid-afternoon her mother was preparing to go to York to do the flower arrangements in her parish church. Local radio was giving live coverage of the *Bedells Beano* in Royal Terrace. Bethany's hand hovered over the telephone to ring Peter and make up, but just as she was about to pick up, it rang. She snatched it up, sure it would be Peter. But it was Josh Pembury.

'Could I drop by, Bethany? I've something important I'd like to discuss with you.'

'You mean, come here?' She glanced across at her mother, who was pottering about in the kitchen wrapping flowers in wet newspaper. There was a laundry basket already half-full of wrapped flowers. Sheets of newspaper were soaking in the sink. Who knew how long it would be before she drove off for the church? 'It's not very convenient.'

'Oh. Well, I can't ask you here, because of course Allie's home from hospital and I don't want her to hear what we say.'

'It's about Allie?'

'Well, yes . . .'

'But how can I be of any help there? You're the best person to deal with her.'

'The fact is, Bethany, I'd like your opinion about something I've done.'

'What have you done?' she asked, alarmed though she couldn't think why.

'Couldn't we meet? How about that bistro on the corner of the old Corn Market?'

'Very well,' she sighed, since it seemed so important to him.

Josh was there before her, solemnly drinking cappuccino with lots of chocolate sprinkle on top. The bistro was only half-full – too early for the evening glass of wine, too late for afternoon tea. He summoned the waitress as she sat down. She ordered a double espresso, then looked at him in enquiry.

'Well, the thing is . . . the thing is, Bethany . . . I've let Allie talk me into resuming the court case against the demolition contractors.'

'What!'

He looked distressed, a big, solid man reduced to absurdity by the moustache of foam on his upper lip.

'I knew you wouldn't approve,' he said.

'Then why did you get me here to talk about it?' she demanded, indignation in every syllable.

'Well, I was hoping . . . I thought you'd be able to advise me.'

220

'Advise you on what?'

'How to get out of it.'

'Get out of the court case? Surely that's easy enough? The lawyer can't have gone far with it, so all you need do is tell him to drop it and ask for the bill for his services thus far.'

'Yes, but . . . you see . . . Allie wants us to go on.'

Bethany paused. 'Because she's going to need the money, I suppose?'

'That's it. You're so quick, Bethany. I knew you'd understand.'

'I understand that she needs the money because she talked about it when I visited her in hospital. She seemed to be under the impression that you were going to get a very large settlement from Barhampton council.'

'Oh, don't,' he groaned. 'When she saw what they were offering she screwed up the letter and threw it across the ward. She got into quite a state. So to quiet her down I agreed when she said we ought to get a lawyer and start up the claim for damages again, and Bethany, honestly, this new man is very steady and reliable – Rosemont, his name is, and he seems to think we could get a sizeable sum if we settle out of court, but the thing is . . . you see . . . the representative from the Association – the man who's dealing with my separation payment – he's quite against resuming the court case because he says it will make the council very difficult to deal with over the early retirement thing . . .' He wandered off into silence.

The waitress, eyeing them with curiosity, came with Bethany's coffee. She sipped a little, to give her time to assess Josh's problem. To her it seemed to arise mainly through his own lack of courage. Rather than have a disagreement with his daughter he'd let himself be led into a dilemma.

'You're going to have to tell her the suit for damages must wait. How near are you to signing an agreement with Barhampton council on your severance pay?'

He shrugged. 'Couple of weeks? A month?'

'Well, then, you tell her that you'll get things going about the court case in a month. And meanwhile you'll have to talk her out of doing it *at all*.'

'But if she's got a good case?'

'I don't think she has, and nor do you, really. She was trespassing, and I know for a fact that warning notices were posted, because I saw them—'

'But not where Allie could see them—'

'So she says.' She hesitated. 'Josh, she seems to live in something of a dream world. Do you really think she saw no warning signs, or has she just talked herself into believing that?'

He bridled a little. 'Allie doesn't tell lies,' he said with indignation.

Heads turned at the raised voice. He was embarrassed so took refuge in his coffee cup.

221

She tried a different tack. 'You could spend a lot on lawyer's fees yet settle out of court for quite a small sum, Josh.'

'We're applying for Legal Aid—'

'Even so, the stress and bother involved would take its toll on you, just when you're trying to start a new career, and I think you ought to consider that the damages might not be great – I mean, Allie will be pursuing her dramatic studies, won't she? How can this Mr Rosemont persuade the opposition lawyers that she deserves a lot in damages when she's not on crutches or anything . . .'

'Ye-es . . .'

'All you've got to do is be firm, Josh. Explain to her that her expectations are too high.'

'I was wondering . . .'

'What?'

'If *you* would do it for me, Bethany.'

'Me?' Now it was Bethany's turn to be embarrassed as people glanced round at her exclamation.

'Yes. I think she might listen to someone like you, a woman who's made a success of her career, someone she could relate to.'

'Nothing would induce me to get involved in this, Josh.'

'But I hoped you'd help me – you've been more sympathetic than most of the others and I was hoping . . . You see, Allie is at a difficult stage.'

'I quite agree, and for that very reason I don't think an outsider should get involved.'

'But you're not an outsider, Bethany. You and I have been friends for a good while.'

'But that doesn't make me any kind of an expert on how to handle a girl like Allie. If you want the truth, she baffles me.'

His broad brow furrowed. 'I don't see what you mean.'

She sighed inwardly. 'When I was Allie's age I was all at sixes and sevens. I knew I wanted to be an architect but I had so much opposition from my father I felt I must be in the wrong—'

'And that's where things are easier for Allie, because I feel she's in the right.'

'About wanting to be an actress.'

'Yes. Surely you can see, Bethany – she's got enormous talent.'

'I can't speak as to that. I've never seen her act, except for one or two of these little snippets from Arabella Bedells.'

'But you must admit she's got all the equipment – good looks, a good figure, a nice voice, tremendous determination—'

'*That's* the bit that worries me, Josh. She's so "determined" she just doesn't listen to anyone else.'

'But she says she has to stay focused – she can't allow herself to be distracted—'

'You mean she can't allow herself to hear anybody else's opinion. She closes her mind to anything that she doesn't want to hear.'

He coloured a little and said slowly, 'You're almost saying . . . that she's selfish.'

'Well, isn't she?'

Josh looked hurt. 'My daughter has a heart of gold,' he declared. 'Why, she's been very, *very* upset about the trouble I'm having over this severance pay.'

'Josh . . . You said yourself . . . she was upset . . . isn't that because it's turning out to be a lot less than she expected? Not enough to pay for all this private treatment and extra tuition and so forth?'

'You can't think that Allie is grasping! Why, the only thing that matters to her is her talent—'

'Right! There you have it. You've said it yourself. The only thing she cares about is being a star—'

'I didn't mean it in that way! I was trying to explain that money was only a means to an end for Allie—'

'I agree with you. The means to get on with this precious career of hers. And to take the cliché a step further, she feels the end justifies the means. She doesn't seem to care what she does so long as she can go on with this dream of being a great actress.'

'Well, you know, Bethany, every great artist has to be a bit ruthless.'

'So you're content to let her run your life for you, talk you into a lawsuit you don't really want, because her so-called talent gives her the right to?'

'You're beginning to sound very critical about her, Bethany. I thought you'd be on our side—'

'I'm on *your* side, Josh. I can't truthfully say I'm on Allie's.'

'But the one is the same as the other.'

'Not at all. I want you to get a good settlement from Barhampton council because I feel you've been caught wrong-footed with them, and you don't deserve to be thrown out. But as to bringing phoney law-suits so that Allie can have funds for special tutors and cosmetic surgery, I'm dead against it. And so should you be, Josh. Surely in your heart you know it's not right to let her go on like this.'

'That's where you're wrong. The doctors told me to encourage her in every possible way to get on with her life, not to discourage her in anything she wanted to try.'

'To get on with her life – yes, of course, but surely not at the expense of someone else's!'

'Oh, it's not as big a thing as that, Bethany. I can go somewhere else, start again—'

'You can go where Allie wants you to go, somewhere where she can get to a good drama school. If you said to her, "I want to use my severance pay to go and live in the Highlands and raise trees" – what do you think she would say?'

'But I'd never do that!' he said, shocked. 'It wouldn't be fair to her. Barhampton was a poor enough choice when I look back on it – no proper theatre, no dance instructor except Miss Delano and occasional master classes in York when there was a ballet company . . . Of course she was only a little kid when we first came. I didn't realise how special she was until later.' He reached out and took Bethany's hand, to impress on her how deeply he meant what he was saying. 'That's why I turned to you. You see, I don't have the sort of sensitivity that's needed. But these practical things about money and so forth – they have to be dealt with. So I hoped you'd take it on, explain to her that she has to be patient with her poor blundering old dad . . .'

Bethany found she couldn't bear any more. She snatched away her hand. 'How can you be so *feeble*?' she burst out. 'You let her twist you round her little finger!'

'Bethany!' He was so startled and upset that he actually jerked back in his chair.

'I'm sorry, it's time someone said it to you. Where Allie is concerned you're as weak as water!'

'Weak? I'm not *weak* – I'm anxious, I'm concerned. I've got a daughter with a very special talent, and like all parents of specially gifted children I want to do what's best for her—'

'What's best for her is to learn she can't have everything she wants! I don't know how long this myth about being an actress has been in force—'

'Myth? How dare you say that! Everyone's who's seen her act agrees she's marvellous!'

'She's marvellous in the context of a small town with an amateur dramatic society, Josh, but it's yet to be proved that she's got what it takes to be a real actress. I'm not saying she shouldn't have her chance, but I can't bear to hear you calling yourself her "poor blundering old dad" – she's made you think of yourself like that, playing second fiddle to her, inferior in some way. Well, it's wrong, and I'm not going to help shore up that image!'

She got to her feet and went to pay at the till for her coffee. By the time Josh caught up with her she was out unlocking the car door. 'Bethany! Bethany! Please!'

She half-turned to him.

'Bethany, don't go – I was relying on you to help me—'

'You rang me to come and give you some advice. Well, here it is. Go home and tell your daughter that you think it's wrong to bring a suit for damages—'

'I can't do that. It would be going back on my word—'

'Which you should never have given in the first place!'

'That's why I thought you—'

'No, I'm not going to get you out of it. You'll have to do it yourself.'

224

She got into the Suzuki and put the key in the ignition.

'But she'd be so upset! And the doctors said I was to avoid putting her under stress—'

'So you're going to take refuge in that, are you? What sort of life is it where you have to find excuses for giving in all the time?'

He was still protesting when she drove off.

The girl at the cash till had found the episode very interesting. Josh had meant little to her, but when Bethany walked in to join him she recognised her at once. That girl with the pretty fair hair . . . on TV about the Town Centre . . . what was her name? But it wouldn't come until she heard Josh call her Bethany. Of course – Bethany Dayton! And there'd been pictures of her in the *Gazette*. And now they were having a right battle, and the girl was shaking her head at the fellow and looking daggers at him out of brilliant blue eyes.

Josh came back in to pay for his cappuccino. 'Lover's tiff?' the girl said jokingly as she took the coins from him.

'Worse than that,' he groaned. 'A court case.' And he wandered out looking miserable.

A court case! It must be worth a fiver or two to let the *Gazette* know. She picked up the phone by the till and dialled.

When Bethany got home she was thankful to find her mother gone, and all the wet newspapers with her. She needed peace and quiet to think.

She had just been given important information – important to the group involved in the construction of the new Town Centre. When Josh recommenced the suit against them – and she was certain he would – there would be media interest.

Had she been told about it in confidence? Had she the right to warn Iris Weston that there might be trouble brewing?

I'll ask Peter, she said to herself. But then she recalled that she'd parted from him coldly last night. If she rang she ought to apologise. But she had nothing to apologise for. Well, if she had nothing to apologise for, why was she hesitating about contacting him? She sat there debating this point, then decided it was all a storm in a teacup, so dialled his number. She got his answering machine.

Disappointed, she left a message: 'I'm sorry about last night. Something quite important has come up, please ring me.'

It was now nearly five o'clock in the afternoon of a humid autumn day. She made herself a cup of tea and a sandwich but just as she sat down to it, her doorbell rang. It's Peter, she thought, and ran to open the door.

It was Jeff Jones, chief reporter of the *Gazette*.

Chapter Eighteen

Jones was ready with his first words. 'Had a bust-up with your boyfriend, I hear.'

Bethany coloured up. Her thoughts flew to Peter. How could Jones possibly know they had parted coldly last night? There had been no one about in the street; they had spoken in low tones.

Seeing her astonishment, he went on, 'About a court case?'

'A court case?'

'The one the little girl was going to bring against the contractors. Is that right? Is it on again?'

Her wits came back. He was talking about Josh, not Peter.

'What makes you think anything like that is happening?'

'My spies are everywhere,' he said with great good humour. 'So you admit you had a row with Pembury about the would-be Ingrid Bergman and her court case?'

'You have some strange notions,' she said.

'Nothing strange about it. The look on your face when I asked my first question told me that I'd got it right.'

'Mr Jones, in that black leather jacket on a warm day like this, you must get very hot – and I think it goes to your brain. If you'll excuse me, I was just about to have something to eat.'

'Not eating alone, are you? That's very bad. Invite me in and I'll keep you company.'

She laughed. 'For sheer unadulterated cheek, you have no equal! Good evening, Mr Jones.'

He put out a hand to prevent her closing the door. 'A colleague of mine is at the Pemburys' cottage right now getting a sob story from the little actress. Don't you want your side of it in print as well?'

'There's no "my side of it". You're wasting your time. And my cup of tea is getting cold.'

This time she succeeded in closing the door. Jones leaned against the bell for a few minutes but gave up eventually, because he had other leads to pursue.

Bethany went at once to the telephone. There was no question now – she must get in touch with Iris Weston. Iris's mobile was engaged so she dialled the number of Alan Singleton's flat, to be answered at once by Alan himself.

'Oh Bethany, there's a great kerfuffle here! Iris is talking to her London office, getting things going in case this gets into the Sundays tomorrow—'

'Exactly *what* is supposed to be the story? I had Jeff Jones here a minute ago—'

'Good Lord, I hope you didn't tell him anything—'

'Of course not. I acted bewildered. And in fact I am a bit bewildered because I don't know how he got on to it—'

'Well, that's the point – what the dickens were you doing talking to Josh Pembury about a thing like that without checking first with Iris?'

Bethany drew in a breath. Don't get annoyed, she told herself. 'Can I speak to Iris?' she asked.

'She's on the other line – no, wait, she's saying . . . hang on . . .' There was a pause while he held a conversation slightly off the phone. 'She says will you hang on, she's just finishing up her London call.'

Bethany fetched her cup of tea, now tepid, sat down with the phone in her hand, and sipped. In about two minutes Iris came on the line.

'What the devil have you been up to?'

Bethany sipped her tea, made no reply.

'Bethany? Bethany? Are you there? Alan, I told you to tell her—'

'I'm here, Iris, but I'm waiting to be spoken to with some manners. Let's go back a few sentences, shall we? Hello, Iris, I was trying to get in touch but your mobile was engaged.'

Iris didn't speak for almost two seconds. Then she said, with much less heat, 'I hear from the press that you and Josh Pembury had a public quarrel in a restaurant this afternoon.'

'Well, it wasn't a quarrel, it was a disagreement. And it wasn't meant to be public but somebody seems to have taken more than a passing interest in it.'

'What were you thinking of, meeting with him to discuss something important like that?'

'I didn't know how important it was going to be.'

'Anything to do with the Pemburys is important to us, Bethany, you surely know that. You should have asked me first.'

Once again Bethany told herself not to lose her temper. 'I'm not in the habit of consulting anyone before I meet a friend.'

'A friend! That man and his confounded daughter have caused us all kinds of damage—'

'And I thought if I met him I could help prevent more – although I admit I got something I hadn't bargained for.'

'He told you he was going to resume the case against the contractors?'

'He said he'd promised Allie to do so and I tried to talk him out of it.'

'But you clearly didn't succeed.'

'Is that definite? He's made some sort of announcement?'

'The *Gazette* sent a woman reporter to chat up Allie – and of course she's easy to trap; she can't prevent herself from starring in any drama that's put before her – and she said her father had hired a new lawyer—'

'Yes, somebody he says is very respectable this time—'

'So of course the reporter asked Pembury to confirm it and he did.'

Bethany sighed heavily. 'Of course he did,' she said. 'He was dithering when we parted, but put him in a situation where he's confronted and Allie is sitting there watching . . .'

'This is very bad, Bethany. You should never have met with him.'

'I should never have met with him where some sneak could ring up the *Gazette*'s gossip column . . . But I'd no idea he was going to say anything about a law suit. I thought it was some problem about Allie's health.'

'Well, you're not to speak to him again—'

'Iris, remember what I said a minute ago about good manners. I'm not about to take orders from you on who I can speak to and who not—'

'Why can't you just show some sense? It's bad enough that you seem to have some soft spot for that idiot and his daughter, but you're snuggling up with the lawyer for the other side—'

Bethany quietly put the phone down. She sat beside it, inactive, for a minute or two, then stood up, picked up the cup of cold tea, emptied it away in the sink, and was going out of the door when her phone began to ring. Ignoring it, she closed and locked her door, ran downstairs, and without thinking too much about it set off along the road on foot. She needed a good walk and some fresh air.

But the air this evening wasn't fresh. It lay like a coverlet of warm tissue paper over Barhampton. Soon she was perspiring and growing weary: it had been a long day, and she still hadn't eaten. She swung aboard a passing bus and was carried to York, where she found her mother still at work on the pulpit flowers in the church.

'That looks very nice,' she said.

Her mother gave a jump of alarm, turning with stems of dark blue Michaelmas daisy in her hand. 'Bethany! What on earth are you doing here?'

'Thought I'd drop in and see how you were getting on.'

'But why?'

'Barhampton's not the place for me today. I'm not allowed to go to the party in Royal Terrace and I'm not allowed to talk to my friends, it seems.'

'And a girl's best friend is her mother – is that it?'

'So I thought you'd like to go for a Chinese meal, maybe.'

Mary's face fell. 'Oh darling, I'm very sorry, but I've got a date for this evening.'

'Oh,' said Bethany. 'Ossie Fielden?'

'Well . . . yes . . .'

'Of course. I should have thought – Saturday night, after all.'

'Why don't you join us?' said Mary, in a desperate effort to be helpful at what was clearly a very important moment.

Bethany laughed. 'What, and go ballroom dancing?'

'Well . . . We needn't go to the ballroom club.'

'But that was what you'd planned?'

'Well, yes.'

'You're awfully sweet, Mother, but it's bad enough being a third wheel on the bicycle without having to do the fox-trot. Oh sorry – I didn't mean that to come out so sour – all I meant was that I don't know how to do the fox-trot.'

'And so much the worse for you,' her mother said, engulfing her in a loving hug. 'Honestly, love, if it's important, I can ring Ossie and tell him—'

'No, no – it's nothing really. And I'll have to get used to the idea that my mum goes out on the town these days. I'll go and have a Chinese meal by myself.'

'What, and eat everything in all those little dishes?'

'Worth a try,' she said, and dropped a kiss on Mary's cheek. 'So long, and have a nice time.'

'Thank you, dear.' And Mary watched with a worried frown as her daughter walked quietly out of the church.

Bethany had once had a recording of Dave Brubeck or someone equally expert playing 'Saturday Night is the Loneliest Night of the Week' but had never realised the truth of it till that evening. She didn't in fact eat Chinese, but went instead to an Italian restaurant for the comfort food that would be less trouble to consume and might, with the help of a couple of glasses of wine, help her to sleep.

She'd left her mobile on the table by her door. When she got home about nine, she found numbers recorded for call-back. The first was her father's: sighing to herself, she pressed the buttons.

'Where have you been?' he cried when he picked up at his end. 'I've been trying to get you for hours.'

'I've been out.'

'I know that! But why didn't you answer your mobile?'

'Never mind all that. What's the plan?'

'The plan?'

'Well, presumably you're ringing about the resumption of the Pemburys' law suit. And the contractors have got to make some sort of response to it. What's Iris decided?'

'She tells me you behaved very childishly on the phone.'

'Dad, tell me what she wants us to do. Are we issuing a statement, or what?'

229

'Billy Wellbrow's to be the spokesman for the contractors. His solicitor has drafted a thing for him to give to the press. But you see, as far as Iris can gather, the tabloids are going to run the item based on you and Josh having a row in a restaurant over it: CLOSE FRIENDS IN CLASH or something like that. They've got pictures—'

'Not from the bistro – that's impossible—'

'No, from one of the times when Pembury was in trouble before and he made a statement – I think it was at Barhampton Town Hall – you were holding his arm and looking very friendly. They're going to say your love life's in a mess these days despite the big success of winning the contract for the Town Centre—'

'Oh, good Lord!' groaned Bethany. 'Haven't they got anything more important to write about?'

'It sells papers,' said her father. 'So Iris says to say nowt, and let the solicitor handle it.'

'Very well.'

'And from now on steer clear of that chap – he's nothing but trouble. Is that clear?'

'Oh, perfectly.'

'Right. Well now . . . is your mother home yet? I know she's been out because no one answered the phone.'

'I'm afraid she's still out.'

'With Ossie Fielden?'

'Dad, if you want to know what Mother's doing, ask her yourself.'

'A chance would be a fine thing. I never can get hold of her. Tell her I want to speak to her.'

'Any other message?' Such as, I miss you, thought his daughter.

'If she's going to church tomorrow, I'll see her there.' After a moment's pause he added, 'It's funny, having to make arrangements to speak to your own wife!' and hung up sharply.

She called some of the other numbers that had been recorded, those that she recognised. They were unimportant, from acquaintances with whom she sometimes went out. Some she guessed to be those of London tabloids and so ignored.

She went to her drawing table to try to do some work on a design that had been waiting for her attention for some days. But she couldn't concentrate, couldn't for the moment summon up the vision of the building she'd intended when she began. She tried calling it up on her computer but there in 3D it looked even more unfamiliar. A day-care centre – why should it now look like a series of unfriendly boxes?

By ten she was trying the television channels for something worth watching, and feeling very sorry for herself. She was at odds with everybody she knew, it seemed – with Josh Pembury, with Iris, with her father, even with her mother who'd been made to feel guilty about going out this evening. And with Peter, whom she tried once more on the telephone. When she got the answering machine she hung up without leaving another message.

By and by there crept into her mind the name of someone who had much better reason for unhappiness than herself – Nancy Bedells. Poor old lady, trapped behind her locked doors, sitting in some room at the back of her house, as far away as possible from the thumping bass of the amplified music and the garish revolving lights that flickered over the furniture in her living room.

Bethany looked up the number in her organiser and dialled. She knew there was scant chance of a reply, for Mrs Bedells seldom answered her telephone. She let it ring ten times, hung up, then re-dialled in case she'd made a mistake the first time.

Nothing.

She tried at intervals until it grew quite late. Her TV set gave her the late-night news, and on the local section there were camera shots of the audience beginning to go home from the *Beano* – smiling at the cameramen, looking faintly foolish in the cardboard hats supplied by the newspaper, pushing baby buggies with sleeping children in them . . .

Her mother still hadn't returned at a little after midnight. Restless, she got up and paced about. She tried Nancy Bedells's telephone once more. No, the old lady was determined not to pick up the receiver. All right, since Bethany was too keyed up to go to bed, she'd go to the house, put a letter of apology through the letterbox.

She wrote: *Dear Mrs Bedells, Please believe me when I say I was as surprised as you when Allie Pembury turned up. I've been trying to ring you, without success. I know you sometimes make outgoing calls so please ring me to let me know you don't blame me. It would be nice to speak to you, and make sure you don't feel too exhausted after all the 'merry-making'. Your friend, Bethany Dayton.*

She added her telephone numbers, the one at the flat, her office, and her mobile. She wrote on the envelope: PERSONAL – IMPORTANT! Snatching up a jacket, she hurried out to the jeep and within ten minutes was at Royal Terrace.

The place wasn't entirely deserted. Workmen were dismantling the stage and taking down the stand holding the amplifiers. Strings of coloured lights were being wound up and stowed away. But in comparison with the uproar of the last two days, the Terrace was tranquil.

She went to the door of No. 15. She knocked – why not? Mrs Bedells might just open the door. But no one came, and after a second fruitless attempt she put the letter through the slit.

With luck, Mrs Bedells might ring her next day.

When she got home her mother had returned and already gone to bed. She made herself a cup of tea, washed up the cup and saucer, tidied up a little by plumping up cushions and squaring up magazines. When she went to bed it was well after one. She didn't go to sleep till almost three.

231

Mary Dayton was reading the Sunday paper when her daughter emerged, yawning and stretching, from her bedroom at a late hour on Sunday morning. 'Good morning, love. Had a nice lie-in?'

'Mmm . . . Did you have a good time last night?'

'Yes, lovely. Did you?'

Bethany avoided a reply by going into the kitchen to make coffee. 'By the way,' she said over her shoulder, 'Dad rang last night. He wanted to speak to you but, when he heard you were out, said he'd see you in church, as the saying goes.'

'Oh, he's going to church, is he?'

'So I gather.' Bethany spooned coffee into the cafetière. She yawned yet again, then eyeing the daylight outside the kitchen window enquired, 'What time is it, anyway?'

'About eleven.'

'Good heavens! Shouldn't you have left for church . . .?' The query died away. Obviously her mother wasn't going to morning service this Sunday. She took a moment to get herself together, then said, 'He'll think you're avoiding him.'

'That's possible, of course.'

'Shouldn't you ring him and say you didn't get the message in time?'

'That would be pointless, wouldn't it? If he's really going to church to meet me, he's already there singing the first hymn.'

'Mother, I believe you're enjoying this!'

'It certainly causes me no distress, my dove.' She folded the paper, laid it aside, and rose. 'I don't know what your plans are for today, but Ossie rang about an hour ago to say you ought to go out to buy the *Sunday Comet* and the *Weekender*. It seems you're featured in them.'

'Oh Lord, what are they saying?'

'Something about you and Josh Pembury, I gather – but I wouldn't worry about it if I were you. My recent experience has shown me that people jump to all sorts of wrong conclusions.'

'I bet Iris is hopping mad. She was doing her best to smooth it all down last night.'

'Ah,' said her mother with a faint shrug, 'Iris . . . Once again, I wouldn't worry about it if I were you. And so I think I'll be off now, dear. I have a lunch engagement.'

'With Ossie?'

Her mother gave a gentle smile. 'No, as it happens with some women friends who've arranged a charity fashion show in Scarborough. If I see anything that would look good on you, Beth, I might splash out some money on it.' She came to the kitchen, dropped a kiss on her daughter's cheek, and next moment was on her way out.

Bethany sank down on a chair. Her world seemed to be changing around her in a most extraordinary fashion.

At first she was going to gulp down a cup of coffee and go racing out for the Sunday paper. But then she thought, Bad news can wait. So she had a bath and a leisurely breakfast, read the *Independent* her mother had laid aside, and was gratified to find mention of neither herself nor Josh Pembury in it.

She was getting dressed to go out when her phone rang. It was her father. 'Your mother wasn't at church!' he stormed.

'No, I never managed to give her your message.'

'Oh, can't you do anything right?' he exclaimed. 'Well, put her on now.'

'I can't, she's gone out—'

'Gone where?'

'To Scarborough—'

'To Scarborough? With Ossie Fielden? Dammit, Bethany, this is beyond a joke!'

'I never said she'd—'

'Give her a message. Write it down, so you don't forget it. She and I have got to talk. Tell her to name a time and place so we can get together. Have you got that?'

'Yes, but—'

'No buts. And another thing, my girl, your name's all over the cheap papers this morning. I don't know what I've done to deserve a family like mine!' With that he slammed down his receiver.

The items in the tabloids weren't nearly as bad as she'd feared. It was true that one had a picture, as predicted, showing Bethany and Josh together, and with Bethany looking concerned and supportive towards him. It was also true that there was a lot of innuendo about the troubles of the new Town Centre parting true lovers, and some hard news about Josh renewing the suit for compensation. But there was no doubt Iris had had some success in damping things down; either that or the gossip columnists had more glamorous names and better pictures to clothe their pages that morning.

By now it was past midday. Most people in Barhampton would be thinking about Sunday lunch. What should she do? It was too close to the large breakfast for her to feel hungry. She rang Alan Singleton in York to speak to Iris. 'What did you think of the morning papers?' Bethany asked her.

'Not too bad. The people who matter won't pay much attention to the gossip stuff, and the financial columns only gave a bare mention to the resumption of the compensation claim. The trade papers may show more interest in their next issues . . . Well, perhaps we ought to discuss that. Are you doing anything this afternoon?'

'Nothing special,' said Bethany, thinking with regret that normally she'd have been going somewhere with Peter.

'Why don't you come here, then – we can talk it through and by then the London office may have a few hints of how things will be handled in the trades.'

'Yes, all right.'

'I'll ask Wellbrow and Emmett Foyle if they can come. And your father, of course.'

'Of course.'

She got ready to leave. The note from her father to her mother was still on the telephone pad. As she propped it up so that her mother would notice it, it occurred to her that she'd written a note last night to Mrs Bedells. By now – and she glanced at her watch, one in the afternoon – she'd have expected the old lady to ring her. That's if she was feeling forgiving towards her. But perhaps she was going to be unyielding. Experience had already shown that Mrs Bedells was a very strong character.

All the same . . . It was worth another try. She dialled the number. No response, still not answering her phone, though she let it ring a long time.

She wrote another note: *I'd hoped to hear from you in answer to my letter. Please ring me, even if just to let me know you've recovered from the turmoil of yesterday. Yours, Bethany Dayton.*

On her way to York she stopped at Royal Terrace. By now the squatters in the other houses were beginning to surface after a very late night and a long lie-in. But the place had a sad look, the movements of its inhabitants lethargic and slow, the only sound a baby crying somewhere, and litter from the party still blowing in the autumn breeze.

Once more she knocked at the door. Once more the door remained shut fast. Sighing, she slipped her letter through the letterbox. Why was she bothering? Everything she did these days seemed to be either wrong or a waste of time. She shrugged, got back into her car, and went on to York.

Iris had succeeded in summoning quite a useful little crowd; several of the demolition contractors were there, the manager of the security firm whose guards had first sighted Allie Pembury on the demolition site, the head of *Dayton & Daughter*'s Legal Department, another solicitor brought by Wellbrow, and Daniel Dayton.

They were already involved in discussion – or perhaps argument – when Bethany arrived. The manager of *Safe-Site* was saying: '. . . can tell you that child is lying like a trooper. My foreman saw her on the CCTV – walking *past* one of the warning signs.'

'But was there light enough for her to see it?'

'You know fine and well that there are high-actinic lamps in those lights, giving good enough brightness to record film – and let me tell you that sign wasn't the first one she'd had to walk past to get to that point—'

'Did you say that to the journalist?'

'Of course I did – well, I didn't say she was lying, that would have been slander, but I told him about the television cameras and that Martin had seen her on his screen.'

'But unfortunately when the tower collapsed it brought down the cameras with it and wrecked them.'

'Aye . . .' Mr Holden sighed. 'A right shambles . . . Still, we're working on it.'

'This Mr Rosemont still hasn't served any papers,' growled Billy Wellbrow. 'We don't know how many of us are going to be defendants in the suit.'

'Oh, you can be sure he's going to include as many as he can,' Daniel Dayton said. 'The more the merrier – and the more money he thinks he's going to screw out of us.'

'The money is bad,' sighed Emmett Foyle from behind his bushy moustache, 'but it's my reputation I'm worried about. I can't allow it to be said that I was running an unsafe site.'

Everybody nodded agreement, although Bethany had a secret thought that the money was the important thing with most of them.

Iris had provided lager and wine together with sandwiches from the local bistro. The atmosphere was more relaxed than the meetings of the Steering Committee but it was also less businesslike. People talked across each other, the two lawyers got into a private tussle about legal safety requirements, Alan Singleton was trying to show files to one of the contractors that monitored the progress of work on the mill site before the accident: 'You see we'd made an actual path with a concrete surface – it's almost certain she walked along that and therefore . . .'

The debate went on, the food and drink were finished. About five o'clock Iris made tea and provided a few biscuits, in a heavy hint that it was time for them all to go. 'Well,' said Daniel, 'we're agreed that we wait for this Mr Rosemont to send us the writ or whatever we get as openers. In the meantime we let our solicitors speak for us, and Iris will do what she can behind the scenes with the trade papers. Those in favour?'

Grunts of agreement, hands raised in assent. 'And Bethany here won't go anywhere near that Pembury lot,' insisted Wellbrow.

'Of course not,' said her father, with a glare in her direction.

'Of course not,' she agreed, gritting her teeth so as not to tell them she didn't take orders.

He was at her elbow as she left the flat. 'Has your mother been in touch?'

'No, I told you, she's in Scarborough for the day.'

'I thought she might have rung or something.'

'Dad, she had no reason to ring. She's off at a fashion show with some friends.'

'A fashion show? Didn't know Ossie went in for that kind of thing.'

'Who said she's with Ossie?'

'She isn't?'

'Not as far as I know.'

'But you said—'

'No, *you* said. You jumped to conclusions and then bit my head off when I tried to explain.'

'Oh,' said her father, for once at a loss. Then he brightened. 'With friends, you say? Lady friends?'

'Well, it's usually women who go to fashion shows.'

'That's not so bad then. She'll be there when you get home, happen. Tell her to ring me, Bethie.'

'I'll pass on the message.'

He hesitated, standing on the pavement as the others got into their cars and drove off. 'Ring her now,' he suggested. 'On your mobile.'

She was going to refuse, but thought, Why not? She pressed the buttons, but there was no reply. 'Not home yet,' she said with a shrug.

'Oh, well then. When she gets back . . . tell her, Bethie . . .'

'All right.'

With a worried cast to his bluff features, and quite unlike himself, he plodded off to his car.

Standing with her mobile still in her hand, Bethany thought to call up any numbers that were waiting for reply. Perhaps Mrs Bedells had rung while she was at the meeting; Bethany had switched it off for the duration, so as not to disturb the proceedings.

But there was nothing, and on the short drive she decided to call yet once more at the old lady's house. Now that there had been several hours of peace in the Terrace, Nancy might feel more like talking.

Once again the familiar series of moves: knocking on the door, calling through it, tapping on the nearest pane of glass in the bay window. But there was no reply. Really, a most unforgiving woman, thought Bethany. She was about to turn away when she decided to give it one more try. She scribbled a note on a page of her workpad – *PLEASE ring me, Mrs Bedells*, with her telephone numbers once again.

She tried to slide it through the letterbox. Lacking an envelope, it hadn't sufficient weight to propel itself through. She stooped, opened the letterbox, and was poking the folded note into the hall when she espied something that gave her pause.

There was a little pile of leaflets and letters on the floor. Among them she could clearly make out the two envelopes she had already put through. The first had been on Saturday night, the second on Sunday about lunch-time.

So the old lady hadn't even come to the door to tidy up the junk mail that seems to come like an unending tide . . .?

She let the last note flutter from her hand and down to join the heap on the floor. She stood, stooping, peering through the slit.

'Mrs Bedells?' she called. 'Mrs Bedells? Are you there?'

Utter silence.

She flapped the letterbox as noisily as she could. 'Mrs Bedells? Please come to the door!'

Nothing.

Now she was hammering on the door with her fist. 'Mrs Bedells? Nancy! Please come to the door! Please let me know you're all right!'

But there was no reaction of any kind from within the silent house.

Alarm and dismay seized Bethany. She ran back to the Suzuki, picked up her phone, and dialled Peter Lambot's number. As it rang she thought, If I get an answering machine I'll throw this thing at the wall!

Peter's voice came on the other end. 'Lambot.'

'Peter, thank God! I've been trying to reach you—'

'Oh, is that you, Bethany? If you're ringing to explain about Josh Pembury, it's really not necessary.'

'Josh Pembury? Who cares about Josh Pembury—'

'Well, you do, clearly.'

'Oh, don't talk such rubbish, Peter! This is serious. I need you here – something's happened to Mrs Bedells!'

Chapter Nineteen

Peter arrived within ten minutes. His clothes – guernsey and slacks – were the clue that he'd perhaps been out of town all the time she was trying to ring him. 'What's happened?' he demanded as he hurried into the Terrace from his car.

Bethany explained.

'But she never comes to her door or answers her phone.'

'But I wrote to her – twice – over the weekend and put the letters through the door myself. And the letters are *still there*, on the floor just inside.'

He went to look. As he straightened he was frowning, half-shaking his head. 'It might mean she's just never bothered to pick them up.'

'What, a housewife like Mrs Bedells? Everything clean and shiny – but she comes downstairs from her bedroom on Sunday morning, sees the letter I left on Saturday night, and doesn't pick it up?'

'Let's ask her neighbours if they've seen her.'

'Neighbours!' sighed Bethany, thinking of the motley crew who had danced and sung at the *Bedells Beano*, regardless of how their 'star' might be suffering. But they went to speak to some of the people who had taken over the other houses.

'Oh, that funny owd soul,' said one. 'Keeps herself to herself, she does, but it takes all sorts to make a world.'

'Her!' said another, with less tolerance. 'We come here to give her a hand and what does she do – turns her nose up at us!'

The consensus was that they'd occasionally glimpsed Mrs Bedells sneaking out either very late at night or very early in the morning, presumably to go to the all-night garage-shop at the crossroads. 'She gets milk and bread there – offered to get it for her, didn't I, but she made out she didn't hear me and walked off!'

The next step was to go to the garage-shop and find out if Mrs Bedells had been there recently. But the girl behind the counter couldn't help. 'I'm "Day",' she explained. 'You want the Night Assistant.'

'And when does she come on?'

'It's a he. Nine o'clock.'

Three hours' time. 'Have you got a telephone number for him?'

'Oh, I don't think we can give out numbers to strangers—'

'Well, will you ring him yourself?'

No, she couldn't without permission from the manager of the station. It took another ten minutes to talk the manager into it, but in the end he made the call. Joe, the Night Assistant, wasn't there. He was at the billiard hall with some friends and would probably go straight to the petrol station from there, his mother said.

'Another three hours,' mourned Bethany. 'And if she's had a heart attack and is lying in the kitchen . . .?'

By now Bethany's anxiety had infected Peter. Yet his lawyer's mind told him there was still no evidence of anything wrong. They drove back to the Terrace and once again knocked on the door. Bethany tried peering through the window panes but the net curtains made it impossible to make out much. No sound came from the house – but that was almost always the case.

One of the squatters sauntered along. 'You really bothered? Think summat's wrong?'

'Perhaps I'm being silly. But I've just got this feeling . . .'

'I'll ring the police,' said Peter, making up his mind all at once. 'They can give permission to call a locksmith.'

'Ha!' laughed the squatter. 'Don't need no locksmith, chum. If you want to get in, I can get you in.'

'What?'

'How d'you think we got into them houses we're living in? Asked the cops to call a locksmith? Do me a favour!'

'But . . . but . . .'

'I'll open the front door to you in ten minutes, if you want me to.'

'It's breaking and entering,' said Peter, shaking his head.

'I promise I'll break nowt.'

'But if she's just . . . having a day in bed . . . got a headache . . . or a cold . . . it'll scare her to death . . .'

'Mister, make up your mind. I've got half an hour before I've got to go home and babysit so the wife can go to bingo. Are you on or not?'

Peter looked at Bethany. 'What do you think, Bethany?'

She knew that if she refused this offer and they left without ensuring that the old lady was all right, she would spend a sleepless night. 'Let's do it,' she said.

'Right,' said the volunteer, hurrying off.

He came back in two minutes, a small dishevelled figure in army-fatigue trousers, a T-shirt bearing the slogan *Loopholes Live*, discoloured trainers, and wearing a baseball cap backwards on his balding head. A spry little soul, he flourished a length of rope and a jemmy.

'Wait a minute, I thought you said you weren't going to break anything!' exclaimed Peter, ever the lawyer.

'Nor I am. I'm just going to lever the skylight open.'

'The *skylight*!'

239

'Yeah, the skylight. Now what I want you to do is knock and call through the door, so she knows nothing bad is happening if she's lying somewhere with a broken leg. Tell her somebody's coming to help her. Okay?' He held out his hand. 'Name's Lennie, by the way. You might say I'm the leader of the Royal Terrace Protection Group, Residents' Division.'

They all shook hands. By now a few other squatters had come to see what was going on. Lennie, Peter and Bethany went up the entrance steps to No. 15. Peter began knocking loudly, Bethany stooped to call through the letterbox. Lennie hopped on to the ledge of the bay window adjacent to the doorway, chimney-stepped up to its sloping roof, caught hold of a drainpipe, clambered up it, and swung himself over the low parapet on to the flat Georgian roof. He disappeared from view.

'Mrs Bedells!' called Bethany. 'It's all right! We're worried about you! If you're all right, come to the door! Mrs Bedells! Nancy!'

'Nancy!' chanted the quartet of squatters who had decided to support the event. 'Nancy Bedells! Who's our star, Best by far, *Nancy Bedells!*'

Footsteps in the hall, a faint flicker across the view that Bethany could see through the letterbox. 'Thank God,' she breathed.

The door opened. There, beaming, stood Lennie.

His friends cheered. 'Get in anywhere, he can!' someone cried. 'Lennie the Loophole, we call him! Let's hear it for Lennie – LOOP-HOLES LIVE! In for a pound, In for a penny, Who's the hero? *Loophole Lennie!*'

'Did you see her?' demanded Bethany, pushing past him. 'Is she lying—'

'Didn't stop to look, miss – I skipped straight down to the door – but she ain't lying in a heap on the stairs, that's certain.'

By now Bethany was going along the narrow hall to the kitchen. It was there she would find Mrs Bedells, she was sure. But the kitchen was empty. She came back to the room next to it, Mrs Bedells's dining room, but that too was lifeless – smelling of beeswax and that airlessness that speaks of windows unopened for days.

No one in either of the two front rooms. 'Upstairs?' suggested Lennie, heading that way.

'I'll go,' said Bethany quickly, drawing him back. This poor old soul, perhaps lying unconscious and only half-clad in her bedroom or, worse yet, in the bathroom – how she would hate to be found by a man in such a state.

She was holding her breath when she put her head round the bedroom door. But the bedroom was empty, the bed neatly made, the curtain drawn back. The other two rooms were empty too, and the bathroom, gleaming with ancient brass fittings, a shining mirrored medicine cabinet, and a brass towel-rail holding neatly folded towels.

'Are you all right?' called Peter from halfway up the stairs.

'She's not here,' Bethany answered.

'Not there?'

'No sign of her.'

'There's a cellar,' offered Lennie. 'Leads out on a little back area.'

Filled with dread, Bethany let him lead the way to it, through a narrow door in the hall. But that too was empty, and when he unlocked the outer door the yard showed nothing but a few pot plants.

Peter looked about. Bethany was already turning to go back upstairs when he caught her arm. 'She's gone away,' he said.

'What?'

'She's left the house.'

'How on earth can you know that?'

'She's put her pot plants out to get watered by the rain.' He nodded at the little group of geraniums standing bravely on the old stones of the narrow backyard.

Lennie studied them, then nodded. 'Aye, I think you're right, lad.'

There was a rubbish sack, neatly tied, beside the back door. Bethany looked inside: an empty milk carton, the remains of a loaf carefully tied in a plastic bag. She ran up to the kitchen, looked in the fridge. No meat, no milk, no perishables of any kind, and the fridge was switched off. She walked quickly past the two men.

'Where are you going?'

'Bedroom,' she said.

It was impossible to say whether any clothes were gone without knowing more than she did about the old lady's wardrobe. But a brush and comb were missing from the ivory toilet set on the dressing-table and there was no tooth-cleaning equipment in the bathroom.

'You're right, Peter,' she said as she came downstairs. 'Mrs Bedells has gone away.'

All three stared at each other. 'Well,' murmured Lennie, 'there's a turn-up for the books!'

Bethany felt a sudden swimminess of the head. She'd been so sure she would find the old lady lying unconscious – even lifeless – on the floor. Peter put out a hand to steady her. When she'd got herself under control again she said, 'What should we do now?'

'How do you mean?'

'Should we tell the police?'

'No!' said Lennie, quickly and anxiously.

'No?'

'We don't want to explain how we got in, now do we?'

'I thought you said it was perfectly all right?'

'That was when I thought we were doing the right thing. I mean, if she'd been ill, we'd have been heroes. But now it seems she's perfectly okay, off on her hols somewhere – and we look like a bunch of Nosey

241

Parkers. No, I'd not like to have to explain this to the cops, Miss Dayton.'

'Besides,' Peter added, 'if we report it – her absence – to the police, someone's sure to get wind of it and then there could be a hoo-ha in the press – they might even start tracking her down—'

'Oh, heaven forbid! The poor soul's had enough of that!'

'Exactly. Moreover, she's got a perfect right to go away if she wants to.'

'So she has,' she agreed, though with regret.

'And I think I said before, we don't actually need her in residence to keep up our protest about the house—'

'Right enough, lad,' Lennie agreed. 'Us protesters want a Conservation Order, whether she stays on in number fifteen or not.'

'But what about those folk outside that were cheering you on? They'll know she's gone—'

'Not unless I tell 'em.'

'But they'll ask you when you come out,' Bethany said, at a loss. 'What will you say to them?'

'I'll tell 'em a lie,' he said, with a grin that wrinkled his entire face. 'No harm in a good lie for a good reason.' He moved towards the stairs. 'Just let me nip up and make the skylight secure.'

Bethany and Peter exchanged a doubtful smile. 'Normally I'd protest about telling lies,' he said.

'Or having someone else tell them on your behalf,' she amended.

'Yes. But as it happens, it may be the best thing.'

Lennie reappeared, the rope coiled about his middle and the jemmy tucked in one of the many pockets in his camouflage trousers. He made for the front door. 'Coming?'

As he went out, his four friends gathered round him. 'Was she in there? She okay? What'd she say?'

'Nothing's changed, folks. Mrs Bedells is all right and still wants to be left alone,' Lennie said.

'Was she annoyed at you for breaking in?'

'I didn't break in,' he protested. 'I effected an entry 'cos her friends thought she might be ill. But she isn't – so come on along to the pub and I'll tell you all about it.' He led the way and they followed like lambs.

'Well . . .' said Bethany.

'Yes.' Peter pulled the door shut. It locked automatically. He stood hesitating.

Bethany too felt a reluctance to speak. But someone had to begin the apology.

'I'm sorry about the way we parted on Friday night,' she said.

'It was my fault—'

'And there was nothing really in that newspaper story about Josh Pembury and me—'

242

'I knew that, really.'

'I did try to ring and explain—'

'And I drove up to the Dales so as to be away all Saturday and not think about you—'

'Saturday wasn't a good day—'

'Not for me either – being in Scannsdale only made me think about you.'

'Let's go somewhere and I'll tell you all about what happened.'

'Damage repairs first, explanations afterwards,' he said with a laugh.

So they went to his flat and made love, and everything was as it had been before, radiant and joyful and full of passion.

It was late before Bethany got back to her own flat that night. Her mother had gone to bed. But in the morning Bethany remembered the promise to her father.

'Dad wants you to ring him, Mother.'

'He does?'

'I was with him yesterday afternoon. He's . . . not like himself, Mother. Shouldn't you talk to him?'

'About what?'

'About . . . well . . . I don't know . . . your intentions for the future?'

'I'm not thinking about the future, Beth. I'm just taking each day as it comes and enjoying it.'

'But Dad isn't enjoying it.'

'Perhaps not. That will be a change for him, won't it.'

'Mother . . . I'm getting a bit worried about him.'

Her mother sighed and smiled. 'If you're trying to make me feel guilty, you're wasting your time. I left your father because I couldn't bear to live with him just then, after the way he sneaked on Mrs Bedells to the newspapers. I still haven't persuaded myself I want to go back.'

'But you *are* going to go back?'

'I suppose so – in the end. But not on the same terms as before, Bethany. And that's why I'm keeping up the separation. I want your father to have time to look at himself, to think things over, to understand my point of view. I want him to realise I *have* a point of view! If I meet him before he's been made to worry about me, he'll just try to steam-roller me as he normally does. So . . . I've got his message, I hear what he wants, and I'm not going to fall in with his wishes. On the contrary, I'm going to Venice tomorrow.'

'With Ossie.'

'With Ossie. And I suppose I'll be gone until at least the end of the week.'

'But when I see him – or he rings – what shall I say?'

'Tell him I've gone to spend a few days with Robert. If he asks when I'm going to get in touch, tell him . . . well . . . tell him you don't know. Which is true, because I don't know myself.'

This was the first day that the reporters could get hold of people to ask for reactions about Josh Pembury's resumed action over his daughter's injuries. Telephones rang, faxes came through, microphones were pushed in front of unwilling spokespersons. But interest waned quickly when news came through of war threats on the borders of one of the African states. Attention was drawn elsewhere: a relative peace was restored among those concerned with the new Town Centre.

Bethany had her usual schedule to attend to, but her thoughts returned frequently to Mrs Bedells. Where could the old lady have gone?

She hadn't any doubt that the departure had been brought about by the arrival of Allie Pembury at the door of No. 15, spouting the words of Arabella Bedells. There was Mrs Bedells, all packed and ready to go with Bethany to a safe refuge for the weekend. All at once her trust in her helper had been destroyed. But nevertheless her suitcase was packed, she'd already cleared out the fridge and poured away the milk – –so why shouldn't she go? What need of Bethany Dayton to help her?

Off she'd gone on her own. But where?

Now, now, said Bethany to herself, it's none of your business where she's gone. As Peter said, she had a perfect right to go away. But all the same it was worrying.

As the week progressed, Peter himself began to express concern. 'I'd have thought she might get in touch with me,' he mused. 'I felt she regarded me as her solicitor, in a way. But perhaps not.'

'It was just bad luck. If Allie Pembury hadn't turned up when she did, it would all have gone like clockwork.'

'You do think she's all right, I suppose?'

'Why shouldn't she be, Peter?'

'Well, we got into the house because you were worried about her. You thought she might have had a stroke or something like that.'

'No, I didn't really – well, I suppose I did – but that doesn't mean she can't pack up and go away on her own if she wants to.'

'But after being cooped up practically all day every day for weeks – mightn't it be a bit of a strain on her?'

'I'm sure she's all right.'

But it wasn't true. Her mind refused to be at rest about Mrs Bedells.

She remembered on the Friday morning that the ladies living in the retirement complex had known Mrs Bedells – or at least one of them had known her – in days gone by. Perhaps there was something to be learnt by speaking to Mabel again.

It had dawned on Bethany that Jephthah would be a restraining influence, so she rang the Home, asked for Mabel Montgomery, and invited her out to tea. Mabel was delighted. Anything to break the routine of life in sheltered housing.

They met in a café in Barhampton famous for its Continental patisserie. Full of glee, Mabel ordered Viennese coffee and a piece of

244

Sachertorte. 'Never get anything like this on the menu at the Home,' she said. 'And as for doing it for myself, I can never get whipped cream to sit on coffee the way they do it in a proper café.'

'You're sure it won't disagree with you?' Bethany said, thinking of all the cholesterol.

'Me? Digestion like a horse, I have!' She forked a piece of chocolate cake into her mouth, then said, 'Well, what's it all about?'

'I beg your pardon?'

'Gerron wi' thee, lass! Young girls like you don't ask old biddies like me out to tea for nothing. What is it you want?'

Bethany blushed, then laughed. 'Well, you're right, of course. I want to ask you about Mrs Bedells.'

'Nancy? Why's that?'

'Well, between you and me, she's disappeared.'

'Goo on! Disappeared?'

'She's slipped out of her house and vanished. I'm a bit worried about her. I wondered if . . . well . . . you seemed to know her from the old days.'

'Oh aye. Nancy Bedells . . .' Mabel scooped up the cake crumbs on her fork and sighed in pleasure. 'That were luvly, lass. Anybody's only got to bribe me with cream cake and I'll do whatever they want.'

'So what about Nancy Bedells then?' urged Bethany.

'Nancy Lee she were then. A real beauty. Proud, you know – raven black hair, flashing eyes, skin like ivory—'

'You make her sound like an Italian or a Spaniard—'

'Well, she were a gyppo, weren't she?'

'A what?'

'A gypsy, a Romany – that's how they met, her and William Bedells. She used to go round selling clothes pegs and bits of white heather at the doors, didn't she? Mobs o' them, there used to be, at Horse Fair time . . . a lot of that's died away now, 'cos of course the chief business for the men was selling horses and everybody in Barhampton's got a car these days.'

'You knew Nancy Bedells?'

'Not well,' Mabel acknowledged, waving at the waitress for another cup of Viennese coffee. 'My husband, bless his heart, were a Welfare Officer and one of his jobs were to visit the gypsy camp to see after the kiddies – you know, to see that they got a bit of schooling and all that. Waste of time, really, poor old Jim . . . they'd send their kids the first day or two after they settled, but the youngsters never liked it . . . They'd missed such a lot of schooling, they felt left out, and of course they talked this special lingo amongst themselves, the other kids didn't like it . . . I think their language has pretty well died out nowadays. Any rate, the kids would skive off, and my Jim would try to round 'em up, and sometimes if he caught one or two he'd bring 'em to me for a cup of tea and a bun, because, you know, they weren't bad kids, just not used to being in one place and making a go of it. Any road, I got to know some of the families that way.'

'And so you knew Nancy?' Bethany said with patience.

'Oh aye, she were a real stunner in those days, I can tell you! It's no wonder William took up with her after his wife passed on. He was lonely and pottering about writing little bits of things about the gypsies and there she was, like the moon and the stars all knit together in a woman. It's no wonder he lost his head over her.'

'But then, why didn't he marry her?' Bethany asked.

The coffee came, Mabel spent a few moments spooning the whipped cream around to her satisfaction – and perhaps delaying her next statement for dramatic effect.

'He did marry her, luv. They had a Romany wedding – jumping over broomsticks or summat like that. I heard about it at the time – a big celebration it were; I think they had to have roast hare trapped by the bridegroom but since William weren't up to that sort of thing, Nancy trapped it for him but everybody pretended he'd done it. Oh aye, it were a regular do. To Nancy's mind they were legally married as if by bell, book and candle. And to his, I dare say, for he'd a great respect for Romany custom.'

So that was why William Bedells had apparently been living outside the bonds of matrimony with Nancy: he regarded the Romany wedding as binding. Nancy, too – but for the sake of legal documents she'd changed her name by deed poll from Nancy Lee to Nancy Bedells. A strong-minded woman all her life, it seemed – and still stubborn and unyielding even now.

'Them gyppos are fierce about independence,' Mabel went on as if reading her mind. 'And secretive . . .? Never tell you owt if they could help it, just on principle – Jim used to say they were afraid to open their mouths in case a fly flew in.' She gave a slightly malicious giggle. 'When I saw that in the paper about the Bedells house, I thought to myself, You'll be lucky if you ever get her out of that, I thought.'

'But what's she been living on all these years?' Bethany wondered. 'She couldn't have applied for a widow's pension – she'd have had to produce a certificate of marriage—'

'Oh, William had money. He had quite a good business for a while, these little books on etiquette and all that – there used to be a market for that kind of thing, but these days nobody cares how you reply to letters or which fork you use. I reckon Nancy kept it going after his death, because it was all mail order, you see, and then when she ran out of supplies of these little books she'd use his savings. Oh aye, I reckon he left her enough in the bank to keep her going a long while and mebbe there was insurance taken out in her name or summat o' t'sort.' Mabel spooned around in her coffee cup for the last of her cream. 'I'm not too

246

badly off myself – my Jim saw to that – but I felt I'd be happier with lots of company, so that's why I moved into sheltered housing. But not for Nancy, never, she'd never budge from her own place. She'd given up the gypsy life for that house; she'd never let anybody else have it if she could help it.'

Bethany was beginning to get an understanding of Mrs Bedells that had been entirely lacking hitherto. 'If she were to go away, just temporarily,' she murmured, 'where would she go?'

'Hmm . . .' said Mabel. She gave it some thought. 'Your first idea is always to say, to relatives or friends. But she left 'em all behind when she married William. And she never made any friends after her marriage. You know, I don't mean to be unkind, but she were never a *likeable* girl. A beauty, of course, and quick in her mind, and with more education than happen the rest of her tribe, but she weren't the sort to have the neighbours in for tea – no, not Nancy. *I* tried to befriend her, 'cos I thought she'd find town-dwelling very strange after the freedom of the road. But after she didn't turn up once or twice for an afternoon's shopping or a visit to the pictures, I just limited it to Christmas cards. And she only kept that up for a few years . . . Nay, I can't think of anyone she were close to.'

There seemed no more to be learned. Mabel said a few admiring things about the cakes on show in the chilled container and expressed gratitude for the outing. 'Eeh, it were grand, lass. Somebody new to talk to, a new face . . . Jephthah's a fine soul, of course, but wearing, wi' all that rectitude . . .'

'She and Nancy would get on well together,' Bethany suggested, laughing. 'Two strong-minded women.'

'Nay! Jephthah thinks Romanies are lawless and deceitful! And she wouldn't like me even talking about them, but—' and here she gave a mischievous grin – 'today she's gone off on a coach trip that takes her near the place where she was born – though why anybody should think all that much of Barnsley, I don't know!'

The next ten days were something of a mixture. Mary Dayton had gone off on her trip to Venice. This was a blessing because Bethany's flat wasn't really comfortable for two permanent inhabitants. Moreover, it released Bethany from the strain of 'looking after Mother' – although quite what that entailed she couldn't have explained. At any rate, she was able to come and go as she pleased, not worrying about staying away overnight with Peter when she wanted to.

But there was her father to cope with. 'Gone abroad?' he roared when she told him. 'Gone where? For how long?'

'She's gone to see Robert in Venice—'

'Robert?' he interrupted in suspicious anger. And then, realising that the Robert in question was his own son, ending sheepishly, 'Oh, our Robert.'

'Yes, she got a note from him a few days ago in mail she collected from the house.'

'Aye, I notice she creeps in and out when I'm not there!'

'Do you blame her, Dad? Look at how you greeted the news I just gave you – you were ready to start a battle right away—'

'But Beth . . . You don't know what it's like . . .' He sat slumped in his office chair, nothing like the big man the public knew, head of that famous and venerable firm of architects, *Dayton & Daughter*. 'When I get home at night, the house is empty. The mail's all piled into the letter-cage, not sorted out on the hall table the way she does it. There's nobody to pour a drink for me, nobody to set the table and put the meal on. There's nobody to argue with about the TV programmes. When I go out to some function, some reception, people ask me what's happened to Mary, and I don't know what to say. And she won't talk to me – she's never there when I ring, and now she's gone *abroad* – with Ossie Fielden, I bet.'

Her mother had said she intended this as a lesson to Daniel Dayton. But Bethany couldn't help wondering if the lesson was proving too severe. Her father had lost weight, his skin had a pallor that signalled too much time spent indoors, not enough on the golf course with his cronies . . . but then his cronies probably asked after Mary.

'Why don't you write to her?' she suggested. 'Write her a nice letter.'

'Saying what?'

'That you're sorry—'

'What am I supposed to be sorry *for*?' he burst out. 'That I used an advantage in business? Good Lord, Beth, you know we do that all the time—'

'But it was how you did it, Dad. You used sneaky tactics against a defenceless old lady—'

'Defenceless! She's caused us more trouble than an army of tanks—'

'That's not what we're talking about here. We're talking about how Mother *felt* about your action—'

'High-minded and unrealistic—'

'And you refused to listen to her opinions.'

'Well, she was talking nonsense!'

'There you are. You can write an apology for saying she was talking nonsense—'

'But I still think so!'

'But you don't have to say so, Dad.' His daughter drew a deep breath and launched on the difficult task of explaining to a self-satisfied man where he had gone wrong. 'There are times when I disagree with you—'

'Oh, I know that – daft ideas about architecture that are going to cost us a fortune—'

'But I don't embark on a war every time our point of view differs. I hold my tongue if it's not important, I try to get round it some other way, I only come to open warfare if it's something vital. I learnt the technique from Mother, as a matter of fact. Now the fact that Mother told you straight out that you were wrong about Mrs Bedells's marriage – or lack of it, as you thought – should have told you it was serious. So you should have backed off, tried to calm things down, and apologised.'

'Apologised! I don't know what I was supposed to apologise *for*! I was in the right!'

'Dad, even if you were in the right – and I disagree with you – you shouldn't be insensitive about how you handle things.'

'Insensitive?'

'Yes.'

'Me?'

'Yes.'

Restlessly, he swung his leather chair to and fro a little. It was clear that his daughter had presented him with an entirely new idea. After a long moment he said, 'So that's what I should say in the letter? That I'm sorry I was insensitive?'

'It's worth saying,' she remarked. 'The more so if you mean it.'

'Oh, I mean it, all right. I'm as sorry as the devil that I ever said anything to set her off on this caper of hers.'

'I meant, sorry that you've been insensitive. And you have been, almost from the time I was in infant school.'

'Me?' he said again. 'But that's not true! If I were going around putting my foot in it all the time, I'd have no friends, folk would avoid me – and nobody can say that Daniel Dayton is an unpopular man, that's just not so!'

His daughter stifled a sigh. Perhaps it was useless to try to make him see himself as she and her mother saw him. But she felt she mustn't give up too easily, or else how were he and her mother ever going to be reconciled? 'Let me ask you two questions,' she said gently. 'And don't get angry or indignant. Think before you answer.'

He gave her an odd glance, almost of defiance. 'Go on then.'

'Why does Mother have to go to Venice to see Robert? Why doesn't Robert come home if he's got some time off from the hospital?'

'Why, because he – well, he talks such nonsense when he's here. I mean, after the first few hours of being glad to see him, we get on each other's nerves—' He broke off.

Bethany said nothing. She let a pause ensue. Then she said, 'The next question is, why have you no friends outside the business world?'

'I've got loads of friends,' Daniel protested. 'Why, our Christmas card list is pages long—'

'Name me two people you know who aren't somehow involved in construction or building supplies or transport or property development.'

'Oh, well, that's easy! There's Ossie – though whether he's a friend of mine at the moment I'm not so sure—'

'Ossie used to be in local government – and still has business contacts you find useful.' She shrugged and waited.

'Well, there's Ralph Bingham – now you can't say he's a business contact, he runs an art gallery—'

'Which you re-modelled for him, Dad. And although he invites you to openings, you never go. Do you?'

'We-ell . . . You know I'm not much on modern art—'

'So he's a friend of yours? When you won't even go and say a few kind words if he puts on a show?'

'We-ell . . .' He pulled himself together to oppose her view. 'All right, so most of my friends are people in the business world. So what's wrong with that?'

'We started this discussion because you wouldn't accept the idea you might be insensitive. But if you think of your friends, Dad, they're people who can't afford to disagree with you. If you say something tactless they can't tell you to drop dead, because you could give your contract to someone else. And you have a lot of prestige, a lot of contacts throughout local government and the quangos. They want to keep in with you because you might do them a lot of good – or bad, as the case may be.'

He stared at her, thunderstruck. He swallowed, then said, 'You make me out to be some kind of bully, lass!'

'Not at all. You're a businessman, and a successful one. But it seems to me that like many others in the business world you've lost the knack of managing private relationships.'

'You've a high opinion of yourself, young woman, standing there telling your own father he's a failure on a personal level! What's so marvellous about you, anyhow?' he cried, indignation getting the better of him. 'You're into your thirties, no proper home of your own, no children, and no sign of a husband to have them with unless this hole-and-corner thing with Lambot is supposed to be leading some-where!' He shook his head, chin up, moral superiority coming to his aid. 'And that's another thing, you're supposed to be so high-minded, I'd expect loyalty to be high on your agenda, but no, you were playing footsie with a man who's preparing to bring a suit against our construc-tion teams – what about loyalty, what about responsibility to our colleagues? Pembury could do us a lot of damage with his law suit!'

'Dad—'

'No, that's enough, I won't have you in my own office talking to me as if it was me that's in the wrong. Clear off and don't try to give lessons to your betters, miss!'

The painful echoes of this interlude stayed with her for days. She avoided going in person to the York office, she communicated by phone. She couldn't even speak about it to Peter. She blamed herself for ever having embarked on an explanation with her father – after thirty years she should have known it was useless.

Then an event occurred that blotted the quarrel from her mind. The Heritage Department made up its mind. No. 15 Royal Terrace was declared a Grade One Listed Building.

Chapter Twenty

The decree caused a big upsurge of activity next day in Barhampton. The Steering Committee of the New Town Centre Development had to meet, in Extraordinary Session, to decide what to do. The advice of Iris Weston was to play it cool. 'The Department of the Environment has made this order because it thinks it's what the public wants,' she remarked with a knowing nod of her head. 'It would do us no good to appear to be against public opinion.'

Barhampton council also went into urgent conference, and reached much the same conclusion. 'We've just got to grin and bear it,' said their Press Officer.

Reporters door-stepped Mrs Bedells but, as always, got no response. 'Miserable old cat,' they grumbled to each other, and dispersed to bother other, more amenable people.

At ten at night, the day's meetings over at last, Bethany sat with Peter in his flat, trying to decide what to do. They were both tired; Bethany's eyes had dark shadows under them, her bright hair seemed to have less gloss, her dress – a business dress for a business meeting – was creased and untidy. Peter's tie was undone, he felt he needed a shave.

They were trying to address the problem which was known only to themselves: the fact that Mrs Bedells was no longer in residence.

'It was all right at first to say nothing about her going away,' she murmured to him. 'But now . . .?'

'I've been wondering about it. The meeting of the Royal Terrace Protection Group was pretty triumphant this evening, pretty content, you know, to sit about congratulating itself and resting on its laurels. But eventually things will move on . . .'

'What actually happens next, Peter? I studied this business of Conservation Orders at university but only from the point of view of what architects could or could not do in a Conservation Area. What actually happens now in the legal sense?'

'The government serves notice on the owner of the property that it's now a Listed Building. From now on, number fifteen is under the protection of the Department of the Environment. Papers will be sent to Mrs Bedells.'

'Who isn't there.'

'Exactly.'

'What does it mean? Under the Department's protection – that doesn't mean she has to move out.'

'Not at all. There are a lot of properties in the UK that are Listed and with people living in them. There are *barns* with Listed status, tractors rolling in and out of them every day.'

'So when the DoE sends notification of the Listing to Mrs Bedells, and she doesn't reply because she's not there to get it – what will happen?'

Peter gave a rueful smile. 'They'll write again. And probably a third time. Then they'll get irritated and send an official, who of course won't get any reply when he bangs on the door. After that . . . I don't know . . . perhaps they'd send a court official to serve the papers . . . But that's in the future, Beth. Officialdom moves slowly.'

'Ought we to tell anyone she's gone?' she wondered.

'We went through all this before, love. She has a perfect right to go away. What happens is still her affair, not ours.'

'But if it's going to get her into trouble with a government department . . .'

'That's for Mrs Bedells to handle—'

'But she's not even *aware* of what's happening, that there could be trouble—'

'Oh, come on, Beth!' he objected. 'She's not senile! On the contrary, she's a very bright old lady, though disagreeable. She reads the papers, watches TV – we know that because she's reacted to events in the past. I bet wherever she is she's keeping an eye on what goes on in Barhampton, and if she doesn't learn within the next few days that her house is now an officially protected building, I'll eat my law books.'

'Ye-es . . . But that doesn't solve our problem. Ought we to tell anyone that the house is empty?'

He considered it. 'Why should we tell anyone? Do we have reason to do that?'

'Well, the Steering Committee has to make decisions about re-planning the Town Centre. The council has turned it over to us – I mean, to *Dayton's* – because of course the design for the Town Centre envisaged the whole of Royal Terrace coming down. It needs a whole new set of blueprints.'

'The council aren't going to appeal against the Order?'

'They decided against it. Their Press Officer said it would be a long wrangle that could make them seem petty, and Bigsby told them it might be a long battle costing them a lot in legal fees. Of course they don't want that. Besides, after the *Bedells Beano* they got the message – the townsfolk and the tabloids are on the side of the Protection Group. It could lose a lot of votes in the next council elections if they fight the Preservation Order.'

'So what are you saying? That you feel you ought to tell the Steering Committee about Mrs Bedells?'

'Ought I?' She was troubled. 'You see, the basis of her support is that she's a doughty old lady standing up to officialdom. But you and I – and Lennie – know that in fact she's abandoned the field.'

He frowned and tugged at his hair in frustration. 'It's a real sixty-four-thousand-dollar question.'

'Isn't it just! Mrs Bedells has a right to her privacy. If she wants to go away, why shouldn't she? And why should anybody be told about it? But on the other hand, there's an awful lot of money tied up in the construction of the Town Centre, and an awful lot being drained away if we have to fossick about waiting for her to sign papers that are lying on her hall floor.'

It was time to call a halt. They were letting themselves be tied up in the detail. He jumped to his feet. 'Are you hungry? It's been a long day and I'm starving.'

'What have you got in the larder?'

'I've got the makings for a sandwich—'

'Not another sandwich!' she cried in dismay. 'That's all I've had all day – cooped up in meeting rooms, chewing cheese and pickle sandwiches and drinking too much cold coffee—'

'Let's go out—'

'But it's getting so late.'

'The Thai restaurant up the road doesn't close till midnight. Do you like Thai food?'

'I like Chinese—'

'Come on then.'

It was a short walk to the restaurant. The crisp night revived them. The weariness of long daylight hours in a stuffy conference room began to fall away from Bethany. Peter felt the frustration of the meetings with the Royal Terrace Protection Group die away. Each of them understood there were further problems ahead: the Protection Group were certain that the Grade I Listing of the Bedells house would be followed by a Grade II for the rest of the Terrace, and Bethany's father was demanding to know where the money was to come from for the new plans needed for the Town Centre.

The meal proved just what they needed. Bethany discovered *satay* and fell in love with it. Several cups of scented tea cleared her head. In the soft light from the restaurant's lanterns, nothing seemed so difficult. She began to feel her brain might function again by next day.

'So the long and the short of it is, the house has a Preservation Order on it, Mrs Bedells isn't there to accept the papers, and nobody except us knows that.'

'Except for Lennie the Loophole,' Peter reminded her.

'But he won't tell anyone because he'd have to explain how he knows – and he doesn't want to do that.'

254

'Exactly. So we have what amounts to privileged information.'

'Should we do anything with it?'

'I'm beginning to think we should keep quiet – at least for the present,' he said. 'Nothing is going to happen *quickly*. The notice about the Listing will arrive at the house. Nobody would expect her to respond immediately. In fact, it would be normal for her to consult a solicitor before signing. So a week or so . . . perhaps more . . .'

'In the meantime, should we be doing anything?'

'Such as what?'

'Looking for her.'

He hunched his shoulders in dismay at the thought. 'Where should we look? If we'd had the police on the job at the outset, they could have asked at railway stations and bus terminals, stuff like that. But now? Asking if anyone saw a little old lady leaving Barhampton with a suitcase a month ago? Hopeless.'

Bethany tried to think of something helpful. 'Could we advertise for her? Law firms do that sometimes, don't they – if they've got a will to settle and they can't find the legatee.'

'We'd have to use her name and address: *Will Mrs Nancy Bedells, of 15 Royal Terrace, Barhampton, please contact . . .*'

'And of course someone would be sure to spot it and put the press on to it.'

'It's likely. And we'd get crackpots saying they're the reincarnation of Mrs Bedells and they deserve the legacy – you always get some of those.'

In the end they decided that for the time being they'd say and do nothing.

'Are you staying tonight?' he asked as they walked back arm in arm to his flat.

'I can't, darling. Mother's due back from Venice tomorrow and I need to be up early to tidy up. I'm afraid I've let myself spread into the spare room while she's been away.'

He sighed inwardly. He had nothing against Mrs Dayton except that he wished she'd stayed even longer in Venice. Her prolonged visit with her daughter was a drawback.

'So shall I see you tomorrow or are you going to be having a welcome-home for your mother?'

'Now, now.' She kissed him lightly on the cheek. She understood exactly what he was feeling, could see the disappointment hidden behind his smile. 'We'll be in touch. It's the same with Mother's problem as it is with Mrs Bedells – we have to wait and see.' They reached her jeep and she unlocked it. 'Good night, my love. I'm so weary it's probably just as well I have to go home to my own bed.'

Mrs Dayton arrived home from Venice with a new hairstyle and many packages, one of them a present for Bethany. 'Robert couldn't be with me all the while,' she explained, 'and Ossie went off to Rome – he'd some friends in a British firm with offices there – really, he's just as busy as before he retired! So I took myself off to Milan for a few days – Bethie, the shops there! Anyhow, I bought you this sweater.'

The 'sweater' was a cornflower blue top, of heavy knitted silk and by a famous designer. 'Mother!' Bethany exclaimed. 'It's fabulous!'

'Yes . . . well . . . you can only do so much sightseeing, and once you get into the shopping area the temptation's too much . . .' Mary looked guilty. 'It's your father's money I'm spending, you know . . . he's never put a stop on my credit cards . . . it's beginning to make me feel guilty . . .' Her grey eyes filled with tears.

'Ah, what's wrong, darling?' Bethany cried, putting an arm around her. 'I thought you'd enjoy being abroad and pleasing yourself—'

'Well, I did, and of course it was lovely seeing Robert. But his mind was on other things, really – he was having meetings with Customs officials about medical supplies that have gone missing.' Mary gulped back a sob. 'And then you know . . . coming home . . . it was stupid but in my mind's eye I was picturing myself going into my bedroom and hanging these things in my wardrobe. But here I am, with all these new clothes, and there's nowhere to *put* anything.'

'I'm sorry, love. I should have made more space for you. I'll clear out—'

'No, don't do that. It's wrong that I'm hanging round your neck like this.' Mary found a tissue, wiped her eyes, blew her nose, and straightened her shoulders. 'If I'm not going to go home, I ought to find a place for myself, a little flat or something.'

'If you're not going to go home – are you thinking of it then?'

'Oh Beth, I *long* to be home in my own place again! But . . . but . . . I don't want to go back for the wrong reasons. Not just to have a proper wardrobe or a garden for the church flowers . . . I want . . . I don't know what I want. Yes, I do. I want some sort of sign from your father that he's going to change.'

'But you won't get that if you won't ever talk to him, Mother.'

'No, I know. I never really thought it through, you know. Well, perhaps it's time for me to do some serious thinking. And to screw up my courage and have a face-to-face encounter with my husband.' She sighed deeply. 'But not yet. Not just yet.'

'No,' agreed her daughter. 'Now wouldn't be a good time. We've got another crisis on our hands.'

She brought her mother up to date with the news about the Conservation Order on the Bedells house. 'It means we've got to make new decisions about the Town Centre, and of course now we'll have to include the Department of the Environment in the planning because we can't do anything to number fifteen without their consent. Dad isn't pleased.'

'And what does Mrs Bedells say to all this?'

Bethany hesitated. 'Mother . . . Mrs Bedells isn't in the house any more.'

'What?'

'She left some time during the weekend of that terrible street party – remember? She's vanished.'

'You don't know where she is?'

'No, and nobody else knows that she's gone – only me, you and Peter.' And Lennie the Loophole, she added inwardly, but thought it best not to mention his part in the proceedings.

Mary nodded in acceptance of the unspoken condition – that no one else was to be told. 'I suppose she's all right?' she ventured.

'Well, she prepared the house for her absence – emptied the fridge, put her plants out in the open air – she didn't have a brainstorm, if that's what you mean. But all the same,' she said with open anxiety, 'I wish I knew where she's gone.'

Her mother considered the matter. 'She might have gone home.'

'Home?'

'Well, looking at it from my own point of view – my thoughts keep turning to my home. She might have felt something like that, for her home-place, for the house where she grew up.'

Bethany thought of Jephthah and her coach trip to Barnsley. Perhaps Nancy Bedells might feel nostalgia too. 'But where is her home? She was born a gypsy.'

'Really? How do you know?'

'Someone told me, someone who knew her as a girl. She used to come to Barhampton for the old Horse Fair – apparently the gypsies bought and sold horses in those days.'

'Horses?' said Mary. 'I remember, when I was a teacher, I used to do lessons about the social history of the North, and of course most of them were about manufacture and so forth, but there were a couple . . . about agriculture and the countryside . . . so of course horses . . . they were part of it . . . There was a town in the North – the Lake District? Appleby, that was it! There was a big trade in horses at Appleby.'

'You think Nancy Bedells's family might be somewhere in the Appleby area?'

Mary shook her head. 'I suppose not. It was all so long ago, after all.'

Later, speaking on the telephone to Peter, Bethany reported this thought of her mother's. To her surprise he took it seriously. 'It's somewhere to start. But the family name wouldn't be Bedells, of course – what was her maiden name again?'

'Lee . . . Nancy Lee . . . let me think . . . Iris Weston did some research and if I remember rightly she said Nancy was born on a farm in – was it Cumbria?'

'Cumberland,' her mother corrected when she was consulted. 'It used to be called Cumberland. And it was right next door to Westmorland – and Appleby was in Westmorland before the names of the counties changed.'

Peter handed this information to a private investigator sometimes used by *Pesh, Samuels & Co.* But after a few days he was advised to call it off. 'Turns out that Lee is one of the commonest names in the Romany world – that and Smith,' said the investigator. 'I showed her picture around but nobody in Appleby's caught on to it, sir. They had a Horse Fair here in June, but otherwise it's a quiet little place. I've tried all the hotels and guest-houses – not a sign of her and though there are several people called Lee in the district phone book, none of them are related to her. You're just wasting your money, Mr Lambot.'

It had only been a faint hope. Peter took the advice and called off the search. Which was made unnecessary, because two days later he received a phone call at his office.

From Mrs Bedells.

'Mr Lambot? Is that you?'

He recognised the thin old voice at once.

'Mrs Bedells! Where are you?' he cried.

There was a minute pause, then she said, 'What makes you ask that?'

'We've been so worried about you!'

'We? Who's "we"?'

'Miss Dayton and I – you remember, we were there that night when Allie Pembury—'

'Don't talk to me about that awful girl! I'm not wasting money on a phone call to talk about *her*.'

'But tell me where you're speaking from! We've been trying to—'

'I'm speaking on my telephone at home, of course.'

In the background he could hear faint sounds – he couldn't quite place them but they were nothing like domestic noises or daytime television. 'No, you're not, Mrs Bedells. You've been gone since the weekend of the *Beano*.'

'And how do you know that, young man?' she demanded, her voice crackling with indignation.

'Well . . .' Now Peter saw what a mistake he'd fallen into. He began all over again. 'Please don't be angry with us about it, Mrs Bedells, but Bethany was so worried! She'd put a couple of notes through your letterbox and she could see them lying there on the floor, so she began to think you'd been taken ill. So we got into the house and—'

'You've been in my house?'

'Yes, and we saw you'd tidied everything up in preparation for going away.'

'How did you get in? If you've damaged my door lock you'll pay for it, Peter Lambot.'

'No, no, we got one of the squatters to slip in through the skylight—'

258

'Oh, him! Clambering about over everything with his ropes and his upsailing or whatever he calls it – thinks he's the king of the castle. If he's broken the glass in that skylight—'

'No, truly, everything is as you left it. When we saw you'd gone, we came away.'

'And so then you went and gabbed about it to all your friends.'

'Not a soul knows you left the house except myself, Bethany, her mother, and the man who let us in, Lennie the Loophole.'

'Lennie the Loopy! He's daft, they all are. They've made my life a misery ever since they got into the other houses. And now there's this thing in the papers that my home is being taken over by the government—'

'No, no, Mrs Bedells – they haven't taken it over—'

'And it's to be open to the public, like them great houses they show on the telly.'

'Not at all. No, nothing like that. The house has been Listed—'

'That's what I say – National Trust or Heritage or summat – and the papers say those protesters aren't going to leave until they get the other houses put under the same thing – and it's never going to end, never.' For a moment the cross little tirade wavered, and he could picture her features creasing in the effort not to cry. 'So I thought I'd better ring you.'

'Yes,' he encouraged. 'Do you want me to do something for you?'

'That girl . . .'

'Allie Pembury?'

'No, no, the architect girl.'

'Bethany.'

'She said . . . she said . . . she could make a retirement flat available to me.'

'Yes, she could.' Hope began to stir in his mind. Could it really be that the indomitable Nancy Bedells was finally going to give in?

'Well . . . I'm not saying I've made up my mind . . . But I can't go on like this, living out of a suitcase, and if I go back to my own place it seems there's going to be people butting in on me . . .'

'There would be officials,' he agreed. 'Inspectors, perhaps. The general public wouldn't have access but people from the Department of the Environment would want to check that the place was in good order—'

'In good order? Let me tell you, young man, that house is in perfect order and not a speck of dust or a trickle of damp has ever gone past my notice!'

'I didn't mean that,' he soothed. 'It's just, if the building is Listed, you can't for instance install central heating without permission – that sort of thing.'

'I don't want central heating, never did. Nasty, stuffy air! If I get a flat from this Bethany girl, it'll have central heating, I suppose, it's the thing these days. But I'd turn it off, me, I'd never live with it. That's if I decide to go along with her offer,' she added quickly, in case he thought she was weakening. 'I thought happen it would be a good idea to sell my house to the council after all and be shot of all the problems. But mind, I'd want you to get a good price for it!'

'I understand. The council would be very co-operative, I'm sure. And Bethany will find you somewhere where you'll be happy and quiet—'

'I won't be happy if them reporters come after me all the time, peeping through my curtains and making a nuisance of themselves. If I give up my house for some place you find for me, you've got to promise I won't be followed and badgered. You won't tell that actress girl, the one that goes on about that wicked Arabella as if she was some sort of angel?'

'No, of course not.'

'Because she was awful, making my doorstep a pantomime show with her daft speeches and hitting people on the head with her placards!'

'I promise Allie Pembury won't bother you, Mrs Bedells.'

'Well then . . . well then . . . you talk to that young woman about the flat, and you go and take a look at it, and we'll see what comes of it. That's all for the moment.'

'Mrs Bedells! Don't ring off! How can I get in touch with you? Where are you?'

'We'll just see how things go,' she said, and disconnected.

'Wait!' But she was gone. Swearing under his breath, Peter hit the buttons for the check-back, scribbled the numbers announced by the polite mechanical voice, and pressed 3. There was a ringing tone; he hoped it had gone through so quickly that Mrs Bedells would pick up the receiver again.

But no. The number rang on and on, and though he disconnected and redialled the result was the same. Off and on, until it was time to go home, he tried the number. No one ever picked up.

He was meeting Bethany at the home of Mr Tallant, president of the Royal Terrace Protection Group. It was her hope to reach some sort of agreement with them on what could be done to preserve the Terrace within the re-planning of the Town Centre. As always, the members of the group disagreed among themselves and went off at cross purposes. Mr Tallant served instant coffee and biscuits at nine o'clock, after which Peter and Bethany said their goodbyes. The arguments were still going on in the living room as the house door closed on them.

Outside on the pavement Peter said, 'I've something important to tell you.'

'What about? I *thought* you looked a bit distracted during the meeting.'

'I've heard from Mrs Bedells.'

260

'What!'

He brought her up to date with what had happened. She stood staring at him in the light of the street-lamp, eyes glinting with the beginning of optimism. She listened, nodding, exclaiming, clasping her hands together in pleasure until he came to the point where Mrs Bedells had rung off.

'But you got her number?'

'Yes, but she never replied.'

'She can be so stubborn!'

'It wasn't just that, Beth.'

'What do you mean?'

'I don't think she was there.'

'She'd gone out? Well, yes . . .'

'Bethany, what kind of phone rings and rings and nobody bothers to answer?'

She wrinkled her brow, thought about it, and understood. 'A public phone.'

'Yes. We've all done it, walked past a phone ringing its head off in a public phone booth. While she was speaking I thought I heard noises that I couldn't place, and now I think she was in the open air somewhere.'

'The clever old thing,' she said, with a sigh that was half admiring and half regretful.

'So I looked up the prefix in the code book and – guess where she is?'

'Where?'

'Blackpool.'

'Oh Lord.'

'You may well say she's a clever old thing. We'll never find her in Blackpool. It's probably full of old ladies on package holidays, come to see the illuminations.'

'So what it amounts to is, we have to wait until she contacts you again?'

'I'm afraid so. But in the meantime . . .'

'In the meantime, let's plan what we ought to do.'

'Exactly. We're not far from the old Victoria. Let's go and have a drink and talk it over.'

Once there, they discussed how to achieve what Mrs Bedells wanted. She had made two demands: that Bethany should live up to her promise of a flat, and that this should be achieved without publicity.

'The first is easy,' Bethany said. 'Barhampton council will want to buy the Bedells house from her. And in exchange I should think they'd be only too pleased to make her the offer of a council flat. If she doesn't want that, I've got contacts among property managers, I'm sure I could get her something nice.'

'But then comes the difficulty. To achieve all that, there's got to be legal negotiations. Someone's sure to leak it to the press.'

'We'll have to put the fear of God into the Legal Department of the Town Council – we'll scare Bigsby with horror stories about her withdrawing from the whole thing if he lets word get out—'

'I'm not so sure it's just a horror story. I think she *would* back out. She's having to give in, which she hates, so the least thing could spook her.'

'We'll take it very slowly, a step at a time, and we'll only tell people on a "need to know" basis. But—' she sighed – 'I'll have to tell Dad. We're going to have to redesign that section of the Town Centre—'

'But that's already the case – because of the DoE ruling—'

'But it changes the possibilities if the council is going to own the Bedells house. We could probably get a lot more co-operation from the DoE on changes if the council is the owner.'

'I suppose so. Your father will be pleased, I imagine.'

'Pleased? He's likely to be euphoric! He's wanted to demolish Nancy Bedells from the minute she got in his way. I'm just so afraid he'll boast about it to his pals.'

'Tell him if he breathes a word, it's all off.'

'He won't take that seriously.'

'Then I'll tell him,' Peter said. 'I've been retained by Mrs Bedells to look after her interests and it's against her interests if he starts bragging. I'll ring him first thing tomorrow and arrange to see him.'

'Ring tonight,' she urged. 'He's probably at home by himself, moping.' She got out her mobile, pressed the buttons, and when the ringing started, handed it to Peter. He took it with some reluctance, but when it was answered, had to speak.

'Mr Dayton? This is Peter Lambot. I have something very important to tell you . . . No, a matter of business . . . Very urgent, otherwise I wouldn't be ringing you this late.' He made a grimace at Bethany and mouthed the words, 'In a bad temper.' After a moment he resumed his conversation. 'I'm ringing to set up an appointment . . . first thing tomorrow . . . as early as possible, then . . . Mr Dayton, stop playing games, I *have* to speak to you . . . No, not on the phone.'

'Let me,' Bethany said, and took the Nokia from him. 'Dad?' she said. 'Stop being difficult. Peter's got some news that will startle you.'

There was a gasp and then there was a faint thump, which sounded as if he had sat down heavily on the chair by the telephone. 'It's your mother,' he said in a faint voice. 'She's starting a divorce!'

She felt a pang of pity. Yet in a moment she was almost annoyed. If Mary Dayton were ever to start divorce proceedings, she would never inform him of it by a casual telephone call late in the evening. Nor would she involve as her divorce lawyer the man her daughter was in love with. Didn't he know that? Was he so out of touch with the way her mind worked?

262

Alas, yes. But that wasn't the point at the moment. 'It's nothing like that,' she said hastily. 'It's about another woman entirely.'

'Another woman?'

'Who is the next most important woman in your life at the moment?' A long pause. 'Come on, Dad, who's the thorn in your side?' Then as she heard him draw breath to say the name: 'Not on the phone, Dad.'

'No. No, better not. But why should we have a meeting about that?'

She handed the mobile back to Peter. 'He wants to know why you want a meeting about that lady.'

'I've been retained on her behalf,' he took it up at once. 'There's been a new development . . . No, I think you'll be pleased . . . That's better, nine-thirty tomorrow . . . Yes, of course I can make it. And, Mr Dayton, perhaps you'd better ask Mr Bigsby of the council's Legal Department to join us . . . Yes, I think so, but this meeting is to lay some ground rules, and one of them is, no one else is to be told . . . No, *no one* . . . Very well, good night, Mr Dayton.'

'He got the message?' Bethany enquired as she folded the mobile to put it away.

'He seems . . . "stunned", is the best word I can think of.' Peter frowned a little. 'By tomorrow morning he'll have got back into his usual stride, I suppose. It might be a bit of a clash . . .' He looked at Bethany in appeal. 'I suppose you wouldn't like to be present?'

'I'd only make things worse,' she confessed ruefully. 'The last time Dad and I had a conversation face to face, he told me not to give lessons to my betters and ordered me out.'

Peter took her hand in a quick, steady grasp. 'I'm sorry. I'd no idea.'

'Oh, it's not unusual. We've been at odds most of my life. But this time it was serious. This time it was about Mother. I was trying to get him to see . . . to see he'll never get her to come back unless he . . . I don't know . . . changes.'

'People don't change much at his age, Beth. He's pretty set in his ways.'

'I know that. But I wanted him to see he has to *try*. It was a mistake.' Tears welled up at the memory.

'Don't take it so much to heart, darling. I think anyone would agree your father's a difficult man and the way things have been going for him the last few months, he's probably ready for a fight with almost anybody – even his own daughter.'

'Well, I hope it goes all right tomorrow. If he crows over his victory, try not to let it annoy you.'

But the meeting next morning was much more subdued than Peter expected. He arrived promptly, dressed in dark legal suiting and carrying a document case. He'd spent an hour earlier that morning typing out a confidentiality agreement, a copy of which he set before both Daniel Dayton and Raymond Bigsby at the outset.

'Before we go any further, I want you both to sign that agreement. By putting it forward I don't mean any imputation against your good faith, but it must be understood that if a word of this conversation gets out and into the media, my client will withdraw at once and totally.'

Daniel, whom he'd expected to bluster, read the paragraphs in silence. Daniel then glanced at Bigsby. Bigsby nodded. 'A bit unusual but I see nothing against it.'

They each signed their copy. Peter received them back. 'I have good news,' he said. 'Mrs Bedells is willing to sell her house to the council and move to accommodation elsewhere in Barhampton.'

'No!' exclaimed Bigsby in astonishment.

Daniel pursed his lips but said nothing.

'What brought this on?' asked Bigsby.

'Partly the Conservation Order. Partly the unpleasantness of having to put up with her "supporters" – she particularly dislikes Allie Pembury.'

'It's nothing the council have done? She's not going to bring any sort of claim against us, for harassment or the like?'

'That I can't say. She hasn't even mentioned such a notion, Mr Bigsby. I should explain that I've had only a short telephone conversation with her, and a lot depends on what you offer by way of alternative accommodation.'

'Oh, we can soon find her something suitable,' the council's lawyer said in haste. 'Good heavens, she's only got to tell us what she wants and we'll sort it out. I could get the Housing Department to supply a list of properties by . . . let's see, today's Thursday . . . by next Monday we could show her some photographs of estates, and there's the Downlands development, sheltered housing. I believe all ground-floor dwellings, no stairs you know . . .' he stopped, aware he was babbling. He was very pleased. Barhampton council had been in great perplexity over Mrs Bedells.

Peter turned his glance on Daniel. 'When Mrs Bedells vacates her house, it should make it much easier for you to redesign the building plans for that area?'

'Daniel gave a heavy sigh. 'My daughter's the chief architect,' he said. 'I leave all that to her.'

'But you agree that this is a very favourable outcome?'

'Oh yes.'

It was strange. Bigsby did most of the talking during the hour that the meeting lasted. Daniel nodded agreement from time to time. When they parted Peter was inclined to think that Bigsby's delight would be more noticeable than any triumph Daniel might be feeling.

The following week was filled with secret activity. Peter expected Mrs Bedells to ring again but for the present she remained stubbornly incommunicado.

Then something happened which took all their attention away

momentarily. The manager of *Safe-Site*, the security firm for the construction areas of the Town Centre, asked for a meeting of Steerco.

'Ladies and gentlemen,' he said with a glance of great satisfaction around the table when they were all assembled, 'I have something very interesting to show you. As you know, when the tower of the old mill collapsed and injured Miss Pembury, it brought down the tall posts on which two of our security cameras were mounted. They were the two with that section under scrutiny, of course. One of them was totally smashed, beyond hope of retrieval. But the other . . . we got experts to see what they could do with the film, and though it was badly damaged they've been able to make it viewable with the help of digital enhancement. And, ladies and gentlemen, something very interesting has emerged.'

He broke off to make sure they were all paying attention.

'The film proves,' he said, 'that Allie Pembury is a liar.'

Chapter Twenty-one

The members of the Steering Committee were here because they were concerned about having to pay compensation for injuries on their Town Centre site. They had been interested to know what Mr Holden, the local manager of the security firm, could tell them. Now they were waiting with bated breath.

'I'd like you to watch what I'm going to show on the screen,' he went on. There was a stifled sigh in the darkened room: in their time they'd seen many demonstration films on small screens, most of them introduced by breezy publicists who wanted to sell them building equipment. Mr Holden was by no means breezy; he was dry, bony, and dull.

This film didn't begin with bouncy introduction music and patterns produced by computers. Instead the screen displayed a typed title: SAFE-SITE RECORDING, *Verified under Insurance Seal, Ref. 122174, not to be taken from premises without prior authorisation.*

There was a flicker of grey and some muzzy noise. Then the bland nothingness of a tape running to its opening scene. Next came some dark grey images. Mr Holden pressed some buttons on his remote, and the picture brightened a little.

'Here you see a view of a length of the recently laid cement path which was for the use of vehicles carrying materials to work-sites. This is where it ends, running into an open area in front of the old mill. Please note the sign on an A-frame to your left.' An electronic arrow pointed it out to the audience. 'This is the section of the film that shows Miss Pembury's appearance for the first time – you understand there was more film, but I won't waste your time showing you the site with nothing happening. Now! Here is Miss Pembury's entry on the scene.'

He paused, halting the tape. A figure had come into the picture, passing the A-frame with a big white board on it. It was impossible to tell whether the figure was a girl or a boy – from the camera's viewpoint it was a young person clad in jeans and a loose white top and with black hair hanging down.

Alan Singleton said: 'She passed the warning notice. She didn't turn her head to look at it so this proves nothing – her lawyer could claim it wasn't prominent enough.'

'Mr Singleton, as Project Manager you know there were warnings at

266

many points along the route she took. Please wait. I only stopped at this point to let you see the first time she was recorded by our camera near the mill tower. She was picked up on other cameras coming into the construction site and she passed other notices, but I didn't want to bother with those shots – you'll see why presently.'

He pressed the remote. The film resumed. The colours were mostly shades of grey, black, and white, although occasionally the bright hues of the construction vehicles showed up as faint echoes of themselves. The figure of Allie Pembury flitted among them and vanished.

'Where's she gone?' Emmett Foyle queried.

'She's out of sight behind the wall now. I think at this point she's scrambling up the pile of rubble behind the wall. You see how Martin – that's the security man in the observation cabin – is panning the lens, trying to find her? Now!'

Once more he stopped the film and used the pointer to draw their eyes to Allie as she emerged on the top of the length of wall still standing.

'Now that wall is dangerous,' Holden said. 'There was a notice on an A-frame at the edge of the rubble that she's just climbed up—'

'But the light?' demanded Singleton. 'Could she say there wasn't enough light for her to read it?'

'She could say anything, Mr Singleton, and we might have a hard time proving otherwise. But let me go on, and you'll see. I haven't brought the film showing our guards coming to stop her – those are recorded on Cameras 3 and 7. Camera 7 shows one of them getting into a dumpster truck so as to move fast, but that's by the way. I can produce those at any time to show solicitude on our part the moment we saw her on screen.'

Once more the film resumed. 'Please watch closely,' Holden instructed. Allie was now making her precarious way along the top of the wall. She was a few feet away from the base of the tower on which she wanted to tie her banner. She paused, and looked down.

The camera didn't show what she was looking at. The manager of *Safe-Site* remarked, 'One of our guards will testify that at this point he's calling to her. He called: "Come down, miss, it's dangerous up there." Watch her response.'

On screen, Allie laughed and shook her head. The movement was clearly visible as her dark hair moved to and fro on the white shoulders of her blouse.

'Our man calls again,' said Holden. 'What he called was, "That wall isn't safe." ' Allie shook her head again but this time emphasised the reply with a very rude two-fingered gesture. Holden froze the picture.

There was a gasp of amazement and horror from the audience. 'By *gum*!' snorted Emmett Foyle, who had a daughter of his own and would have been stricken to think she even knew anything so crude. Wellbrow broke into derisive laughter. Alan Singleton gave a groan of relief. Iris Weston said, 'So much for our little martyr!' Daniel

267

Dayton said with great satisfaction, 'Got her!'

Holden gave them a moment or two to express their feelings. Then he said, 'The rest of the film that we were able to reconstitute shows the wall beginning to shake. One of our men was scrambling up the rubble on the far side, the same route Miss Pembury took, and his head is visible for a second as he reaches the top and then the wall goes down – taking him with it, of course, and let me remind you, he suffered some injuries himself in trying to get to her. And of course our camera ceased to record when it fell. But I think you'll agree the film proves beyond reasonable doubt that Allie Pembury heard the warnings being shouted to her and responded to them with contempt.'

'So that disposes of the claim for negligence on our part.'

'Absolutely, I should think. *Safe-Site*'s lawyers have seen it and so have the legal people from our insurance firm. They had no doubt that this discounts Miss Pembury's version entirely. And if you want to hear what they said about her . . . well . . . it wasn't very complimentary.'

'She's a little swindler—'

'Hang on,' Bethany said, having got her breath back after the revelation of the TV film. 'She probably believes it happened the way she says. She persuades herself that things are the way she wants them to be—'

'Oh, nonsense, she's nothing more or less than a cheat and a liar—'

'And when we give this to the press, they'll have a field day with her – they love anything like this.'

'Iris, you can't do that.'

'Why on earth not? This vindicates us absolutely—'

'But there's no need to hold her up to public scorn—'

'After what she's put us through, I'm happy to see her hung, drawn and quartered,' Wellbrow growled.

'This girl bopped you on the head with a placard!' Iris said in amazement. 'You're not actually *defending* her?'

'No, of course not. I think we all knew from the outset that what she was saying wasn't true—'

'In other words, she's been lying—'

'But the point is, I don't think she knows she's lying,' said Bethany. 'Her hold on reality isn't very firm.'

'Well, that's got nothing to do with us,' Iris declared, her black eyes glinting with the light of victory. 'Her mental state isn't our concern. We've got to make the most of the evidence Mr Holden's provided.'

'I agree,' he broke in. 'The efficiency of our service and the truthfulness of our men were brought into question, and although as yet the case hasn't come to court, even the preliminaries damaged our reputation—'

'Mine too,' Alan put in. 'As Construction Manager I'm responsible for the running of the site, and her accusations—'

'Cost us sleepless nights,' Wellbrow put in. 'And don't forget, she and that father of hers were probably planning to settle out of court, hoping to screw a lot of money out of us without having to go to court at all—'

'I say make that clever little minx pay for what she's done,' snorted Daniel Dayton.

'But not by running a press campaign against her,' Bethany insisted. 'Think about it.' Her mind was racing, trying to put together a case that would keep them from the attack. 'We already look mean-spirited for getting her father sacked. His severance settlement wasn't as big as it might have been because the council were annoyed with him over restarting his daughter's claim.'

'Well, what did he expect?' her father returned. 'Did he think Barhampton council would be pleased with that?'

'Josh Pembury is a bit of a fool,' she replied, 'and very much under the influence of his daughter. I agree when you all say she's caused us a lot of trouble but what I'm trying to point out is that she's a pretty, young and charismatic girl who's been injured on one of our sites. If we start giving interviews about how wicked she's been, we're going to look like great big bullies. We can't show that bit of film in all the cinemas to back up our claim that she lied.'

'No, but we could supply stills.'

'And how would they look – dark and grainy, and she'd say they were tampered with – and in fact, they *have* been computer-enhanced, haven't they?'

'But only to make them suitable for viewing.'

'So you say, Mr Holden, and I believe you. But if it got into the media it would be accusation and counter-accusation. Is that what we want?'

Iris was piqued. 'We don't have to look like bullies. I can do it so that it sounds as if we're more in sorrow than in anger—'

'But why do we have to do it at all? For revenge, public revenge?' Bethany hit the arm of her chair with the palm of her hand. 'Revenge shouldn't come into good business. I say *Safe-Site* invite her lawyer and her father to watch this film, give them a polite interval in which to withdraw the case, and be done with it.'

'Give away our hand?' Daniel cried. 'You said yourself she'd say the film was doctored—'

'I'm not suggesting it's shown to Allie. I think she'd dream up something to work her way out of it. But I know Josh. That film will horrify him.'

'He may refuse to believe it—'

'If he sees it with Mr Rosemont, it will embarrass and shock him. To have someone there, seeing his darling little girl behaving so badly . . . And Mr Rosemont isn't going to start making accusations about tampering with the film. I don't know him but I hear he's a very respectable man who'd understand that a firm like *Safe-Site* isn't going to undertake a fraud.'

'That's certainly true,' Holden acknowledged. 'Our reputation is second to none . . .'

'We have a site in the middle of Barhampton that needs a new design, a new concept,' Bethany insisted. 'That's what we should be concentrating on, not getting our own back on this slip of a kid who's been a nuisance to us.'

'You're only saying this because you're soft on Josh Pembury,' her father said.

'Nothing of the kind. But even if that were true, it's still good advice. Do we want a public war-dance? Do we want to shoot arrows at the Pemburys and see them hurt? I say that's beneath the dignity of the team of architects and builders who are putting up a new Town Centre for Barhampton.'

Alan Singleton, once her ally in the firm of *Dayton & Daughter*, was nodding his head. 'I think Bethany may be right,' he said slowly. 'We certainly don't want to look like a bunch of wolves pulling the kid out of the sleigh—'

'But she can't be allowed to get away with it—'

'No, no, Daniel, I agree. But what we want is a dignified statement from her solicitor saying they're dropping the case, then when we're asked for our comment we say that absolutely *no* compensation is being paid—'

'And that she lied her head off,' Wellbrow put in.

'No, perhaps as a result of her injuries her memory was faulty—'

'Alan, that means letting her off completely—'

'No,' Bethany said, in a voice of such sad conviction that they all paused to stare at her.

'Look at it from the point of view of the Pemburys,' she said. 'Josh Pembury is going to see this film and know – *know* – that Allie has been lying all along. He's got solicitors' fees to pay – no doubt he and his solicitor imagined they would get a settlement out of court, a big one which would pay all the bills. But that's not going to happen now, is it? They won't get a penny, not even an ex-gratia payment.'

'Not a sou,' growled Emmett Foyle. 'Not a stunted cent.'

'So there you are – Allie wants special tutors which she's not going to get, she'll find she can't rule her world the way she used to, Josh has lost his job, and what's more he's lost his daughter—'

'What do you mean, lost her?'

'Lost in the sense that she's not . . . she's not the darling he imagined. Something will be destroyed when he sees that film.' She felt her throat constrict with sorrow at the thought and ended, 'Isn't that enough? Do we have to punish them more?'

There was a silence, a sense of shock that slowly turned to consideration of her view. It was Holden of *Safe-Site* who spoke first.

'Well . . . speaking on behalf of my firm, I would be satisfied with a

270

declaration from the Pemburys' lawyers that they agree they have no case against us.' He hesitated, then ended, 'But I'd need a statement to the technical and trade papers that cleared us – I don't insist that it has to go to the nationals or be made a big issue, but the building trade has got to be told that *Safe-Site* were not in any way to blame.'

They looked about at each other.

'I'd go along with that,' Wellbrow said, much to Bethany's surprise. 'It's not out of any pity for that wicked little snip, mind you, nor for that stupid father of hers. I'm just fed up of the whole thing. Like Bethany says, let's get on with building this Town Centre.'

She turned to her father. He could and might still turn them back towards reprisals. But he wasn't quite the blustering bear of a man of a few months ago. He rubbed at his broad chin in doubt, then shrugged. 'All right, let's show the lawyer the film and get it all closed up.'

'You don't want to go for defamation?' Foyle said to Holden. 'That girl implied your firm was responsible for her injuries.'

'We never like to take anything to law,' Holden said drily. 'It only costs time and money.'

'You go along with that, Iris?' Daniel asked.

'I handle publicity,' she said in her cool way. 'Tell me what you want and I'll do it.'

'Right. Then, easy does it, a nice quite settlement, and we get back to our jobs.'

Holden extracted his film from the VCR; the gathering began to break up. Alan Singleton made his way to Bethany's side.

'That was a nice thing you did, Bethany,' he said, 'sticking up for Pembury's daughter.'

'I thought it was a bit unrealistic,' said Iris Weston, joining them and laying a possessive hand on his sleeve. 'But it came off – you got what you wanted.'

'It made good sense, Iris. We don't want any more sourness in our media management – I begin to feel there's been a bit too much of that.'

She coloured. 'Are you criticising my PR methods?'

'No, no, not at all – it's not your fault that the Town Planning Department made a hash of purchasing the Royal Terrace properties, nor that Allie Pembury was determined to hog the limelight. But the emotions that seem to be to the fore these days are quite different from what we intended when we were getting the design ready – aren't they, Bethany?'

She gave a sad little nod. 'You weren't around much then, Iris. Alan and I were full of hope and ambitions. We wanted to bring some warmth . . . some enjoyment . . . into the lives of the Barhampton people. It was a dreary little town in many ways, you see. It had lost its main industry, the surroundings had got run down . . . My design was sort of . . . it was an attempt to lighten their world . . . I'm not explaining it well. I'm better with

271

a set square and a ruler than with words, I suppose. But hitting back at people was never part of my view of things.'

'Oh, thanks for the lecture,' Iris riposted. 'I only did what I was asked to do – and let me point out, it wasn't me that gave the story about Mrs Bedells's marriage to the press – that was your father.'

'You don't have to remind me.'

'Iris, don't take what Bethany said as a criticism,' Alan insisted. 'You're very clever at your job, and I know you'll get a good, dignified report into the trade papers if Pembury drops the case – and of course he will. I just wanted to let Bethany know I admired what she did. She changed the whole atmosphere of the meeting.'

'Maybe Bethany should take up the public relations job, then, instead of me,' Iris said crossly.

Alan put his arm round her. 'Come on, Iris,' he soothed. 'You know you're talking nonsense—'

'Nonsense?'

'You tend to do that when you're uncertain—'

'I'm never uncertain!'

He laughed. For the first time in their relationship he felt that he, and not Iris, was in control of it. 'Come along and let's have a quiet drink with a lot of ice in it,' he commanded. 'I think you need to get your temperature down—'

'Don't talk to me as if I'm half-witted! I don't want a drink and—'

'Well, I do, so come along and stop being crotchety—'

'Crotchety?'

'And we can work out whether you should speak to Pembury's lawyer – Rosemont, isn't it?'

'I don't need any help in planning what to do, and I'm *never* crotchety—'

'Oh yes, you are,' he said as he led her away. 'In fact, I think there's a chance you may turn out to be another Mrs Bedells when you're old and grey . . .'

Bethany smiled to herself. That partnership was developing into something that might be more equal and long-lasting than she'd thought.

Early next morning she had a frantic phone call from Josh Pembury. 'Bethany, you've got to help me! Allie is *so* upset—'

'So she should be,' Bethany replied.

'She never slept a wink last night, and this morning she's got the most dreadful headache.'

'Josh, why are you telling me about it? Take her to your doctor—'

'But she needs someone who understands her—'

'*I* don't understand her, Josh. And I don't want to get involved.'

'But you must help me – that dreadful film – of course when I told her about it I was quite angry and she almost fainted – she needs someone to help her get over it—'

'Get over it? What on earth do you mean, get over it? Josh, that film proves that Allie lied—'

'Oh, of course, I know that, and of course Mr Rosemont had us both in his office and told us we'd have to drop the case, and Allie has faced that, even though it means there'll be no money for all the things—'

'Wait a minute, wait a minute – you understand that Allie was lying when she claimed she didn't know it was dangerous to be on that site – you know she was willing to sue the construction firms for a lot of money on the basis of a lie – and you just pass over that as if it were run of the mill?'

'That's not what matters now – she's making herself quite ill—'

'Are you sure she's not just acting?'

'Bethany! How can you! If you could see her, so pale and trembling . . .'

'If you're asking me to rush over and sympathise—'

'But *someone's* got to help us.'

'I agree, Josh, I agree one hundred per cent. You should get help. You should see someone professional, a family counsellor or a psychiatrist—'

'A psychiatrist? What are you saying? My little girl isn't a mental case!'

'Your little girl is drifting further and further into a fantasy world, Josh, and if you really want to be a good father you'll do something to stop it. It's no good asking me for help, I've no idea what to do. The first step is surely to take her to your doctor.'

'The doctor! She needs someone who'll listen to her, sympathise with her – a doctor will see her for three minutes and give her a sedative—'

'Take her to the hospital, then. She has a specialist there who's treating her—'

'But that's a bone specialist. Besides, he's always been very brisk and businesslike, and that's not the right attitude for her at the moment—'

'The right attitude at the moment is to get her to accept that she's done wrong—'

'Well, I'm disappointed in you, Bethany. I thought I could depend on you for some sympathy—'

'I sympathise, I do, indeed. But I can't help, I don't know how. And neither do you, Josh – that's what you have to face. You don't know how to handle Allie. At this very moment she's got you in a tizz, so that you don't even remember that she's been very wicked.'

'Wicked? My little Allie?'

'You've *got* to ask for professional help, Josh,' she insisted, sickened by his over-protective tone.

'You've grown very hard, Bethany,' he said sorrowfully. 'I never expected this of you.'

'I'm sorry, Josh. Good luck.' She replaced the receiver, deeply depressed at the conversation. She was determined not to try to help, because she knew she couldn't do any good. The Pembury family were beyond the reach of what ordinary friendship could do.

Later in the day, Raymond Bigsby got in touch. 'First of all, congratulations on a very favourable outcome as regards Josh Pembury and his daughter,' he said.

'Oh, you've heard?'

'On the grapevine, you know. We on the council were influenced by Pembury's intention to go to court – it hardened our attitude, I think, with regard to his severance pay. But that's not why I'm ringing. I handed over the list of properties that might suit Mrs Bedells to Peter Lambot yesterday,' he reported. 'I wonder if I could ask you to use your influence for a quick response from the dear lady?'

'Er . . . We all want this problem resolved quickly, Mr Bigsby.'

'Of course. So may I leave it with you?'

'Well . . . yes . . . I'll see what I can do.'

She felt she ought to confess that she had no real idea how to get in touch with Mrs Bedells. But she'd better consult Peter about that.

'It's certainly getting complicated,' he said when they discussed it that evening. 'We've got something she wants but we don't know how to get it to her!'

'What did she say about getting in touch? Did she say she'd call again?'

'She said, "Let's see how it goes," as far as I remember. I was still asking for her phone number when she rang off. And the number I tracked is useless . . .'

'Bigsby is very anxious to move things along, Peter.'

'I understand that, but my client is Mrs Bedells. Things have got to move at her speed.'

'That's all very well,' Bethany said, 'but there is another side to it, you know! Us poor construction types are waiting to get on with that bit of the Town Centre. I don't know if you have any idea of what the delay can cost us per day.'

'Thousands?'

'Tens of thousands, especially as we move into bad weather conditions. We switched priorities around to accommodate the problem about Royal Terrace but we're falling behind schedule and if we don't finish on time there are big penalty clauses. I'm sympathetic to Nancy Bedells, love, you know I am, but our construction group is suffering and going to suffer even more – and there are jobs at stake, there are people waiting to start work in the office blocks, the shopping mall, they're waiting for housing that we're engaged on . . .'

Her earnestness was impressive. Although his first duty was to his client, he understood that something had to be done. 'What about . . .'

'What?'

'We've got the promise of a flat . . . She wants it, we've got it. The difficulty is letting her know, isn't it. But she reads the papers, she watches television. Could we go public?'

'But one of her conditions—'

'Is that we don't let anyone know where she is or where she's going to live. Right. Can we go public to the extent of . . . I don't know . . . saying we're offering her a new home . . . that she's considering it . . .'

'But the minute the press got hold of it—'

'I know, they'd bang on her door and call through her letterbox – but they've done that before and got nowhere so that wouldn't be unusual. The difficulty as I see it is that whoever made the statement would be badgered and pressed until perhaps they let something slip—'

'Not if it was well managed.' Bethany thought about it. 'Iris Weston could handle it.'

'She's been very much against Mrs Bedells, the way I read things—'

'Yes, but if we explain to her that this is for the eventual good of her clients, the construction group . . .'

'Could you ask her?'

She looked reluctant. 'She doesn't like me much.'

'Why not?'

'I've no idea. We just seemed to get off on the wrong foot and then when I tried to cool things downs over Mrs Bedells, she perhaps got the idea that I was against her . . . Well, this is different. This time when I ask her to do something that will benefit Mrs Bedells, it will benefit her clients too . . .'

'Could you ring her? Ask for a meeting?'

'It's worth a try. She's back in London at the moment, getting out a press release for the trade papers about the Pemburys' withdrawing. I think I've got that number on my organiser.' She burrowed in the capacious shoulder-bag that went with her everywhere on weekdays, came up with the organiser, found the number and dialled it on Peter's phone.

Iris was very surprised to hear her voice. 'Has something happened?' she asked in startlement.

'Yes, but it's something quite good so don't get worried, Iris. I'm with Peter at the moment and we want to ask you—'

'Peter Lambot?'

'Yes, and there's something—'

'Bethany, I thought you had more sense than to keep that thing going.'

'Iris, this isn't about my private life. It's about Mrs Bedells.'

She heard Iris give a little groan of frustration. 'What now?' she demanded.

'We need to put out a statement or something—'

'Who's we?'

'Well, it's Peter really—'

'Listen, Bethany, I'm not hired to represent you or Peter Lambot and if it's anything to do with Mrs Bedells I don't want to be involved—'

'Iris Weston!' Bethany said at the top of her voice. 'Will you stop interrupting me at every minute and hear what I'm trying to say? Peter is acting on behalf of Mrs Bedells and wants to tell the press something important, something that will help and not hinder the work of the construction group.'

There was a long pause.

'What's got into you?' Iris said at length. 'I never heard you raise your voice to anyone before.'

'It seems to work,' Bethany said with a sidelong grin at Peter. 'Are you paying attention now?'

'Well . . . yes.'

'Peter wants to tell the press something in the interests of his client, Mrs Bedells. You know how much local interest – and sometimes even national interest – her name arouses. Peter wants to avoid a grand opera. He just wants to make an announcement but in such a way that it will . . . reach all sections of the public.'

'An announcement about what?'

'I can't tell you that over the phone.'

'Did you say this was something helpful?'

'Yes.'

'Peter Lambot wants to make a press statement about something to do with Mrs Bedells – and it won't make us look bad?'

'Not at all.'

'Why didn't you mention this yesterday, when the Steering Committee was in session? I could have cleared it with them.'

'We don't want Steerco involved. We want this done quietly, Iris.'

'Why?'

Bethany hesitated. 'I can't tell you that.'

Iris said briskly, 'Is Peter there?'

'Yes.'

'Let me speak to him.'

Bethany handed over the phone. Peter announced himself and then Bethany heard his end of the conversation, which consisted mainly of, 'I can't tell you that . . . That's confidential . . . No, it will be a beneficial act, I believe . . . No, no one else must be consulted . . . Yes, very important . . . Yes . . . Very well, at my office. Thank you.

'She's taking the first train in the morning,' he said as he hung up. 'I think she's so eaten up with curiosity she's just got to come.'

At mid-morning next day they met in Peter's office at *Pesh, Samuels* in Barhampton. Even after a train journey and a long taxi ride from York, Iris still looked one hundred per cent the trim young executive, in a short-skirted grey gabardine suit and an emerald green blouse.

276

Bethany, in her work outfit of slacks, shirt, and boots, felt like a country bumpkin by comparison.

'I hope you haven't wasted my time, bringing me here,' Iris said by way of introduction.

'I hope so too. Can I offer you coffee, Miss Weston?'

She waved it away. 'What's this about?'

Peter explained that what he was going to ask was difficult, and that he himself was hampered by his duty of confidentiality to his client. 'It comes down to this. Barhampton council are offering Mrs Bedells a new place to live, and I want to make that fact known to the press.'

'But Barhampton council have been willing to give that old nuisance a new place to live for months, and she keeps saying no. What's the point of saying it again?'

'I can't tell you that. I'm asking you to help me put the news out to the press. We have some pictures from Barhampton council showing the accommodation, and I'd like if possible for one or two of them to be published—'

'Don't be silly. Newspapers aren't going to give up space for pictures of blocks of flats—'

'No? Well, I suppose not. But a few words of description—'

'What's the intention?' Iris interrupted. 'That's the point a press agent has to ask. What are you trying to achieve?'

'I want to show the sort of place Mrs Bedells will be living in if she accepts the council's offer.'

'To *show* something – a visual effect – television is better.' She mused for a moment. 'Local TV is quite interested in Mrs Bedells. You could probably get a spot in the regional news slot.'

'Wider coverage would be better,' Peter said.

'Oh well, if TV takes it, some newspapers will probably pick it up—'

'Prominently?'

'You're joking, I imagine. Why should anyone bother to give it prominence?'

'What makes a national newspaper put an item on the front page?'

'War, disaster, scandal or money.' At the dismay on their faces, Iris smiled and shrugged. 'The tabloids will go for a human-interest story. Cat down a well, twins meeting again after a parting of twenty years . . . Mrs Bedells has a fair amount of interest for the columnists. If we could dress this up somehow . . .'

'But how?' Peter said in perplexity. 'We can't say much—'

'*Why* can't we?'

'I can't explain. You have to take it on trust. If there's too much publicity Mrs Bedells will take fright and everything will fall to pieces.'

'What we're trying to achieve,' Bethany said, having thought over Iris's query, 'is to help Mrs Bedells to accept a new home, so that the Royal Terrace section of the construction can be planned and recommenced.'

'But without giving too much away,' Peter added.

'Giving too much of what away?' Iris demanded.

'I can't tell you that,' he said. 'I'm sorry to keep harping on it, but you just have to trust us that it will be a good thing.'

'Huh!' said Iris. But she was greatly intrigued. It was a fascinating problem in PR. 'What we need is a touch of poign,' she said.

'Of what?'

'Poign. Poignancy. Nothing the tabloids like more than something that makes their readers say, "Awww . . ." '

'And what makes them say that?'

'I told you. Dog walks a hundred miles to find its master, injured man awakes from ten-year coma . . .'

'Cat down a well,' Bethany quoted.

'Yes.'

'Mrs Bedells had a cat.'

'Don't I know it! The rotten thing scratched me.'

'It ran away. She said it couldn't stand all the noise and uproar in Royal Terrace after the squatters moved in.'

Iris put out a hand, as if to capture Bethany's words. 'Hang on. This new place . . . will she be able to have a cat there?'

'Certainly,' said Bethany at once. If the council had some rule against pets, she knew of properties where they were not only permitted but encouraged.

Iris Weston's face took on a dreamy look. 'GRAND OLD FIGHTER GETS NEW FRIEND,' she murmured. '*Mrs Nancy Bedells, whose fourteen-year-old cat Tommy or Spot or Dinkie ran away because of the upset in Royal Terrace, will be able to have a cat in her brand new home. Supporters of Mrs Bedells have clubbed together to buy her a Siamese kitten* – no, a Persian, that's fluffier, looks better in pix – *a Persian kitten worth . . .* however much a Persian costs, let's make it a hundred. How about that?'

'Can you get that in the tabloids?' Bethany asked.

'Watch me,' said Iris.

Chapter Twenty-two

The item appeared two days later in the *Daily Comet*, the tabloid which had subsidised the *Bedells Beano*. Low on the front page, it featured a cropped photograph showing Mrs Bedells at her door – this was the picture caught when Iris got scratched by Tibbles the cat. Alongside was a photograph of a very pretty model girl holding against her cheek an endearing white Persian kitten. The caption read: *Nori is for Nancy*. The headline running above the two photos was: NEW HOME, NEW PAL *(see p. 2)*.

On page 2 was a description of the kitten, its pedigree and its price. *The* Comet *feels Mrs Bedells, a Grey Panther as the Yanks would call her, deserves a new feline friend*... Then came the interview with Raymond Bigsby and Peter.

Bigsby was quoted as saying that he was very glad to respond to the invitation from Mrs Bedells's lawyer to offer possible domiciles. '*There are six within the council's domain, mainly on the outskirts of the town. Our good friend Mrs Bedells only has to let us know which she prefers.*'

The journalist handling the interview, who had made flying visits to each of the sites, then supplied a few sentences describing the one she liked best: '*... Super kitchenette*... *pretty garden for Nancy to sit in the sun with Nori, our Persian Present to this feisty old lady, on her lap*... *Public transport nearby*... *Bingo at the local church*...' She ended with the rousing tag: '*Town councils sometimes get it right, chums! Well done, Barhampton!*'

'It's awfully clever, Iris,' Bethany said when she rang to thank her. 'Particularly the idea of getting the *Comet* to buy the kitten.'

'Oh, I knew that would sell them on it, dear. The editor can never resist anything to do with pretty little animals, and it was a chance to appear generous. So – it's what you wanted?'

'Couldn't be better. Thanks a million.' They chatted a few more minutes, then rang off. The fact that Iris had actually called her 'dear' echoed in Bethany's mind for a long time. Was it possible that Iris was beginning to like her – or at least not dislike her?

That day was a flurry of phone calls among the members of the construction group, Barhampton council, and various local interests. But the one phone call they were hoping for didn't come. Mrs Bedells didn't respond.

'Do you think she hasn't seen it?' Peter wondered, laying the paper on his desk so as to display the text to its best advantage.

'Perhaps not yet.' But it was already past lunch-time. The paper had been out for at least seven hours. The item had been picked up by the local radio news and the phone-ins, but there was no way of knowing if Mrs Bedells – off somewhere in the vicinity of Blackpool – was able to tune in on Barhampton's local wavelengths.

Early afternoon, Yorkshire Television rang to invite Peter Lambot – and the kitten – on the early evening newscast. Peter rang Bethany. 'What should I do?' he begged. 'I've agreed to appear because I think Mrs Bedells probably watches television even if she doesn't always buy a paper. But I don't want to make a mess of it!'

'Ring Iris Weston. She knows how to handle things like that.'

Iris was delighted to be asked. 'Wear something lawyer-like – dark suit, good tie, plain shirt—'

'What I'm wearing now, in fact—'

'But have the jacket unbuttoned, and get them to let you hold the kitten—'

'But its fur will come off on my jacket—'

'All the better. Makes you seem approachable.'

'All right, I can do approachable. And what do I say?'

'Not much. It's a lovely kitten, how kind of the newspaper, how good of Barhampton council to come to the aid of Mrs Bedells . . .'

'But I don't want to say much about Mrs Bedells—'

'Well, I think you'll have to say whether she's chosen any of the places she's being offered—'

'I can't talk about that. Mrs Bedells doesn't want anyone to know which address she's going to.'

'Hmm . . . She doesn't make it easy for anyone, does she? I know for a fact they've been knocking at her door in Royal Terrace all day begging her for a picture, but she won't even speak through the wood. Well, you'll have to fall back on how shy she is, how she's never sought the limelight but of course she loves cats, the kitten is delightful, and her life will be brightened by this little treasure.'

'In other words, be soppy about the cat?'

Iris laughed ironically. 'Nobody ever went wrong by being soppy about animals in front of the great British public.'

Peter went through agonies of apprehension, sure that someone would trick him into saying Mrs Bedells had left her house and was now off in Blackpool. But in fact the link-woman was rather sweet to him, petted the kitten a lot, and asked only one awkward question: 'Which retirement flat has Nancy chosen, Mr Lambot?'

'She hasn't made up her mind yet,' Peter said with perfect truth. 'The properties the council has offered are so good, making a choice isn't something you can do in a couple of hours.'

'Of course. But when she's chosen and is moving in, perhaps we can come and film Nori in her new home?'

'You never know,' he said with a smile of complicity, thinking meanwhile, Only when pigs sprout pink wings. He was rather ashamed to be complimented later by friends and acquaintances on how well he came over.

Because of the interruption caused by the TV interview, he had things to catch up on at the office. He was still there at eight o'clock when his phone rang.

'Well,' said the cross voice of Mrs Bedells, 'that wasn't very canny, now was it?'

'Mrs Bedells! So you saw—'

'Aye, I saw it, and daft it seemed to me. Didn't I tell you I didn't want everybody to know where I were going?'

'But you weren't getting in touch. Barhampton council were very eager to let you know they had flats to offer, so we thought that a bit of publicity in the media—'

'That's bad enough, but letting on that I might be going to a council flat? For heaven's sake, anyone that wants to know my new address has only got to look at the pictures in their housing department window – they're right there at the front of the council offices, on the street, showing everybody how wonderful the council is, putting up flats for us old and half-witted – they only have to note down the addresses and they know I'm somewhere among that lot!'

'But there are other premises.'

'And that soppy cat! Who in their senses wants a daft little cat like that, all blue eyes and white fluff? Get white hairs over everything, you would—'

'No, no—'

'Don't tell me "no, no" – I saw white hairs on your sleeve, I haven't lost my eyesight even if I am losing my home! I don't know why you lowered yourself by appearing with that thing – if you're going to talk about cats, why don't you get a proper cat with some character?'

'But it was a nice affectionate little—'

'Bundle of fur, that's all it was. And if that newspaper thinks I'm accepting anything from them . . . They're the ones that drove me out of my home, with all their noise and kerfuffle!'

'Mrs Bedells,' Peter said, getting over his surprise at her attack, 'I presume you're speaking from a public phone booth again and you'll be running out of coins—'

'Huh! I bought a phone card, didn't I?' she said with some asperity.

'Well, it's costing you money so I presume you wanted to talk about something more important than the cat?'

'Didn't I tell you to wait to hear from me?'

'No, you said we had to wait to see how it goes—'

281

'Well, why didn't you wait?'

'Because you're not the only person involved,' he said with as much asperity as she had shown. 'The construction group—'

'Whose lawyer are you? Mine or the construction group's?'

'Yours, it seems, but I can't represent you unless we're in touch—'

'We're in touch now, aren't we? And what I want to say is this: I don't want a flat provided by the council. They're going to want to get a lot of credit out of it – you could tell that by the way that newspaper carried on – "Well done, Barhampton" – what a nerve!'

Peter stifled a sigh. 'So what do you want, Mrs Bedells?'

'I want to talk to that architect girl—'

'Bethany Dayton.'

'Yes. She said she could find me a home, once when we were talking a while ago . . . I didn't think too badly of her . . . She's not so much on the make as the others . . . So if she's got a place to offer, I might think on it.'

'I'll give you her number so you can ring her.'

'If I wanted her number, young man, I could get Directory Enquiries and ask them! I want to see her face to face while we're talking.'

'Oh,' said Peter, rather taken aback. 'Well, of course, that's no problem—'

'You come too. I want your advice on whether it's a good offer, about the lease and all that—'

'Of course. We can easily drive up to Blackpool—'

'Ah!' It was a little gasp of surprise. Then she said, 'Well, aren't you the clever clogs! Right, so you'll drive up to Blackpool, and we'll talk about a new place to live. You'll want the address, I suppose, even though you know the town!'

'Let me write it down.'

'The Woodlawns, it is, and if you ask for me when you get there—'

'The Woodlawns – you're staying at a hotel?' he asked, writing.

'You'll find out, won't you, when you get here.'

'Mrs Bedells, if you can get Bethany's number from Directory Enquiries, I can get Woodlawns' and ring to ask whether you're really staying there—'

There was a little pause. Then she said, 'You're not dim, any road. Well, I'll tell you, but don't you let on to anyone else except that architect girl.'

'I promise.'

'It's a caravan park.'

A caravan park! Where else would you expect to find a daughter of the Romanies except in a caravan?

'What's the name of the road?' he asked.

'What are you smiling at?' she countered.

'I'm smiling because at last you're beginning to show some sense.'

'Don't you lecture me, young man!' she snorted, quick as always to take offence. 'I could easily go off you, you know!'

'Tell me how to find The Woodlawns. We don't want to waste time driving all around Blackpool looking for it.'

'But you're so clever you'd ask at the Information Office, wouldn't you?' But she gave directions; they arranged a time for the following day.

'Who shall I ask for?' enquired Peter. 'You're not staying there under your own name, are you?'

'And what name should I use, then?'

'Lee, perhaps?'

She gave a little grunt of amusement. 'Been digging, eh? Well, if you know I was born a Lee, you'll know us Romanies always stick together. The feller that manages this caravan park is a Lee, son of a second cousin of mine, and he knows who I am – he isn't going to let on to anyone if I ask him not to, is he? But I'll tell him to let you in and point you in the right direction.'

Before she rang off she added, 'I thought you did quite well on the telly, as a matter of fact.' He could hear a sort of own-back amusement in her voice.

He replaced the receiver, reflecting that he had his share of difficult old ladies as clients. But at least Mrs Crowther paid him . . . Whether he would ever get a fee from Mrs Bedells was problematical.

Bethany lit up with pleasure when he told her. She was already at his flat when he got there, with a towel tied round her as an apron, preparing a meal in celebration of his debut as a TV star. She'd rushed out to buy his favourite food and bring it with her. By this time she had a key so that she could come and go as she pleased; it was understood between her and her mother that she might not always be around at her own place.

'Can you get pictures of the properties?' Peter asked, coming to steal both a kiss and a taste of the sauce she was stirring.

'No problem. I'm pretty sure to have them in my files because I was involved in their construction . . . If not, we can collect some on our way. There's one in particular I think she would like – protected housing, used to be a mansion in its own well-wooded grounds. There was a cottage for the gardener and another for the gamekeeper, which I turned into separate homes for the more sprightly of the residents, and stables with accommodation above for the grooms . . .' She stirred thoughtfully, adding more tomato concentrate. 'If I remember aright, that's now four flats in a separate block, and then there are ten flats in the former mansion. What I'm saying is that it doesn't look institutional or purpose-built. I took a great deal of trouble over the re-modelling.'

'Is there anything available there?'

'I'd have to find out. Can you keep an eye on the pasta while I telephone?'

283

The upshot of her phone call was that there was one flat available at Allenham House, in the Stable Block. 'Mrs Greshen says it's the upper left that's vacant . . . Nancy Bedells might like the idea of being a bit away from the main building. Of course it's linked by alarms and personal radio to the main house . . . has good views of the lawns and the woods beyond . . . Mind you, it's not cheap . . . But if you make Barhampton council pay a lot for the house in Royal Terrace . . .'

'We'll find enough money to finance the thing,' he assured her. 'That's if she'll agree to take the flat! She's the most stubborn, self-willed old thing.'

'We'll just have to talk her into it.'

Easier said than done. Mrs Bedells had made up her mind to give them a hard time.

They were directed to the 'leisure centre' of the caravan park. This consisted of a covered swimming pool, a large hall with a stage, a snooker room, and a café. Near the car park was a quite capacious shop and post office – with, Peter noted, a public telephone. This wasn't one of the more luxurious set-ups with acres of sculptured shrubbery and an adventure playground for the children, but the park had a licence for permanent residency so that a sprinkling of owners were pottering about, tending little gardens or doing repair jobs. Though the sea wasn't in sight, there was a tang of salt in the air and the trees were turning golden brown. On the whole, the atmosphere was cheerful.

This was the first time that either of them had seen the old lady out in the light of day. She was waiting for them at the café, sitting straight-backed at a wooden table in the late autumn sunshine. Her dress was a chain-store print, a dark blue check cotton, and over it a chain-store cardigan of cerise cotton-knit. Her shoes were sturdy rather than fashionable. Her black hair, only faintly sprinkled with iron-grey, was dressed in the way they already knew, parted in the middle and coiled in 'earphones' at her ears. Her ears had been pierced but she wore no gypsy hoops, only tiny gold keepers. Her hands were folded in her lap, their sole decoration her wedding band. She seemed thinner, though there was vigour in the flash of her eyes.

Beside her on the table lay a discarded newspaper and an empty coffee mug.

'You're late,' she greeted them.

'I'm sorry, it was my fault,' Bethany said. 'I wanted to get up-to-date information about vacancies.'

' "Vacancies"! Sounds like hospital beds! Are we talking about homes for old has-beens?'

'You can make your own assessment,' Bethany said, producing a thick envelope from her shoulder-bag. 'Those in the yellow folder have vacant accommodation at the moment. The ones in the blue folder have nothing available, but that changes quite often – people move out to live with relatives, or perhaps want to be closer to town.'

'Humph.'

'Can I get you more coffee?' Peter suggested.

'No, I only allow myself two cups a day and I want the second one to be after my lunch.'

'Isn't it time for lunch? Would you like something to eat?'

'No, thank you.' She gave a critical study to his clothes – corduroys, a flannel shirt, and a thin Shetland sweater. 'You're not so tidy as you were on telly,' she remarked.

'I plan to wear this next time I appear.'

She almost smiled. 'Think you've a career on the box?'

'Not if I can help it.' He picked up her empty coffee mug and nodded towards the café. 'You won't mind if Bethany and I have something? We've had quite a long drive.'

'The café's open to the public,' she said dismissively. She was already opening the envelope and taking out the folders. She might try to disguise it, but she was eager to see what was on offer.

Bethany made a little grimace at him telling him to make himself scarce. She watched as the old lady took out the yellow folder. There were brochures published by the managements of the properties, colour photographs, sketches she herself had done in the course of the construction or redevelopment of the dwellings. The settlement where Mabel and Jephthah lived wasn't included; she could imagine how Nancy Bedells might react if Mabel tried to renew old acquaintance.

She knew the accommodation was attractive because she had made sure of that herself; she knew also that it was comfortable, each unit easy to run, all with the lifestyle of elderly people in mind. Yet her aim had always been to offer an everyday setting, nothing hospital-like or institutional.

Mrs Bedells turned over the glossy leaflets, squinting a little in the sun. 'What's it going to cost me to live in one of these?' she demanded.

'Well, they're not cheap. Some are to rent, and some you have to buy a lease. But you understand that it's an all-in rate once you're there – heating, lighting, cleaning, repairs, porterage, care of the grounds, all of that is included in the contract. There's a café or a meal service attached to most of them. With some there's also an arrangement with a bus company to run a regular time-table to the nearest shopping precinct—'

'Shopping precincts!' snorted Mrs Bedells. 'That's what everybody seems to be mad about these days! I wouldn't choose a place to live for the sake of getting to a shopping precinct.'

'What would you want as a requirement?'

'Well . . . peace and quiet. Nobody playing pop music at one in the morning. Good light coming in the windows for my plants. Nice walks nearby, like the riverside at Barhampton – I'll miss the river,' she mused. 'Shops . . . I prefer small shops really but I'd put up with a supermarket if I had to. I could bring my own furniture?'

'Of course. But not all of it, you know – most of these flats are one-bedroom—'

'I understand that, I'm not daft!'

'And in most of them, you can have a pet—'

'I don't want that chocolate-box kitten!'

'You don't have to have it. There are plenty of cats in the cats' home looking for someone to love them.'

'I miss Tibbles,' said Mrs Bedells, and her deep brown eyes filled with tears.

'I'm so sorry,' Bethany said, putting a young hand on the old veined one lying on the folders.

'Oh, animals have their own lives to live,' said Nancy Bedells. 'We had cats and dogs and ponies and trained jackdaws and all sorts when I was a kiddie, and it was a fact of life, you lost them along the road as you travelled. Not ponies, you couldn't afford to lose a pony, but the dogs would often go dashing off after rabbits, and vanish. So you collected another pup from the next farm you worked at ...' She brooded a moment. 'I suppose I could get another cat. I wouldn't have a tabby next time. I fancy a black and white. Neat little white socks.' She sniffed, blew her nose, and looked up as Peter arrived with a plastic tray of coffee and sandwiches. 'You took your time,' she accused.

'I thought you ladies would like a little while to look at the brochures.'

'What's in the sandwiches? Tuna? Tibbles liked tuna but I think I'll feed the next one on cat food.'

'Would you like a sandwich?' Peter offered. 'I got extra just in case. Tuna, and egg mayonnaise, and turkey.'

'Oh, you don't want to eat the turkey, it's not real turkey, it's only that stuff from packets ... I'll try the egg mayonnaise. And I'd like an orange juice to go with it.'

'Back in a minute.'

The old lady smiled. 'He seems all right. Biddable, at least.'

'I like him,' Bethany agreed.

For a moment or two they sat in silence, the autumn sun warming Bethany's back through her silk shirt. Then Mrs Bedells said in a low voice, 'My William was a fine man. I had to stand up to my whole family to wed him, but meeting him was the best thing that ever happened. I held on to the house because it was his, you know ... It was the place where he'd lived, it was full of memories of him ... But I can take my memories with me to a new place, after all. When you get to my age, lass, memories are important. See you make good memories with that lad of yours.'

They looked at each other, dark brown eyes gazing into sea-blue. Then the old lady smiled, patted Bethany's hand, and looked up to greet

Peter with a sharp admonition about spilling her drink.

Bethany noticed that during the conversation carried on through lunch, Mrs Bedells's hand would fall on the advertising brochure for Allenham House. But each time, she would put it aside as if somehow it was untouchable. When Peter had collected up the crockery and gone to return it to the café, she said: 'I think you ought to take a look at Allenham. It's nearer Barhampton than some of the others – you could take a bus in, and walk by the River Barr if you want to.'

'Allenham House . . .' Nancy Bedells flipped the brochure open, then closed it. 'Nay, one of those flats would cost a pretty penny.'

'Not so much as you might think.' And in any case, thought Bethany, we could probably come to a special arrangement on behalf of someone so important. A firm like *Dayton & Daughter* could pull a few financial strings. 'Do you like this setting? It's more spacious than some of the others – when I did the revamp, that was one of the aims – to keep it looking like a country mansion with its own woods and a view.'

'I remember the view well,' said Nancy surprisingly. 'When I was a lass, in good weather I'd be let sleep on the roof of the van. And in the morning when I woke I'd sit up and look over the grounds, and think how grand it was—' She snapped away from her reverie. 'Too grand for the likes of me,' she ended.

'You knew it in the old days?'

'Aye, my father and mother used to work for the estate agent – Mr Crickieth – seasonal, it was, of course, putting up stakes for the runner beans, picking up the spring bedding and planting lobelia and heliotrope for the summer . . . then picking the peas when they came ripe, and the strawberries . . . ah, the strawberries . . .'

'I'm afraid the kitchen garden is gone now,' Bethany said with regret. 'But the flower beds are still there at the front of the house. I don't know what they plant in them – at the moment I suppose they'll be full of chrysanthemums.'

'Chrysanthemums,' sighed Nancy. 'The gardener used to bring them on in the glass-house . . . His name was Ned Parker . . . And the head groom was Mr Vickery, knew all about horses, he did . . .'

'It would be nice to live there, then, wouldn't it, since you've got a link with it?'

'But what would they charge, luv? I know I'll be getting money from the sale of the house but otherwise there's not much left in the bank these days . . .'

'I think you should let Peter deal with that,' Bethany said. 'He's really very bright, you know. I'm sure he'll make a profitable deal on the house and as to the new place . . . well, it so happens there's a flat going, in the Stable Block.'

'In the Stable Block?'

287

'No horses there now, I'm afraid. But it's mostly the same building, only converted into modern flats.'

'By gum! That must have taken some doing?'

'You'll see when you go to look at it. We've kept the clock in the little tower on top – it even keeps good time.'

'Well I never,' cried Nancy Bedells, and Bethany knew she was going to choose Allenham House for her new home – the stable clock had sold her on it.

Peter brought Nancy her second mug of coffee of the day before they left. They promised again to keep everything very hush-hush. After they had safely negotiated the Blackpool traffic Bethany said with a little sigh of satisfaction, 'I do believe we've solved the Nancy Bedells problem.'

'I think you're right. And she's made a good choice – it seems a lovely place. All she needs is some of her furniture and a cat, and she'll be as happy as she was in Royal Terrace – perhaps happier.'

'That's what I'm hoping.'

They agreed to tell only a few members of Steerco about Mrs Bedells's decision; Cyril Ollerton and Alan Singleton because of the re-planning that must now be immediately undertaken, and since Alan knew, it was clear Iris Weston would also know. But Iris could be relied on for reticence and so could Raymond Bigsby, the head of the Council's Legal Department. 'He'll have to convince the Town Planning Department to pay a very good price for number fifteen,' Peter remarked, 'but I don't think they'll quibble when I tell them the sale has to cover the cost of the new flat and leave a bit over – otherwise, I shall say, Mrs Bedells of course won't sell.'

'And nobody's paying you a penny to do all this!' Bethany said, and kissed him on the cheek.

'Don't do that – you'll distract me from my driving!' But he was laughing.

Bethany decided to stretch a point and tell her mother the good news. There was no danger of Mary passing it on to anyone else and, besides, Bethany sensed that she needed cheering up. There was something melancholy about her these days.

'Well, that sounds marvellous,' Mary declared when she heard the story next morning. 'So she actually knew the place in the days when it was a mansion? There's something ... I don't know ... *fitting* in the idea that she should go there, don't you think?'

'Peter's already begun the negotiation to sell the house in Royal Terrace. He got in touch by phone as we were driving back yesterday. I gather Bigsby promised the council would be very co-operative.' She hesitated before saying the next words. 'I phoned Dad last night. He's very pleased about it.'

Her mother gave a little shake of the head. 'He feels he's won, I suppose – the enemy is leaving the field.'

Bethany laughed. 'I can't deny there's perhaps a little bit of that in his view of the thing. But he's not so much given to feeling triumphant these days, Mother.'

'No?' Mary Dayton pushed away her plate of toast and marmalade. 'How interesting.'

'He's very subdued.'

'Subdued? That's not a word I ever thought to hear about Daniel Dayton.'

'Oh, Mother, don't you think you ought to talk to him? The weeks go by, and matters don't get settled—'

'It's not an easy thing to settle, Beth.'

'I know that – it's just . . . it's not even as if you're happy either, now is it?'

'I'm perfectly happy.'

'Really? Ever since you came back from Venice you've been . . . less amused by the situation, more troubled.'

Her mother said nothing.

'Isn't that true?'

'I'm perfectly all right, thank you.'

'What is it? Is it something to do with Ossie? I notice you don't see him as often as you used to.'

'Bethany! Mind your own business!'

Bethany flushed and got up from the breakfast table. 'Sorry I spoke,' she said. Really, life was quite difficult these days with her mother. If the flat were bigger, or if her mother had something definite with which to occupy her time . . .

She went to her computer in the living room, determined to give her mind to the vexed question of how to sort out Royal Terrace, even if she couldn't sort out the problems of her parents.

No. 15 was now a Class I Listed Building and could not be significantly altered, couldn't even be refurbished without specific permission. The rest of the Terrace was likely to be Listed also, although not perhaps as Class I.

That meant, in Bethany's view, that the whole Terrace had to be incorporated – more or less untouched – into the plan for the New Town Centre. The Town Council were in a quandary. No money had ever been set aside in the building budget for the preservation of Royal Terrace and so they were begging their architects to come up with a solution that would cost the very minimum.

In the place where Royal Terrace stood, Bethany's design had called for a shrub-bordered walkway and a little piazza of boutiques. This couldn't now be built. Yet is was essential to have something light and with a feeling of relaxation before the pedestrian entered the busy commercial area. To ditch the pedestrian area and join Royal Terrace on to the busy traffic of the modernised Town Centre seemed brutally abrupt.

She was rotating an outline sketch of the Terrace to see whether isolating it would help, when her mother came to stand at her shoulder.

'I'm sorry I snapped at you, dear.'

'You never snap, Mother.'

'But I wasn't very nice to you, was I?'

'That's all right. I can see you're a bit distressed.'

'You were right. It is about Ossie.'

'What about him?'

'He . . . well . . . he wants to get serious . . . and Bethie, you know . . . I don't want that, I never did. I mean, I never thought for a moment that Ossie . . .'

'You thought of him as a good companion.'

'Yes. I was silly, I suppose. But at my age, who'd think a man would want to . . .'

'Come on, Mother, there are romances at every age!'

'Well, the long and the short of it is, I've had to tell him it's not on, and so we've sort of stopped seeing each other because . . . well, it's so awkward, knowing he's not getting what he wants out of it and . . . well, it's daft, isn't it? Here I am like a teenager trying to get rid of a boyfriend who's got the wrong idea . . . Don't laugh, Beth, or say "I told you so".'

'Wouldn't dream of it. But Ossie's a nice man, after all. He's got the message, I'm sure.'

'Yes, he's making himself scarce. But then, you see, I don't go out with him, and so I fall back on my women friends, and they're not exactly giggling in front of me but I know they think I'm a fool—'

'Not at all! They probably admire you—'

'Well, I don't admire myself, I think I'm a ninny! I did all this to make your father sit up and take notice, but now I'm stuck. He's taking notice, I gather – but I don't know what to do next.'

'What do you want to do?'

'I've just told you – I don't know!'

'No, I meant something else – something Iris Weston said to me. "What do you want to achieve?" That's the question.'

Mary leaned against the computer desk for support. 'I want to go *home*!' she sobbed.

Her daughter jumped up to put her arms around her. 'Don't, Mother. Don't cry. Come on now. Don't cry, we'll sit down and talk it out.'

It was some minutes before Mary Dayton got enough control of herself to move to the sofa and collapse into it. She mopped her eyes. Bethany went to the kitchen to heat up the remains of the breakfast coffee in the microwave. She brought a cup to her mother who accepted it, sipped a few mouthfuls, then gave her a rueful smile.

'What a fool,' she said.

'Don't say that. You've done well so far but perhaps now's the time to . . . review the situation.'

'It's a situation, all right. I want to pack in all this woman-on-her-own stuff and go home. I know it's cowardly but I . . . I want my own place. I want to have a house to look after, meals to plan, friends dropping in, my garden . . . it all sounds trivial, I suppose, but I was good at it, and now I'm aimless, useless, drifting about serving no purpose that I can see, doing a couple of hours a day in a charity shop, hurrying home now and then to do the church flowers . . . If I'd had a plan, when I walked out, it would be different – somewhere to go to, something definite to do . . . But I feel I'm just wasting one day after another. I want to get back to a life that has some purpose in it.'

'So that's what you want to achieve.'

'Yes, and what good does it do to say so? To get it, I have to go back – eat humble pie – admit I was wrong—'

'But you weren't!'

'No, I think I was right – but there's the problem. I don't want to go back to the way things were before. I look back and think I should have protested years ago. But I can't imagine your father ever accepting my view of the matter.'

'You could be wrong there, Mother. You haven't seen him lately—'

'Because I've been avoiding him. I told you – I'm a coward.'

'Perhaps if you were to meet?'

'God forbid! He'd only need to raise his voice and I'd cave in.'

'Perhaps not. You'll never know until you try.'

'I couldn't face the encounter – if I set up some sort of meeting with him I know I'd get the shakes on the way there and turn back . . . Because, in a way, I want to give in. Strange though it may seem to say so, I miss your father, Beth.'

'Despite his domineering ways?'

'He has a lot of good points – he's old-fashioned in his outlook, of course, but then so am I. He's strong and forthright and determined . . . and clever, good at business . . . good company, when he's in the mood to relax and chat . . . and still a handsome man even though he's got a bit thick around the middle . . .'

There was a wistful note in Mary's voice, backed with a surprising affection. Beth reminded herself that, after all, these two had once been passionately in love, had bred three children and brought them up. Perhaps the years hadn't been as fulfilling for Mary as they might have been if Daniel had been more sensitive to her needs, yet it seemed they belonged together – at least, Mary didn't feel she belonged anywhere else.

What was to be done about it?

Chapter Twenty-three

No. 15 Royal Terrace had been Listed as Grade I. On a dismal day in November the rest of the Terrace was announced as Grade II Listing.

Bethany, having waited for just that result, arranged an appointment with her father. It was several months since they had had an encounter tête-à-tête: she had preferred to see him at meetings of the Steering Committee or to communicate by telephone.

'Glass?' he scoffed when she explained her plan. 'What are you going to put up – a conservatory?'

'Come and look at the sketches. They're on an easel in my room.' They were in his office at *Dayton & Daughter* at mid-morning.

Daniel was not in a good mood. The toaster had refused to work so that he had had to breakfast on cornflakes and plain bread and butter. No one cooked bacon and egg for him these days; no one bought the special marmalade he liked.

He looked with a jaundiced eye on his daughter's work and barked his disapproval. 'Looks like the Leeds bus station!'

Bethany refused to let herself be vexed. 'I like the Leeds bus station,' she said.

'Hardly a suitable model for a big-scale project like Barhampton, though?'

'Then how about the Trafford Centre in Manchester? That's mostly glass.'

'Don't get delusions of grandeur, girl. This is hardly a Chapman Taylor concept.'

'No, it owes its inspiration to Victor Horta's design for the Hotel Tassel in Brussels.'

'Horta? Horta?' cut in her father, who had had a good grounding in architectural history. 'The Belgian fellow? Died just after the war. I associate him with... what?... ironwork? Ironwork clothed in mahogany, or something.'

'That's the man. His work on the Hotel Tassel—'

'You're not suggesting *we* use ironwork clothed in mahogany, Bethany! Have some sense – it would cost a fortune!'

'No, no. This is more than a century later than Victor Horta. I'm suggesting we use steel.'

'Steel?'

'And glass. You see, the idea is to protect the façade.' She tapped the first of her drawings, which showed a front elevation of Royal Terrace as it was at present.

'I can't see why we should bother! Let the Town Council pay for its upkeep if it needs protection!'

Bethany chose to disregard this. 'I got quite a lot of help from Mr Tallant and the Historical Society. They've done a lot of research on Royal Terrace. Some of the houses have been quite badly treated. Number seven was used as a skirt-making factory in the 1890s so it had a lot of heavy old sewing-machines. They went through the floor and wrecked the room below. Then number four had a fire in the 1920s, and its roof came in. I'm afraid the repairs weren't done with any great efficiency so for most of the houses there's a lot of restoration and repair needed.'

'So what?'

'Once that's been done, the council will, as you point out, be liable for its upkeep.' She drew him to another of the sketches on the easel. 'What Victor Horta did for the Hotel Tassel is one of the great elegances of architecture, Dad. He took an ordinary town house in Brussels and with beautiful glass extensions turned it into a handsome and efficient hotel. We could do the same for Royal Terrace.'

'I don't think the Barhampton Town Council will be too impressed with Victor Horta, lass,' said her father with a dismissive shrug.

'But it will help them save money.'

He cocked an eye. 'Now you're talking. How exactly?'

'Putting the front façade behind glass is going to save on maintenance.'

'Ah?'

'Moreover,' said Bethany, holding up a finger for his attention, 'their original requirements for the New Town Centre demand a Museum and an Art Gallery for local landscapes, plus an Information Office—'

'Yes, yes, in River Walk—'

'Well, if we put those in the restored buildings of Royal Terrace, we release that expensive new construction which the council can rent out for prestige offices.'

'Ah,' Daniel said again, in a tone which held some satisfaction. The money aspect was always very important to Daniel, lately to the extent that it cramped his architectural outlook.

'Mr Tallant has been in touch with some colleagues in Germany,' she went on. 'They've managed to find two not awfully good portraits of Arabella Bedells, done during her career as mistress to the Duke. Then Mr Tallant says they can find a couple of costumes she might have worn, and they have bits of manuscript from her plays and a few letters – put them in glass cases, and one room in the museum could be dedicated to Arabella Bedells.'

'Humph,' he said. A tribute to Arabella Bedells, his *bête noire*, didn't tempt him.

'You can grumble,' she responded, 'but the rest of the Barhampton Museum is going to be mainly industrial archaeology and old wool-spinning machines. It'll brighten it up a lot if it can have a bit of scandalous romance attached to it—'

'Scandalous romance? Scandalous nonsense – it's the Historical Society making itself important!'

'Nothing wrong with that. They're entitled to be pleased with themselves.'

'Well, I don't agree, and if you think I'm going to endorse something that makes them look big—'

'Dad, this has nothing to do with personalities – it's a way of making use of Royal Terrace without antagonising the Conservationists,' she said patiently. 'Now the Museum would take up all of number fifteen. Then numbers fourteen and thirteen could be the Information Office, and number twelve could be the Art Gallery – or number eleven as well if they need a lot of room.' She was pointing at her sketches as she spoke. 'The next two or three houses could be an up-market café—'

'A café!'

'Ironwork tables and chairs, perhaps. Good coffee, Continental pastries. The rest of the premises . . . I don't know. Shops, perhaps, if the council want to rent them out.'

'Yes . . . Boutiques . . . jewellery, posh antiques . . .' Despite himself, Daniel was beginning to see possibilities in the scheme. At least it was less costly than some things his idealistic daughter might have suggested.

'In the evenings the Galleria could be used for receptions, you know. Or fashion shows . . . Things like that. It could be quite a prestige venue.'

She could sense that his resistance was lessening. She'd known, of course, that he wouldn't care for the design. He thought her work 'frivolous', not solid and heavy enough. What could be more frivolous than glass? Yet she'd known that if it could please the Town Council and save money, he would at least listen.

'It means calling in specialists,' she acknowledged. 'None of our present contractors know how to put up glass and steel—'

'I bet they would charge us a pretty penny.'

'But if we can sell the Town Council on it, it's more likely to please the Department of the Environment.'

'Oh, the Department of the Environment,' her father groaned. He knew from experience the frustration of dealing with their experts.

'I've put out a few feelers,' she said, 'and it seems there's a group there who feel Listed buildings should be *used*, not treated as monuments. If I can show their consultants that my idea will help to preserve

294

the façade and make it available in good weather and bad to the citizens of Barhampton, they may be quite taken with it.'

She nodded at another of her sketches, which showed the glass frontage in use. Pedestrians strolled, customers sat at the tables of a café drinking coffee or reading the newspaper. Here and there flowering shrubs flourished in handsome pots. Part of the existing Terrace garden, retained in her plan, led the eye to the new Town Square, skirted by a pedestrian walkway to encourage the shopper en route to the department stores.

'I've got a 3D simulation of the Galleria interior on the computer,' she said, turning to it. 'But you can't get any feeling of *style* from that. I think the glass shows up better using sketches.'

'The DoE people aren't going to like modern glass and steel.'

'Yes, they will, because although most of the glass pieces will come from stock, I'll have some specially made. I agree we don't want it to look too rectangular and hard – it's got to blend in with the buildings, it's got to have reference to the Georgian architecture. Some of the steel is going to be contoured.'

He gave her an ironic smile. 'Isn't that pastiche? I thought you were against pastiche.'

She could only nod and shrug. It was true she didn't like putting decoration on buildings merely for the sake of decoration. 'In this case, needs must.'

Having scored a hit, her father was more inclined to discuss things. 'You think they'll go for it?'

'I think they will.' She could tell he was on the verge of approving. His first instinct was to say no because it was so unlike anything he himself could have designed, yet he sensed her solution might be right.

Now was the moment when she had to enlist him on her side. If anyone were to walk in now and say, 'How silly!' he would turn against her work at once. So she said quickly, 'I haven't costed it out properly yet. I've made some educated guesses but it would have to be done in detail before we could show it to the council.'

'Head in air as usual,' he said. 'You never were much good at the facts and figures.'

'No, because you always did it so much better.'

He favoured her with a glance that told her he knew he was being flattered. But already he was beginning to work out the cost of transporting fragile glass to the site, wondering how much the specialist construction would cost. It was a pity he had no contacts among firms of that type – if they'd been old cronies he might have been able to twist their arms a bit on price.

'Let's have the others in to look at this,' he said.

She nodded gravely, careful not to show her pleasure. He was going to approve it. She didn't remind either of them that his approval one way

295

or another was meaningless, for Bethany was the consulting architect to the New Town Centre. Nevertheless, it was better to have him on her side than continually grumbling about the work.

On the whole the staff of *Dayton & Daughter* liked her design, especially Alan Singleton and the younger members. 'I hear the council repair men are going to start making the Terrace weatherproof,' Alan remarked. 'The squatters moved out the day after the Conservation Order was announced – they didn't want to end up in court with the DoE against them. But they've left a bit of a mess behind them.'

Bethany groaned. 'I'm taking Mrs Bedells there to sort out what furniture to take to her new home,' she explained. 'It's going to look really dismal, especially in all this grey weather.'

'She'll probably feel she's well out of it,' he comforted her.

That more or less summed up Mrs Bedells's view as she clambered down from Bethany's Suzuki. 'It looks a right mess,' she announced.

'And it'll look worse once the workmen get going on it, I'm afraid. But when it's all been done and dusted, you can come back and admire it.'

'I never want to see it again as long as I live,' said the old lady crossly.

Inside the house, Bethany began to stick labels on the pieces Mrs Bedells selected. 'I hope that's not those permanently sticky things,' she scolded. 'You can't get that glue off furniture!'

'No, these are old-fashioned gummed labels. Warm water will take off the stickiness.'

'I don't use warm water on my furniture, girl! Where did you learn your housekeeping?'

'I never learned any, I'm afraid.'

'Humph. So how are you going to manage when you marry that young man of yours?'

Bethany had no reply to this. She didn't feel like explaining the complexity of the situation to this strait-laced old lady. The fact was, announcing a forthcoming marriage, or even an engagement, between herself and Peter would be very difficult. They were still to some extent on the wrong side of each other's fences. Bethany was the architect for the New Town Centre of Barhampton. Peter still represented not only the troublesome owner of No. 15, but also the Royal Terrace Preservation Group, who might still put a spoke in the wheel of any plans.

Moreover, Bethany had doubts about running a career and a marriage. There was no question of giving up her work as an architect, and perhaps if she had been with some other firm the difficulties would have seemed less. But to have to handle Daniel Dayton all day and every day, while still being a lover and companion to a husband at night . . . It seemed an impossible task.

'You are going to get married, aren't you?' insisted Mrs Bedells.

'We haven't discussed it.'

'Why not, I'd like to know? If people are serious about each other they ought to get married. That's one of the things I have against all the hoo-ha that's going on about Arabella. She was a *wicked woman* and it fair puzzles me why anybody should want to do anything in her memory.' Nancy Bedells shook her dark head in perplexity. 'That silly young girl, for instance, the one that nearly got herself killed trying to put up a banner about Arabella – someone should have told her not to waste her devotion on a dreadful woman like that. By the way, what's happened to that child? She's walking again and all that, is she?'

'Yes, she's quite mobile, I hear. I believe they're leaving Barhampton, she and her father.'

'Best thing, probably. Get her away from bad memories.'

'Yes, best thing,' agreed Bethany. She had come to terms with the fact that any friendship with Josh Pembury was impossible while he still remained devoted to his daughter. His going or his staying was no longer her concern.

She helped Mrs Bedells pack some clothes and some personal things for immediate removal. The furniture van was to come on Thursday, the furniture to be arranged in the flat at Allenham on Friday, and Mrs Bedells was to move in on Saturday. 'Mrs Greshen, the manageress of the Allenham Estate, will have some groceries and things delivered for your immediate use,' Bethany explained. 'And there's the café if you want to go there for weekend meals, or they'll bring something over on a tray if you'd prefer.'

'Thank you, I can manage for myself,' said Nancy Bedells with unremitting tartness.

'She's always like that,' Peter remarked when Bethany told him about it. 'Always taking a snap at the hand that feeds her. I'm trying to get her to apply for her Old Age Pension – she's fully entitled to it, but will she take it? "Never took charity in my life!" she keeps saying. Absolute idiocy!'

'But it's good that she's so independent . . .'

'Cantankerous is the word, darling.' But he laughed as he said it. Despite the problems, he had a great regard for Mrs Bedells.

He'd arranged a handsome price for her house in Royal Terrace and a very advantageous lease on the flat at Allenham House. This left a reasonable sum to add to her existing bank balance, which consisted mainly of what William Bedells had left her by means of his insurance policy. All the same, she couldn't keep whittling away at her capital to live on. Judging by the way she was going, she would live to be a hundred and one – and there wasn't enough in the bank to keep her going that long. But Peter hoped to wear her down so as to get her to sign the documents that would gain her a pension.

The Town Planning Committee of Barhampton gave their blessing to

Bethany's scheme for Royal Terrace. They were delighted at the idea of having the Museum and the Art Gallery in that prestigious precinct so as to free up a large footage of prime office space on the River Walk.

Bethany then prepared two sets of plans for the conservation of Royal Terrace besides the glass Galleria frontage. The other two were somewhat less costly to put in train and involved no glass and steel. The Galleria looked rather expensive but had the blessing of the council. The experts from the Department of the Environment came to look at her plans, heard what the Town Planning Committee thought, looked intrigued, and went away saying they would let them know in a short time. If the DoE gave its approval, Bethany was hopeful that the Royal Terrace Protection Group would approve also, and go into voluntary dissolution.

'I don't quite understand why you drew up those two other schemes, dear,' her mother said when Bethany told her of it.

'Because if a solution to the Royal Terrace problem looked too cheap, they'd think we were skimping somewhere. But the Galleria, with the extra expense of experts to erect it . . . that makes them feel it's the best.'

Mary gave her daughter an astonished glance. 'There's a lot of your father in you, my girl,' she said with a shake of her head.

'But, Mother, the Galleria *is* the best solution.'

'But you've manoeuvred them into it.'

'Sometimes,' said Bethany, 'a little manoeuvring is necessary.'

She was about to manoeuvre her mother into a meeting with her father.

The construction of the New Town Centre had been progressing well in those areas not hampered by the Royal Terrace dispute. One of the low-rise buildings, a block of shops with flats above, had its roof on. Billy Wellbrow, in an unaccustomed fit of generosity, decided to hold a 'topping-out' party.

Topping-out is a very old custom attached to the building trade, not always carried out these days. It used to be regarded as essential that, when the last tile was placed on the roof of a new building, a ceremony was held on site asking for the blessing of some local saint. Gradually, the ceremony turned into a celebration involving drinks and food brought by the builders' wives. And latterly, when observed, the celebration was mainly a drinks party.

If tradition were strictly observed, Billy Wellbrow's completed roof didn't allow a topping-out. Only the tallest building on the site was supposed to be eligible and so they should all have waited until the buildings on the River Walk were roofed.

'But we've had such a bad time this year up to now,' remarked Billy, 'that I thought we'd have a mini-topping-out – anybody going to vote against it?'

Certainly not. Everybody was delighted with the idea. There did

298

indeed seem to be a lot to celebrate: the dreaded Mrs Bedells had taken herself off to a retirement home, the whole of Royal Terrace now belonged to Barhampton council and Bethany Dayton's design for it would make it an asset; Josh Pembury and his troublesome daughter had withdrawn all charges against the contractors and left for parts unknown, and a dignified statement in such journals as *Construction News* had let the trade know that the builders putting up Barhampton Town Centre had spotless reputations.

Added to that, leases and sales on the property being erected were better than expected. The publicity that had crackled around the New Town Centre had done it no harm in the end. The Job Centre had future openings for all kinds of staff – shop assistants, buyers, computer experts, secretaries, cleaners, supervisors, bus drivers, van-men, office managers, warehouse managers – after several decades of decline, the job market in Barhampton was looking up.

Billy Wellbrow organised two parties, one for the builders them-selves, who were offered tins of beer and lager and hearty sandwiches on the fourth floor of the empty building at knocking-off time. The symbolic 'last tile' was put in place by the youngest member then on site – he happened to be an apprentice brickie. He was helped down the ladder rather more quickly that he would have liked and rewarded with a can of ale poured over his head and a voucher to be used at the local wine shop.

These celebrations were mainly over by six of a dark November evening. The men strolled off home in a merry mood. In their wake appeared the catering firm hired by Wellbrow to make the ground floor fit for his more important guests.

This was by no means an easy task, for the block of property was empty, windowless, and had the night breeze blowing through it. But the caterers were under the guidance of Mrs Wellbrow, who had done this kind of thing before. She had brought in a troop of helpers who, that morning, had put up boarding to keep out the draught, installed enormous agricultural heaters to blow warm air through the ground floor, fixed up a portable lighting system, and set out picnic tables and chairs.

Swags of cloth in the colours of Barhampton's coat-of-arms disguised the unplastered walls, a drugget was laid on the concrete floors, red-checked plastic tablecloths hid the picnic tables. The caterers brought salvers of cold meat and smoked fish, enormous bowls of bright salad, sparkling wine glasses, pretty crockery, cutlery, ice buckets to chill the wine, and great round cream gateaux like cartwheels.

The guest list consisted of all the members of the Town Council, members of the Town Planning Department, the Legal Department, the Publicity Department and any others who had helped during the Bedells crisis. Next came the Steering Committee, senior members from the construction firms, representatives from the suppliers of materials and transport, reporters from trade and professional journals, and anyone else Wellbrow felt had helped cope with the difficulties of the last six months.

Naturally not everybody accepted; there were those who didn't fancy the idea of standing about with a plate of cold meat and a glass of wine in the shell of a building. Iris Weston had sent an excuse about having to attend a publicity conference in London. She was determined to lure Alan Singleton away from the uncivilised North as soon as possible, to the world where parties were held in comfortable hotel suites.

But those closely involved with the New Town Centre wouldn't have missed it, and of these Bethany Dayton was one. She had invited her mother as companion. Her mother had accepted.

It was of course understood by Mary Dayton that her husband would be at the party. It was also understood that neither she nor Bethany was to say so, because once the fact was put into words, Mary would have to take it into account, and would decide not to go.

Mary knew she had to encounter Daniel at some point. She had long ago decided she would not meet him alone, because no matter what Bethany said about his having changed, she was afraid of being steam-rollered into going home. She *wanted* to go home, but she wanted to make her husband see that things had to be different. How this was to be achieved was still moot. By going to Billy Wellbrow's topping-out party she would be in the same room yet protected by the presence of others.

I'm not going to make anything special of it, she told herself. If we talk to each other or if we don't, it doesn't matter . . .

That being so, it was difficult to explain why she took so much care over her appearance that evening. She had bought a dark wool dress in Harrogate not long ago, which disguised her plumpness rather charmingly and went well with her ash-grey hair. She put on sensible shoes, because experience told her that getting to half-finished buildings involved walking in muddy terrain, but though they were sensible, they showed off her trim ankles and still-shapely legs.

'Well, you do look nice,' said her daughter when she emerged into the living room of the flat.

'And I have to say the same of you, dear,' said Mary.

Bethany was wearing the heavy knit top of cornflower blue silk that her mother had brought back from Milan. With it she wore a wine-coloured wrap-around skirt, held with a big gold clasp. She had found time during the afternoon to have her hair done so that the short fair crop gleamed smoothly under the light.

'We'd better take jackets,' she advised. 'Billy says he's had heaters going, but you know how draughty it can be . . .'

They used Mary's car, since climbing into the worn old jeep in their finery seemed ill-advised. Cars were already parked in a line along the perimeter of the construction site. All the security lights were turned on; great hovering shadows of the construction vehicles stood like sleeping dinosaurs around the site, though in the distance machines could be heard working by night on the River Walk buildings. A security man was waiting to escort them to the party over a path of duck-boards.

They could hear the noise and laughter before they reached the building. Wellbrow caught sight of them as they came in, and surged forward to greet them. 'Here's our architect!' he exclaimed. 'And Mary – it's ages since I've seen you, luv! How are you?'

Mary said she was well and allowed herself to be embraced. Others pressed forward to greet her. It was clear many of the guests had already been celebrating to good effect, but Mary had been to parties of this kind before and had known what to expect. She always felt that a gathering with too many men and too few women tended to become boisterous.

Ossie Fielden appeared at her elbow. 'This is a nice surprise,' he remarked. 'And aren't you a sight for sore eyes!'

'How are you, Ossie?'

'None the better for not having seen you in weeks. Have you been enjoying yourself?'

'Yes, thank you. And you, what have you been up to?'

'Well, I organised a Guy Fawkes party last week for an orphanage, and I'm doing some work for the student-exchange programme – but you don't want to hear all that.' He paused. 'I saw you came with Bethany. Still staying with her?'

She nodded. A waiter came with a tray of drinks, so to get away from an uncomfortable topic she took a glass and sipped. 'Quite a nice set-up for the party,' she said.

'Oh aye, Billy's missus knows how to run these things. She's over there, talking to Daniel.'

Despite the fact that she'd known he was to be here, the saying of his name gave her a little thrill of apprehension. Here, in the same room, after weeks of angry separation . . .

Others joined the conversation. From time to time she sensed her husband watching her from across the open area of the shop. Why didn't he come up and speak? Didn't he want to? Or did he expect her to make the first move? Well, I won't, she said to herself with desperate firmness.

The fact was, Daniel had had no idea his wife would be here. He was still trying to come to terms with the thought.

Bethany had left her mother among the group of acquaintances. She was fairly sure that if she herself stayed by Mary's side, her father would never approach her. She sought out Peter, who was in conversation with two of the town councillors.

They kissed in greeting. If it caused raised eyebrows, it didn't matter any more. The problems keeping them apart were being solved, so that there was no need any longer to be circumspect about their relationship.

'I'll fetch you a drink,' he said, and moved off. Her gaze followed him. He was really looking very good, in his lawyer's suit of dark worsted and his tie of muted blue silk. Better, to Bethany's mind, than Alan Singleton in all the glory of Armani jacket, CK slacks, and Gucci shoes – and looking lost without Iris.

The councillors wished to know if she'd heard whether the Department of the Environment were going to give their blessing to her scheme for Royal Terrace.

'Not yet, but my spies are everywhere, and they tell me that it's being viewed very favourably,' she said. 'I'm hoping to hear soon. The minute I get word, I'm going to send in the order for the materials for the Galleria. I can tell you, I've got it typed out, all ready to fax.'

'I must say it looks as if it'll be right pretty when it's done,' said Councillor Penshall with a nod of approval. 'You *are* a clever lass.'

'Thank you,' said Bethany, resisting the urge to tell him you didn't get to be architect to a project like the New Town Centre by being a *stupid* lass. Seeing Peter out of the corner of her eye, she made her escape.

'Your mother's here,' he remarked as he handed her her glass of wine. 'You didn't say you were bringing her?'

'No. I thought it best to keep it a secret.'

'Oh?' He studied her, thinking about it. 'Is it ... Ah, your father's here, of course ... Is it to give them a chance to get together?'

'Hit it in one.'

'Well, it isn't working. He's over there talking to Mrs Crowther and she's trapped with Mrs Wellbrow being told how she organised all this.'

Bethany gave a weary shake of the head. 'There's nothing to be done about it. They're both grown-up people. If they can't manage to have a word with each other, then it's a lost cause.'

'Do you think she wants to speak to him?'

'I'm sure of it. But not alone, at least not the first time. She's scared of him, you know – oh, not in the sense of expecting violence, nothing like that. But he domineers, and in the main she's tended to give in ... So she thinks she might find herself back home again, with everything just the way it was before, and nothing gained by the misery of the past months ...'

'What she needs is a marital agreement,' said Peter.

'A what?'

'A marital agreement. It's quite the done thing these days. I've drawn up quite a few – not usually for couples already married, you know, but before the wedding. To say who's to do what, and whose property is whose, and what will happen if they split up ...'

'Really? I'd no idea.'

'Perhaps I ought to suggest it to your mother. I mean, if she's afraid of losing verbal battles, she could arm herself with a list of conditions that had to be adhered to—'

'Peter!' She was laughing.

'I'm serious,' he said, though he too was smiling. 'To have something down in black and white is a great help – it clears your mind, it steadies your nerve.'

'Well . . .' As she thought about it, she could see it had possibilities. One of Mary Dayton's problems was that she couldn't hold her own under verbal attack. In the past, she'd given in and then by subterfuge or gentle persuasion gained her point sometimes. She knew her own failings, and it was this that made her nervous of having a meeting with Daniel. But if she had a list, a written list of the changes she wanted to see in her life . . .?

'Shall I go and speak to her?' Peter suggested. 'In any case, she needs rescuing from Mrs Wellbrow.'

'That would be a good deed.'

He laughed and made his way through the press of people to Mary Dayton's side. Their hostess, surprised but pleased to have a new listener, was about to launch on a second report of her organising skills, when Peter said apologetically, 'I have to borrow Mrs Dayton for a minute, Mrs Wellbrow.'

'Oh? Oh, of course . . . I ought to see how the food's holding out, in any case.' She bustled off, and Mary turned in enquiry to Peter.

'Borrow me for what?' she asked.

'To have a conference. I thought you might like to hire me.'

'*Hire* you?'

'I'm a solicitor. Solicitors are often involved in solving family disputes—'

'If that wicked daughter of mine has suggested any such thing—' Mary began, flushing with embarrassment.

'No, this is my idea. I asked Bethany why she'd brought you here and guessed the reason. So then we discussed your problem a little and I wondered if you'd like me to draw up a marital agreement for you.'

'Eh?' said Mary inelegantly.

'Have you heard of the idea? In these days of rather muddled relationships, couples sometimes—'

'I read something about them in the *Guardian* the other day,' said Mary. 'I thought it a strange thing.'

'Not at all. It used to be quite common, you know, to sort out what was being brought to a marriage by either side and what was expected. It still goes on in many countries – France still has it, and of course it is normal in the East.'

'But this isn't France or the East, and I never even thought of such a thing. What would be the point?'

'Well, you see . . . Forgive me for blundering into your private affairs, I'll try not to make it too tactless . . . If you and your husband were to want to resume . . . er . . . what is legally termed cohabitation, it might be a good idea to have a plan, a set of rules—'

'Oh, no!'

'Don't dismiss it out of hand. It would be something to fall back on if . . . er . . . you know . . . if things didn't go too well after you went back to Mr Dayton.'

'It's not likely to happen. I can't bring myself to even say good evening to him.'

'Why is that?'

'Because I know he'll make me feel in the wrong and before I know it I'll be walking in my front door again to my old life.'

'Not if you have a list of demands ready to put to him.'

'What?'

'A list of demands. It's quite usual in a negotiation. Employers versus trade unions, parliamentary committees, head-hunters speaking on behalf of candidates for important jobs . . . If you like, I could draw up a list for you.'

'I never even thought of such a thing.'

'Think of it now. Or for the future. You see, before you commit yourself to any reconciliation, you could say you want a delay to have some conditions drawn up.'

'Daniel would go through the roof if I so much as suggested it.'

'That would be one of the conditions – no going through the roof.' Mary laughed despite herself and Peter went on. 'I think you really need a list of demands and a marital agreement, Mrs Dayton. You need all the support you can get.'

She looked at him in astonishment, shaking her head and looking bewildered. 'You're a live wire, aren't you?'

'A live wire, full of power,' he agreed, 'the power of the legal system. You should think about using it, even just as a . . . a bulwark, if you know what I mean.'

'Oh, I do, believe me. A bulwark, that's what I need. Thank you, Peter. You're making me look at things in a new light.'

They were joined at this point by Billy Wellbrow, who wanted to be congratulated on his party. Others joined them, so that Peter could make his escape to Bethany. Mary stayed, chatting with acquaintances from the world of architecture and construction.

A fiction was maintained among them that Mary Dayton was staying with her daughter in Barhampton so as to help furnish and decorate her flat. No one ever said that Mary had left Daniel – certainly not within the hearing of Daniel. So now they stood with glasses of wine and plates of food, pretending everything was just as usual.

Wellbrow went to fetch another drink and on his way back, from

304

sheer mischief, collected Daniel. Daniel, as it happened, wasn't unwilling to be collected. He'd been looking at Mary from various spots, distant and semi-distant, without being able to get himself close in a casual manner. He was certainly not going to walk up to her in any direct manner.

'Well, Mary,' he said as he joined the group.

'Well, Daniel.'

'Your wife's been telling me she's supervising the redecoration of Bethany's flat. Won't be long till we have to start thinking of Christmas decorations, will it, lass?'

'Oh aye, Christmas!' Everybody began bemoaning the fact that the newspapers and TV kept reminding you how many shopping days were left till Christmas, and here it was only the first week of November. By and by Mary edged away from the group, and to her satisfaction Daniel did the same. They moved little by little to a secluded corner.

'It's a fine thing when you can only get to speak to your wife by coming to the same party,' Daniel grumbled.

'Aye, it should make you value the opportunity, I imagine.'

'Mary!' He was startled at the tone of reprimand.

'Here we are together, and you start straight away to complain.'

He blew out a breath. Her attitude took him aback. He'd many a time imagined himself at this first meeting, reproaching her and making her see it was time to stop making a fool of herself. He'd been sure she'd be immediately contrite – but no, she seemed rather sure of herself, ready to hold her own against any of his usual arguments.

Mary, for her part, was a little shocked at the change in him. He had lost quite a lot of weight, which in fact suited him, but there was a sag to his shoulders and a weariness in his manner that was quite unlike him.

He began again. 'How are you?'

'I'm well, thank you.'

'Aye, you look well. That colour suits you.'

'Thank you.'

'It's a new dress, isn't it?'

'Yes, and that reminds me to say – I'm still using the credit card that draws on your account. We need to come to some arrangement about that.'

'What on earth for?'

'Well, I can't go on using your money.'

'Why shouldn't you?'

'If we're going to live apart—'

'Mary,' he burst out, 'we're not going to live apart. This has got to end!'

She said nothing, and for a moment he was too upset at her suggestion to continue. He felt helpless, and blurted out: 'Be a bit kind to me, Mary. I've been having a terrible time of it.'

305

'Have you, lad?' Against her own wish, concern came into her voice.

'You've no idea! The house is so empty without you, and that woman who does the cleaning moves everything so I can't find things, and though she's supposed to do the shopping for me, there's never anything decent to eat—'

'You should hire a proper housekeeper, then,' she said, recovering herself.

'*Oh!*' He threw up a hand to his forehead as if he wanted to smite himself. 'I didn't mean it like that. I don't know why I talked about the cleaning – Mary, my world is turned upside down and I don't know how to cope. And then all this kerfuffle about the Conservation Orders on Royal Terrace, and Bethany staying out of my way as if I had the plague, and Allie Pembury wanting to sue over her injuries and making us look bad—'

'But Daniel, all that's been sorted,' she pointed out. 'The Pemburys have admitted there was no negligence and have gone away, Bethany's design is going to solve the Royal Terrace problem—'

'Yes, and I ought to be as tickled with myself as Wellbrow, but I'm not. Mary, I'm not.'

She put a hand on his sleeve. 'Calm down, lad. People are looking.'

'Oh, let them, let them! I don't care any more. Come home, love, please come home. If you don't, I'll either take to drink or chuck myself off the top of the Minster.'

'Now, now, Daniel, don't talk daft. We're two sensible people, we ought to be able to sort out our problems without dramatics—'

'Dramatics! Is that what you call it? I mean every word of it. I'm trying to tell you that everything's turned to ashes since you left.' He gave a shiver of fear. 'It's too bad to contemplate. I didn't know . . . I never knew . . .'

'What?'

'How much you mean to me,' he said in a whisper.

Mary was astonished at the revelation but hid her feelings. This meeting, dreaded for so long, was turning out utterly different from her expectation.

She must be careful what she said now. To show how much his words had shaken her would be a mistake. There was still enough of the old Daniel there to take advantage of any weakness.

She remembered what Peter had said, that a list of conditions could be a bulwark. So she began, slowly, 'Well . . . I won't argue that this situation can go on indefinitely . . . and I would quite like to—'

'Yes? Yes?'

'Get things back to normal—'

'Yes!'

'But "normal" means something different from the old ways, lad. I'm not coming back to be a doormat again—'

'Oh, now, Mary, you were never that—'

'It depends on how you see it. From the doormat's point of view, Daniel, all you see is heavy feet coming down on you.'

'But I've never – you've always—'

'Had to play second fiddle. Had to see my children leaving home because you wouldn't let them have the lives they wanted.'

'But children always leave home, Mary—'

'But they stay close in a happy family! I have to go to Venice to see Robert, and you said yourself Bethany was avoiding you like the plague. If I come back, Daniel, I want your promise that you won't order everybody about, that you'll show consideration for the views of the other members of the family. I want Robert to come and stay without arguments breaking out every ten minutes. I want Bethany's talent to be acknowledged without that grudging tone in your voice. I want freedom for myself—'

'To do what?' he demanded, more to stop the extraordinary flow of criticism than from any real belief that she needed freedom.

'I don't know yet. What I do know is that there's a world out there beyond the household of Daniel Dayton, and I've begun to take part in it – a bit late, but I've still got something to contribute. I'm looking for a job—'

'A *job*?'

'Oh yes, there's a million things in the world that need doing, but young people are too busy making careers and bringing up families to do them—'

'Oh, you mean volunteer work – oh, that would be all right.'

'Daniel!' she said, and raised a hand in warning. 'I'm not asking your opinion or your permission. I'm telling you. I want to make use of my abilities. If I decide to join the *Folies Bergères*, that will be none of your business.'

He stared. 'The *Folies Bergères*,' he repeated, and grinned.

'Oh, you can laugh,' she countered, smiling too, 'but I've revived my dancing skills since last we saw each other.'

He glowered. 'With Ossie Fielden.'

'Yes, with Ossie. He and I make a good partnership. I might decide to go on with my evenings at the dancing club.'

'Mary! You can't – you can't feel anything serious for Ossie Fielden?'

'Why not? He's a very nice man.'

'But – but—'

She decided not to let jealousy spoil this chance of reconciliation. She said gently, 'Ossie is a nice man and a good friend. That's all it is, Daniel.'

'You swear it?'

Once more she held up a warning hand. 'Think on, lad. I've told you, and you either believe me or it's never going to work. Now, what's it to be?'

307

'You're right. I'm sorry. I should have known better. All the same, Mary . . . Promise me you won't go dancing with Ossie Fielden!'

'Why, Daniel,' she replied, with a little laugh, 'there'll be no need to go with Ossie. You can take me yourself!'

'What?'

'Have a night out. Not just a formal dinner with forty construction company executives and their wives, but supper in a cosy restaurant with candles on the table and a disc jockey playing tunes that you can sing the words to.'

Daniel stared at his wife in bewilderment. Had she always been there, this romantic woman with romantic longings? How was it that he had never known her? To him she had always been that quiet, pretty, intelligent schoolteacher he'd swept off her feet during a short courtship.

She could see it was hard for him to take it all in. She said, still remembering Peter's advice, 'You won't want to rush into anything, love. Think it over. If you want to start again on a new understanding, well, we can talk about it. You know where I'm living at the moment.'

That said, she moved away, leaving him at a loss.

Mary left the party almost at once. She was exhausted after what had been for her an ordeal. She went home to Bethany's flat, wondering if she would be staying there much longer and thinking that, if Daniel would only see sense, she could be back home by the weekend. But that was too much to hope for.

Bethany, at the party's end, saw that her mother's car was gone, so drove off with Peter. They went to his flat, swept away by the longing to be together again in mind and body. They made love with that constantly renewed passion that had come to them like a gift from the gods. At last, for the time content, they lay wound about each other and, as always, began to talk in quiet tones. Peter wanted her to stay till morning. Bethany said she ought to go home.

'But why, sweetheart? As the song used to say, it's cold outside!'

'I saw Mother having a serious talk with Dad. I want to know what happened.'

'Couldn't you wait till morning to find out?'

'It's important to be there, Peter. She needs someone to hold her hand.'

'And what about me? *I* need you—'

'Yes, but you haven't got a shaky marriage to take care of.'

'I haven't got any kind of marriage,' he rejoined, catching at the word. 'And that's a point I think we should be considering. What about us, Bethany? Are we going to get married?'

She laughed, her breath tickling his ear. 'Don't sound so *enthusiastic* about it. "After due consideration . . ." '

'I *am* enthusiastic. Just give me more time and I'll show you.'

'No, seriously, Peter. Are you really thinking about something permanent?'

'I certainly am. Always have been. Haven't you?'

'I don't know . . . Yet Mrs Bedells said—'

'Mrs Bedells? What on earth has she got to do with it?'

'Oh, a lot. I've been thinking about what she said.'

'But what did she say?'

'She said that people who are serious about each other ought to get married. Yet it's a big commitment.'

Peter held her closer. 'But we're committed, aren't we? To each other?'

'I feel that we are. Only . . . so many people make a mess of it.'

'We're different from other people.'

'Oh, Peter! You seem so sure.'

'I am sure. How can I persuade you to be sure?'

She sighed and shook her head. 'I don't know. It wants a lot of thinking about. And now I've got to go, it's nearly midnight.'

Reluctantly he let her leave. When she got home she found her mother still up, as she'd expected. 'Well, how did it go?' she demanded, knowing her mother would understand her meaning.

'I think it went well. I hope so . . . I remembered what Peter said to me.'

'What did he say, in fact?'

'He told me I could make conditions, that I could have a legal document if I wanted, and that I should think of it as a bulwark when it came to speaking to your father.'

'A marital agreement?'

'Oh, I'm not thinking of having one drawn up. Somehow that's a bit . . . bizarre. But I kept reminding myself of it, Beth, while we were talking. It did me good.'

'And Dad? What about him?'

'He was . . . "perplexed" is maybe the word. But you're right, Beth, he has changed.'

'For the better, do you think?'

'At this moment, yes. The difficulty is to know how long it might last. Still, I made my point with him, and told him to think it over. And we'll see.' They chatted on for nearly an hour, Mary trying to recall what was said and Bethany making sounds of approval. It certainly seemed as if a new beginning might be possible between these two.

And for herself and Peter? Should there be a new beginning? She went to sleep still mulling over that point.

They were rather late in rising next morning, and were still at breakfast when Bethany's doorbell rang. On the threshold stood a young man with an elaborate bouquet wrapped in cellophane and bound with many ribbons.

'Mrs Dayton?'

'Er . . . that's my mother. Thank you.'

She carried the bouquet into the kitchen, calling as she came: 'First flowers, then boxes of chocolates.'

'What?' said her mother, then gasped with surprise as the huge bunch of flowers was placed in her lap.

'There's a card.'

'Oh. Just a minute.' Mary detached the little envelope from the wrappings, took out the card, read it, then blushed with pleasure.

'What does it say?'

'Never you mind!'

'Oh, like that, is it? They're from Dad, of course.'

'Yes.'

'Mother, he's *courting* you!'

'Yes, he is, and I like it.'

They both laughed as Mary put the card back in its envelope and tucked it out of sight in her dressing-gown pocket.

Bethany was dressing for the day's work when the doorbell went again. Halfway into her sweater, she called through its thickness, 'Get that, will you, Mother?' She was pulling on her trainers when her mother came into her bedroom.

Bearing a bouquet of flowers.

'What is this, Support-a-Florist Day?' Bethany asked.

'They're for you.'

'For me? Oh – thank you.'

This was a much less exuberant token, twenty crimson roses in cellophane tied with a single red ribbon bow.

'There's a card,' Mary urged.

Bethany found the envelope, opened it, and took out the card. The message ran: *Mrs Bedells is right. Let's lunch and discuss her views.*

'I won't ask what it says,' Mary remarked. 'I can see it's something good.'

Bethany hesitated. 'Peter wants us to get married.'

Mary clapped her hands in delight. 'Perfect!'

'But Mother . . . I'd be running a career and a marriage . . . I don't know if I'm up to it.'

'Don't be silly. Plenty of women do it—'

'But they're not partners with a man like Dad!'

Her mother sat down beside her on the bed and took her hands. 'You can do it, lass. You've done wonders so far, and you'll do better yet. And you said yourself, your father's changed. Perhaps he's learned a lesson.'

They gave themselves up to their thoughts for a while. Then Bethany said, 'Peter will help. I'm no great business mind, but he will help me to sort out business problems. That way, Dad won't have to be so obsessed over financial matters. I'll try to take responsibility for things a bit more, so that it really will be *Dayton & Daughter*, a real partnership and not a second-best thing on his side.' She rose. 'I'm going to telephone Peter.'

'And say what?'

Bethany smiled. 'Yes – I think.'